Edith Courtney, the da[...] Lancashire woman, ha[...] insurance, worked in [...] postmistress. Yet writing has always been her main interest. She has had many short stories printed, was on the staff of a Swansea newspaper for some years, had broadcast and had three volumes of autobiography published.

Edith Courtney founded the Swansea & District Writers' Circle of which she is president, and is also a vice-president of the South & Mid Wales Association of Writers. She and her husband live on the border between Swansea and the Gower Peninsula. They have three grown children and one granddaughter.

THE PRICE OF LOVING

Edith Courtney

CORGI BOOKS

THE PRICE OF LOVING

A CORGI BOOK   0 552 12719 1

First publication in Great Britain

PRINTING HISTORY
Corgi edition published 1986

This book is set in 10/11 pt Plantin
Corgi Books are published by Transworld Publishers
Ltd., 61-63 Uxbridge Road, Ealing, London W5 5SA, in
Australia by Transworld Publishers (Aust.) Pty. Ltd.,
26 Harley Crescent, Condell Park, NSW 2200, and in
New Zealand by Transworld (N.Z.) Ltd.,
Cnr. Moselle and Waipareira Avenues,
Henderson, Auckland.

Printed and bound in Great Britain by
Cox & Wyman Ltd., Reading, Berks.

TO ALL THOSE WHO HAVE PAID
THE PRICE OF LOVING

THE PRICE OF LOVING

CHAPTER ONE

Bertie Hemsworthy wondered ever after why fate hadn't warned him about that October morning in 1931, why a streak of lightning hadn't shot at the front door as he opened it, because all he did was decide to wear his homburg, dust it with his hand, put it on, pick up his gloves from the drawer in the hallstand, admire his dark laughing eyes and clean white smile in the mirror and call 'Cheerio' to Kit. Then he opened the front door.

Normally the front door would be open anyway and he would have seen the outline of anyone standing there through the inner glass door. As it was he saw nothing but the morning gloom of the passage, until he opened the front door and the autumn sunshine acted like a halo around Elsie Buckley. He raised his hat quickly, instinctively, and the breeze lifted his fine greying dark hair slightly, so that she saw a halo too.

He saw her legs first because he was looking down, and they were legs with slim ankles and small feet, the calves shone because of silk stockings, and reached gently to dimpled knees. Then there was the hem of a shabby tweed coat and a small black patent handbag shaped like an envelope. It was clutched by a small white hand that had long red nails.

Bertie looked up to the face and smiled. He became unaware of the weather or of anything except the pleasure this girl gave him, and she laughed, caught up in the same excitement. Neither of them sensed any danger in the attraction. She, because she was too young, and he, because the army had come first until 1918 and the end of the war, the end of his period of serving king and country, and he had married Kitty Nolan out of loneliness and a need for a home of his own.

Elsie was no more than five feet high and smelled of Phul-Nana perfume: it was musky and cheap and advertised by an Arab carrying a beautiful girl off on his white charger. Her face was small and naive and trusting and knowing all at the same time. It was also inclined to be plump with a rounded chin, and a mouth made for laughter with corners that quivered easily. He saw the badly-placed rouge, and the too harsh lipstick making a rosebud mouth, the over-plucked brows; and he ignored them for the happiness of her smile.

'Mr Hemsworthy?'

'Guilty.'

'You're the manager?'

She gestured to the brass plate on the wall beside the door, and he was proud it shone with so much effort.

He said, 'I am the manager, and this is the office of the South Wales branch of the Unicorn Insurance Company. What can we do for you?'

He was smiling, his expression teasing a little, in case she was a policy-holder with a complaint and he had to charm her out of it.

'I want to be your secretary.'

'Secretary?'

His dark brows went up in astonishment.

'You've advertised,' she accused. 'I saw it in the paper –' She stuttered on the last words, very near to saying, in the paper we had chips in.

'Yes but – ' He surveyed her more materialistically now. She was not a complaining policy-holder, she was a half-baked kid looking for a job.

'You're too young. I need someone to run the office while I'm out.'

'I'm twenty-one.'

'It's still too young. Too young in the head.'

'I am nothing of the sort. Try me.' She stepped forward a little and he stepped back. A tram came around the bend in

10

the road. It was empty and made a lot of noise, its over-head wires singing. The driver stamped on his bell to draw Bertie's attention, his red fingers jutting through red swollen half-mitts on the brass controls. Bertie moved his right arm in acknowledgement, then looked back at the girl. He said, 'Who put all that muck on your face?'

'I did. It's the fashion.'

'It makes you look like a tart.' He watched her flush and her eyes narrowed in suppressed indignation. She said, 'I can type and I can do shorthand.'

He laughed at her and she laughed back, open-mouthed. She had big teeth, which was something of a shock in one so dainty.

He moved further back. 'You'd better come in.'

He called to Kit, 'It's me again,' and shepherded the girl into the front room of the house; it was large, high, furnished like an office with white ceiling and cream walls. He put his homburg on the pink blotter on his desk and sat before it, opening his overcoat. He put his hands in his trouser pockets and nodded the girl to a small hard chair beyond him. She sat upright, feet together, her knees rounded in the silk stockings beneath the hem of the tweed coat.

'Well,' Bertie said, 'it's kind of you to call, but I can't give you a job. You are too young by far and you lack experience.'

Her face tightened again and the blobs of red rouge on her cheeks became more prominent. He said casually, 'Move your chair round a bit. The light there makes you look ninety.'

She did so.

He said, 'How old are you?'

'Twenty-one.'

'You're a liar.' He slid further down in his chair, aqui-line-nosed and narrow-faced. 'Now. How old are you?'

She looked down at the black patent leather bag in her lap. 'Seventeen. I'll be eighteen soon.'

He sighed with exaggeration, 'Too young. Much too young.'

'I'm not you know, and I'll thank you to stop being so rude, just because you're a manager,' and her accent became recognisable. He said, 'You're from Port Tennant.'

'St Thomas.'

'Same thing.'

'It's nearer the docks.'

He took his hands from his trouser pockets and sat up. He yawned; St Thomas, Port Tennant, the docks, one struggling gritty area where mulattos and Arabs lounged in doorways and seamen found girls.

'I need a job,' she said, and leaned her head on one side, unconsciously pleading.

'Why stick kiss curls in front of your ears like that?'

She fingered them quickly. 'They're nice. Like Spanish girls. It's the fashion.'

'What? Stuck to your skin?'

'Yes, of course.'

'What d'you use? Glue?'

'Sugar and water. I did them special.'

His tongue was in his cheek. She looked common, cheap, yet was attractive, enticing. He wondered why. He said, 'If you work for me you wash that muck off your face – or learn to put it on properly.'

She humphed quietly.

He said, 'I'll pay you five bob a week.'

She flinched and blinked, then looked down at her bag again. 'I want ten.'

'You aren't worth ten. I'll be training you, teaching you a job.'

'I have been to Gregg College, my shorthand speed is – '

'Don't tell me, show me. There's a pad and pencil on the other desk. Get a move on. What other jobs have you had?'

She didn't answer. She deliberately put her handbag on the edge of his desk then sat with the pad and pencil ready.

'You haven't had a job since you left Gregg, have you? You're unemployed.'

'That's not my fault.' She lifted her head, indignant, staring at him. She had large grey eyes and a turned-up nose. 'Everybody's out of work these days. Millions. All living on bread and spit.'

'Dear Madam.' Bertie turned from her, his wooden chair squeaking on its axis as it swivelled. 'You haven't told me your name or your proper address. I need references. If I employ you – and I emphasise the if – you will be here by nine on the dot every morning, no excuses will be accepted about the New Cut Bridge being up for ships getting into the dock, and you won't leave until I tell you to. The only day you will not be obliged to work is Sunday. Your salary will be five shillings a week until you have proved you are worth more, and you will always remember that I am the boss. Yours etc. etc.'

He watched her pencil moving; it did so lightly and easily, then she looked up. 'Shall I read it back?'

'No. I want you to run an errand for me.'

'What? Out?'

'Out. You know the meaning of the word, I assume? You can get me some more cigars. There's a box in the small cupboard behind you. I want the same sort again.'

She moved quickly, putting the pad and pencil on the desk beside her handbag, then bending to the low cupboard and getting the shallow wooden box. She smiled directly at him and said, 'Right then, if you give me some money I won't be long.' And Bertie was never certain how it happened, but in that instant he knew she had the job for as long as ever she wanted.

She didn't stride as Kit did, her thin heels were too high, but neither did she mince. She paused at the door, looking back, silently laughing, unwittingly flirting, young and vital. 'D'you want a whole box?'

'Heck no! A packet will do.' And she went, the doors thudding behind her. Bertie went to the kitchen and Kit was ironing, one long thin arm pushing the heavy flat-iron over the winceyette nightie. For a while he stood in the doorway watching her. She had lost weight, gone from the fashionably slim to an angular skinny. She overworked, and Bertie felt it was his fault; he couldn't provide her with the standard of living she had been born to.

She glanced up, folding the nightie, placing it on a pile of other finished garments on a chair. 'Was that a policy-holder?' Her accent struck him as more cultured than it really was, because he had just been listening to Elsie Buckley, and he stepped further into the room, closing the door behind him, parrying her question.

She readjusted a padded holder in her hand then took one flat-iron off the fire and stood it, end up, on the hob beside the black iron kettle, then she gently turned the coals with the long poker, bringing new orange-coloured heat uppermost, and placed the cold iron into the formed nest. She tested it for safety but moved her hand fast, away from the burning. 'Coo! That's a good bit of coal. Ought to be, at the price.'

The room smelled of hot cloth and warmth and Bertie sniffed appreciatively. Kit straightened herself and, for a moment, stood eye to eye with him. She said, 'Well?'

'An applicant for the post of my secretary.'

'Good heavens!' she exclaimed. 'After all this time? I'd given up hoping.'

He smiled at her, a little wryly. 'Oh, come on Kit, there have been applicants.'

'Oh, come on yourself. It's six weeks since you advertised and all the applicants, as you call them, wanted a bigger salary than you get.'

'Well, if you want someone with qualifications and experience – '

'Has this one the qualifications and experience?'

He clicked his tongue and rocked back on his heels. 'No. She's got plenty of nerve though. She wouldn't take any nonsense from stroppy policy-holders.'

'We don't get many of those.'

'I think she'd be a worker. She looks tough.'

Kit said flatly, 'Is she pretty?'

'No. Got a face like a painted doll, actually. Bit of a kid.

14

Seventeen. I suspect someone deprived themselves to send her to Gregg College. Unless she got a scholarship –' The flat-iron was put on the upturned saucer that acted as a rest and Kit lifted the small yellow dress that she was ironing and shook it. She admired it and examined it, then she placed it back on the sheet that was spread as an ironing base on the table. 'We've had all this argument before,' she said.

'A man would want a quid a week. Hell! I can't afford that.' He wanted to add, I've given you my all, Kit. The girls could have been educated without a private school, and we don't need carpets in almost every room. I've given in to you every time. Pay out. Pay out. I just don't have the sort of money your father has.

Instead, he said quietly, 'I even begrudge the five bob. It would buy over three hundredweight of coal or three weeks' electricity, but we must have help.'

'Where is she from?'

'St Thomas.'

'Phew! That sort.'

'There's nothing wrong with St Thomas.'

'Of course not.' Kit was not going to argue.

'I sent her out. When she comes back I'll see if she can read her own shorthand.'

The iron explored small puff sleeves, and Bertie went on, 'We won't get anyone else for – ' he paused, then upped Elsie's salary ' – six shillings.'

'I don't like the sound of her.'

'You haven't seen her.'

'I don't need to see her. I have this feeling, a type of instinct.'

'Kit,' he sighed, 'what has got into you lately? You watch me like a hawk. You didn't use to be like that. Have I suddenly grown rolled gold toenails or something?'

She didn't look at him. Her head with the thick glossy black hair piled on top in Edwardian style stayed bowed over the ironing, the back of her neck long and slim and white with its enticing little hollow in the centre.

15

'I don't know,' she said slowly. 'I've gone all possessive, haven't I?'

'You have.' It was an indignant accusation. 'The one thing we promised when we married was that we would never try to possess each other.'

She suddenly turned and laughed, a beautiful mouth in a model face. 'It must be my age. Forty and all that.'

'Kit, it's not as if we are lovelorn kids.'

'I know. But we are happily married. Aren't we? After thirteen years. And I don't want it spoiled.'

'We are happily married. And let's hope it stays that way.'

'Do you ever regret marrying me?'

'Good God! Why should I?'

'Oh, I don't know.' She shrugged and held the base of the iron close to her face, testing it for heat.

'Kit.' He frowned. 'Are you getting soppy in your old age?'

'Soppy? Me?' It was her turn to accuse. 'Of course not. We married because we liked each other, respected each other – '

'Admired each other, needed each other.' He moved to her, standing close behind her. He put his arms around her, gently kissing the nape of her lovely neck and she said calmly, 'Now who's soppy in his old age?'

He sighed and stood back, hearing the wooden clock on the mantelpiece ticking methodically. He moved his shoulders as if to throw off a mood. 'I suppose I'd better get out today, do some cold canvassing.' He watched her, brooding, resenting her busyness, and she kept ironing, moving her head as if trying to remove his touch from the back of her neck. He listened for the clang of the gate and he was in the passage, waiting, when Elsie Buckley returned.

She opened the glass door, laughing, calling, 'Can I come in?'

'Of course,' he laughed back. 'There's no need for you to ring the bell. Come right in. Be one of the family.'

16

She followed him into the office, and he enjoyed the warmth of excitement. She gave him the cigars and he looked at the dark brown cardboard cylinder, checking they were what he wanted. She said coyly, 'You didn't really need those, did you?'

'I had to get rid of you while I talked to my wife.' He looked down at her and she said, 'You like me, don't you?'

'Not particularly.' He was amused at her brazenness, but he had met others just as brazen, and accepted it as part of her.

'I like you all right.'

'So you should. I'm a likeable fella.'

He took a cigar and put the tip between his teeth, and bit, then spat the piece to the waste basket. Elsie Buckley watched with an inquisitive glow in her eyes. 'You're very handsome, aren't you?' She said it shyly, but honestly.

'Yes, aren't I?' He laughed back at her, whimsically. He gestured her to the small desk. 'Read it.'

'Now?'

'Now. I suppose you've forgotten what you wrote.'

'No. You wanted my name and proper address. I start at nine on the dot every day except Sunday, and I don't leave until you tell me to. I get ten shillings a week – '

'Five.'

'Six. And you can ring Mr Willerby for references.'

'Who's Mr Willerby when he's at home?'

'The vicar.'

'Don't say you're church?'

'My mother's church and my father's Catholic.' She lifted her head, challenging. 'So what's wrong with that?'

He stared, temporarily off-balance. Kit wouldn't tolerate church-goers. Kit found her God in chapel and was convinced that any other temple housed the devil in disguise.

He heaved his shoulders, disgruntled at thoughts of Kit's displeasure invading these moments. He said sharply, 'Raise your voice to me again and you'll be out of the door P.D.Q.' And he was gratified to see her cheeks flush. She looked down. She was easily scolded, and he felt better.

He waited, smiling, and when she peeped up she burst into laughter. They stood enjoying each other, until he said, 'Right then, let's see if you can type.' And the door slowly opened. It was Kit carrying a tray set with cups and saucers. Her pale mouth was set in a smile and she had taken off her apron. Her reddy-brown gaze settled on Elsie. She said meaningly, 'I am the manager's wife. Mrs Hemsworthy.' Elsie nodded, but some of her sparkle had gone, there was a wavering in her eyes.

Bertie rubbed his hands as if to rub the sudden tension away. 'Well, come on then, let's have a cuppa. Elsie, help yourself. Make yourself at home.'

'Elsie can stay where she is,' Kit said. 'I am quite capable of passing her a cup of tea. With sugar, Elsie?'

'Yes please.' And Elsie took the cup and sipped slowly, tasting, then she smiled. 'D'you mind if I type this letter out? Then it's done.' She turned to the machine without waiting for a reply and Kit stared, her classical features blank. Bertie puffed the cigar, watching through an aroma of smoke. He said, 'Nice cup of tea, Kit.' And she marched away, the door thudding on its draught excluder.

Ten minutes later Elsie Buckley had gone. The office was silent, the house smelling of hot newly-ironed clothes, and Bertie liked the odd feeling of excitement deep within his loins.

He went to the kitchen and the table was cleared, the irons cooling on the fender but there was no sign of Kit, so thoughtfully he tinkled the change in his trouser pockets, his fingers caressing the little silver fiddlers amid the heavy, rough-edged half-crowns, while he listened. Any moment now Kit would let him know where she was without calling, expecting him to extend the gestures of attention that she could accept without losing face.

The sound soon came. She stamped along the passage upstairs, going from the bathroom to the front bedroom. He looked at the clock, then took the gold watch from his waistcoat pocket, checking the time. He ought to be off.

Get some new business in. Earn enough money to pay his new secretary.

He went up the stairs like a panther, easily and silently on the thick carpeting. Kit pretended not to be aware of him as he walked in on her.

She wielded a duster energetically, supposedly angrily, flicking it between the heavy china pieces on the dressing-table, avoiding seeing him in the three hinged mirrors before her.

He said, 'Well, that's a good job done. We've got help in the office at last. It'll take a lot off you, Kit.'

She frowned, still not looking at him, and he moved behind her, his hands catching her hips. 'She's not a patch on you.'

'The devil sent her, Bertie. I'm warning you. I have a feeling, and she snubbed me. She did. She snubbed me.'

'Tripe. She's still a kid.' He leaned his face towards her neck, then changed his mind; he turned her round and kissed her, but she didn't respond. He pretended not to mind, and when she pushed him away he tapped her on the bottom so her smile became a reticent laugh; her inhibitions were like icicles.

He said, 'I'll be off then.'

'Will you be late home?'

'Depends on the weather.' When, a few moments later, he left the house, he looked up, and Kit was at the bedroom window waving to him. She blew him a kiss and he blew one back. He buttoned and belted his overcoat, then reset his homburg on his greying head. He knew the neighbours envied him. He had a wife who saw him off each day, and she never failed to blow a kiss. The tram came up the road noisily and empty. It didn't stop. He caught the brass rail and jerked himself aboard.

'Nice day,' the conductor said, 'but cold.'

'Yes.' Bertie struggled to reach his trouser pocket beneath the overcoat to get his money out. 'Yes,' he said, 'nice, but cold.'

19

That night he lay up on his pillows with his hands behind his head. The brass knobs shone at the four corners of the black iron bedstead, and Kit slowly undressed, her poses deliberate. She was doing a private, silly battle with Elsie Buckley for Bertie's attention, and Bertie watched, wondering what it was all about.

He wondered if tonight would be different, if tonight Kit was about to say yes, maybe even say 'Let's', if the sense of excitement he had felt since seeing Elsie Buckley on the doorstep wasn't just his but everyone else's as well. His face was without expression as Kit drew her dress up over her head, her arms crossed before her as she gripped the beige woollen material. She put the dress on a hanger, gently shaking it into place, then she put it into the wardrobe, her legs poised and stretched beneath the white petticoat, her toes prodding into her green furry slippers. Bertie's elbows jutted on the white pillow, his eyes darkened by shadows. Kit removed her petticoat then stood in her vest and knickers, they were rayon, shimmering like silver water. She removed the knickers, rolling the legs with their elastic edges from her thighs, then she undid her suspender belt and peeled off her dark stockings. Bertie's tongue pointed into his cheek, roaming and wandering, afraid to expect too much, yet hoping. Kit put her head into her nightie then let the blue chiffon flounce to her feet, while an expression of approval flashed in and out of Bertie's dark eyes. He had chosen well when he bought her that.

She loosened her hair and shook it back, then laughed. 'Like it? Pretty, isn't it. Thank you.'

He scratched his nose, wondering if even doing that would frighten her off. It was like enticing a deer in a dark forest.

Kit flicked the light switch near the door then ran in the ensuing darkness to the bed. She cuddled into him, gasping, 'Ooh you're lovely and warm.'

He waited, hearing the silence of the dark beyond her little noises, and when she relaxed and sighed he turned towards her and let his hand slide from her waist to her breast.

'Bertie.'

'Mm?' He deliberately sounded dozy, afraid of rushing her.

'You can stop that.'

'You shouldn't tease, Kit.' His nose nuzzled her ear.

'I have never teased in my life.' She stiffened, repulsing, and he rolled himself away from her. 'I'll run off with my new secretary.' He brought a low chuckle into his voice, and Kit humphed. 'To her you're an old man, more than twice her age.'

'Maybe. But I'm not dead yet.'

'You are forty-seven. Soon be fifty.'

The darkness wasn't so dark now. He could see light on the mirror, the slits between the curtains.

He said, gently threatening, 'I will, you know. I'll run off with her. If a man doesn't get his dinner at home, he'll eat out.'

'It's astonishing how vulgar you can be.'

He let his hand rest on her hip bone, then slide to the gentle curve of her belly. He felt her tense, but she didn't push him away.

There was a minute of stillness, of silence, then, 'Oh, all right.' She was martyred, condescending, 'If you must, you must, but get on with it.'

He did as he was told, then he mused, 'I suppose that was my Christmas present?' And Kit lay inert.

'Be thankful you get such a Christmas present,' she murmured, 'a lot of men don't.'

And Bertie believed she really believed it.

He turned over, preparing for sleep, but the bright painted face of Elsie Buckley was in his mind. It had young lips that quivered with laughter, young clear eyes that enticed, and a young throat with soft skin that asked to be touched. He smiled, remembering, unaware that she had needed courage that morning.

21

She had come on the tram, her heart thudding more loudly the closer she got to Prince Edward Road.

She had regarded her old tweed coat as new. She and her mother had paid twopence for it the week before, in a church jumble sale, but as she stepped from the gloom of the tramcar onto the kerb and the sunshine hit her, she knew how shabby she really looked.

She took her cotton gloves off so Mr Hemsworthy wouldn't see the darns in their fingers, and she stuffed them into the black patent envelope-shaped handbag.

The houses here were splendid. Elsie gazed at them open-mouthed as she saw some had sun blinds – very posh, that, like in a magazine – and some had sun curtains covering the front door. Wide stripes of bright orange and greeny colours.

She walked along, noting the numbers. It was an endless terrace, and every house had a garden and a silver-painted gate.

She paused at number 300. It was on the corner of the crossroads, high, wide, yellow-bricked with black paintwork, and imposing. Beside the front door was the brass plate telling her she had found what she sought. The local office of the Unicorn Insurance Company Limited. District Manager: A. H. Hemsworthy.

The bell-pull was brass and the front doorstep was black and white marble.

Elsie hurried away. She was so frightened she could hardly breathe. She stood on the other side of the road, in the shade, where the early October air was made cold by a breeze coming in from the sea. She took the too small square mirror from her handbag and examined her face. She sighed as if bereft. The cloche hat didn't make her look twenty-one. They would guess she was only seventeen. Her lipstick was the wrong colour. It wasn't dark enough, not dried-blood enough, not fashionable enough. They would guess she was poor. Her feet hurt. The Spanish heels on her shoes were like stilts and made the calves of her legs ache. She thought for a moment of taking the shoes off, going barefoot. She did at home. Then common sense took over. She needed a job.

She tried not to compare this street with hers, not to think of the flagstone floors her bare feet were used to, the continual stink of caustic soda in boiling water, used for scrubbing and washing everything.

She hurried back to number three hundred Prince Edward Road. So all right, these people had money, and she wanted a slice of it.

She pulled the bell and waited.

All the rest of her life she would remember the look on Bertie Hemsworthy's face as he opened that big black door and saw her. There was disbelief, charm, amusement and, Elsie always vowed, disdain and arrogance.

After the interview she walked away with rapid short steps on the Spanish heels, in her size two shoes, and she sang a little to herself.

She had got a job at six shillings a week. She would have taken anything at five. She smirked a little, her head on one side as she waited to cross a road. There were horses snorting, harnesses jingling, and hooves clattering. There were wheels rattling, and the dung dropped on the cobbles was a haven for bluebottles that shone like purple and silver glass.

She could twist that Albert Hemsworthy around her little finger. It was as if she knew him, had known him all her life, and in lives before that.

She had seen pictures of men like him in *Peg's Paper*, men with high cheekbones and dark deepset eyes, men with straight dark brows and straight thin lips, men who were tall and lithe and – she bit her lower lip and crossed the road quickly – looked passionate. In *Peg's Paper* such men were dressed in a burnous; they rode galloping horses across the desert while quelling rebellious tribesmen, and in between adventures they carried the terrified white girl to their tent.

Elsie stopped to look in a window. Low in her belly there were the lovely feelings that had first developed when she

23

was about eleven years old. They came quite often now, and she stood enjoying them and thinking about Mr Hemsworthy, then she ran. It was an awkward mincing movement because of her shoes. It gave the impression her knees were tied together, but she was running away from her feelings, from the sensation creeping up and over her. She never minded the feeling when it was low down, isolated, nice and controllable, but when it grew and her mouth went dry, and she longed for a man from *Peg's Paper*, she always had to think of something else; run, sing, scrub the flagged floor again, anything to kill the feeling.

A tramcar rattled past and she wondered, momentarily, whether to catch it, but it would mean another penny gone. She kept running.

In Oxford Street she eased up, panting and flushed. Little globules of perspiration stood out on her crude make-up, causing her tip-tilted nose and puckered upper lip to glisten.

The street was wide, teeming with people and traffic. There was even a car, big and black and open, with some posh people sitting in it arranging their shopping all around them.

Elsie's eyelids drooped a little over her large grey eyes. One day she would have a car. One day she would have so much shopping that she would have to arrange the bags around her. One day she would be so stinking rich that no Albert Hemsworthy would look down his nose at her.

She paused at the main gate into the market. The man with no arms stood there. He had a string around his neck that held a cocoa tin on his chest and a card saying 'Thank you'.

Elsie put a half-penny in his tin. He was a big man, broad, thick-necked. She asked, 'Do you hate the Germans for what they did to you?'

'The bastards,' he said, and his voice tumbled up as if from the pit of blackness.

'It's the government,' a cockle woman said from her stool, her basket of goods set before her. 'It's the rotten

24

government done it – like it's made millions unemployed. They done it. Not the Germans.'

Elsie went into the corner behind them and leaned against the wall. Life was bloody sickening. Some people had sun blinds and canvas curtains to protect the paint on their front door, and others had no arms or had to go picking cockles to sell them in the market.

She bent her knee up and took off her shoe and her stocking. A youth let out a wolf whistle, and when she looked up he gave a large cheeky grin and a wicked wink. 'Bit of all right,' he approved.

Elsie looked at him sourly and waited until he had gone before removing her other shoe and stocking. She stuffed her stockings into her coat pocket, then buttoned the straps of her shoes together and put them around her neck.

'I've just got a job.' She came back to the cockle woman. 'As a secretary. I'm going to be private secretary to a very important man. He's in insurance.'

'Oh aye,' said the woman, not believing, but indulging, and Elsie ran back to the pavement, no longer moving as if her knees were tied together. She dodged around people and laughed, the cloche hat in one hand and the black patent bag in the other, her made-up face clownish on the young body.

'I'm going to be rich,' she repeated loudly. 'Me. Elsie Buckley. I'm going to be rich.'

She scampered down Wind Street, almost unnoticed by people who were used to seeing others barefoot and running.

She paused on the New Cut bridge and stared through the trellis of steel at the dock water below her. It was green, oily, scummy, tranquil, and she breathed in deeply, loving it all. She smiled at the sky, at the white clouds over the black cranes, then she was running the last lap to home.

The house was in the middle of a dozen others called Salubrious Terrace. It was grey with cracked walls, standing precariously above tall narrow worn stone steps, with bits of moss oozing from the supporting wall.

25

'Hi Elsie!' Another youth stopped whistling, his cap on back to front. 'How'z it looking?'

'The same as it's always looked,' Elsie called back, 'clean.' And she ran up the steps.

The passage into the house was narrow, dark and cold. She yelled. 'I'm home,' and continued through the little bare kitchen to the scullery. She looked in the galvanised bucket then yelled, 'Who's used all the water?' She sighed a huge sigh then grabbed the bucket handle so it swung and clanged, and she went out of the rickety back door. She hurried down the path, her dirty feet going thump thump on the hard cinder path, then up the narrow rutted lane.

Two women were at the tap, one watching her bucket fill, the other with arms folded over soft hanging breasts that were barely hidden beneath the sleeveless overall, which was all she wore; her protruding stomach not recognised as a sign of malnutrition.

'Good God,' she growled at Elsie. 'What you done to your face?'

'I've got a job.' Elsie smiled, smug, superior. 'I'm going to be private and confidential secretary in a very important insurance firm.'

'Oh aye.' Both women were disbelieving. People didn't get jobs that easily. 'What insurance firm is that then?'

'The Unicorn.'

'I've heard of it.' One woman took her filled bucket, and the second woman filled hers, watching Elsie's face, then she sighed and went.

Elsie squelched into the cold mud, feeling it ooze between her toes, then she put her head under the tap.

She enjoyed the rushing force of cold water and she rubbed her scalp hard, then she wiped her face with a tiny handkerchief. She made loud brr brr-ing noises as she did it, then she shook her head and fingered back her short brown hair. With the kiss curls and the make-up all gone she looked what she was; a mentally bright street urchin. She clanged her bucket in place and stood with her hands on her hips as it filled, then she heaved it up the lane, up the cinder path and into the back kitchen.

'Ma!' she yelled. 'I got more water. Don't you let our Tommy wash in it. He can go up the tap hisself like I did. It's fer drinking and cooking. That's all.'

She listened for a reply and there wasn't one.

'Ma? You in?'

She went to the kitchen, the passage, then up the bare wooden stairs. 'Ma?'

Gwen Buckley was sitting on the big bed, her small sunken face ashen.

'Ma? You all right? You tired again?'

'The doctor been,' her mother said. 'He left me some Parrish's Food. He got it hisself for me.' She sat placidly with her hands between her thighs, sunk deep in the folds of her grey flannel skirt. 'He says I got consumption – '

A dog was barking in the lane. It sounded far away and unreal, while the noises of the street went on unhindered: horses, children, bicycle bells.

'Consumption,' Elsie said, and stood in the gloom beside the chest of drawers. 'Did he say how bad?'

'Only one lung. Just the top of it.' Gwen's smile was more of a grimace. 'He said it's not galloping. If I don't worry it'll heal up itself.'

'Yes,' Elsie said, 'yes.' Then she brightened artificially brittle in her attempt to be cheerful. 'And I got the job.'

'You did?' Gwen Buckley's eyes lit up like bright crescent moons. 'What's he like? Your new boss.'

'Oh.' Elsie moved to the bed and sat, holding her mother's hands. 'Scrumptious. Handsome. Arrogant. Rich. And he likes me.'

'Of course he does.'

'His wife doesn't. She's tall and dark and skinny. I think she's a cow.'

'Did he say – did he –?'

'Yes Ma. Six shillings.'

'Ooh.'

They fell towards each other, crooning with pleasure.

27

'You see Ma,' Elsie said, 'in a couple of months I'll be getting ten.'

'Oh Elsie.'

'I will. I saw it in his face. He likes me.'

'Now you be careful, my girl. Well-off men are not like the boys around here, mind.'

'And you be careful too, Ma. Get into bed now and I'll make some toast. I'll put some jam on it. Right?'

'Right,' her mother chuckled, and she climbed towards the pillows. Elsie pulled the dark grey blanket up over Gwen's shoulders. 'Now you rest,' she ordered, her chin set in determination. 'You've had a shock. Tomorrow you'll feel better.' And she went back downstairs, smiling.

Ten shillings a week! Soon she would ask Mr Hemsworthy for ten shillings a week, and not everybody died of consumption. Sometimes they hung on for years. She had heard about it.

CHAPTER TWO

Elsie was early for work on Monday morning and every morning after. She got up at six and washed herself into pink shiny glowing happiness, then she emptied the bowl over the hard earth that sprouted clumps of wild dog-daisies outside the back door, wiped up her splashes in the scullery, and hung the face flannel and towel on the string line over the Dover stove.

She found the half of a discoloured broken mirror, balanced it on the small scullery table against the wall, then sat on the rickety broken-backed wooden chair and gazed at her blurred reflection.

Carefully she painted herself. Arched thin eyebrows, lifted as she concentrated, rounded painted doll blobs of rouge and carefully shaped rosebud lips. Then the powder, flicked on so it clouded around her head, smelling strongly. For her kiss curls she dissolved sugar in hot water and told herself it was all for a good cause.

She smiled to herself, locked in the world of illusion. Unable to see herself properly in the old piece of mirror, she was content to believe she had gilded the lily and was beautiful enough to drive men mad. Especially rich, successful men.

She ran in her stockinged feet for her Phul-Nana and tipped the cheap little bottle onto her finger, then dabbed the finger behind each ear and between her breasts.

Her blouse was low and had cost all of three and eleven-pence. Elsie was ready to face the world.

She was convinced Bertie was fascinated by her, lusting after her. To a certain extent he was, but usually only as one might be fascinated by a new creature in the zoo. Sometimes he thought about it. He wanted to stare at Elsie as he had once stared at a gaudy parrot. Its colours had been exotic, but it had cunning, darting eyes, whereas Elsie's eyes were big and grey and naive and trusting.

It was early December and Elsie had sat at the smaller desk near the window every weekday for over two months. Bertie was getting used to her, even learning to forget she was there, but she often leaned against him, maybe to get a paper clip. He was irritated by it. The girl lacked manners and, at times, when she forgot herself, her diction was deplorable.

On one occasion he turned to her in exasperation and his gaze was riveted by her breasts. The deep neck of her blouse hung loosely as she bent, and her bosom was there, soft and smooth and young. He felt his body react and he laughed impulsively. 'Oh, I can see your tummy. Yum yum yummy.'

Elsie's face screwed into laughter and the tip of her tongue shone quivering and scarlet between her lips. 'Oh Mr Hemsworthy. You are a devil.'

'Me?' he teased. 'Bend over the agents like that and the company will be bankrupt. I'll never get them back to work.'

She flushed with pleasure, and Bertie said more seriously, 'I would prefer you without make-up.'

'How d'you know? You've never seen me without it.'

'Try me.' He was assessing her now, his tongue poking inside his cheek.

She moved to her own desk with an exaggerated swing to her hips and Bertie got up.

He went to the kitchen unwittingly like a small boy avoiding temptation.

Kit was making bread, kneading and bashing, her black hair coiled in two small plaits against her ears. She paused and looked at him. 'What do you want?' She hadn't meant it unkindly but it came out a rebuke, and Bertie shrugged.

'Nothing.' He looked at the wooden clock on the high

30

wide mantelpiece. He stood before the fire, watching her, aware that soon she would drop the dough into the big yellow mixing-bowl and stand it on the fender with a linen tea-cloth over it.

He wondered what he was doing there, why he had left the columns of figures he had been checking, and he tried not to remember Elsie's breasts, the sudden unexpected shock of seeing them so close. If he had made a quick movement of his head he could have almost bitten them.

Kit jerked her head to where he was standing. She said, 'I'll want to come there in a moment.'

'Yes. All right.' He swayed back a little on his heels, feeling the heat rising from the black-leaded cast iron of the oven. 'I suppose I'd better get back to the office.'

Her reply was cool, impersonal. 'I'll make a cup of tea in a while.'

He nodded and watched her; long floured fingers, strong and deft, then bare fore-arms, the sleeves of her beige dress rolled up above her elbows. Funny how Kit always wore dull colours. Elsie always seemed to wear yellow or pink or green. Come to think of it, he liked the girl in that mauvy colour best. Made him think of sweet peas on a June evening, when the sky was purple and the moon was full and hot and low.

He rubbed his hand over his chin and frowned. He was getting maudlin.

Kit slapped the dough, then felt the bowl. It was the correct degree of warmth and she sighed, then she dropped the dough into it.

'Out of the way,' she said, and he moved, his hands in his trouser pockets. It was odd the way Kit concentrated so hard on what she was doing, blocking him out. Elsie couldn't reach for a paper clip without seeming to entice him.

His mind balked on the idea. Enticing? Was she? Or was she just a kid unwittingly using a power she hadn't yet realised she had? He pursed his lips and began a doleful little whistle.

31

Kit put the bowl on the fender, her usually pale face made pink in the fire's glow. She arranged the tea-cloth as a cover then stood, tall and straight. She looked at her hands then went to the table and rubbed them together, removing the remnants of dough. She said suddenly, 'I'm pregnant.'

'Oh yes,' Bertie said politely, then realised what she had said. There was a shocked hesitation while his lungs felt empty, and he slowly filled them, doing it quietly, as if afraid any noise would be disastrous.

She stood with her back to him, ram-rod straight, silent fury and fear like an invisible aura about her.

His lips were apart, dry, then he licked them and gave a grunting little laugh. 'You can't be – unless it's the Holy Ghost. I haven't been near you – '

'October,' she said. 'The day you made Elsie Buckley your secretary.'

'The day *we* made her my secretary. You were referred to.'

Kit shrugged and began clearing the table, the paper of the flour bag noisy as she folded its top in, the knife clinking against the basin that had held the yeast as she moved the cutlery. 'I am not going to carry it.'

'You can't be sure!' He felt he was drowning in her silent accusations. The words she had thrown at him during her previous pregnancies, the taunts about men being like animals, filthy beasts expecting wives to succumb, submit, suffer the torture of lust and labour for the satiation of men's desires.

His shoulders moved helplessly. The room seemed full of heat, the smell of yeast, and Kit's misery. He moved to her, ready to cuddle, to soothe, to comfort.

'Don't touch me,' she warned. 'Go away. Go and ogle Miss Buckley. She'll go to bed with you. And with any other thing in trousers.'

'Did the doctor say when? I mean – '

'I haven't seen the doctor. I don't need to. I've had two miscarriages and two babies. D'you think I don't know when I'm pregnant?'

32

'Maybe – ' he sought words of help, 'you have been overdoing things – '

'Not for two months. For two months Miss Buckley has run that office. Miss Buckley answers the telephone, the letters, Miss Buckley sees to the agents . . . ' Her voice was rising and Bertie hurriedly closed the door between them and the passage, neither he nor Kit realising it was jealousy provoking her.

'Kit. I'm as stunned as you are. Hell, I'm forty-seven, I don't want a baby screaming all night.' He was trying to soothe her. Deep inside him there was a tiny thrill that he was still capable of doing the trick, of putting a woman in the club.

He thought momentarily of a little one taking his hand for its first steps, of seeing a tiny wet baby mouth framing the famous word 'Dadda.' God, it might be a boy!

Kit turned and saw the light in his eyes, the hunger that every man feels with the hope of reproducing himself.

She said, 'Oh Bertie,' and they came together, clinging. 'I can't have it. I can't. I'm terrified.'

'Oh come on.' He was caressing her neck, nuzzling his cheek against hers. 'Maybe this time it won't be so bad.'

'Oh it will. It will. You don't understand.' Her tears were wet between them. He could taste them. His quiver of delight at the thought of fatherhood was suffocated almost before it was born. Kit was unhappy and so he needed to be unhappy too. They couldn't afford a baby. He could survive without a son. He had two daughters.

'Oh Bertie. Why did you do it to me?'

He squirmed inside, guilty, bewildered. 'Maybe the doctor can help.'

'Yes, of course.' She moved from him, taking the white handkerchief from his breast pocket and blowing her nose in it. She snuffled, 'I ironed the others. I'll get you one.'

'No. You sit down.' Subconsciously he hoped to put things right, to elevate her opinion of him from the depths to which it had sunk, to be forgiven.

'Sit down. I'll make us both a cup of tea. Unless you'd

33

like a drink. A whisky?' God, he thought, I need a whisky. I need a thousand whiskies.

'Tea will be nice.' Kit sat as though exhausted, her hands still floury. 'I'm sorry, Bertie. I'm sorry. I'm a coward, but I can't – ' She began to snuffle again, her amber eyes even darker than their shadowed hollows, the crow's feet deepening as she grimaced.

He jammed his teeth together as he found the teapot still held stale tea, then went to the scullery and emptied it in the sink. He waited for Kit to rebuke him, to complain, but she didn't. She sat, limp, spent, as if the weight of her condition had truly proved too much.

She called, 'I think I knew last month. I waited to make sure.' Her hand squeezed one breast through the thickness of clothing as if re-enacting something she had done often recently. 'They were sore. It's always a sign. With me anyway.'

He came back to the kitchen and made tea, avoiding the bowl of dough on the fender, glad the kettle was always ready, hissing steam. He fumbled, making a lot of noise as he prepared the cups, and had a vague idea a bell was ringing. It was far away, part of another life, and he was startled when Elsie knocked on the door. She opened it and stuck her head around.

'Bertie, it's Head Office on the phone. They want to talk to you.'

'Blast!'

Her head bobbed as if she wanted to withdraw quickly, her gaze taking in the scene, her senses knocked by the atmosphere of tension and stress. 'Shall I tell them you've just gone out? I'll say I didn't know – '

'It's all right. Tell them I'm coming.'

Elsie smiled politely, curiously. This was a new picture of the Hemsworthys. She wanted to know more, but she nodded, agreeing with anything and everything. 'Yes. I'll tell them.' She hurried away, the Spanish heels tap-tapping on the linoleum then silent on the mats.

Bertie gave Kit her cup of tea. 'Shall I get you an aspirin?'

She shook her head. 'No. It's all right. I was tired. The bread. The kneading. Once it's in the oven I can open the back door, cool the place down – I'll see the doctor tomorrow – '

He kissed the top of her head and left her. He went back to his other world, to the scent of Phul-Nana, of paper and ledgers, of red and blue inks, of cigarette smoke and the noise of trams, carts and horses rattling past the window.

Next day Kit donned her tight little felt hat, put on her grey woollen suit beneath a grey coat and went to see Dr Sullivan in the centre of town. His waiting room was small, airless, and crammed with people in shabby clothing. Kit always longed to transfer to a better class practitioner, simply because she longed for a better class waiting-room, preferably with a large, fringed, oriental carpet and a large, round, mahogany table bearing glossy magazines.

As it was, Dr Sullivan and Kit's mother had known each other in the old days, and so Kit had remained loyal to him all her life.

Now she drew her feet in even closer under the bench she sat on, so another smelly man could squeeze past her into the surgery. She smiled up at him, feeling kind and condescending. The poor man could probably not afford a bar of soap, and a not-so-little surge of satisfaction flooded through her. How nice not to be like these people. How nice to be comparatively well-off.

Her smile became even more kind, more condescending, and she bestowed it on everyone, those who cared to stare at her with unveiled curiosity and those who knew she was Mrs Hemsworthy, the lovely woman who wasn't too grand to have the same doctor as they.

She had waited almost an hour when her turn came and she went into the surgery.

Dr Sullivan sat amid his glass-fronted cupboards that were full of bottles and jars, and peered up at her from under bushy, gingery eyebrows. His lashes were almost white, a phenomenon that fascinated Kit whose own lashes like those of everyone else she knew, were dark.

'Hm,' he said, and his fine head moved up and down as his eager gaze sought sign of Kit's need for medication. He saw none so he sat back in his wooden armchair and clasped hairy red hands across his chest. 'Hullo Kitty.' His voice was gruff. 'How's your mother?' He took moments to remember when he and Kit's mother were at university, different subjects, of course, but they were good days.

'Fine.' Kit smiled, as much in awe of him now as when she was a child.

'Huh.' His heavy head seemed too big for his frail body and it moved up and down again. 'What's the trouble?'

'I'm pregnant.'

'Huh.' He unclasped his hands, and lowered his eyes to hide any expression that might show in them. 'Albert pleased? It might be that son he keeps wanting. Maybe another colonel in the family.' He looked at her now, prepared for anything she might say. 'Your father would be pleased by that, wouldn't he?'

Kit licked her lips. Her father would be pleased, and so would her mother. And so would everyone except herself. She said, louder than she intended, 'I do not want it.'

Dr Sullivan nodded again and pursed his lips. He was a bent man, crouched in his chair, dressed in tweeds as gingery as his colouring. 'A bit late to think of that, Kitty.'

'You know I never wanted another one. Why can't they invent something that stops women having babies all the time?'

'Hm.' He was watching her keenly now. She was bony, pasty, nervous, scared out of her wits, but she was strong, wiry, and her recuperative powers were good. 'You never wanted the two girls, Kitty. D'you regret having them now?'

She tried to avoid an answer, then gave one that was not completely true. 'No.'

'There then.' He shrugged. The problem was solved.

'I do not want it,' she repeated. 'I've thought about it. I've lain awake night after night thinking about it . . .' She licked her lips again, fear beginning to deepen in her unusual eyes. 'I can't go through that again. I can't. Honestly – '

Dr Sullivan kept looking at her. He was used to hearing women say they couldn't go through that again, but they invariably managed it.

He patted her knee, 'It's natural to feel like that at first, Kitty girl, but you'll be all right. I'll come as soon as you need me.' He was smiling now, liking her, remembering her as the skinny child presenting her teddy bear for a cursory examination.

He lifted the ends of his stethoscope from around his neck and plugged them into his ears. 'Lift up your jumper, Kitty. Let me check on you.'

Kit's long thin fingers fumbled, the knowledge that he was not going to help her making her face taut. 'I can't have it, Doctor.' She struggled to control her desperation. 'I can't. Give me something to shift it. Please.'

Both his ears were plugged. He didn't hear her. Her heart beat strongly and purposefully. Many of his patients would willingly bear the pain of childbirth in exchange for such a heart.

He removed the stethoscope. 'Open your mouth, Kitty. Good girl. Say ah. Hm. I'll give you a tonic – '

'Give me something to shift it. Please.' It was a hoarse, muffled shout, and his gaze locked with hers. His was reprimanding, hers was defiant, determined.

'Kitty! Now pull yourself together.' He spoke sharply, a man who might have married her mother, but lacked the ambition Lorraine Nolan adored, a man who had brought Kit into the world, and felt it his prerogative to treat her like a distant relation. 'You are a strong, healthy young woman. There is no reason why you can't have another strong, healthy child.'

'They might use instruments again. I'm small there. You said so. My babies are always big-boned. Emma was ten pounds – '

He sighed and took her hand, changing his tactics smoothly. His voice became calming. 'How far gone are

37

you? Two months? Well then, seven months and it will all be over.'

'I'm not having it.'

He drew his pad towards him and scrawled out a prescription. Consumption, fever, pregnancy, starvation, or just no further will to live, the palliative was a prescription. He ripped it off the pad and pushed it towards her. 'Come and see me again in a month, Kitty my dear. You'll be feeling your old cheerful self by then.'

Kit avoided looking at him. At that moment she hated him. He was a hypocrite, pretending friendship when he had none to give. She took the prescription quickly. 'Thank you. Goodbye.'

'Remember me to your mother.'

She swept out, her head high. To hell with the man; she should have known better than to come here in the first place.

She threaded her way between the packed benches in the waiting-room, and ignored the receptionist behind the high insulating counter. She felt near to tears, to heaving great sobs, and thought she saw pity in a woman's eyes. The woman wore a man's tweed cap and a checked flannel shawl over a black dress that was greying with wear, but Kit appreciated the woman's smile, the woman's sympathetic voice as she murmured, 'Never mind, love.'

It didn't matter what was wrong. In such a place they were two women drawn there by trouble, and Kit smiled in return. She swallowed the lump in her throat, the fear like maggots in her blood, and went out into the street.

With a shock she realised that life was going on as normal out there. A policeman watched the traffic, the light catching his buttons, the spike on the crown of his helmet seeming to wait for hoopla rings, and Kit began to giggle as tears began to fall. She hardly saw where she was walking, but she knew where she was going.

To see Mrs Skummings in Lone Row.

The small white cottages known as Lone Row were hidden. They ran obliquely from a north side main road

38

that had no tram lines. Their front and back gardens were narrow, but long, full of tall trees: lilac, laburnum, sycamore, and at least one mountain ash, so unless one was looking for the narrow opening in the rampaging privet hedges, Lone Row was never disturbing.

Kit knew where it was. In the early days before they had enough work to offer a full-time agent, she had collected premiums for three days a week. And one of the best payers had been Mrs Skummings, of number three, Lone Row.

Now Kit approached the shining, half-glassed door with defiant courage. There was a huge spider plant hanging inside the window, and the lace curtains were white and frilly and new, held back loosely with blue ribbons.

Mrs Skummings had seen Kit coming up the narrow, twisting crazy paving, where the lavender and rosemary fought for prominence. When she opened her front door her thick, steel-grey hair was combed freshly back to its bun, and her nose heavily powdered.

'Well . . . .' Her face was alight with feigned surprise, but her eyes sparkled with real pleasure. 'Mrs Hemsworthy! Come in. Do come in.' She stomped into the parlour, her size dwarfing its beamed quaintness, her composure as one with the highly polished furniture. There was a round gate-legged table with four matching chairs. They were straight-backed and leather-seated. There was a tall bookcase her father had bequeathed her, the set of encyclopaedias standing with the black family bible like ornaments.

There was no empty space for the two women to stand together, so Kit stood one side of the gate-legged table and Mrs Skummings stood the other. They spent a moment looking at each other. Kit had lost the attitude of defiance provoked by Dr Sullivan. As she came through the cottage door her head had instinctively lifted to the arrogant position, but her face was more pale than usual, and her nostrils were slightly dilated with nervousness.

'Well, let's sit down,' Mrs Skummings said. 'Would you like a cup of tea? I have Mazawattee or China. As you like.'

Kit thought fleetingly that Mrs Skummings seemed to be a darn sight better off than the Hemsworthys. There was not, and never had been, any sign of shortage in the cottage.

'No thank you,' she said, and both women sat on the edge of big leather armchairs, their knees and feet together, their hands in their laps.

Mrs Skummings waited, a woman of experience where other women were concerned.

Kit said, 'It's a lovely day, isn't it?'

'Yes,' smiled Mrs Skummings, and still waited.

Kit admired the spider plant framed by the glistening multi-paned window, and commented on the busy lizzy that stood on the sill, still a mass of pink flowers. 'They're perfect,' she said. 'It's a sunny window.'

Mrs Skummings nodded. 'Would you like a glass of port, Mrs Hemsworthy? I have tawny or ruby.'

'Thank you.' It was almost a gasp. 'Yes, please. Sweet. That would be very nice.'

Kit removed her brown kid gloves as she watched Mrs Skummings open the cupboard at the base of the bookcase and take out a dark bottle and glasses. Then the ruby red wine flowed and a glass was handed to her.

Mrs Skummings held her own glass up and looked across at Kit. 'Here's to the end of all worries, Mrs Hemsworthy. And to the new worries that'll take their place.'

'Yes,' Kit smiled weakly, lifted her glass in acknowledgement and sipped.

The port was rich and potent. Kit savoured it, then she carefully placed her glass on one of the neatly crocheted little place mats on the table. 'Mrs Skummings,' she said, 'we have known each other a long time.'

'Eight years or more.'

'And I have never found you to be a gossipy woman.'

'Heaven forbid!' Mrs Skummings poured herself another glass of port.

'I want you to do me a favour.'

'Yes?' Mrs Skummings put the bottle back in the

cupboard and grunted as her corset bit into her ribs. 'Anything I can do I will do.' She stood, again waiting, and as Kit said nothing more she sat, this time well back in the chair, her thighs apart for comfort, her skirt and purple apron not quite covering the elasticated legs of the pink directoire knickers that covered her knees.

Outside the sun shone and the trees shuddered. A bush of Michaelmas daisies looked unreal.

Mrs Skummings said gently, 'You can talk to me, my dear. There is no one else here. We are quite alone.'

Kit licked her lower lip then suddenly looked right into Mrs Skummings's cat-like eyes.

'I'm pregnant.'

Mrs Skummings blinked, but any expression on her face was immediately smoothed away.

'Yes dear?'

'I want you to move it for me. Get rid of it.'

Mrs Skummings moved uneasily, lifting one shoulder then the other, the glass turning slowly in her fingers. She said shrewdly, 'What makes you think I can do such a thing?'

'You're well known – '

'Oh. Am I?' Mrs Skummings swigged the dregs from her glass and said, 'That could be defamation of character you know. I could sue the person who said that.'

'Not if it's true.' Kit faced her like a terrier with a poised snake. 'I will pay well, and I'm told you are reliable.'

It sounded as if Kit had discussed the matter with a third person, but she hadn't. She had come to the cottage on the strength of whispered gossip, the threads of rumour that could have meant nothing.

Mrs Skummings put her glass on one of the ecru cloths, then stretched her fingers and looked at them. 'Does your husband know you are here?'

'No. No one knows.'

Mrs Skummings watched Kit thoughtfully, then she relaxed her hands and said, 'I will have to come to your house – '

41

'Of course.'

'The sooner the better.'

'Yes.'

'Tomorrow?'

'All right.'

'In the morning. About eleven o'clock. Can you be alone then? What about the children?'

'They'll be at school. My husband will be out. He's arranged to go canvassing tomorrow.'

'What about that girl who helps him in the office? Miss Buckley.'

'She'll be out, too. He's taking her with him to teach her the business.'

'Right then.' Mrs Skummings stood up. The interview was over. 'I want the money in the morning. Before I do anything.'

'How much?' Kit was tense now, her shoulders ached. She was frightened, but being frightened of tomorrow was preferable to being terrified of seven months from now.

'Ten pounds.'

Kit gasped. It was a month of Bertie's salary, but she nodded, then her head came up again and she stood, tall, thin, but confident, and with a certain air of elegance, of refinement. 'I'll expect you, Mrs Skummings.'

Neither woman deferred to the other. In their own ways they each regarded themselves superior. To Mrs Skummings Kit might be a manager's wife with a big Edwardian house the monied side of town, but, she, Mrs Skummings, owned half a dozen houses, small but excellent investments, and people like Mrs Hemsworthy soon lost their hoity-toity manner over a bucket of soapy water and a quick sharp haemorrhage.

To Kit, Mrs Skummings might be spotlessly clean and highly solvent, but she was still a back-street abortionist, a spider gloating over the blood of her victims.

Mrs Skummings stomped past Kit to the minute passage, and opened the front door. The scent of wet gardens flooded in and a sparrow fled from the crazy paving.

42

'In the morning, then,' Kit said, and stepped out. The air smelled good. She had made a decision and stuck to it. Her fear was mingled with relief. This time tomorrow it would all be over.

At the wicker gate she turned and waved. Mrs Skummings waved back. Both women smiled, then Mrs Skummings went back into her cottage and Kit walked fast, seeking a street where tramcars ran. She wondered why God had arranged for chickens and fish to reproduce so easily, while women had to suffer so. Maybe, she thought, it was Eve's fault, for luring Adam on.

CHAPTER THREE

Bertie awoke but felt he hadn't been to sleep. He was still wretchedly tired and already he had a headache. He listened for Kit, her body curled up away from him, and heard her deep exhausted breathing.

Stress could do this to you. Stress could suddenly cripple your days and torture your nights. He pulled himself up slowly and tried to peep at Kit's face in the December morning darkness, but it was covered by her loose black hair, and her arms and shoulders were well covered by the rose-coloured quilt, where she had drawn it higher against the cold.

It was as if his heart became tangled with his lungs as he wondered where their marriage had gone wrong, why he had failed to make Kit happy. Maybe it was because they had never loved each other. He lay quietly back on his pillow and thought about loving; about Kit on the day they married. She had worn a big cream hat of soft straw; there had been real pink-tinted cream roses beneath its wide brim, and her complexion had been as soft and lovely as their petals. Her brown eyes had glowed in reflected light and as she held his hand, coming from the chapel altar, he had sensed her happiness as one senses a vibration. He, too, had been happy, filled with the completion of an ambition: to belong and to have someone belonging. He had been so sure that a lifetime of good companionship, an affectionate relationship, stretched ahead, yet now, thirteen years later, they irritated each other.

He tried not to think of separation. People didn't separate, at least, not decent people. Tawdry people did: those who went on the stage, or those who had so much money they could ride the scandal, flee the country until everything died down.

He moved his legs out from the warmth of the bed and sat with his feet on the multi-coloured rag mat he and Kit had made during the first year they were married. He had given her almost all she had said she wanted, he had kept his side of the bargain: a nice house, the sort of neighbours her parents could approve of, a private school for her children . . . There had been only two things that had been in her dreams that he hadn't yet attained; a car and holidays abroad.

He rubbed his hands over his face. He dammed any thoughts of what his own hopes had been. He knew them too well: a warm, soft bed containing a warm responsive woman, meals when he needed them. Help when he needed it. And a wife he could take anywhere without feeling embarrassed or ashamed. He also wanted a son: a fine strapping boy who would make him proud and carry on his name.

He sighed and shivered. It was cold, and he stood reaching for his heavy dressing-gown from the nearby basket chair. He supposed both he and Kit had been idealists, expecting too much of each other. He turned to look at her, his gaze accustomed to the dark now, and her eyes were open, glittering as she peered over her shoulder. She said softly, 'Penny for them,' and he chuckled ruefully.

'You go back to sleep,' he said, 'I'll see to the kids.'

She turned on to her back, stretching her legs. 'You are going to Port Talbot with John Davies today?' It was a statement because she knew it was true, yet it was a question because she needed to be sure.

'I had hoped so.' He watched her, the concern cloying inside him, the headache piercing. 'Will you be all right?'

'You've spent all night worrying?'

'Not really.'

'Liar.' She pushed her hair back off her face. 'Your eyes are lost in big black holes.'

He tied his dressing-gown about him and picked up his

46

clothes. 'I'll get dressed downstairs, so you go back to sleep,' he ordered. 'Go on. You need enough sleep for two.'

She moved the edge of the sheet from against her chin. 'What worries you most? Me expecting another baby, or me not wanting it?'

He snorted derisively. 'Both, I suppose. It would be easier if we could be happy about it. If I could throw a party to celebrate, instead of feeling a sinner for creating it.'

Her retort was just as derisive. 'Oh God, beautiful dreamer.'

He got to the door. 'D'you want a cup of tea? Or what?'

'Or what,' she said.

'Stop being funny, Kit.'

'All right.' She sounded mollified. 'I'll stay here a while, if you don't really mind. I don't want a cup of tea.'

Downstairs he raked the ashes out of the grate while waiting for the small kettle to boil on the stove. The wood was already chopped and dry on the fender. He arranged it in the well of the grate with newspaper and coal, then drank his first cup of tea of the day as the flames licked and caught. He washed at the sink, glad of the hot water from the tank. He wondered if his two daughters would settle for boiled eggs and toast, and in the back of his mind the sadness persisted that neither he nor Kit seemed to know what married love was all about.

He had had a crush when he was seventeen. He had whispered, 'I love you' to many women during the war. Sometimes the endearment 'chérie' came after it, and once he had found it prudent to add 'liebchen', but he had known, and had assumed that they too had known, that these words merely helped the moments along, a little magic in a world of meetings and sudden partings.

Yes, his daughters would settle for boiled eggs. Linda had another stye on her eye. At twelve she seemed all bones and moods. Bertie told himself she took after Kit: skinny, often pasty, but as strong as an ox.

Emma was five and inclined to be a fatty. She was delightfully knock-kneed and dimple-faced. She talked a

47

lot, confidently, and, Bertie thought sadly, would have become a crack canvasser if she had been a boy. Now she chirruped as she chewed, 'Miss Jones said that all school fees will have to go up. It's the books and the balls. She said they all cost money. Nobody looks after books properly and the balls keep getting lost.'

Bertie grimaced obligingly. 'Fancy that. Did Miss Jones say what did not cost money these days?'

Linda pushed her plate away. 'That was scrumptious Dad. You boil eggs better than anyone I know.' She lifted her face and he kissed her nose. Linda needed loving too. He sensed it every time he kissed her, she needed loving more than Emma. Unless, he watched his two daughters leave the table and start getting into their coats, unless, he thought, Emma was unaware of love because she never lacked it. She was confident of her safety among them. So was love merely a confidence in another? And if so, was it possible he loved Kit? If so, it was disappointing, too mundane.

He made the girls tiptoe through the passage, and whisper their goodbyes, and as they went, their hands waving small and white from the open top of the tram, Elsie came. She stood at the gate with him watching the tram rattle down the road and disappear around the bend, then she laughed. 'I like your pinny.'

He looked down at himself, then laughed with her and took the apron off. 'Kit's having a lie-in. I'm doing my good deed for the day.'

They went into the house quietly and she took the mail off the hallstand where he had put it.

'Shall I attend to this?' Her voice was hushed but her Phul-Nana was strong this morning, and she had added a fur collar to her coat; it curved softly round her neck and he wanted to touch it.

She knew and said, 'From a jumble sale in the church. Ma got it.'

'Nice.'

They nodded, enveloped in the silence as if in a conspiracy.

She followed him to the kitchen and shut the door. It closed off their sound from Kit, but closed them in together.

She said, 'What time are we going? There's a train about ten.'

He began clearing the table, carrying too many dishes at once, laying them noisily in the sink in the scullery. 'You aren't going.'

'You promised!' She followed him again, and there were two crease lines between her thinly arched eyebrows. 'You said I could learn. I need to know what it's like working outside.'

'You are staying here.'

'Why?'

'Because I say so.'

'That's not fair.' Her rosebud-painted mouth pouted.

'You do as you are told, madam, understand.'

She scowled, a seventeen-year-old with one hand on a postured hip. 'You promised.'

'Well, it'll teach you not to trust men, won't it?'

'There isn't much to do in the office today.'

'Find something.'

She undid her coat and shook it off. 'You can leave those dishes then, I'll do them.'

'Good girl.' He smiled at her. 'I don't want Kit left on her own. Not today.'

'Why?'

'If I wanted you to know I would have told you. Now get into the office and I'll wash and shave.'

She smiled quickly, flirting again, then hurried away.

He cut his chin and stuck a piece of cotton wool on the slit before putting on a clean starched collar, cursing the back stud and front button. He combed his thick dark hair, noticing the grey at the temples, then he crept up the stairs.

Kit was asleep, her breathing deep. He stood watching her in the pale light from the doorway, then he crept back to Elsie in the office. 'Anything interesting in the post?'

'A fire claim on John Davies's book. The woman says

49

she's burned a lot of stuff. It was on a line over the Dover and the string broke.'

'I'll tell John this morning. Who is she?'

'Travers. A Mrs Travers, Number one, Wern View.'

'Right. Drop her a line. Tell her the agent will be calling within a few days.'

She made a note, and he gave instructions on other tasks to be done, then he went.

In the street he looked up at the bedroom window, but it remained curtained and blank. He looked down, at the office window, and Elsie was there. She smiled and waved, then she blew a kiss. Without thinking he blew one back, then watched as she caught it in mime and put it down the neck of her blouse.

He tossed his head and grinned, some girls had odd ideas, then he was running for the tram, his briefcase swinging and his homburg on the back of his head.

Elsie turned from the window and listened to the silence of the house. To her, the rooms were huge, the windows light and splendid, even on this dull, grey December day. It wasn't the first time she had been left alone and, normally, she didn't mind, but today she felt restless, vexed. Bertie had promised to let her learn the insurance business from A to Z, and she had been anxious to see just how canvassing was done, to hear the patter.

One day, she vowed, she would canvas her own book. One day she would be a manager. The first woman manager the world had ever seen.

She sat at Bertie's desk and swivelled around in his chair. She fingered one of his cigars and wondered who she could telephone, then she wondered about Christmas; it was three weeks away, and she needed money.

She mused on the price of chicken. She had seen the advertisement in Lipton's window, ORDER YOUR CHRISTMAS POULTRY NOW, and she longed to order a chicken. Last year the Buckley family had had a rabbit. This year Elsie dreamed of walking into the little terraced house with a bag full of shopping. There would be an iced cake, stuffing, and some crackers. She smiled, lost in the illusion of her family pulling crackers, of placing gaudy paper hats on their heads and eating chicken. Even her father would be laughing.

She ought to ask Ma about a pudding. Ma usually made a pudding in the cast iron boiler on the stove. She hadn't this year. Not yet.

Upstairs Kit got out of bed and went to the bathroom, and Elsie heard her. She hurried from Bertie's chair to her own. She sighed and sorted through the paperwork he had left her. She hadn't done the dishes as she had promised. She made as if to go to the kitchen but already Kit was coming down.

Kit was singing in a low busy voice and Elsie sat in silence, listening. Kit didn't come into her, didn't call 'good morning'. Neither had anyone explained why Elsie needed to stay in today. What was wrong with Kitty Hemsworthy that Bertie didn't want her left alone?

The atmosphere seemed to retain the secretiveness that Bertie had generated when he first put his finger to his lips, gesturing Elsie's arrival to silence, and Elsie felt no desire to break it.

She stared at the window. How clean it was, the panes practically invisible. The street was quiet. The end of a lace curtain fluttered from the bottom of an open attic window across the road.

Elsie looked again at the letter from Mrs Travers. It was badly written, illiterate. Elsie wondered if the fire was genuine. With Christmas so close it was no sin to burn a load of old clothes and snap the line over the stove yourself. Ma did it once, and the Prudential paid out.

Elsie kept herself busy, clearing old stuff from the pigeon-holes, filing papers she had hoped would just go away of their own accord if she ignored them.

Kit went up and downstairs a few times. She sounded very busy, very pre-occupied. Elsie wondered about the time. She didn't possess a watch and the office clock had stopped, but Kit usually either called her to the kitchen for elevenses, or brought in a tray, depending on the day. On Wednesdays and Fridays, for instance, there was no time to leave the office. It was a case of sup tea while working.

Elsie fancied a cup of tea now. It must be eleven o'clock. She sat and wondered what to do, and why she seemed to be hiding, yet to walk boldly out became a more challenging task every second. Wouldn't Kit say, 'Oh Elsie, I didn't know you were there,' and wouldn't Kit want to know why she had been so quiet?

Elsie opened her bag and drew some more lipstick onto the rosebud mouth that was wearing off. Then she decided to type. If she made a noise Kit would be bound to come to her. Elsie could claim to have been so busy she had been unaware of time passing. It wasn't the most brilliant idea ever, but it appealed to Elsie and she rolled carbon and papers into her machine. She drew Mrs Travers's letter to a more convenient position and prepared to answer it.

That was when the gate clanged, the kitchen door opened, and Kit came quickly up the passage.

Elsie's fingers were above the typewriter keys. She was tense, like a dog with its hackles up yet not seeing the intruder. And she heard Kit saying breathlessly, 'Oh, I thought you had changed your mind – '

There was a bustle of someone coming in, taking off their hat and coat and placing them on the hallstand.

Kit was frightened, effusive. She rubbed her hands together then rubbed her arms as if to hurry her circulation.

'Would you like a cup of tea first?'

'No thank you. We'd best get on.'

They went upstairs and Elsie quietly opened the office door and peeped out at the ascending women. Her jaw dropped.

She knew Hettie Skummings. Jesus! Everybody knew Hettie-the-shift-it. Elsie thought she had recognised that voice, muted as it had been through the closed door. Now she spoke to herself quietly. 'Thank God I opened the door and had a peeper.' Did Bertie know? Was this why he had made her stay in? What did he expect her to do? Call the dicks?

She looked at the telephone. Should she phone Maggie Davies? Tell Maggie to get on her bike and find her husband, John, and Bertie?

She moved to the telephone. But what if Bertie knew Hettie was coming? He'd play merry hell if she made a fuss for nothing.

Fancy Mrs Hemsworthy having an abortion! You never could tell with these posh types. They were no better than anyone else if the truth be told. All plum-in-the-mouth talk, yet running to Hettie Skummings just like the women in Salubrious Terrace.

Elsie shivered. Annie Dawkins had died after Hettie-the-shift-it had shoved her enema into her. No one had split on her. No one knew anything. The time might come when you were glad of Hettie's knock at your door. Sometimes life got so unbearable that dying trying to shift a kid was better than living and trying to rear it. And Hettie was supposed to be cheap.

Oh Mother of God!

Elsie stood against the wall of the office and unconsciously prayed.

Hettie Skummings went to the bathroom. Elsie could imagine her filling the white enamel bucket, swishing the suds in it, squeezing the enema in it, trying it out, and Elsie crossed her own legs hard.

'God,' she whispered, 'if ever I'm in the pudding club I'll keep it. I'm warning you now, God, I'll keep it. So don't you let me click till it's a good man who'll look after me and the kid.' She listened hard for a while. A board creaked above her, but the bedroom carpet deadened other sounds, and her blood stopped pounding so hard. She became less apprehensive, more impatient with stupid rich people.

If Kit Hemsworthy didn't want more children she should have made him use something. What are French letters for anyway? Nobody has to have kids. And why go

53

to Hettie, of all people? There were others, better, safer.

The thoughts calmed her even further. The idea that Kit had brought it on herself acted as a balm. Then she heard the handle of the bucket clatter. And she thought she heard Kit moan.

She edged to the foot of the stairs, looking up, the kiss curls stiffly in place, her fingers clasped tightly before her, and in the bedroom Kit tried to cover her face with one hand in shame.

Hettie was on her knees beside the bed, and Kit sat before her, naked from the waist down, her knees wide apart.

Kit closed her eyes, trying to block out the horror; that dreadful woman with the creased, over-powdered face and grey bunned hair staring at her private parts, concentrating. The humiliation! The degradation.

'Bertie,' she thought, 'you swine! You swine. You did this to me.'

The suds were warm inside her. She waited for the sharp pain, the piercing, and when it came she tried not to faint.

'You all right?' Hettie looked up at her. The suds were escaping again, running around Kit's buttocks, dripping noisily to the newspaper spread beneath the bucket.

'Yes. It's all right.' Kit was gasping, leaning back, supporting herself with stiff, cold, skinny arms.

'D'you want a drink? Water?'

'No. If you've done, you can go. I've got tea in the flask. I put it ready – '

Hettie looked back at the job in hand. She liked the feel of warm suds, so soft about her fingers. She liked squeezing the enema. She would get the blasted womb clean. Why should women have to suffer this? It was always women who went through the mill. Her lips tightened with the thoughts, her face-powder standing out like sand. Men! Damn them all, and the things they forced into women in pursuit of pleasure.

'Are you all right Mrs Hemsworthy?'

'Yes. Yes. Don't worry.'

54

'I'll leave you now then.'

'Have you done it?'

'I think so. You know what to do?'

'Yes.'

Hettie took the bucket to the bathroom and emptied it. She rinsed her enema and wiped it, then folded it back into its red box. She put it into a brown paper bag and dropped it into her shopping bag.

She dried Kit briskly with a big blue bath towel and tucked her into bed.

A minute late Elsie Buckley was in the doorway of the office and Hettie saw her as she rushed downstairs.

'Well,' Elsie said, more calmly than she felt. 'Well well.'

'You keep your mouth shut, girl. D'you understand? You haven't seen me.' For a second Hettie's eyes threatened into Elsie's, then she had gone, the glass door banging, the front door agape, caught by the coconut mat, and the gate clanging shut. Elsie hissed, 'Filthy bitch,' and Mrs Skummings walked up the street as respectable-looking as any comfortably off married woman.

Kit lay in bed and shivered. She stuck her knuckles against her teeth, and all the fears of death crammed into her brain.

She shouldn't have done it. She was sweating. She was ice-cold between her breasts. The house was silent. Like a morgue. What if something happened that made her unconscious and she died? The girls would be home first. The vision of what they might find swamped her. Blood. Soaked through the bed. Her, lifeless, among it all.

And men did this to women! Tears oozed from her eyes and her nose was running. She groped under the pillow for her handkerchief then looked at the flask on the wicker table before her. The table was yellow, its top eight-sided. It was discoloured. She would have to scrub it one day. Stand it in the bath.

Then, suddenly, as though she hadn't been waiting for it, the pain came across the small of her back. It echoed in the pit of her belly, dragging her guts down, and a sob of terror ground from her throat. She lowered her head so her crying was muffled. She cried for her mother, 'Oh Mam, oh Mam,' then the bleeding began and she felt sick as her head began to swim.

She felt the warmth trickle, menacing, slow, onto the folded towel between her thighs, and she wriggled up. All she had to do was get to the lavatory. All she had to do was get to that hard, cold, wooden seat and sit on it, lean against the wall, her forehead against the cold of the white gloss paint.

The next pain was longer, stronger, tearing her apart.

She left the bed, crouched, holding the towel in place, and the bleeding was too fast, flooding.

She tried to hurry, and the landing swam in a grey mist. She clutched the banisters and was only partly aware of her fingers slipping on their polished surface. She was vaguely conscious of the landing carpet scrubbing against her face, and the pains were killing her, excruciating, coming in sickening spasms. The blood ran over her legs. She heard a voice struggle through pain calling, 'Bertie! Bertie! I need you. Bertie . . . . Why aren't you here . . . ?'

Elsie heard her. Elsie standing at the foot of the stairs longing to run away, to the street, to Salubrious Terrace, anywhere but up the stairs.

'Bertie . . . . Bertie . . . . Please come home . . . .'

Elsie's scalp was prickling and her feet were joined to legs she couldn't lift.

'Mrs Hemsworthy?' Her voice sounded thin, wavering, ridiculous. 'Are you all right?'

There was silence, and Elsie climbed slowly, shakily. She peered through the banisters, then sobbed, 'Oh Jesus.' Her feet became light, difficult to control, and she winged her way downstairs again, to the office and the black candle-shaped telephone.

'Ambulance please. We need an ambulance – ' Then she hurried back upstairs. She pulled the rose-coloured quilt off the double bed and took it to the landing. She put it over Kit and tried tucking it in.

'Don't die, Mrs Hemsworthy. For Jesus's sake don't die. Not here. Not while I'm on my own.'

The ambulance took Kit away and Elsie tried to clean the carpet. She knelt there scrubbing, the water oozing all around her until exhaustion suffocated her panic.

Then she went to the telephone again, her hands red and cold and wet, her mascara run into her rouge, her lipstick smeared up her cheek where the back of her hand had tried to move tears that had itched her skin.

The shaking had stopped. She found a telephone number. 'Will you take a message to Mrs Maggie Davies please? This is the Unicorn Insurance office. It's terribly important. I think the manager's wife is dying – '

She never remembered much more than that. She went to the kitchen and put coal on the fire. She made herself a cup of tea and found biscuits in the pantry, then she washed her face without having to carry water up the lane.

She sat down to wait.

*   *   *

Maggie Davies was buxom with a cleavage she was proud of. She often said that one day she would diet, but in the meantime the cawl, made basically from fat bacon, was forever in the cauldron hanging on the chimney hook over the fire.

She was at the bowl of water on the table now, cleaning yet more vegetables to go into the pot: onions, swedes, carrots, cabbage, potatoes; anything John brought in from the half-acre black-earthed garden. Anything she could swop flowers or vegetables for among her neighbours. Last week it had been strips from a dead ram. The rest of the animal hung in two pieces, salted, at the side of the beamed kitchen where they didn't dangle in people's way.

She heard the banging on the front door and yelled, 'Come in. Who is it?'

'Oh Maggie, fach – ' It was Sion-the-Shop and he came creeping in like an ageing, withered gnome in the white cap he wore in the name of hygiene.

'Aye,' Maggie said, 'there's eggs for you. In the basin in the pantry. Two bobs-worth, but they aren't laying as well just lately. Too cold.'

'Thanks Mag.' The gnome, familiar with Maggie's kitchen, went to the pantry and took the basin of eggs.

'And your mother already owes me two and sixpence for the last lot.'

'I'll remind her, Mag.'

'I need that two and sixpence.'

'Yes Mag.'

'Got to keep my stocking filled for a rainy day.'

'Shouldn't think you'd need more money, Mag.'

'Don't you be bloody cheeky now Sion. Take the eggs and remind your mother I need money too. Just like you capitalists.'

'We're not capitalists, Mag.'

'I still need money.'

He crept back towards the front door, then remembered the reason he had come. 'Someone just phoned a message for you, Mag. Is John out then? Gone with his boss?'

Maggie took her hands from the water and wiped them on a tea-towel. 'For me, Sion? What sort of message?' Her voice became less demanding. Sion wasn't too bright, not a quick thinker, and she didn't want to scare any memory of a message out of his little head.

'A young woman it sounded like, Mag. Upset she was. Crying I think.'

Maggie put her hands on her ample soft hips. 'What did she say? Can you remember?'

'Of course I can!' Sion spoke sharply with indignation, then blinked. If he carried on like that he would soon forget what the girl said. 'A matter of life and death. Mrs Hemsworthy is dying.'

'Wh-att?'

'Don't shout, Mag. It unnerves me.'

'You sure that's what she said?'

'Oh yes.' But Sion wasn't sure any more. He backed

58

through the doorway and out to the front garden. 'I must get home to Mother now Mag. The shop's busy – '

She followed him to the door, calling, 'Thank you for coming. Tell your mother I'll be seeing her.'

'Oh yes. When Mag? When will you be seeing her?'

'As soon as I've something to tell her. Ta ta. Good boy. Thank you for coming.'

Maggie ran for her coat, then to the shed and humped out John's bicycle. She ran with it down the path and out through the gate, leaving the front door of her pink-washed cottage wide open.

There was no pavement, just a pitted track running down the side of the mountain, swerving here and there to meet other cottages, squat amid their cabbages and sprouts. Maggie hopped on to the bike and held her feet out while the machine kicked and bounced and ran. The pedals sped around of their own accord until, at the bottom of the track, she put her slippered feet on them and rode like mad between the banks of grass. She sighed and readjusted her shapely bottom on the saddle as the wheels met a pavement. Cycling on a cobbled road was not for Maggie. She bent low, all breast and good intentions.

She came to her first call.

'Mrs Harris! Mrs Harris!' She banged at the front door and opened it at the same time, so Mrs Harris came running.

'Good God almighty Maggie Davies, whatsamatter? A fire or something?'

'Has John been here? He's out canvassing with Mr Hemsworthy – '

'Oh yes. Ages ago now – '

'Thank you.' Maggie stumbled in her anxiety to get back on the bike.

'What's the matter – ?' It was a cry.

'Tell you after. Tara – '

It took Maggie half an hour to find John and Bertie. By then her face was florid with effort and her dyed black hair stuck out from her head.

'John! Bertie!' She saw them sauntering up the street, both men tall, their overcoats open, their hats at an angle, their faces interested and intent as they talked to each other.

'Bertie! Cooey!' She didn't have much breath left, her hands hurt on the ridged rubber grips, and she doubted her legs would ever be the same again. 'Thank God I found you. There's been a message –'

Bertie was frowning, staring at her, frightening in his intensity, instinct telling him something was wrong with Kit. 'For me?'

'Yes. Ooh my God! I'm sweltering. You'd better get back home Bertie. Take a taxi. Don't wait for a train–'

'What's happened? What did she say?'

'I don't know. She phoned the shop –'

'Kit phoned the shop?'

'No. I don't know. Oh Bertie, just go. Sion came down and said a young girl phoned –' Maggie stopped. She was not going to tell Bertie his wife was dying.

Bertie looked up and down the street, his lean face suddenly yellowish in the December light. 'Where do I find a taxi?'

'Get on the bike,' John said. 'Turn second left. Go on for about a mile.'

Bertie passed his briefcase to Maggie and took the bicycle. 'Phone home. Tell them I'm coming.'

'Yes,' they both said. 'Yes, of course,' and they watched him cycle away with such speed his legs moved like pistons, his coat skirt flapping behind him. Maggie and John looked at each other.

'There's a phone box down the road,' Maggie said, and she and John began to walk, their minds travelling the miles to Swansea.

They telephoned 300 Prince Edward Road, and Elsie answered.

'What's happened?' Maggie urged. 'Was it you phoned?' And John held the kiosk door open to make more room.

'It's Mrs Hemsworthy.' Elsie was glad of the call, their

60

voices coming tinnily over the wires. 'She's been taken ill. I called an ambulance – '

'But what's wrong with her?'

Elsie couldn't think of an answer, not then. She covered it by saying, 'Is Mr Hemsworthy there?' And John sneezed.

Maggie turned to him and realised for the first time since catching up with him that he looked unusual. His long, crooked face was hot red, and so were his eyes.

She said, 'John! Have you got a cold?' And he nodded. She glared, furious that he dared do such a thing.

'I think so, I – ' and another sneeze came.

Maggie gave a short exasperated sigh. 'You haven't got your longjohns on, have you?'

'Maggie! I don't need longjohns.'

'You're not right in the head Johnny Davies. You've got to be watched every minute of the day.' She remembered the receiver in her soft fingers, and turned back to it. 'Elsie? Don't worry, love. Mr Hemsworthy's on his way. He'll get a taxi.'

'If he's lucky,' John said, and buried his prominent nose in a big blue and white spotted handkerchief. 'I didn't like to tell him . . . .' He blew his nose. 'But they've only got one taxi and that might be out somewhere.'

'Oh darro!' Maggie said, then back to Elsie, 'Well at least he's got John's bike. He can cycle home on that. All right, love?'

Elsie said yes, but wondered how long it would take Bertie to cycle thirteen miles.

It took him almost two hours, pushing the bike up hills and freewheeling down them, ears jutted against it, and the sweat ran inside his vest and pants so he felt he was sticking even to the saddle.

He propped the bike against the wall beside the front gate and strode fast into the house. 'Kit!' he bellowed, wanting her to know he had arrived, wanting her to know she was safe now he was here. He took off his overcoat and jacket and hung them up with his hat. Cold air hit his shirt and he pulled off his tie.

'Phew.' He bent his knees and hips then straightened again, releasing sweat-soaked clothing from skin, and made for the stairs, but Elsie was at the kitchen door.

'Bertie. Mr Hemsworthy.'

'Yes?' He stood looking at her. 'Where's Kit? My wife? In bed? What happened?'

'Shall I pour a cup of tea?'

'Tea?' The suggestion was good, comforting. 'Now? Will my wife have one?'

'She's not here.'

For a few moments he remained there, frowning, dark brows low over dark, deepset eyes, his thin mouth tight as he tried to understand. 'Where is she?'

'She's all right. I just phoned, checking.' Elsie turned back into the kitchen. 'I made you some sandwiches. The water in the tank's hot if you'd like a bath.'

She was proud of herself. It sounded wealthy to be saying such things. At Salubrious Terrace there was no tank to get hot, no bath to get into, and never any proper sandwiches.

Bertie followed her, worried and perplexed. The fire was roaring, banked high with lumps of best coal. Kit would have a fit. The stuff was over two shillings a hundred-weight. Both kettles were boiling fast and noisily on the hobs.

Elsie turned and looked up at him. 'Kit's in the hospital.' She was barefoot, tiny now, relieved he was there to take the responsibility from her. 'Sit down. They won't want you visiting just yet. She's in the theatre.'

She watched him as he sagged into his old armchair, its base collapsed almost to the floor, and its seat reinforced with cushions in various states of wear and textures.

He had his lips apart now, like a man suffering from asthma. His hair hadn't been cut for a while, it flopped over his shiny forehead. He sat with his legs stretched out, apart, and for a second his hand touched the button on the waistband of his trousers, going to open it for comfort, then he remembered that even now good manners prevented some things, and his hand drew away.

62

He let his head fall back and he let out a long exhausted 'Aah . . . ' while Elsie poured his tea.

She put in extra sugar, saying, 'It's best to have it sweet after a shock. They did it like that for my dad when his hand came off in the works.'

'His hand came off?' Bertie sounded choked.

'Yes. The flywheel done it. He didn't feel a thing at first.' She gave Bertie the cup and saucer. 'A cigarette?' she asked. 'Would you like a cigarette?'

'Can a duck swim?'

'Where are they?'

'In my jacket pocket. On the hallstand.'

She got them, feeling relaxed now, at ease, as if previous happenings had been a dream and only this was real, this was to be relished and absorbed.

In a strange way she felt she had taken Kit's place in this house. She could run it, care for this weary, handsome man and his two daughters.

She sat opposite him, looking at him. He had filled the room with something completely male. There was the smell of his sweat, the vibrations of his voice, the instincts of togetherness, and the lovely little feelings began in the deep pit of Elsie's body again. Her face went soft, winsome, and her big grey eyes went gentle and wistful with longing.

Bertie flicked out the match he had used to light his cigarette, then looked at her. The cigarette tasted good, the smoke sucked deep into his lungs.

She waited until he had drunk half his cup of tea and he no longer looked like a man with asthma. He drew up his legs and composed himself and, without him asking, she guessed the time had come to tell him the whole story.

He listened as though she were five-year-old Emma telling her dad tales, and when Elsie had finished he lit another cigarette, but this time the striking of the match was vicious.

He stared at the fire, and Elsie sat on the edge of Kit's armchair, her bare feet thrust out, her hands clasped childishly between her thighs as she had seen her mother do.

She said after a while, 'Was that why you made me stay here? Wouldn't let me come canvassing?'

His thoughts weren't with her so his face was blank, uncomprehending, and she bent her head. 'Because you knew Hettie Skummings was – '

'Good God no!' The words spat at her and she recoiled, lifting her hands and shoulders in soundless defence, and he eased his voice. 'No, I didn't know. Kit seemed odd this morning. I guessed something was up . . . . God no! I had no idea she'd . . . .' His thoughts went on as his voice stopped. Kit had seemed almost serene. The panic over the pregnancy had been muted, or had gone altogether. He couldn't put a finger on his reasons for making Elsie stay. He had only known Kit couldn't be left alone.

'Would you like your sandwiches now?'

He rubbed a hand over his face. What the hell was up with Kit? Didn't she realise having a baby was as natural as a tree bearing apples? Couldn't she accept that God had created man and woman for a purpose? Why did she have to make everything so blasted difficult?

'Would you?'

'Heh?'

'Your sandwiches – '

'No thank you. No. I'll have a bath and change. Make me feel better. Then I'll get to the hospital.' He smiled abstractedly. 'If I'm not back – will you see to the kids when they come in from school?'

'Yes. I'll get dinner too. About half-past eight, is it?' Again she had the feeling of wealth. Dinner at Salubrious Terrace was in the middle of the day. 'What would you like?'

'Oh – chips,' he said easily. 'We can make do tonight. Chips. There's steak somewhere. Steak and chips.'

'With pickled onions,' she said, and felt she was nearing paradise. She had never tasted steak. 'Do I fry it or – '

'Grill it,' he said. 'With a bit of butter,' and she nodded, not daring to ask how long it took. He caught the little look of worry on her face and he laughed. 'Have you ever grilled steak?'

'No.'

'Then let Linda do it. She'll help. What about your people? If I'm very late getting back?'

'I'll phone them.'

'They're on the phone?' He was startled.

'No, but I'll find a shop near them that is.'

He drew a chestful of breath with relief. He was glad he could leave such matters to her. She was quite a kid. He looked hard at her, remembering, what was she? Seventeen?

For a short while he stopped thinking of Kit, stopped feeling the discomfort of his overheated body in this overheated kitchen, and he smiled at her, then he winked. 'Good girl Elsie. Remind me sometime to give you a rise,' and she said demurely, 'Thank you Bertie, you are very kind to me,' then the big grey eyes held his gaze until he turned and strode away to the stairs and the bathroom.

The rest of that day was so stress-filled for Bertie Hemsworthy that it wasn't until much later he realised it was one of the milestones in his relationship with Elsie Buckley.

He used John Davies's bicycle again to go to the hospital, and almost immediately wished he hadn't. Either side of the cobbled roads were strips of comparatively flat surfaces, but he still found the cycling experience bruising, and wished he didn't panic so easily when things happened to Kit or the kids. He wished he could stay as rational and calm as he always did if things went haywire in the office.

As it was he sat on the small hard chair beside Kit's bed as though his raw bottom was on sandpaper, and wondered how patients were expected to recover when they spent all day in such overpowering smells of Dettol, bedpans and porridge.

Kit still smelled of ether and she looked as if he would soon be calling the undertaker.

Her eyes opened drowsily and her hand on the white patterned counterpane barely lifted. 'Hello,' she murmured.

'Hello,' he replied, and took her hand in his.

He sat and she slept. He looked at the chrysanthemums in white enamel jugs on the white tables down the centre of the ward. He looked at the white screens that had been drawn from around her even as he entered the ward, and he looked at the other women. They all had babies. They all had soft, lovely faces with alive eyes, and they all smiled at Bertie.

He looked back at Kit and knew he could never experience this again, never hold Kit's hand, trying to be kind, after she had murdered his child.

He moved restlessly, his bottom needing easement, his legs aching from the unaccustomed pedalling, and Kit opened her eyes again and looked at him.

'Hello,' she said.

'Hello,' he answered, and he smoothed her fingers, feeling guilty that he couldn't be effusive, kiss her, reassure her. God, she probably expected him to apologise, say it was all his fault and he shouldn't do such disgusting things to her. He wondered why women weren't made more like men. What was nature up to, making men hot-blooded and women frozen? If nature wanted procreation then nature should make women want men . . . .

His mind wandered back. The German girl had been hot-blooded, strong-limbed. And those French girls . . . . Maybe it was just that Kit was Welsh . . . .

'Bertie . . . .'

'Yes?' He lurched his chair nearer to her head.

'I'm sorry.'

His hand tightened on hers. 'So am I. I'll never touch you again. Never. I promise.'

She smiled without showing her teeth, white lips in a white face, and the nurse came, all starched white and rustling skirts. 'You had better go now, Mr Hemsworthy. Come again this evening.' She smiled, young, looking vaguely like Elsie, yet not like Elsie at all. Then he remembered what it was.

Elsie had had a clean face. Elsie's face had been as devoid of paint as this scrubbed nurse. Elsie had been smaller than usual too, looking lost, vulnerable. He kissed Kit's cold damp forehead and left her. He knew he ought to ask to see the doctor, but what would the man say? What could the man say? 'We have to inform the police about this woman Skummings?'

Bertie back-tracked quickly, his long slim legs taking him to the side of the bed as the nurse move away. 'Kit.' He whispered, his lips to her ear, 'Do they know you invited that – that woman – '

'No.' Kit looked up at him. 'No. I told them I did it myself.'

He felt embarrassment colour his face. Did all the new mothers in the ward know what had happened? He kissed her forehead again, then left her.

He ignored the bicycle in the hospital yard and caught a tram. He went to his club in Wind Street and sank into the old blue plush chair.

Harriet came to him, in her black dress with a deep V neck showing hollows like discoloured salt cellars, her thin white hair caught in a top-knot with thin black ribbon. 'Would you like something, Captain Hemsworthy?'

'Whisky, I think, Harriet. Neat.'

'Very good, Captain. Are you taking food today?'

'Food?'

'Some very nice Cornish pasties, just out of the oven.'

'Yes,' he said without interest. 'Yes. Two Cornish pasties, please Harriet.'

She smiled, liking him, his chiselled dark good looks, the deep even timbre of his voice, the way his clothes fitted about him, the air of breeding that so many men lacked today; and the pasties brought were the fattest and brownest on the baking tray.

He went to see Kit again in the evening. He was feeling calmer, able to smile, and she was propped up on two pillows, the ward garish under electric light.

Maggie Davies was there, sitting on the hard chair beside

the bed, a huge bunch of yellow chrysanthemums wrapped in newspaper on the locker.

Guilt again swamped Bertie. He should have brought flowers, or a box of chocolates, or something.

He thought Maggie had been crying. She said, 'Hello Bertie,' and he got the impression she was being brave.

She was wearing a red coat that had a black velvet collar, and she opened it a little wider so she could push her damp handkerchief down her cleavage. She patted it into place, and as Bertie sat on the edge of the bed, she said, 'I was just saying, Bertie, what a topsy-turvy world we live in. Kit loses a baby and doesn't mind.' She sniffed and drew the handkerchief out again. 'I'd be heartbroken. The poor little mite.' She dabbed the corners of her mouth, her lipstick as bright as her coat. 'Me and John would love a baby . . . . Love one . . . .'

'There's still time,' Bertie tried lightening the atmosphere. Other beds had cheerful visitors. People all over the ward were laughing and talking, cooing at minute babies.

'Oh, go on.' Maggie glowed. 'Know as well as I do, you do, I'm past it. Past it, I am . . . .'

Bertie thought they kept the conversation going rather well. Maggie loved to laugh until she throbbed all over, and Bertie loved to see her laughing, all open red mouth and cream teeth. She looked cuddly and comfortably and always had a faint clean soapy smell. She kept gazing at Kit, a sadness creeping into her eyes, and she would sigh so her big bosoms rose and fell, then she would look at Bertie. He would wink, and they would laugh again as though they knew of hilarious things.

Kit knew they knew nothing. She believed that Maggie was the silly, laughing sort, and Bertie was the type who pandered to the wives of his agents, so let them wink and glow and act like schoolchildren. She felt terrible. Was it her punishment, being in here, this ward, with so many satisfied, gleeful mothers? Didn't anyone understand she didn't want to kill a baby? She didn't want to be in here. She didn't want that vile woman with her enema.

Without a face muscle moving Kit began to cry, and both Maggie and Bertie left their seats to tend to her.

'Oh cariad,' Maggie soothed. 'There there then.'

Bertie smoothed Kit's brow and wiped the tears from her cheeks. He longed to say, 'It's your own damned fault,' but he sensed she was the most confused female he knew, and he accepted it.

When the bell finally rang Maggie stood up. 'I'll take the push-bike, Bertie.'

'All right – how – ?' He was holding Kit's hand.

'Sion-the-Shop and his mother are picking me up in the trap.'

'Are you sure? Shall I get a taxi for you?'

'No, no. I'll see you again.' She kissed him, her lips soft and warm and full beside his mouth, her closeness almost overpowering, then she went, all laughter and vitality, waving all the way to the doors.

Kit waved back languidly. 'Poor Maggie – '

'Poor Maggie, my foot!' Bertie said. 'She's all right.' He kissed Kit again. The nurse was getting impatient. The supper trolley was rattling in, and he left.

He ran down the stairs and out to the street with a sense of elation, of freedom, of a duty well done, and he went home to Elsie Buckley, to a big fire and a bright kitchen. She was darning one of his socks, sitting in Kit's armchair with her bare feet tucked under her.

At the two tables behind the door Emma and Linda swotted on their homework.

'Hello Daddy.' It was a chorus.

'Hello kids.'

Elsie asked, 'How is she?'

'Fine. Coming on fine.'

Emma pursed her mouth as she gazed up. 'Will Mummy be home for Christmas?' The light reflected in her round eyes.

'Yes of course.'

'What did the doctor say?' Elsie was brewing tea.

'I didn't see him. He wasn't there.'

Emma said, 'How d'you spell "very".'

'Vee,' Elsie said, 'ee, arr, why.'

Emma bent to her work again, the pencil moving carefully on the faint blue lines, and her lips shaping the words she drew as she concentrated. 'Then the very said to the elf – '

Elsie burst into laughter. 'Not very. You must mean fairy. A beautiful silver lady with golden gossamer wings like a magic spider's web.'

'Yes.' Emma looked up, her round face full of wonder. 'How do you know a very got golden wings?'

'Oh I know.' Elsie's face was young too, smooth, filled with an illusion of childhood and happiness. 'And they are fairies. Say Ff. You spell it . . . .' Bertie watched her and listened. He smiled. He liked the aura about her, the easy way his daughters laughed with her. He mentally made excuses for the tension Kit created, but was relieved it was absent now.

Emma said, 'Can I read you a new poem? Miss Davies taught us it today.'

Bertie nodded. 'Aye, go on.' He was able to laugh too. 'Is it a long one?'

'No.' Emma lifted her book importantly and left her seat. She came to the fireplace and took her position on the rug before Bertie, while Elsie went back to Kit's chair.

Elsie clapped and called. "'Ere, 'ere. Ladies and gentlemen, please welcome the famous Miss Emma 'Emsworthy,' and with all the seriousness of a five-year-old, Emma bowed to her father, then read from her book. 'Under a toadstool crept a wee elf. Out of the rain to shelter himself. Under the toadstool fast asleep, sat a big dormouse all of a heap.'

Then she bowed again and marched back to her chair and card table.

'Well?' Bertie exclaimed with mock bewilderment. 'What about the rest of it?'

'There isn't any rest,' Emma said, no longer interested. 'That's all there is.'

'Oh!' Bertie said, then Elsie clapped again, calling, 'Well done. Encore. Encore.' Until Bertie and Linda joined in and Emma smiled coyly, picking up her pencil again. 'Now I'm going to do my sums.'

'Do them quick then,' Elsie said. 'You've got ten minutes to bed.' Bertie cringed a little as her grammar strained, but her laughter, her youth, was all about him, and years later, when he looked back, he remembered that at that moment, in spite of his concern for Kit, he was happy for the first time in a long time.

CHAPTER FOUR

Bertie was in a foul mood and he tried not to blame the general gloom that had settled over the house with Kit's return. She had been in hospital three days, and by the second week in December was in charge of her home again. Weak, miserable, and martyred, she wanted to stay in bed every day. She longed for the luxury of doing nothing, being waited upon, but she punished herself. Bertie chopped sticks and carried coal. Elsie washed dishes, cleaned vegetables and bundled up washing for the laundry van to collect. She and Bertie watched in horror as Kit dragged her anaemic body around, and Dr Sullivan prescribed iron tablets and Parrish's Food.

Kit hoped to attract Bertie's sympathy, his attention. All she did was alienate him still further. She was a constant reminder of things he would prefer to forget, but he said nothing. He rushed to help if he saw her carrying a tray of tea, he rushed up and downstairs to save her legs, and he wished she would smile now and again, but he lacked the courage to say so.

On the Wednesday morning, ten days before Christmas, Bertie sat in his office feeling cold, while opposite him Elsie sat with her face plastered with make-up, the kiss curls increased, their stiffness stuck securely around her face.

He heard the wood in the low black grate behind him crackle and fall, the coals collapsing. A gust of wind hit the house and a cloud of smoke came from the chimney like a dark blanket to suffocate them.

'Damn and blast!' He sat up straight in his swivel chair and banged the papers on the desk before him. 'Am I supposed to work in here or am I not?' His gaze surveyed the smoke as it rushed past and around them.

Elsie demurely crossed her knees and looked at her pencil. In Salubrious Terrace the chimneys smoked all the time, for those lucky enough to have coal.

Bertie said, 'You look about ninety. All that muck on your face.'

'I feel about ninety. That's why I got the muck on my face. It hides things.'

The smoke settled. Bertie felt the first warmth of the fire begin to touch his back, and rain hit the window. The gate clanged and an agent entered the house. They heard him burring and gasping as he stopped at the hallstand.

'See who it is,' Bertie said. 'Get his book.'

Elsie went casually and Bertie watched irritably. She had a nice bottom on her, a neat waist – he stood up, pushing his chair back awkwardly, and went to the window. Look at it! Grey sky, grey houses, grey road, weary-looking horses with sacking on their soaking backs . . .. What had possessed him to get married in the first place?

Even as he thought it, he quelled it. Kit was all right. She was a home-maker, a responsible mother, a bloody marvellous hostess. But he might as well be a monk. In fact, as a monk he would know where he was. He wouldn't be expected to kiss a woman and say nice things, though not be allowed to fornicate with her.

Blast everything, the weather, Christmas, the bloody chimney. He would have to get a cowl for it. More money. Who had money this time of the year?

Bertie turned as Elsie came back into the room. She laid an account book on her desk and smiled at him. 'I'll check it now.' The telephone rang.

Bertie wandered back to his desk and she took the earpiece to the side of her head. 'Hello?'

He sat feeling less irritable. Life wasn't really so bad, he supposed, and he drew the papers strewn with fingers towards him.

Elsie covered the mouthpiece with her hand and leaned

74

towards him conspiratorially. 'Mrs Travers, Number one, Wern View.'

Bertie frowned, trying to remember, and Elsie whispered, 'That fire on John Davies's round.'

'Hasn't it been seen to?'

Elsie shook her head, grey eyes uptilted. 'John's on the sick. Got the – '

'Ah yes, yes, got the flu – '

Exasperation rose again in Bertie. He didn't want to bother with the woman. He didn't want to bother with anyone. Not then. 'You see to it. Tell her you will attend to the matter.' He smiled unexpectedly. The new idea sounded fine. 'Tell her you are my secretary and you will attend to the matter personally.' The expression in his dark eyes danced, and the good humour that had not been so far away, bounced back.

Elsie's face flirted with him, the corners of her mouth twitching, her tip-tilted nose wrinkling a little. He expected her to gasp teasingly, 'Oh you – ' but she didn't. She let the tip of her tongue wander around her bottom lip as she looked at him. She thought him terribly handsome, all clean-cut and elegant, his hands, on the blotter, white and slim, perfect, sensuous for caressing. She said, 'Shall I go there tomorrow?'

Bertie nodded. 'Aye, all right.' He mused a moment, then said, 'The round will be going to the dogs with no one collecting it. If John is off too long people won't be able to afford to pay off their arrears. Especially with Christmas on top of us.'

Elsie cocked her head on one side, her painted face bright, her plucked thin brows lifted archly. 'I could collect it.'

'And pigs might fly.'

'I could. I'm not as daft as you think, mind.' She edged nearer his desk, nearer him, her right hand extended as if to touch him, persuade him.

He sat back, as though away from those inviting fingers. 'Women don't collect books. It's a man's job.'

She stood, half smiling, while he watched her, trying to analyse her.

She lifted her face challengingly. 'Try me.'

'And what about the office? Kit can't come back in here. She hasn't the strength.'

'Agents don't collect on Wednesdays and Thursdays. I can be here then, and some of Friday. They do most on Friday evenings and Saturdays. I can come in on a Saturday if you like.'

'Oh yes,' he said with some amusement.

'And what I can't do in the office I'll leave till John comes back.'

The tip of Bertie's tongue rolled against the inside of his teeth, his eyes gleaming with the admiration and the attraction he no longer hid from her. 'All for six shillings a week?'

'I can have the commission off John's book. After all, I'll be collecting it.'

For a while longer, he watched her. She was little. She was young. But she was willing, even daring.

He jerked his jacket down and sat up straight. He spoke abruptly. 'Forget it. John will be back. He'll have to be.'

Elsie grinned, suddenly a street urchin with make-up and high spiky-heeled shoes. 'How's about a cuppa and an aspirin, then, heh? Make you feel less crusty.'

He didn't cringe inside at her accent, he felt too grateful to her. He smiled, seeing the clear greyness of her large eyes, the brown curling lashes, the worldly wisdom mingled with the innocence of youth, and to indulge her, to make up for his early surliness, he said, 'Isn't your birthday somewhere around?'

She nodded, pleased he remembered. 'It was yesterday. The sixteenth.'

'And you were eighteen.' He sat back again, smiling.

'Yup.'

'An old lady.'

She laughed and the closeness between them grew warm.

'We must have a party,' he said, and he was aware of her breasts again, the pale smooth line of her throat disappearing into the square neck of her over-washed green jumper, the rounded, almost plumpness of her hips in the shrunken green woollen skirt.

'For me?' Her eyebrows soared, her expression was of amazement and disbelief and delight.

'For New Year's Eve,' he replied, the amusement making his chiselled face kind, his lips quirking. 'To cheer up my wife.'

'Oh yes,' Elsie said, and the delight fled. 'Of course. It'll do 'er good. I'm glad. Honest now.'

'Who was it just came in?'

'Jim Thomas.' They became formal again.

'Get the tea. Pass me his book. I'll check it.'

As she left the room she stopped at the door to look back at him and he looked up at her.

'Well?' he said.

'Sometimes I don't like you.' She was a painted child, sulking.

'And other times?' He encouraged her, his gaze teasing now, waiting.

She wriggled as if wanting to avoid the question, but then she said, 'I fancy you,' and Bertie jerked his head in playful derision before attending to Jim Thomas's book.

*   *   *

Tom Buckley put the last morsel of kipper into his big mouth and savoured it. He hadn't seen Gwen eating any breakfast. Come to think of it, he hadn't seen her eating much for weeks.

'Gwen?'

'Yeh?' She was in the scullery.

'You had grub today?'

'Don't feel like it.'

He belched and stood up, the chair legs scratching on the flagged floor. 'Tommy give you any money this week?'

'Yeh – ye-es.'

He went to the scullery doorway, almost filling it with his height and width, his Welsh flannel shirt open to the waist,

77

the black hairs on his chest curling. 'I'll box his bloody ears when he comes in.'

'You'll do nothing of the sort. Keep your maulers off of him.' Gwen put her fists on her hip bones where they jutted in the thin shapeless black flowered dress. 'I told you afore. He's a man now. One day he'll bash you back, and it'll be your own fault.'

Tom Buckley belched again, not interested in her advice, his big bald head square and belligerent. He poked his stub of a left hand towards her. 'It's the only thing them kids understand. He's got a firewood round. He can give you money.'

'You, you mean. Give you money. Go and see what you done last night when you come home. Go on! Look at the front room winder. You done it. Coming home in a taxi, all la-de-da, then raising 'ell. And whose money was it you swilled away, heh? Our Tommy's hard-earned cash, that's what.'

Tom Buckley stuck out his bottom lip. 'I didn't have much. One pint.'

'And bollocks to that for a laugh,' sneered his tiny, shrunken wife. 'You were bloody drunk. If it weren't for our Elsie – '

'Oh Gawd – ' He turned away, his arms raised high. 'If it wasn't for our Elsie . . . . And Tommy got rays of sunshine sprouting from his arse.'

'Shut up.'

'I suppose she's gone to work all done up like a bloody tart again. Getting fancy ideas.'

'I said shurrup and wash yer mouth out with carbolic.'

There was a long truculent silence, then Gwen stole a glance at the giant she could manoeuvre so easily. She said, 'That egg boiling on the stove is for our Elsie. I put the tray ready. So you put the egg in the egg-cup on the tray and take it up to her.'

She watched disbelief grow on his veined, ruddy, heavy face, and the stump lifted. 'Me?' he cried. 'Take it up? You mean she's lyin' in bed?'

Gwen sighed hugely and spooned the egg from the pan herself. She tipped it onto the tray and held the lot out to him.

'Our Elsie is going to be an insurance agent one day. D'you know what she's got to do terday?'

'Get outa bed.'

'Investigate a fire claim. Mr Hemsworthy told her she needn't go to the office first thing terday. She c'n get the train ter Port Talbot then go to the office after.'

'Well, well.' He was scorning. 'You pays every bloody stever of your old man's savings for her to go to a fancy college, and now you expects me to wait on her. Just because she investigates some poor bugger's fire claim.' He bent his bald square head low, emphasising. 'With her education our Elsie ought to be running for Parliament. Get some jobs for those millions thinkin' a stickin' their 'eads in the gas oven. She oughter be on her knees to you. What you done for her.'

Gwen smiled up at him and patted the hand already taking the tray from her. She gently pushed him around and away. 'An' knock 'er door afore you go in. She's a big girl now.'

'Bloody 'ell.'

'She's learning manners, and it won't do you no 'arm to do the same. Might even help you land a job.' She kept smiling until she heard him tramping up the bare stairs, then she coughed, and wished her lungs didn't ache.

Elsie enjoyed her breakfast in bed, then spoiled herself a little by heating a pan of water to wash in. She didn't refill the bucket at the tap. Dad could do that. He could get up off his lazy fat backside and do something. Not leave everything to her and Tommy. And Ma.

She enjoyed the train ride even more, and pretended she was going a long way. Maybe to London to have an audience with the King. She hadn't been on a train before and found the noise, the clackety-clack, the hissing of steam, enchanting. She sat with her silk-clad knees

79

crossed, and cotton-gloved hands clasped, pretending she was wealthy.

Black smuts flew in through the open window and sprinkled on her nose and forehead. She left them there. To prove to any nosey parker that she was not lying, when she said she had travelled by train to investigate a business matter for the Unicorn Insurance Company.

She almost bounced to Number one, Wern View, though her toes were clamped in the brown size two shoes with Spanish heels.

'Mrs Travers? Good morning. I am Mr Hemsworthy's private secretary.'

'Ooh.' Mrs Travers had not been expecting an over-painted, just-eighteen-year-old. 'You'd better come in.'

The house was no better than Elsie's. Mrs Travers had sand on the floor, and small logs were waiting beside the Dover. Five small children sat on a rush mat, their feet bare, their noses pink and wet, their eyes enormous in pale faces.

'Out!' cried Mrs Travers at them, and her long red finger pointed to the back door. 'Out! I got business to attend to.'

The children went slowly, filled with curiosity. One smiled wickedly at Elsie and she smiled back. Was he insured? When the claim was paid she could come back, get Mrs Travers to insure all her kids. That will be a shaker for Bertie.

'Would you like a cuppa tea?' Mrs Travers twisted her cracked, chapped hands together. This slip of a girl could deny her compensation for the loss of her clothes.

'No thank you. Is this where the fire occurred?' Elsie tried speaking precisely, imitating Kit on her good days.

'Yes.' Mrs Travers became animated. 'This line was 'cross here. You c'n see where the hooks're still in the wall . . . . It just snapped. As my husband says, the whole house could of gone. Burned to death we'd a been.'

'Can you show me the clothes, have you kept them?' Elsie became prim in her pseudo-efficiency. 'I'll need to make a list.'

'Yes, yes, of course.'

The discoloured bolster case produced from under the stairs, and the stink of stale smoke, of burning quenched with water shocked the air as Mrs Travers shook out the rescued bits and pieces onto the sanded kitchen floor. 'This was a lovely dress, this was. Cost every ha'penny of five bob.'

'Five bob?' Elsie eyed the remains of the dress.

'Well,' Mrs Travers conceded. 'Four and elevenpence.'

'Hmm.' Elsie felt powerful. She could say ay or nay to this woman. Bertie would accept her valuation. The firm would pay this woman what she, Elsie Buckley, recommended they pay. She took the claims form from her black patent handbag. 'Right then. You call them out and I'll list them but – ' she paused for effect. 'You know we can't pay the full price you paid for the goods. We have to allow for the wear and tear that you had out of them.'

'They'd cost a lot more to buy now. To replace.'

'Yes, I know.' Elsie shrugged helplessly. 'But it isn't up to me. I'd give it to you if I could.'

'Hmm, well, mm yes,' said Mrs Travers, and turned once more to the clothes piled on the floor. 'Well, one pair of man's trousers.'

'When did you buy them and how much did you give for them?'

'Oh, about seven an' 'leven. Last year.'

'Hmm,' said Elsie thoughtfully. 'Shall we say eight and eleven last month?'

'Oh,' said Mrs Travers and thought about it, then her face lit up. 'Yes, of course. I remember now. They were eight and 'leven and I did get them just four weeks ago.'

'Good,' said Elsie, and put on the form, Trousers. Men's. And in the next column 8/11 and in the estimated allowance column 7/11. 'Next?'

'Two pair a knickers. Phoo, dear! Look at 'em.'

'Ladies'?'

'Little girls'.'

They worked assiduously, and when the list was completed Mrs Travers stood among her wet, smelly rags, wringing her hands again and saying, 'Please love, I need one pound ten. It's the grocer. I haven't been able to pay him – and Christmas coming.'

Elsie smelled the poverty she knew so well, hot water, strong with soda, burning your hands into great torturous cracks as you scrubbed the wood of the stairs, the table, and even the draining board into near whiteness. It was almost the only thing you had to be proud of, your scrubbing.

Mrs Travers's hands were burned deep red, the cracks raw, her nails bitten down to a painful depth.

Elsie totted up the list quickly, then looked up. 'I'll try and get two pounds for you. Any good?'

If Elsie had offered a thousand pounds the reaction could not have been more instant. Mrs Travers began to giggle. 'Oh Gawd! Can you?' Her eyes were like stars. 'My my, fancy a young girl like you able to do things like that. I'll be ever so grateful. You'll 'ave a cuppa. Oh do 'ave a cuppa.'

Elsie had a weak cuppa made with condensed milk before she left Number one Wern View, and in the train back to Swansea she looked at the list of clothes that were supposed to have been on the broken string line over a Dover stove. She would have to say some of them fell on a wooden clothes horse that was also laden, and the lot collapsed into the Dover.

The train wheels went clackety-clack. There were black and white cows in a field, and a river ran fast and clean around a bend banked by trees. It didn't look like December. With a blue sky like that it could be any time, not nearly Christmas.

'I need the money, love.' Mrs Travers's face floated before her mind's eye. 'With Christmas and all.'

Elsie nodded in the empty carriage, thinking of the five frozen-looking children, then she took out her pencil and added two nighties – cotton, one lady's dress – silk, and a blanket – wool. She nibbled the end of her pencil working out the cost of these extra casualties, then totted up the bill. It might even come to three pounds, but with a list like that surely head office would grant two pounds. That should see

Mrs Travers right for Christmas, and also gain her some new business when she came to pay the claim.

Pay the claim? Maybe John Davies would be back before the authorisation came through and he would pay it out. It was his round, his agency.

'Ah well.' She sat back contentedly and watched a white cloud seeming to rush across the lovely sky. 'That would be that, but it was worth a try.'

Back at the office she laid the list before Bertie like a presentation. 'I done it.'

'You did it. What's she like?'

'Very nice. Needs the money.'

'Don't we all?'

'She's different. Got five starving kids and sand on the floor.'

Bertie nodded. A woman spreading sand on her floor was trying. Pity she couldn't have carpet, but that was the way of the world, some had and some hadn't. Thank God he had, at least, enough to be getting on with. He rubbed a hand over his mouth, then settled to discussing the list with Elsie.

He queried, 'She's got sand on the floor yet she could afford eight and elevenpence for trousers? You can get a whole tailor-made suit with a waistcoat for thirty bob.'

'It was special. For a wedding.' Elsie's face was concerned, wary. Was he going to cut her valuations much? Maybe she should have added a couple of sheets and towels to offset any deductions.

'Hm.' Bertie went down the list, then he drew his hand across his mouth again. 'Any idea how much she's paying us? Those five kids. They insured?'

'No. Only her and her husband on a death policy, and this fire and accident.'

'Right then, get this posted as soon as possible. Tell Head Office I want the woman paid before Christmas. John can get those kids booked up as soon as he's back.'

'Good.' The warmth of satisfaction, smugness, felt nice inside her. 'How is he? Have you heard?'

'Maggie phoned this morning. She's got a doctor's note for him. Looks like he'll be off for a while.'

'What about this round? Who'll collect it?'

'Someone has to, that's damn certain. Kit can't. It's taking all she's got to stand up these days, and she's not doing that properly. So – me, I suppose.'

'I could do it you know, Bertie.' She put her head on one side, wheedling, her rosebud lips tilted in anticipation.

He sat back, wanting to laugh at her. 'You couldn't collect for toffee. Walk miles in those shoes?'

'I can. You said I couldn't be your secretary, but I am,' and her head lifted, the streak of defiance very evident now.

Bertie stood up, stretching. He thought of the streets in the little town of Port Talbot, of the wind blowing in from the sea, the December weather, the wet, the discomfort, the need to smile, laugh at policy-holders when you would rather be at home. 'All right. Start on it tomorrow, Thursday, but remember it hasn't been collected for two weeks. Everybody is in arrears. Get those arrears off them.'

'All at once?'

'All at once.'

'They won't have it. It's Christmas!'

'You're the agent. I've given you an order.'

Her grey gaze dropped before his. 'Yes. All right. I'll try. Do I collect during next week, Christmas week as well?'

'You'd better.'

She didn't argue and he smiled.

'Good girl,' he said, and wanted to hold her, to kiss her. It wasn't passion. Maybe, he thought, it was pity. Or admiration. Or relief that he wouldn't have to walk the streets of Port Talbot just yet. Or maybe it was a strange sense of loneliness, as though his marriage had finally died sometime last week and he needed another woman to comfort him.

Elsie walked the streets of Port Talbot lightly. She had gone wild and bought herself a pair of white daps. The posh folk wore them only when playing tennis, but the poor wore them until their big toes poked through the canvas,

84

and the cobbles seemed so sharp they might as well have been barefoot.

Elsie whitened hers afresh each evening. She mixed the whitening powder with water to a creamy consistency, smeared it on the daps with a piece of cloth, then she left them to dry on the black fender before the kitchen fire. Each morning she went out the back to put them on, because there was always that shower of surplus flaked whiting falling from them, until she had jumped up and down and loosened it all away.

Then she put on her make-up. She did away with the kiss curls, and cut herself a small fringe, promising herself a proper mirror for Christmas.

The claim came through for Mrs Travers at unusual speed, arriving in the office on the Tuesday, two days before Christmas, and Elsie made a detour from that day's calls to pay the woman.

On the way she passed a smallholding. Two pigs honked and snuffled somewhere, and Elsie halted to absorb what she told herself was the true smell of the country.

'Ah.' She took a deep breath. The rain had stopped. There was a piece of blue in the grey sky big enough to patch a man's trousers, and that, Elsie knew, meant the rain had cleared for the day. She had worked fast. Her collections were good considering folk needed money for Santa Claus, but not as good as Bertie demanded.

The thought of him gave her those lovely cuddly feelings again. She had already proved expert at getting new business, and Bertie's attitude had been warm, indulgent: even, Elsie was sure, affectionate. Her world seemed to be brightening all round, although Ma had coughed a lot last night. Elsie wondered if the owner of the smallholding was insured, and how much a week it would cost for Ma to stay on a farm until she was better.

She went up the track to the cottage, skipping over the dark mustard-coloured puddles. She stopped to pat the nose of a flea-bitten pony that showed its yellow teeth in appreciation, while half a dozen Rhode Island Reds scuttled noisily out of her way, and the cottage door opened.

The woman was as wide as she was high, and she was no higher than Elsie's five foot three. She had a huge black eye, her cheekbone cut and stitched. As she saw Elsie gaze at the wound she touched it gingerly and said, 'I fell off a bloody ladder.'

Elsie's sympathy was almost tangible. Tom Buckley had ladled out a couple of black eyes in his time, often to Elsie and her brother, Tommy.

Elsie drew a deep hissing breath and peered harder at the poor woman's face. 'Have you claimed off your insurance?'

'What insurance?' asked the woman.

'Haven't you an insurance against accidents?'

'Never heard of them. I got the old man covered though. Enough to bury him.'

Elsie smiled and the woman said, 'You come about a turkey?'

Elsie thought quickly. 'A turkey?'

'We got just two left. That's all. Fresh killed yesterday.'

Elsie wondered, then visualised her mother's face if she, Elsie, walked in with a turkey. A whole, real turkey! Not a rabbit. Not a chicken. A turkey.

Elsie had never tasted turkey.

'How much are they?' She followed the waddling woman around the side of the cottage and into a corrugated iron shed. A pair of plump turkeys dangled heads down, legs stretched. Elsie tried not to look at their eyes, not to wonder what they thought when they knew they were about to die.

She shuddered. She thought, 'I don't want to die . . .' but then the thought had gone and the woman was saying, 'Ten shillings. You can have the biggest one for ten shillings. There's a bargain for you.'

Elsie felt her mouth was moist, drooling. Roast Christmas dinner with Brussels sprouts . . . .

'Yes.' She sounded breathless. 'Oh yes, that'll be lovely.' She fumbled for her wallet, for the day's collections. She said quickly, 'If I pay you now, can I come back later for the turkey? He'll be heavy to carry around and I'm on my way to pay out a claim. I'm an agent you see for the Unicorn Insurance Company.' The woman's expression was inquiring, not believing, but the money was real, in this young girl's wallet.

'Oh yes?'

'A woman fell downstairs.' Elsie looked at the black eye and her story dripped easily from her tongue. 'She's bruised all her hip and twisted her ankle. I'm going now to pay her out.'

'How much then?' The woman's thick arms hung to her straight sides.

'Ah well – ' Elsie went cagey. 'That always depends on your premium. Your weekly payment – '

The woman plodded beside her, back around the cottage. 'I'll put the turkey in a bag ready for you. I got a carrier somewhere,' and Elsie ran up the track and onto the street. She felt jubilant. What a tremendous, thrilling, exciting, Christmassy thing she had done. The only thing wrong was that she didn't have ten shillings. Not of her own. She had given the woman part of her collections. Somehow she had to pay it back. Bertie would want it on paying-in day, Wednesday.

She got to Number one, Wern View still pondering. She had chewed her bottom lip so it was bereft of lipstick, and the little voice inside her was appealing, 'Please God, send me some money, a pound note will be fine. Just one pound note.' She had watched the gutters as she walked, the daps that were far from white now going slap slap, but she hadn't found even a halfpenny, never mind a pound note.

Mrs Travers opened the door to her and almost swooned with joy. The red cracked hands gripped Elsie's arm and dragged her in quickly. 'Here Mr Jeffreys.' She faced a big-bellied man who sat near the table, his macintosh tightly belted. 'Didn't I tell you she'd come? Didn't I say I'd pay you ternight? Didn't I say I'll never come inside your shop again, not even fer a box of matches? Here – ' She turned on Elsie, 'Miss Buckley, you give this man who doesn't trust

87

me – no Mr Jeffreys, you don't trust me. You said as how you'd take me to court, well now it's my turn. You treating me like I wasn't right in the head. Watch us starve you would.' Her feverish gaze settled on Elsie's wallet as Elsie prepared to pay out, and the red fingers quivered and waited to snatch. 'One pound ten you said love. Did you get one pound ten?'

Elsie handed over one green and one brown note then four half-crowns. She said tremulously, 'I've brought you two pounds, Mrs Travers. Our firm looks after its policy-holders,' and she watched the delighted Mrs Travers pay her grocery bill, then shoo the apologising man out.

That night Elsie lay awake thinking of what she had done. She had paid Mrs Travers two pounds, but Head office had allowed three. She hadn't presented Mrs Travers with a receipt. It had three pounds printed so clearly on it.

'That's all right,' Mrs Travers had soothed after Mr Jeffreys had gone. 'You forgot it. Don't worry. I'll come into Swansea if you like, to the office.'

'Oh no, no.' Elsie had smiled brightly, the receipt intact in her handbag. 'No, no, I'll bring the receipt next week.'

Next week Elsie again knocked on Mrs Travers's door. The wind gusted paper along the pavement and, goose-pimpled, Elsie shivered. 'I've brought the receipt,' she smiled. 'For the two pounds.'

She had typed it out herself on coloured paper bought from Smith's.

Mrs Travers signed willingly. 'Did you have a good Christmas love?'

'Yes. Yes, I did.' The turkey had been delicious. Even she and Tommy and Ma had belched after it. They had had tinned fruit and cream for tea, with a cake that had marzipan and icing.

'That's good then, see you next week.'

Elsie hurried away. She had signed the official receipt herself, using her left hand, and Bertie hadn't queried it. It had gone, with her account sheet and her collection, to Head Office in London.

CHAPTER FIVE

'A party?' Kit had said before Christmas. 'You want us to throw a party?'

Bertie was perplexed; she wasn't as enthusiastic as he had anticipated. 'I thought you'd like the idea.'

'We haven't had a party for years.'

'Two years.' Bertie smiled gently, encouraging. Kit looked ghastly. She had lost yet more weight and her face continually looked ill-tempered. 'We had one for New Year's Eve two years ago. Remember, it was the time we took John Davies on? Our sixth agent.'

'Is that all it is? Two years?'

Bertie nodded. When he had mentioned the party to Elsie it had, to him, been merely an idea, but her reaction had been so gleeful that he had immediately decided it was a splendid idea, one of his finest. It was a bit of a blow to find that Kit wasn't hopping with delight.

She turned from him, towards the fire, and the flat-iron that seemed inevitably waiting. Her two daughters sat squashed into her chair, their childish faces uplifted as they listened, their dark fringed hair thick and glossy.

'Can we Mummy?' Emma was ready to hug herself. 'Can we have a party?'

Kit almost smiled. 'Why should you want a party like that? It won't be a children's party.'

Emma and Linda stole a slow look at their father. Linda wiggled her foot. Emma said, 'We can stay up late. Can't we? We can hold hands, and everybody sing Auld Lang Syne. Like we did before.'

Kit began the never-ending task of ironing. Emma's pyjamas with the tiny teady bears printed all over were first. 'Did we let you stay up then? We must have been mad. What were you? Three and Linda was eight.' She concentrated on the ironing, pressing her weight onto the flat-iron, half wondering if she had let it cool too much. 'I'll see.'

The children smiled and sighed. Looks of anticipation flashed between them and Bertie. They were confederates. They all had to be very, very good so Mum didn't get rattled, and Dad had to sweeten her around. There was a quiet confidence in the way Linda and Emma's hands groped towards each other, then clasped. There had to be a party. There had to be. To bring the New Year in.

There was.

Kit had Elsie Buckley come to it at seven o'clock, and gave her an apron. 'I'll cut the bread, and you can butter it.'

Elsie didn't demur. It had sounded important when she said to her mother, 'Mrs Hemsworthy needs my help, Ma. She still looks awful. She lost a lot of blood, mind. And I'll get paid for it.'

'How much?' Gwen Buckley was round-shouldered, growing to look like a very old crone.

'I didn't ask her.'

Gwen Buckley sucked her teeth. 'They're good to you, I got to say that fer 'em. But there, the gentry allus 'ave been like that. It eases their consciences.'

'How?' Elsie was interested.

'Well they're better off 'an us and it pricks their conscience, so then they gives to charity and things like that.'

'We're not charity.'

'To them we are. Like St Dunstan's.'

Elsie frowned. Being a charity was degrading. She said quickly, 'We're as good as them any day. Maybe better.'

'Don't talk like that, love. The vicar always says it's best to know our places in this world.'

'At least I wouldn't murder my own unborn baby!'

'Sshh.' Gwen looked around quickly as though the ponderous vicar was listening. 'I was only saying as 'ow they've been kind to you. Did you thank them fer the turkey and that?' Gwen watched Elsie anxiously. At times she felt her only daughter was getting big ideas and, as Tom kept saying, heading for bloody trouble.

'Of course,' Elsie returned. 'And don't you go mentioning it to them. They'll get embarrassed and never give us anything again.'

Gwen Buckley nodded and looked at the wooden crucifix on the dark green wall opposite the fireplace. She sighed. Tom had nailed that there years ago, but sometimes Gwen wondered if it was worth the hole it made in the wall.

Elsie followed her mother's gaze and a condescending gentleness entered her voice as she agreed, 'Yes, Ma.'

So she set to, cutting the bread for Kit and ignoring the fact that Kit regarded her, at that hour, as a maidservant.

'Make the mustard, Elsie. Do you know how to make mustard? No, not water. Always use vinegar. Tastes better.'

By nine o'clock the glasses and tumblers were arranged, the bottles opened, the decanters full. Cups, saucers and plates of china so thin that one could see the light through them were stacked beside the sandwiches, the various cakes and biscuits. The fruit bowls were piled high, and the family's outdoor clothes were removed from the hallstand.

All ladies were to be shown into the back bedroom, the spare room, where extra lighting had been arranged around the dressing-table mirror. Elsie changed into her emerald green party dress in there. The dress was too short for her, with no waist, its skirt starting at the hips, exceedingly full and cut into petal-shaped pieces.

She gazed at herself in the long mirror of the wardrobe. She looked stunning, absolutely stunning. The cheap light-coloured stockings wrinkled a bit at the knees when she stood up, but nobody would see that if she sat down a lot, and her feet looked nice in silver sandals. The heels were a bit high at three and a half inches, but the extra half-inch made her look heaps taller. Her kiss curls had returned for the occasion, and she licked a thumb and forefinger then applied them to reshaping one that was out of line. She dabbed more Phul-Nana on her wrists and behind her ears. She was glad she had gone to that jumble sale. Sometimes the church had scrumptious things there, and this dress was one of them. She twirled, smiling at her reflection. The skirt lifted and her new suspenders were black. Black satin, holding up the near-white stockings.

Elsie Buckley was happy.

As she left the room Kit was coming across the landing, wearing a dress that covered almost all of her. In mauve jersey it was cut on the cross and clung to her body, yet the hem of the skirt waved expensively about her knees, and the high neck was softened by a satin cowl collar. The dress was basically simple, but optically lust-invoking. As she walked one was reminded of the sinuous movements of a slick cat on the prowl.

Kit smiled as she and Elsie met at the top of the stairs. 'You look charming, Elsie.' But she was concentrating on clipping a gold bracelet into place. Her words were polite. 'How are your parents getting here? Will they get a tram this time of night?'

'No.' Elsie stepped back to let Kit descend first. 'They'll get a taxi.'

'Oh!' said Kit, and her voice rose in surprise.

Elsie followed her, smiling, thinking how elegant Bertie's wife was, how beautiful with that thick, burnished black hair so expertly Marcel waved and drawn back into a low chignon tonight, how lucky the woman was to have Bertie and this house and all her money, and how selfish she was, and arrogant, and skinny. Elsie said politely, 'It was good of you to ask them.'

'Not at all.' Kit was equally polite. 'A pleasure. Will you go back up and see if the two girls need any help?'

Elsie stopped on the last stair and Kit swept away, to the kitchen where Bertie stood arranging this tie.

'Darling,' Kit said to him. 'Why not wear your dicky bow? The white one.'

'It's an informal party.' His voice was edgy.

'All right. All right,' she retorted. 'Wear a bathing-costume if you like. I don't care.'

Elsie went back upstairs to the girls' room, knocking on the door before being called in. She knew Ma and Pa would be walking to the party, and it was a hell of a long way.

She hoped Ma wouldn't drop dead doing it, and she hoped to God Pa didn't call in every pub on the way. He would surely say it was to give Ma a rest and he couldn't refuse to have one at the same time.

Her trepidation was justified. Tom Buckley was already swaying, laughing uproariously with his square rough-skinned face a heightened red, and his hefty left hand slapping everyone on the back. Gwen Buckley wanted to take him home but he wouldn't go, and she was too tired to manipulate him.

'Tom, don't drink any more, there's a good lad.'

Standing together, his size dwarfed her, his broad chest threatening the buttons on his second-hand blue serge jacket. 'After this one Gwen. No more. After this one. On the wagon.'

In yet another pub he met yet another acquaintance, another man ready to extend Christmas cheer, and the beer disappeared down Tom Buckley's gullet as easily, as smoothly, as cream off the back of a silver spoon and, like each time before, he smacked his lips, then licked them, then wiped them with the pink stump of his right hand and effusively thanked the buyer. 'My turn next year!' It was a huge joke. 'Next year, boyo, I'll buy you one – '

Gwen tried not to mind, but the Hemsworthys were high-class folk, and she didn't want Tom shaming Elsie in front of them. 'Don't drink any more, Tom – ' She sat where he had placed her, at a corner table, jammed in by woolly-minded men, almost suffocated by smoke and smells in a low unventilated room.

'One more, Gwen.' He was becoming lyrical, the stage before he became obstreperous. 'Dear Gwendoline, your eyes they shine, right into mine – '

'You're bloody drunk already.' It was a hiss, her eyes rolling signals, warning him not to make a fool of himself, not to attract more attention.

'Gwendoline. Beloved rose. Not me. Sober as a judge.'

'Balls ter that for a joke.'

'Merry maybe, but it's a party we're going to. A party. Needs cheering up. A party.'

'Let's go back home, Tom. Phone 'em. Say I'm bad.'

He put his arm about her and bawled 'goodnight' to the pub. 'And a happy New Year.'

'Happy New Year Tom, boyo . . . .'

Gwen walked more urgently than she should, bullying him along. 'You sober up now fast or yer'll make fools of all of us. The Hemsworthys are posh folk.'

'For Christ's sake shut up woman about the bloody Hemsworthys. They're just luckier than us, not better.'

'They've been good to our Elsie.'

'And what for, I'd like to know.'

She stood in the light of a lamp, panting, but ready to fight. 'Just what d'yer mean by that Thomas Buckley?'

'Why should that Bertie Hemsworthy – Bertie, pah! Bloody sissy name – '

'Shurrup!'

'Why then? You tell me why? Why's 'e give 'er a turkey and a puddin' an' that, heh?'

''Cos she's a good girl. A good worker. She's there now, helping them. They like her, that's why.'

He leered, putting an arm about her. 'Oh aye.'

'You got a rotten mind. Like all men. You got one thought. It's our Elsie yer casting a slur on. Yer own daughter.' Gwen pulled away from him. Her lungs ached. Talking had roughened her throat so she wanted to cough. She leaned against a wall, and the street lights made her face look like a skull of bleached white with black hollows. She let the attack of coughing come, then she took the arm he offered. He soothed, murmuring, his face screwed up in an effort to fight the beer. He wasn't an intelligent man. He was often confused. A man's lot in life was to work and

94

booze, and a woman's to slave over the kitchen stove. There was no work, he was bullied if he boozed, and his wife was in no shape to slave over a kitchen stove. He sighed and adjusted his step to hers. He hoped these knobs had good beer on tap. Be waste of a night if they didn't.

They arrived at 300 Prince Edward Road at the same time as Kit's parents, and Maggie Davies opened the door to them.

Maggie wore scarlet taffeta with a neckline so low that Tom Buckley always swore she damaged his eyesight. The waist was around her magnificent hips, emphasised with a band of wide black ribbon tied in an enormous bow at the back. Tom Buckley cut the deep burp that rose to his lips and went towards Maggie's widespread, bare dimpled arms. 'Come in! Come in!' Her welcome was expansive and genuine. 'I'm Maggie Davies. I'm married to John. One of Bertie's agents.' She had no idea who Tom was, and didn't much care. He was another man at the party. She hugged him to her warm softness and smelled the pubs he had visited.

'Attaboy!' she laughed, 'and this is – ' She held her arms out to Gwen who was near to curtseying.

'How do you do?' Gwen murmured, and Colonel and Mrs Nolan stood waiting on the black and white marbled doorstep, aghast at the crew their daughter and son-in-law could invite into their home.

The colonel coughed discreetly and fingered his moustache. 'If you'll-uh-allow us to-uh-pass Miss-uh – '

'Call me Maggie. Everyone does.' Maggie drew in breath to let Kit's parents pass her, and Tom Buckley went with them.

There was uproar in the passage. Elsie was crying, 'Pa! You've been swigging it again,' and the colonel was saying importantly, 'A party eh? You're having a party? What what?' And Kit was trying to hide her confusion.

'Father! I didn't know you were coming. Why on earth didn't you let us know?'

Her mother stood, immaculately silver-haired, her face

95

peach-powdered, looking bewildered. 'We won't stay my dear. It's inconvenient for you, isn't it.' She pulled her fox fur closer about ther shoulders, and a sudden rush of obscene laughter roared from the middle room. Kit guessed someone had just told another joke, and she brought her hands together in a silent hope that everything would be all right. She tried not to sway back from Tom Buckley's breath, nor let her parents know she would rather they were anywhere than here, crushed between the hallstand and staircase with the big-mouthed and big-breasted, blowsy Maggie Davies, and these dreadful people who she assumed were Elsie Buckley's parents. Dear heaven! It was Bertie's idea to have the party – blast him.

'No, no,' her voice urged her parents. 'Of course you must stay. Bertie will be delighted to see you. It's the office party.'

'Ha hum,' said her father, the back of his forefinger stroking his moustache, instead of twitching it, and he eyed Tom Buckley. Tom Buckley eyed him, and the animosity grew thicker by the second.

'Bloody snob,' Tom thought.

'Bullying layabout,' thought the colonel. 'Can pick them out anywhere.'

Elsie hopped up and down, the emerald green petals on her skirt flapping about her thighs. 'Pa, you put your things on the hallstand.'

'What things?'

She laughed, then giggled at her stupid remark. Her dad didn't possess any things, no hat, no overcoat, and certainly no gloves or walking-stick. The colonel had the lot and he handed them to his daughter, who dutifully deposited them on the hallstand.

Kit licked her lips quickly, then introduced everyone. She said brightly, 'Elsie, if you take the two men in to my husband and see they get a little refreshment, I'll take your mother upstairs.' She smiled, then put her arm about her own mother, a protective gesture, unintentionally blocking Gwen out.

The men went with Maggie, not Elsie, all doors open and any inhibitions of those already there fast drowning in drink. Elsie watched her mother climb the stairs. Gwen looked weary, frail, sick and overawed, her senses taking in the smells, the warmth, the comfort: her feet feeling the carpet, her fingers the wallpaper, and her ears the accents of the two women ahead of her. She had been right to give Elsie a chance at Gregg College. These people had all the good things. Her Elsie ought to get her finger in here good and proper, and keep it in.

She sat in the pink wicker chair in the spare back bedroom and felt deliriously happy. She didn't have to worry about Elsie any more. Elsie was doing all right.

Kit spoke to her, remembering she was consumptive, so patiently offered her a cup of tea, then went to get it. Gwen was wearing her best black dress, and her black elastic gusset shoes were shining, but they were old; they had sockets worn into them that fitted her bunions.

Mrs Nolan sat at the dressing-table and combed her gleaming silver hair. She patted the waves and curls into place and watched Gwen in the mirror. She admired her own daughter tremendously; Kit could get on with absolutely anyone. She looked down at her hands, the diamond rings gleaming, and worry was in her eyes. Just who was that dreadful little tart in the obnoxious green dress? Not Albert's secretary, surely. This woman's girl? Dear, dear! She smiled at thoughts of Maggie Davies. She supposed one did have to associate with all sorts in the insurance world. Keeping the common touch and that. Then she shrugged imperceptibly. Kit had looked elegant enough. She hadn't lowered her standards. Pale maybe, but still interesting.

She said to Gwen, 'I am going downstairs, would you like to come?'

'No thank you.' Gwen watched her go with relief, then she climbed onto the bed amid the women's coats, Mrs Nolan's fox fur against her cheek, and fell fast asleep.

Kit came with the cup of tea, gazed in amazement at the

97

black-clad, fur-cuddling, open-mouthed Gwendoline, left the tea on the table, and crept away.

Downstairs the colonel was standing straddle-legged before the white marble fireplace. He liked this room. Always had. Fine structure. French doors to the – er – garden. He supposed Kit had to live in a terraced house. Her husband did. Good boy, Albert, bit of a mug, but one must make allowances for those not born with the necessities of life. Guts and such like. He tried to avoid looking at Tom Buckley. The man was an oaf; why the devil couldn't he stand up straight and stop glowering at people. Did he think the loss of a hand was the end of the world? Damn fool! Never been in the trenches. That was his trouble. Too mollycoddled. Should have joined the army. Seen men who were men. Who was he exactly? Kit did say . . . . Buckley? Buckley? Where had he heard that name before?

'Ah –' Pleasure and pride enveloped Colonel Nolan as he watched Kit go to Tom Buckley. She was smiling. Charming girl, Kit. Fine daughter. By God, Albert was a lucky chap. Lorraine appeared, a wine glass in her sparkling hand, her tweed skirt, cashmere jumper and pearls not the outfit for a party, but she had the breeding to look unselfconscious, and the colonel's heart swelled with pride.

The party seemed to advance without him and Lorraine. They were two people who didn't fit in, who shouldn't be there, so they stood, side by side, watching the others. They had been acknowledged, but they knew nothing of insurance or the laughter of insurance men and insurance men's wives, so they were left alone.

Bertie had sensed it all before. As a sergeant, then a subaltern, then a captain, he had been caught between the two; depending on the respect, the obedience of 'the men', but also depending on the good will of his superior, the colonel. Now it was here again, and at a party, as though his men were on parade before the commandant, and he was unable, unwilling, to call them to order. Elsie smiled at him, her eyes as bright as his mother-in-law's rings, and he went to her, drawn by the signals of approval.

'Enjoying yourself, Elsie?'

She giggled, and moved her shoulders as if in a hug. 'Mrs Hemsworthy's parents are nice, aren't they?' She was being polite again.

'They're all right.'

She moved closer to him, secretive, the top of her head barely as high as his shoulder. 'They scare the pants off me. They're awfully posh, aren't they?'

He instinctively, generously, put an arm about her and gave her a party squeeze. 'They're not so bad. They were born into a different world. That's all.'

'Like the King and Queen,' Elsie said, and looked up at him. Her painted face wore the tremulous expression he had seen there so often. Was it fear? Fear of life, of being lost in the midst of it because of things she couldn't understand? He caught sight of John Davies. He and Maggie were whispering, close, laughing and loving secretively, their lips touched, more in a gesture than a kiss, then they drew apart. John looked rough. His already long face was hollowed. Could his chill turn to pneumonia, or, more easily, consumption?

Bertie resoved to tell him not to come back to work yet, not during January. It would be too risky, foolhardy. Elsie was collecting his book all right. Elsie was doing fine. Bertie was surprised at her capabilities, her willingness, and his heart went gentle for her, his hand firm on her waist.

He noticed his two young daughters. They both wore pink taffeta with white shoes and socks, and pink ribbons were slotted through their thick dark brown hair, with big bows arranged above their straight fringes. Little Emma concentrated on the plate of sandwiches she held out to her grandparents, while Linda stood, as slim and straight as Kit, offering mince pies. It was a scene, a cameo, that impressed itself on Bertie's brain, formed by the noise of men singing 'Nellie Dean', and women delightedly joining in or calling 'Well done, boys, well done'. A wave of tenderness swept through him that he had rarely known before.

He was forty-seven and everything seemed to be going his way. Maybe an easier, much bigger territory once the depression was over. He looked at Kit. She was pallid but laughing. In bed she was useless, but as a spur to his ambitions she was unrivalled. Why the hell couldn't the National Government get the country back on its feet, give people a chance to build, to extend?

His gaze moved back to Maggie Davies, her expansive body, all oozing breasts and spreading hips, her scarlet mouth open as she yelled in enjoyment at her husband John. They were an ambitious pair, hard-working, willing, helpful. Maybe John would be a manager one day. Maybe in a year or two Bertie could recommend him for a district. Up the valley perhaps, Pontypridd way.

Then he looked at his daughters again. Emma would soon be six, still tubby and knock-kneed, too young to be afraid of life, as yet unhurt; and Linda, already developing her mother's amber-eyed, sombre-faced elegance, straight-backed and gently confident.

Another wave of tenderness enveloped Bertie; maybe it was the drink, the heat, the noise, the ending of a year, but at that moment he loved everyone, his family, his friends, his agents. His arm tightened on Elsie's waist. She was light, supple, and bent to him. He wanted to kiss her at that moment more than he wanted another drink, simply because she was there, and he sensed that she would reciprocate, but Elsie's father materialised before him, blocking out the rest of the world, and Elsie's father was as tippled as any foundry worker could be before he actually fell down.

Tom Buckley growled, 'Keep your bloody maulers off her, mister.'

Bertie's arm dropped and his face flushed. He moved a little to one side and his in-laws were watching, intent. He said, 'It's all right Tom. No harm meant,' and he moved further away. Elsie came after him. Her little rounded face

100

was hot and furious. 'Don't let him bully you, Bertie. He's a rotten coward. He's drunk.'

'Sshh. This is a party. We're supposed to enjoy ourselves.'

Kit was against him. 'A stiff drink, darling?' She smiled at Elsie, but her red-brown eyes were saying, 'Keep away, m' girl. Go on. Now!' And Elsie went. She pushed through a group, and Maggie held a glass out to her. 'Here, Love, swig up. Soon be next year.' They drank together and Lorraine Nolan gazed up at her ever-military husband. Her immaculate brows rose gently towards her silvery widow's peak. 'Do you think – ?'

'Hm.' The colonel stroked his moustache and moved his bottom lip out and in thoughtfully. He didn't like what he had seen. He had seen many things in his time. Pukka white men with black girls, that sort of thing, but none had appeared as tawdry as the green-clad tart being clasped by his son-in-law. Albert wasn't a bounder. Never had been. Middle-aged, maybe. Had to be some explanation.

Lorraine Nolan said quietly, 'We'll have to do something. Will you talk to him?'

'By Jove, old girl. Want my nose bitten off?' He drank the last of his whisky and soda and relished its flavour. 'Good stuff.' Then, 'You can handle this. Have a chat with Kit. Find out who the girl is.'

'Albert's new secretary.'

'Heavens above!'

A group swayed, laughed, and moved nearer the Nolans. The colonel whispered darkly, 'You, Lorraine. Have a tactful chat with Kit,' and their gazes locked in understanding and a desire to save those racing towards scandal.

At midnight they welcomed the new year in. For them 1932 arrived in a cacophony of ships' hooters, church bells and Auld Lang Syne. All the men were locked out, the little front lawn full of laughter, talk and the smell of drink and cigarettes and cigars.

The neighbours came out and were invited into number

300 for a quick one, which became the first of many slow ones.

Bertie was aware of an impending anti-climax. 'A game!' he called, and laughed as though he had said something hilarious. 'A game. Let's play a game.'

'Oooh Bertie!' Maggie screamed, her scarlet lipstick gone, washed away by numerous glasses of port and lemon. 'Suggest the vilest things, you do.' Her voice carried an innuendo, and only the two children missed it as they stared with red eyes that were forced to stay open.

Tom Buckley sat in a chair and glowered. All these bloody nobs. All with bloody good jobs. Not jobs. Positions. All with bloody good positions. Look at that tin soldier with fungi on his top lip. He hasn't stopped eyeing our Elsie. Tom knew the type. Heard of them. Do anything if it didn't hop. Well, none of them would lay hands on Elsie. They might rule India but he'd see them in hell before they ruled him. 'Elsie?' It was a bawl. 'Elsie?'

'Yes Dad?' She rushed to him, anxious to avoid him attracting the wrong attention, and he held out his hand to her. 'Give your old Pa a kiss. It's a bit late but I'm saying it now. Happy birthday, gel, happy birthday.'

She giggled and flushed, surprised and delighted. She bent and kissed him and a young man turned to watch. Elsie's short skirt left her French knickers and black suspenders on view, and the young man whistled in appreciation. Others turned to look and Elsie put her hands to shield her bottom, but didn't spring up to pull the emerald green petals into place. Her father scowled, suddenly furious, and turned his head from her. Her expression of pleasure died and a brooding came into her grey eyes. 'I'm eighteen, Dad. I been eighteen for three weeks now.'

'Slut.'

She stood, insulted, rebellious, unhappy, and a circle formed around her.

'More drinks!' Maggie yelled, her scarlet taffeta rustling, her dyed black hair gone wild, her movements unsteady, and Linda brought her drinks, her tray loaded.

102

'A toast,' Bertie called. 'To the baby on our staff. She is just eighteen and a bit.'

'Happy birthday – when was it?'

The agents liked Elsie. They liked the way they could tease her, the way she had collected John's book while he had been ill, the way her happy attempts at glamour brought colour and conversational speculation into their cold, damp winter lives, the way she flirted and made them all think they could bed her when the right place and time occurred.

'To Elsie.'

The colonel raised his glass and Kit stood near her mother. They drank, but said nothing, didn't cheer, or sing, 'For she's a jolly good fellow.'

'A game,' Maggie yelled. 'The plate. Spin the plate – '

Everyone laughed, bleary-eyed now, the men bereft of jackets and ties, the women shoeless, all pals together. God, it was 1932, another year gone, another year towards the end of life. Over three million unemployed and half of them in South Wales. Let's drink up. Have some fun.

'A plate! Ah – '

The plate was enamel, blue, and they sat in a large circle around the smoke-filled room, the fire long dead, the ashes grey and powdery.

Bertie gave everyone a number. 'And if you don't catch the plate before it stops spinning, you pay a forfeit.'

'Aye aye.' They knew the rules.

He spun the plate in the centre of the grass-green carpet and yelled, 'Three,' and John Davies's long legs uncurled him from the floor, his long arms caught the plate and he yelled, 'Twenty-three.'

Amid shrieks of laughter Bertie had to twist back again, grab the plate and call. The time rushed by and, one by one, the men, too, removed their shoes and their white starched collars. Their braces were of many colours, their armlets of expanding silvery fragments, and all their socks were navy blue.

Lorraine Nolan laughed and the colonel gasped as they

too joined in the game. 'By Jove, I'm a bit old for this lark m'boy,' but the laughter went on and rank didn't count any more.

The forfeits were collected: a stocking, a hair-slide, a fountain pen, a pair of cuff-links . . . . They grew into a pile on the table amid the last of the iced cake and the almost empty bottles.

'Bertie can do the forfeits.'

'Not me.'

'Yes, you can. You're good at it.' Tonight Bertie was not the manager. It was one of the secrets of his popularity, the reason he succeeded at a time when others in the insurance world failed. He was one of them.

'Come on Bertie. On your hands and knees, boyo.'

He obliged, sagging in the middle like an old horse, his thick hair flopping over his forehead, his chest heaving as he panted. Women rushed to the bathroom, to the bedroom, to comb their hair and gasp with excited dismay over shiny noses and puffing faces. 'God, I'm tired.' 'So am I – marvellous isn't it?'

'I'll sleep for a week after this.'

Gwen awoke and listened and watched. They had seen her, whispered about her, and now they smiled at her. 'Feel better love?' They hoped her consumption hadn't spread to their coats, and they silently resolved not to wear them until they had been sponged down with Dettol and left out on the back-yard line for a couple of hours.

'The germs can't hurt you when they are dry,' one whispered in the bathroom. 'It's only when they are wet that they are contagious.'

'It's when they're dry that they fly about,' said another. 'That's why it's against the law to spit in the street. When it dries it flies. Onto other people.'

They all shuddered, wished their heads would clear and stop spinning, dreaded tomorrow's hangover, and rushed back downstairs for the forfeits and a hair of the dog.

Gwen followed them. She was hungry. She sat by the tables and drew the remaining mince pies and tattered sandwiches before her. She felt fine, and wasn't this room beautiful. Look at that mirror over the mantlepiece, all gold. Cost a fortune. Must have done.

'Here is a thing and a very pretty thing. What must the owner do to receive it?' Bertie was on his hands and knees and Maggie held the forfeit over his bent shoulder blades. He stared at the floor between his supporting hands and said, 'Ah – ' He couldn't think clearly. 'Push themselves through the keyhole.'

There were shrieks of laughter and he wondered who the owner of that forfeit was.

'Here is a thing and a very pretty thing. What must the owner do to receive it?'

'Stand on one leg with their eyes shut and drink a tot of whisky.'

'Oh!' More shrieks.

Bertie was tired. Being on his hands and knees made him want to sink down, further, gradually succumb to the greenness of the carpet completely, and just sleep.

'Here is a thing and a very pretty thing. What must the owner do to receive it?'

He had to think, to stretch his eyes open, to moisten his mouth. Think. Think. 'Stand on their head against the wall for half a minute.' He chuckled over that one. He hoped it was Tom Buckley, or Lorraine. Lorraine? Ye gods, Lorraine upside down against the wall . . . .

'Here is a thing and a very pretty thing . . . .' It went on, and on. Were there so many forfeits? Were there as many people as that at the party? Then came relief. 'All right Bertie, that's the lot.'

'You mean I can get up now?'

'Yeh. You can get up now,' Maggie said. 'Come on, old man. Help him up everybody. Cor, you can hear his bones creak.'

He stretched, grinning, the blood no longer running to his head, and he noticed Tom Buckley glowering, Tom Buckley sitting forward on the settee, his great shoulders in the striped Welsh flannel shirt hunched. Tom was in his cups, his big rough face almost the colour of Maggie's dress, a haze in his eyes emitting resentment, envy, jealousy. Bertie wondered whether to go to him, to try and be a friend, then he realised it was he the haze was concentrating on. It was he, Bertie Hemsworthy, more than anyone else in the room, that Tom Buckley resented.

Bertie tried to shrug the feeling off. He looked at Gwen Buckley sitting by her husband, a Victorian parody, her hands thinly clasped on her black-dressed lap, her consumptive cream and pink face set in polite weariness.

Everyone else was laughing. Maggie Davies had to push herself through the keyhole, but she was an old hand at parties, and Bertie leaned against the wall while Linda brought him a cup of coffee. She and Emma were red-eyed, yawning, but determined to miss nothing. 'Coffee!' they chorused, and Bertie wondered fleetingly if his two daughters had stolen more than one taste from the many bottles strewn around. 'Who wants more coffee?' they called. 'More coffee. Fresh now.'

There was an odd, momentary silence and someone said, 'It's gone two o'clock. Over two hours of 1932 gone already.'

'Sshh,' someone else said, 'the angels are passing over.' And everyone looked at her. It was Gwen Buckley and her face brightened. 'Haven't you 'eard that before?' She gazed up at them all, her neck grey and stretched. 'When a silence falls at twenty past any hour it means the angels are passing over.'

Tom Buckley crossed himself, then growled. 'Shut your trap, woman,' and she subsided.

Maggie drew a fat woman on a small scrap of paper, wrote her name on it, rolled it tightly, then threaded it through the keyhole, and everyone clapped.

The party spirit rose again, the momentary flagging forgotten, and the colonel drew loud claps and yells of 'Encore' as he stood on one leg, very wobbly, blindfolded, and drank a tot of whisky.

Tom Buckley watched. He was given five matches on a

106

table and told to make them into any part of a woman. He stood looking at them, sullen, feeling inferior. Soon they would all know he couldn't do it. Soon this crowd of bloody nobs would crow over him. Maggie put her shoulder against him, trying to hint, to give him a clue. She heaved her bosom and everyone chortled, 'Go on Mag. Give him a hand. Look at Maggie, Tom. She'll tell you.'

Tom looked at Maggie and saw only a woman tormenting him, a woman sent by the Devil to stab urges into his great body, and him with no right hand to touch her, only a stump, a pink, gruesome, obscene stump God had seen fit to curse him with. To hell with them, hell with them. Christ, he wanted to heave.

'Come on Tom, love.' Maggie touched the matches. 'I'll do it for you, shall I?'

She did it, the matches sliding on the white cloth amid the bread and cake crumbs, the drink stains and empty glasses. She made a word, TIT, and Tom glared at it, his nostrils inflating. Bertie Hemsworthy had done it on purpose. Tom was convulsed with rage. He was certain. Bertie Hemsworthy had seen which forfeit was held over him. Paper through a keyhole for this woman, whisky for that bloody moustached colonel, but obscenity for him. Vulgarity. There, on the table.

Gwen was beside him, holding his good arm, clinging. 'Oy,' she cried too loudly in her effort to soothe, 'isn't that clever?' And Kit knew what was happening. She called, 'Right. Who's next?'

Her black hair was brushed loose now. She looked younger than her years, beautiful in her elegant calmness. 'Elsie! Elsie! You're next.'

Elsie stepped forward, no sign of tiredness or nerves. She was excited, expectant, her make-up worn thin, her kiss curls gone in the excitement and turmoil of the night. This was her birthday celebration.

'Come on, Elsie. Your turn.'

'What do I do?' She was laughing, half shy, but willing.

'Stand on your head for half a minute against the wall.'

Elsie put both her hands to her mouth and squealed. She hadn't done a headstand since she left school, four years ago. This was fun, this was gaiety, this was living. Her eyes danced at Bertie and he grinned back, a link that was strong, still threaded even amid a few dozen people.

'All right!' she called. 'Clear the decks everyone,' and they moved from the one wall that was clear of furniture. She hopped a little, gauged her distance, then sprang, her hands to the carpet and her stockinged feet to the wallpaper.

Laughter roared, clapping broke out. Some would have liked to do the same, others regretted that, for them, that age, that accomplishment had gone. And Elsie's emerald green petalled skirt had fallen back to hide her squashing, reddening face. Her new satin French knickers draped back in lace-trimmed folds from her thighs; her crotch was scantily covered between the black satin suspenders.

'Down now!' Maggie yelled uncharacteristically, panic-stricken. What possessed such a kid to wear French knickers? Surely to God she knew directoire were the best, at all times, especially in the cold of winter. 'Elsie, get down, *fach*. You've done the forfeit. Get down!'

''Alf a minute,' Elsie's muffled voice came in defiance. ''Alf a minute Bertie said. I gotter be 'ere 'alf a minute.'

Stunned, awed, aware things had gone too far, the guests watched, then Elsie gracefully separated and spread wide her legs, bringing them gently back to the floor. Her petalled skirt flopped back into decency as, with a slight bound, she stood erect, feet together, hands at her sides. She awaited the applause, the laughter, and it came, so did her father's left hand. It whipped across her face so she heard her neck click, and his eyes were murderous with fury, his teeth gritted in a snarl. 'Slut! Whore! – ' and she toppled back against the open door, her eyes wide, startled, terrified.

Pandemonium broke out, and Gwen clutched Tom's arm. The colonel bellowed, 'Control yourself man,' and others were tutting, soothing, agreeing, disagreeing.

Elsie ran from the room, up to the bathroom. She sat on

the lavatory and sobbed. She felt she had wanted to cry for a long time and hadn't. She felt, as her father did, that life was rotten. Life bashed those who were down so they never had the chance to get up, but those who were born in feather beds alway had it easy, always had bathrooms with rugs, and their own toilet seats. They didn't have to run down the lane to a lavatory used by the whole street, and they didn't get bashed by their dads. 'Oh Pa, I hate yer bloody rotten guts, I do. Oh Bertie, don't you be mad at me too. Please love me, love me all over . . . . Oh why doesn't somebody love me? If only somebody would love me . . . .'

When no more tears came she washed at the pedestal, using Kit's Pears soap with a mixture of envy and indulgence, then she went to the children's bedroom. She didn't want the spare room, the intrusion of guests' coats and dressing-table lights. She went to where the two small beds stood with a board and easel, and a number of dolls and a teddy, a room with shelves filled with books: *What Katy Did* and *The Heroes*, and *Alice in Wonderland* and *David Copperfield*.

At home there was no light to switch on, so she didn't seek a switch here. She collapsed onto the furthest little bed, the one against the wall where the light slicing gold from the landing didn't reach. She heard the party going on downstairs. They were singing. 'Come, come, come and make eyes at me, down at the old Bull and Bush, ta ra ra ra ra – '

They all had partners. Everybody had somebody else. If only Tommy had come with her. Brothers could be nice. She lay on her back. One day she and Tommy would give Pa what for. One day she and Tommy would beat hell out of him. She turned face down again, sobbing dry-eyed because she knew nothing of that sort would happen, because they understood Pa, the frustration, the feeling of being useless, unwanted, of seeing people with money, with carpets and bedrooms with satin quilts, of seeing Ma going so small it was like the consumption was eating her away, and no one really cared. To hell with all rich people.

To hell with the King and Queen because they had more than anybody . . . .

She fed her chagrin, and downstairs Kit and Maggie were fussing over Tom and Gwen Buckley. Kit came upstairs, rushing past the room where Elsie lay listening, and got Gwen's thin black coat.

Kit wondered what she had in her wardrobe to give the poor soul, and rushed back downstairs to pack a cake and a tin of ham. 'Because we don't use it,' she explained as she pressed it on Gwen, and Maggie let her eyes be naughty and laugh at the mollified, ever-confused Tom Buckley.

Bertie had called a taxi and it chugged and spluttered outside the door.

'Our Elsie,' Gwen cried. 'Where's our Elsie?'

Tom clutched her arm, his size such that he could almost have gripped her whole body as easily. 'Let her walk. She'll learn.'

'Oh Tom – '

'Shurrup. She's a slut.'

'You shurrup. You disgraced her.'

They got into the taxi. Kit was saying, 'Elsie will be all right. Don't worry.' But she was feeling nauseated by the Buckleys, and the more upset because it had happened in front of her parents. Goodness knows what they would think.

Gwen seemed too limp to lift her head properly. 'But I'd like to see our Elsie – '

'She's all right,' Maggie lied. 'I just saw her in the bathroom.' In the lamplight of the street she stared into the darkness of the taxi. 'She'll stay here the night.' She didn't look at Kit. It was a case of getting rid of the Buckleys, and the promise seemed the quickest way of doing it.

The taxi rumbled over the cobbles and tramlines, the driver already paid by Kit, and she and Maggie made for the kitchen. 'Duw, it was cold out there. If ever a cup of char was needed, it's now,' Maggie said, and set to while Kit began clearing stale bread away.

Bertie loped upstairs, long-legged, lithe, frowning. The

troubles of his employees were often his. An unhappy employee did poor work, let the team down. Not even then did he acknowledge that he found Elsie special. He was too tired, worried, irritated, even deflated now the party seemed to be breaking up on such an unusual note: a low, common, ruffian note. The arrogance he hid so well from himself was objecting, not only to the degradation of his hospitality, his home, his business, but to his secretary: a kid who had no way of retaliating.

'Elsie?' He stood on the landing, calling softly. He could hear Kit rattling dishes in the kitchen. There would be more tea or coffee all round, a post-mortem on Tom and Gwen Buckley, then quiet chats, reminiscences of others who had once behaved the same way.

'Elsie?' The light was still on in the back bedroom, the bed strewn with coats, the washing-stand heaped with hats. His in-laws would sleep there tonight. What a time for them to arrive. At this party, on this night. Never before had they 'surprised' them on New Year's Eve. No doubt they would be most frightfully tactful and all that, stiff upper lip, as well as deeply, snobbishly disapproving of the types Bertie invited to Kit's home. Blast Tom Buckley.

'Elsie?' He crept through the open doorway of his daughters' room, and Elsie was curled up on the furthest little bed, her outline dark against the pale pink quilt.

'Elsie?' She moved slightly, and he went to her, sitting looking down at her. 'Do you feel better now?'

'Yes.' It was hesitant. 'There was no need to come up.'

He took her hand. It was small and cool and rough. He said, gently teasing, 'Have you been washing dishes with soda in the water? It's bad you know.'

'No.' She turned on her back, limp, watching him. 'I only use soda on the woodwork.'

'The woodwork? What's wrong with polish?'

She laughed deeply and softly at his ignorance. 'We don't have any polished furniture. I scrub the stairs and the kitchen table. And things like that.'

He was glad the semi-darkness hid his face. He had been

111

into so many houses of poverty, but had never wondered at the whiteness of the wood. He had only ever wondered at the smell, the stench, of continual caustic soda wetness.

She wriggled to one side of the bed. 'You look buggered. Lie down a minute.'

He hesitated, wondering if he was needed downstairs, but he could hear the wireless. A French accordion. Maggie was calling as she hurried along the passage, and Colonel Nolan laughed, a deep haw-hawing sound as though the absence of the Buckleys had left him more at ease.

Bertie lay down and sighed as his head settled on the coolness of the linen pillowcase. Then he grinned as Elsie turned on to her side and cuddled into him, her hand gently moving inside the top of his white cotton shirt. He felt needed, adequate, as if for the first time in a long time he was doing the right thing – comforting this girl on the first day of 1932.

He looked down at her and her eyes were large, the whites almost luminous as she stared up at him. Her face was clean, shining, and so young he felt a stab almost of pain where his heart should be. His sympathy for her, his pity, almost choked him, and his arm instinctively tightened about her.

'Bertie?'

'Yes?'

'Will you kiss me?'

He didn't answer. He was puzzled. Didn't she realise it wasn't wise to go around asking men to kiss her?

She snuggled closer, her face naive, trusting, pleading. 'Just this once . . . . I feel terrible . . . .'

He whispered, 'Oh, come on . . . .' His arm jogged her slightly as if she were a small baby about to cry.

'I need loving, Bertie. Just a little bit of loving.' She moved higher, towards him, and her lips brushed his chin.

'Elsie!' He spoke more sharply than he intended.

'Only your closeness, Bertie. Nobody ever holds me close.' Her hand went to her cheek where, even in this

112

shadow, away from the stream of landing light, he could see the bruising beginning to appear.

'Does he often hit you?'

'Always. Tommy too. He broke Tommy's nose once – '

'Can't you go to the police?'

'D'yer think they care? It'd kill Ma, wouldn't it?'

Her little kisses caused tingling, her lips moving slowly, sensuously down the side of his neck. 'Bertie.'

'Hm?' He was relaxing and the bed was soft. Downstairs the French station had someone singing, 'Amour, amour, amour . . . .'

'People do get better from consumption, don't they?' She leaned up, looking down into his face, and her hair that was usually so stiff with sugared curls was soft, falling forward. Her Phul-Nana had been washed from her wrists, but it still wafted from her ears.

She kissed him. Her mouth, at first, was undemanding, whisper soft as if he would hit her away, then the love she had so often sought in *Peg's Paper*, the lovely, exciting sensations in her crotch, pulsating warmly, made her mouth more hungry. The food her emotions needed was here, at the tip of her pointed, seeking tongue, and Bertie's arms were wrapped around her.

It was almost three months since a woman's breasts had sent their pleasure, their powers of awakening, to his skin, and his flesh quivered with the unexpected anguish of it.

'Elsie.'

She smiled down at him, her white teeth big, even, her mouth and eyes eager for muffled laughter.

'You'd better get off me or there'll be an accident.'

'Love me, Bertie. Love me.'

His tongue met hers.

'Are you a virgin, Elsie?'

'No, my darling, no.'

'Good lor!'

She sat up, astride him, and took off the emerald green dress. 'Not since I was thirteen.' Her skin was white, ivory smooth, her breasts more perfect than sly peeps down her

113

neckline could ever imagine. She rolled onto the bed beside him, and he lifted himself up, his lips took a pink nipple and his tongue caressed.

'Bertie, oh my love, my darling. Bertie, d'yer mind me loving you, loving you? Loving you till I die?'

She was like a butterfly emerging from a chrysalis, beautiful, perfect, small. Her belly was smooth, her hips softly rounded, her skin silken to his touch. The satin French knickers slid away, and when Bertie too was finally naked, and took her, he didn't care if the world crucified him.

Here was relief. Here was love, and he groaned as he entered her.

'Elsie.' It was a low, guttural escape of tension, an absorption into pleasure. 'My love, my love.' And Elsie was enslaved. Drawn into the very centre of her deepest emotions, this man was not like the sniggering, bragging, inexperienced boys she had experimented with before. Here was the tall, dark, handsome lover of *Peg's Paper*, whose passion was blinding, whose hands were manipulators of magic, and as all the beauty of every fairy story, every love story Elsie had ever read burst into her brain, she gave herself completely, trusting that he was hers for evermore, and that she need never again seek another lover.

*   *   *

Elsie slept what was left of that night on the settee in the middle room. First she had cleared the place of glasses, bottles, plates. She had washed the ashtrays and got onto her hands and knees and swept the carpet, enjoying its greenness, pretending it was a vast meadow where it was always summer, and that beautiful things like hummingbirds and blue butterflies lived in its boundary hedges.

When Kit and Bertie called 'goodnight' from the passage, their voices were formal. Elsie got onto the settee, aware of the chill creeping through the house now the fires had died. She wrapped herself in a blanket and slept the sleep of complete satisfaction.

* ★ ★

Breakfast was at lunchtime and the spasmodic conversation was polite. Lorraine's eyebrows seemed a little higher this morning and the corners of her lips a little tighter. She disapproved of the staff sitting at the table with their betters. Elsie ran to and fro like the servant she had temporarily become, and kept her gaze on her plate when not at someone's beck and call.

Colonel Nolan noticed her scrubbed face, remembered the happy sounds coming through the bathroom door early on, and nodded as if he had known all along that this child came from a bathroomless house. People did, of course. They didn't mind, most of them, they bathed in the sink, didn't they? Or something. Still, she had a dainty pair of breasts on her. He wanted to smack his lips beneath the newly-combed moustache. When he was younger . . . . By Jove . . . . She wasn't unlike that little girl in Poona . . . .

'Cedric!' Lorraine said sharply. 'Kitty asked if you require more coffee.'

He shook his head brusquely, and when Elsie gave a shy smile around the table and said in her best party manners voice, 'That was a very nice meal, thank you Mrs Hemsworthy. May I leave the table?' only Bertie and the colonel failed to feel the awkward silence. Elsie, as a junior, an inferior junior, should sit quietly, her hands in her lap, until told she could move, and certainly not be the first to retire. She remembered it, then, and stayed. Bertie smiled at her. Today his tensions had gone. Today Kit was a fine wife and mother who was still unwell after her recent suffering, and his in-laws? Well, it was damn good of them to come. They lived in Worcester and must have driven the old Bentley for some hours to get here.

Emma and Linda sat at the table spooning marmalade onto their toast. They had enjoyed the party, had enjoyed going to bed at goodness knows what time, and their grandparents had brought them gifts.

Gifts! Linda looked at Emma, and Emma, thinking she

115

was about to be scolded by her older sister for taking too much marmalade, stared into her eyes.

'I just remembered,' Linda said, and her adoring grandmother smiled benignly on her. 'Yes, my darling? And what did you remember?'

Linda glanced sideways at Elsie and said stoutly, 'Elsie is eighteen now. She had a birthday. And nobody bought her a present.'

Kit moved her own plate quickly. 'You mustn't worry your head over Elsie.'

Bertie said easily, 'I had thought of that,' and his high cheekboned face expressed indulgence all round. 'I thought of some flowers.'

The Colonel pouted and nodded, pleased the onus wasn't on him, pleased their visit was short and he and Lorraine would be back home at The Gables tomorrow. 'Splendid idea. Splendid. Do you know we saw daffodils in bloom on the way here. Where was it Lorraine? Malvern? We had to slow down didn't we? Cows all over the road.'

'Oh Malvern is lovely.' Lorraine almost clapped her hands, and the silver waves of her hair caught the light as immaculately as a brand new half-crown. 'A friend of ours has gone to a farm there. Poor darling has this frightful consumption complaint.' She nibbled her toast, genteel. 'The doctor, dear man, was so tactful. He didn't tell her, did he Cedric? He told her husband. She had an awful shadow on the lung. I cried when I learned about it. I really did. I cried for her. It's such a terrible death. Terrible. They linger on, you know, linger and linger.'

Elsie's hands gripped each other tightly under the table. This was the first she had heard of the way they died. Oh yes, people died every day with it, but not the people she knew closely, and up to now, she thought, she had never seen a dead person. She had always refused to visit coffins when the rest of her family went. Her big grey eyes watched Lorraine's carefully peach-powdered face, and she asked softly, almost frightened, 'Is your friend going to die?'

It was the wrong question. Lorraine put an anguished hand to her narrow forehead. 'I hope not, oh I do hope not.' Kit made soothing noises and the colonel lowered his head and peered at Elsie.

'No, no, m'dear girl. The lady in question has money, stacks of the stuff. The farm she is staying at has every requisite. Specialists call there regularly, and she will have the finest country food: milk straight from the cow, fresh eggs, butter made on the spot. She can't possibly fail to survive.' He had an urge to hold Elsie's hand. The poor child was obviously upset. How remarkably sensitive of her. And what a complexion she had. Alabaster. By Jove just like alabaster. Thoroughly touchable, in spite of her home obviously lacking a bathroom.

Bertie stood up, pushing his chair back, becoming irritated by the self-centred egotism of Lorraine's anguished face. He looked at his watch. 'Elsie. There isn't much we can do in the office today. What if you go along home? Is there a tram? Are they running today?'

Elsie smiled, eager to escape. Looking at him made her happiness rise like a rose-pink cloud around her heart, and the loveliness of it almost choked her. She tried to send a message with her eyes, to say, 'I love you. You're wonderful.' But he was ushering her down the passage, helping her on with her frayed tweed coat, and walking with her to the tramtop. As he went Emma and Linda slid from their chairs and went up the stairs to their gifts. The colonel moved to Bertie's battered chair and lit his pipe. The smoke clouded before him. He stretched his legs, crossed his ankles and sighed. It was just a case of sticking the visit out now, what? Wait until tomorrow brought release and all that sort of thing.

He saw his wife begin to finger her knife and the prickles rose on the back of his neck. Lorraine was about to be up to something. Lorraine was coming all over, 'This hurts me my darling more than it hurts you.'

He was right.

Lorraine said in a restrained voice, 'Kit, you know I

117

would never wittingly hurt you?' Kit blinked then stared at her mother; she too could recognise her mother's wiles before any actual words slid forth. 'That girl.' Lorraine half smiled. 'That Elsie. What does she do here? Who is she? What is she?'

Kit tried not to sound stiff. She was tired, weary, starved of the blood lost during the abortion, laden with guilt over her lack of courage in childbirth, her inability to enjoy lovemaking, her feeling her marriage was crashing about her, and what she saw as her helplessness. 'She's Bertie's secretary.'

'She's – er – ' Lorraine missed the hint of defensiveness in Kit's voice, 'a little young for such a position dear, don't you think?'

'She's all we can afford. We pay her six shillings a week and she works all hours. At the moment she is even collecting a book for an agent on the sick.' Lorraine's gentle rebukes, her disapprovals, had always dripped about her daughter, and Kit had never openly rebelled, but the rebellion had been there, like a tiny tumour ready to erupt if fed too well. If Lorraine had cared to criticise Satan, Kit would have risen to his defence, and now she did it for Elsie Buckley. 'She's a good, hard-working girl. We would be lost without her.' Which, Kit told herself, was perfectly true.

'Well, well.' Lorraine shrugged and carefully replaced her knife beside her fork on her empty plate. Then she said slyly, her eyebrows high, her mouth in a tight smile, 'You know they sleep together, don't you?'

Colonel Nolan choked on his pipe-smoke and suddenly leaned forward coughing and heaving, his eyes and nose running, the pipe held at arm's length, his free hand scouring his jacket pocket for a handkerchief. Was his wife the finest bitch the good Lord had created?

'How interesting,' Kit retorted. 'You saw them? They performed in the middle of last night's party?' She got up from her chair. 'You should consult someone about your mental state, Mother. Your own life is so barren you invent intrigue for others.' Her amber eyes shot sparks of warning.

'Oh Kitty, darling. I was only trying to help.'

'When? When did Bertie and that girl ever make love? You witnessed it?' Kit's heart was hammering. She had seen the closeness growing between Bertie and Elsie, but she wanted no one to put it into words, no one to say what instinct had warned her about for some time.

Lorraine glared at her, then at the colonel, unalarmed at his paroxysm, not particularly interested, wondering what the fuss was all about. The colonel was purple. He tried clutching his heart.

Lorraine turned back to Kit. 'I'm only warning you, darling. I did see them looking at each other.'

'Looking at each other!' The shock of her mother's unexpected attack was wearing off. Kit was derisive.

'Oh come now, darling,' Lorraine smiled and examined her finger-nails; they were shaped and buffed. 'Someone has to warn you. If it hasn't happened already, it soon will.'

Kit stood, stiff, more elegant than ever before, even superior to the woman who had bred her. 'Understand one thing, Mother. Bertie has never been unfaithful to me. He never will be. He is not at all like Father with his silly little concubines in every inch of the British Empire.'

The Colonel's heart banged, jumped, swayed, stopped and went again. Surely his daughter was the second bitch the good Lord had made. He thought his moment had come.

'That's just what I mean,' Lorraine said sweetly. 'All men are like that. You must not be upset when it happens. For six shillings a week you are most fortunate. Most concubines cost a lot more.' She too stood up and began collecting the plates. 'As I have told you consistently, no decent woman ever allows herself to be used in such a way. It's so, well, it is, isn't it? Such a dirty, animal busines. Degrading. On the few occasions I have been to London I have seen girls standing around, just begging men to pay them for it, and you should see their faces. It shows on a woman's face you know, ruins her looks.'

119

The Colonel stood up and tapped his pipe out on the hob. This subject had always been the core of trouble between himself and Lorraine. He often thanked God for the army and the pretty little girls it had led him to. He said firmly, 'Their bank balances are jolly healthy though.'

'Be quiet, dear.' Lorraine smiled at him. 'I have never complained about your wanderings. Just as long as you made no attempt to touch me afterwards.' She grimaced and turned back to Kit. 'Now, shall we get these dishes swilled? It's a housekeeper you need really, darling. Someone to ease your life, not Albert's.'

Kit turned from her quickly, furiously. God help Bertie, she thought, if he ever did sleep with that girl, and God forgive her for what she might do to that girl if ever she found them together.

Bertie came back to the house whistling. He had waited with Elsie for the tram to come, and as she stepped on to its platform she had half turned to him, smiling, impish, the tip of her pink tongue deliberately suggestively placed between her silently promising lips, and he had nodded, just as meaningfully.

'See you Monday.'

'Another three days.' She gave an exaggerated sigh.

'Make the most of it.' His dark eyes were laughing, his thick greying hair lifted gently in the wind.

CHAPTER SIX

Maggie and John Davies's bedroom was low and long with a beamed sloping ceiling. On that mid-January morning Maggie could hear the infinite silence that told her last night's rain had stopped, and in its place was the mist, the cloud that came so low on the mountains it enveloped the cottage in a grey velvety isolation.

It was cold, the air damp, and Maggie's flannelette nightgown was voluminous. She got into the wollen wrap-around blue dressing-gown John had bought her for Christmas.

She shivered as she plodded down the narrow winding stairs, feeling the warmth of the kitchen gradually rise to her, and she guessed the fire was still in, banked with wet small coal.

There had been no real reason to get up yet. John was still weak from the chill he had contacted in December, still tired from the New Year's Eve party at Prince Edward Road, and lately complaining of sharp pains in his right lung when he breathed.

Maggie dreaded consumption, and she lay awake at night telling herself not to worry: spring would soon see John putting on the weight he had lost, getting out on the knocker again, building up his book and his self-esteem, heading for a district of his own.

There were two things Maggie longed for; a baby, and to be a manager's wife. Sometimes she stood with the long ladle held in the cauldron of cawl over the fire for minutes at a time, unaware she had stopped stirring, that her fleshy, usually merry, face was going scarlet and puffy in the heat, and the highly respectable, unfashionable, winter warm, full black skirt she had only ever left off for Bertie's parties was scorching into a permanent, patchy brown.

At these times Maggie was daydreaming of being a manager's wife, and of having a baby. As the former she would never again have to wear the black skirt type of clothes. She would become more fashionable, more modern, wear the scarlet taffeta dress more often, and because she would live in a more modern area, the neighbours would not look askance at her desire to bare her cleavage. They would understand that big women need the freedom in which to breathe.

As to a baby . . . . Her dreams usually folded themselves away then, the ecstasy of the dream and the sadness of the futility mingling and, as she put it, bringing her back to her senses. Financially she and John were comfortable. They had almost half an acre of back garden, so when they had a good crop they sold a lot of stuff to Sion-the-Shop and his widowed mother. The profit was all tax-free and tucked away in various parts of the house. But there was one thing that niggled Maggie Davies: one thing she felt 'awful' about, and John was the only person on earth who knew about it. It was her jealousy of Kitty Hemsworthy. Sometimes it swept over her so strongly she had to grip the back of a chair, John's hand, or her umbrella, depending on where she was, lest she go rushing to Prince Edward Road and wallop the smug, skinny, born-with-a-silver-spoon in her mouth Kitty Hemsworthy. Then, as the emotion ebbed away, Maggie would shudder so her pectoral muscles hurt with the sudden shaking of her massive breasts, and she would console herself with the thought that Kit Hemsworthy hadn't enough life in her to suckle a cat, whereas she, Margaret Ann Davies, could have supplied milk to quins for a year if only God had given her a chance. But she hadn't had a baby. Neither did she get any letters. Until now. And there was one on the cold red and black tiles of the passage floor at the foot of the stairs where it had flown from the letterbox.

Maggie gave a fleeting thought to the postman who must

122

have pushed his bicycle and laden satchel up the mountain in the thick white mist that she could see through the fanlight, then she was bending, gasping, lifting the long white envelope.

The postmark was London, and the M in Mr and Mrs was made with a great flourish. The handwriting, in bright blue ink, told of a big person with big opinions, and the only person Maggie knew of in London were those associated with Head Office.

She went to the kitchen, stood before the grate with its gently glowing fire, and quickly made her cold, plump fingers rip the end off the envelope. The letter was short, the letter M still as beautifully made as Maggie had ever seen. She read quickly, scanning more than reading, then going over it again, more slowly.

Dear Maggie and John,

May I take this opportunity to wish you a highly prosperous and joyous 1932. I know of no valid reason why my wishes should not become realities as long as John keeps his nose to the grindstone and gets the new business in.

It was with regret I heard of his recent illness and trust he has new fully recovered.

Sometime during the next few weeks I shall endeavour to visit South Wales and shall arrange a day or two with him.

We have become concerned at the number of fire claims on his book this season, but have no doubt both John and Mr Hemsworthy have looked into each one meticulously.

Thank you for your usual Christmas card. I accept it with the same sincerity as it was doubtless sent. As you are fully aware I never send the things. Your letter was most informative. I had not previously had the pleasure of hearing about Miss Buckley.

Yours,

Then followed a large signature that Maggie recognised as Z. Carruthers.

Like everyone else involved in the local branch of the Unicorn Insurance Company she and John sometimes wondered what the Z stood for. Was it Zacharias? Even now Maggie quivered with mirth at the thought, then she hurried back upstairs. 'John. We've had a letter. From Carruthers.'

'Who?'

'Carruthers. Head Office.'

John woke himself properly and sat up. 'He's written to us?'

'I'm thinking the same thing. I've sent him a card each Christmas since you started with the firm and he went out that first time with you, remember? And this is the first time he's ever acknowledged it.'

Maggie sat on the bed that clanged as it took her weight, and John reached out for the letter. 'Big man. Big writing,' he said.

'Maybe we're in at last.'

'What d'you mean? In at last?'

'Maybe there's a new district going.'

John stared at the letter, speculating, then stretched his upper lip down over his crooked teeth. 'So you wrote to him.' His tone was dry. You're sucking up. Now look Mag. When I get promotion I want it because I'm good, not because you write to the old man's lapdog.'

'It was only a chatty note about the party.' Maggie was unrepentant. 'He didn't have to answer.' She swept her fingers up the sides of her neck and through her dyed black hair. 'Can't have done any harm.'

They sat in the cold grey dampness for a while, and she put a shawl across his pyjamaed shoulders. 'You've got to look after yourself. Get better properly. There's bound to be a vacancy soon.'

They sat looking first at the letter, then at each other, until Maggie heaved a huge breath and said, 'Funny Bertie hasn't said Carruthers is coming down.' She gave a little sniff. 'Maybe we are making a mystery over nothing. He comes down each spring anyway.'

'It's not spring. And I've been home from work over a month. Over five weeks. And he says about too many fire claims.'

'Head Office wouldn't send Carruthers down for that!'

'Bertie told me Elsie Buckley's doing fine on my round. And I bet she's cheaper. Some firms are starting to employ women just so they can save money. For all we know I'm due for the push, not promotion.'

Maggie frowned, trying to understand, not prepared to acknowledge that her dream of being a manager's wife might be fading. 'Oh John! Feeling in the dumps, you are. They wouldn't sack you. Bertie wouldn't let them.'

'Bertie wouldn't have any say in the matter. It's the Old Man. The bearded old goat whose picture hangs over Bertie's filing cabinet who decides.' John's sallow bony finger prodded the blankets over his knees. 'And he'd send Carruthers. Poor bloody Carruthers. He gets some dirty jobs, that bloke does. Lapdog or not.'

'At least he's got a job. I'll write to him again. Just friendly like.'

John slowly folded the letter and pushed it back into its envelope. 'We'll wait and see.'

'Wait and see what?'

'See what happens.'

'Aren't you going to ask Bertie?'

'Ask him what? Why Carruthers decides to honour us with a letter? If I'm getting the poke? Don't be daft, woman.'

'What'll you tell him then?'

'Nothing!' John looked directly at his wife. 'There's nothing to tell.'

'If he learns we're corresponding with Carruthers . . . .'

'We forgot to mention it. That's all.' John got out of the bed which clanged and sprang as Maggie rushed to help her serious-faced husband into a dressing-gown the same as hers but smaller. 'Let's go and have a cuppa,' he said urgently. 'Then I'll get down to the doctor. See if he can give me something that gets me back on my feet.'

'D'you fancy breakfast? I've got lovely brown eggs there. Sion hasn't called for them yet.'

'Aye,' John nodded. 'We'll have eggs,' and as she went he grumbled, 'Eggs. And cawl. Every day. Eggs and more bloody cawl.'

* * *

Bertie hated January. Swansea seemed to huddle in on itself, unable to retreat from the dark, wet, greyness of the Bristol Channel because of the cloud enshrouded hills that encased it. Business was bad. No matter how little people had spent on Christmas, it had been too much, and now there was no money left for the extra coal, the extra bedding, the extra woolly needed for the snow that might always come next month, and so they tried clinging to life and waiting for the first signs of spring.

As it was, that first Tuesday in February Bertie saw daffodils on sale in a florist's window. He stopped to admire them, just to gaze at their brazen yellowness, their sheer audacity for being alive and beautiful at such a time. He wondered if Kit would like some, then he remembered Elsie. As long ago as the New Year's Eve party, he had promised her flowers for her birthday, and he had done nothing about it.

Now he went into the gloom of the shop and it smelled of ferns and fertiliser. He asked that a bouquet be made up and delivered to Salubrious Terrace, then he bought daffodils for Kit.

He walked home whistling, his trilby on the back of his head, his long legs covering the ground easily, his overcoat open, swinging about him like a cape.

It would soon be spring. He felt more optimistic already.

He went in through the doorway of 300 Prince Edward Road and didn't pause at the hallstand. He went straight to the kitchen, where Kit had her hands deep in a bowl of flour and fat. Her black hair was plaited tightly, the two

126

plaits caught on top of her oval head. Her skin was matt cream and her eyes lit up as they saw the flowers. Bertie held them as if in triumph. 'Voilà!' he cried. 'Spring has arrived,' and for a moment she thought how young Bertie looked, how vibrantly alive and ready to face life.

'Bertie! You goose!' And she was beautiful in the calm, almost perfect-featured way that had first attracted him. She held her hands up from the earthenware mixing-bowl, and rubbed the mixture from them. She took the flowers and held her face for the chaste kiss he always gave her when he came home, and her second reaction took over: what did he want? Why flowers now, at this time of the year, when they were expensive? And some of her pleasure ebbed. Lorraine had taught her, years ago, that no man gives a gift for nothing, never from the sheer goodness of his heart. Lorraine. In flashes Lorraine often entered her daughter's head. Lorraine, laughing, hinting, warning. And as Bertie took off his hat and coat, his face grinning with the happiness he had found outside the florist's window, she realised his hands looked nice. His hands looked unusually nice.

She said suspiciously, 'Have you had a manicure?'

'Yes. Like it?' He spread his hands, palms down, for her to see. 'The barber is trying to drum up business and has this manicurist there, so while I had a shave she did my nails.' At that moment Bertie was completely naive, unsuspecting the trap she was leading him into. He kissed her again, his lips jutting like the mouth of a tied balloon, passion as far from his mind as the next New Year's party, and he didn't see Kit's eyes film over.

Never before had she known Bertie have a shop manicure; a shop shave, yes, because he disliked nicking himself with the cut-throat razor, but a manicure – was that to make his caresses more acceptable? Was it something Elsie had requested? And flowers early in February? She said lightly, 'Have you seen Elsie?'

'No. Why?'

Her question startled him, then he said, 'Oh, I sent her

127

some flowers too. For her birthday. From us. I did promise them a month ago, then forgot.'

Kit looked at the daffodils, then rushed them to the scullery. She plonked them in a vase. The flush of pleasure was dead, now she felt only emotions she didn't understand. Jealousy and hatred. She leaned against the edge of the sink for a moment, feeling its coldness bite through her.

In the kitchen Bertie was whistling, making tea. Kit wanted to ask him about Elsie Buckley. How advanced was his friendship with her? Was he in love with her? She turned on the cold tap and held the vase of daffodils under it. Logic was telling her to control her mind, to stop imagining things that had not occurred. Bertie could be happy because winter would soon be over. He could be happy because he had a good home, fine daughters, and a good wife . . . .

And there Kit had to bite her lip. She put the vase on the draining-board and her wrists under the cold tap. She was not a good wife. She was like her mother. She remembered her father taking her into his confidence just before her wedding. It was, Kit always thought, a few moments of her father's loneliness, an emotional loneliness; he had filled his pipe, squashed down the tobacco in the bowl, then said heavily, 'Kitty, your mother is a fine woman.' He had drawn the back of his forefinger along under his moustache as if afraid the pipe might singe it. 'She understands my peccadillos and I'd appreciate it if you did too. If a man's not at home, or if, for some reason, his bed isn't kept warm as often as nature intends, then he'll be driven into other arms.' He had peered at her, hoping to teach her about men without being obvious. 'Nothing in it, you understand, not basically. I mean, by Jove, I couldn't marry any of the little girls. That position belongs to your mother. It's a throne she occupies admirably.' He had lit his pipe then, and half smiled, as though he was forgiving Kit for not being the type to whom he could speak more bluntly. Then he had said quickly, 'The truth is, your mother won't let herself enjoy it.'

Now Kit thought of those words. Was it true that

Lorraine deliberately didn't want it? There were times when Kit yearned for loving, when her thin hands caressed her own body, moving firmly from her breasts, down the concave of her waist and out over her hips, and she longed for the kisses that could bring to the surface the ardour that felt stifled inside her. Did other women have a secret, a way of bringing to life the passion that could match a man's? Did prostitutes have a secret that decent women lacked?

And so her thoughts came back to Elsie Buckley, and she wondered if Elsie would have run to the scullery with the daffodils, or whether she would have run straight into Bertie's arms with warm, passionate kisses.

The hurdy-gurdy man was at the side of the road when the pony and trap stopped below the supporting wall of Salubrious Terrace, and the man in the navy blue uniform with a peaked cap got down from the driver's seat. He reached into the trap and lifted out a bouquet of flowers, and the children around the hurdy-gurdy stopped dancing to stare, all big eyes and curious expressions.

The hurdy-gurdy man kept turning the handle and the spindly, tinkly music kept filling the air. 'It ain't gonna rain no more, no more . . . .' The man with the flowers walked up the worn stone steps and banged the knocker on Elsie Buckley's door. Already the neighbours knew about it and women gathered, wrapped in their Welsh shawls to watch surreptitiously as Elsie appeared, barefoot all shiny pink face and shocked eyed as the bouquet was handed to her.

First she saw the man's ruddy, peaky-nosed face beneath the navy blue uniform cap, then she saw the flowers; a mass of yellow and golden splendour, daffodils, mimosa, chrysanthemums, shivering delicate fern, and her hands shook.

She knew at once who they were from. Each day she had gone into the office expecting, hoping for, the birthday present Bertie had so easily promised her; and now they had come, on a Saturday afternoon when, it seemed, all the street were out to watch.

Elsie lifted the flowers to her face, wallowing in their cold softness, their particular perfume, then she watched the man walk away, and she lifted the white card tied with a thin yellow ribbon to the stems and read: BELATED BIRTHDAY WISHES FROM KIT AND BERTIE. She stepped off her doorstep, further out, into the early February chill of the smoke-scented street, and she heard the hurdy-gurdy. She hurried to the wall, her skirt too short, too tight, above her young knees, and as she watched the delivery man raise the long whip and flick the pony, the trap, and himself away, she waved to the hurdy-gurdy man. Not because she knew him, she didn't, but because he was laughing, and scruffy, and ragged and cold, with a red, wet nose, and because she was up on the grey stone wall, while he was below her and she was happy. He waved back and his tiny monkey stood in its blue velvet trousers on the hurdy-gurdy and stared, brown-eyed, unblinking, at the children. Beside the monkey lay an upturned cap, and Elsie suddenly ran into the house, took the penny gas meter money off the mantelpiece, and ran back out.

'Hoy!' she yelled, and threw the penny. It fell into the road and the children pushed and fought for it, bare bottoms thrusting from ragged trousers, and bare dirty feet and hands everywhere.

The hurdy-gurdy didn't stop. The man kept turning the handle, and it seemed a dozen kids were needed to flick Elsie's retrieved penny into the cap.

Elsie turned proudly to her neighbours, the flowers nestled in her arm, her voice as grand as she could make it, 'From the manager of the Unicorn Insurance Company. I'm his confidential secretary, you know.'

Their eyes were knowing, their world-weary minds a few jumps ahead of Elsie's words. They nodded grudgingly, then they watched her go back into the house with the cracked walls. They supposed her father knew what was going on. Fine one he was to allow it.

Elsie took the flowers to the scullery and sorted them, her inside full of the lovely cuddly feelings, and her lips smiling with tenderness. The card said 'From Kit and Bertie', but that, Elsie felt sure, was for prudence's sake,

130

nothing else. The flowers were from Bertie. From Bertie, her lover, to her. She arranged them in what jugs and jam-jars she could find, then put them on the tin tray and carried them upstairs.

Her mother spent a lot of time in bed these days. She said it was warmer and Elsie believed her. Gwen watched the flowers being placed about her bare dim little room. 'Oh, our Elsie! Where d'yer get them then?'

'Bertie sent them.'

'Oh, isn't he kind?'

Elsie nodded. She was blushing, her mouth slightly open, her tongue full as it rested on her lower lip. Her body felt as if Bertie had a warm hand on her breast, his thighs so close she could feel the heat of him. 'I'll pay him back, Ma,' she said, 'there's no reason for you to feel obligated.'

'Oh,' Gwen's eyes were enormous, 'aren't they a lovely colour. Oh, like in the fields in summer. Did he send them for me then?'

Elsie turned and looked at her, her own face in shadow with the small-paned window behind her. 'Ma, if Bertie could get you on a farm in Malvern, would you go?'

'Malvern?' Gwen could only absorb so much. 'Where's that then?'

'Not far. Mrs Hemsworthy's parents got special friends there.'

'Oh,' Gwen's grey hands came together as if in prayer. 'D'you think they'd give me a 'oliday then? On a farm?'

Elsie smiled, kissed her mother, and said mysteriously, 'We'll see . . . we'll see . . . .' And in her innocent belief in the rich always giving to the poor, she went to the office early on the Monday, typed the necessary letters, then, after Bertie had left to go canvassing, Elsie too, hurried off to get the train to Port Talbot and started collecting John Davies's book.

During the second week of that February Elsie was still smiling over the flowers. They were wilting now, but she was loath to throw them out, and in Port Talbot a pale, white sun tried to shine over or under heavy clouds, but

Elsie had a good morning. Collections were up, the round was beginning to recover from Christmas. A few people had even paid a little off their arrears. In her last call before the universal lunch-hour, she sat gratefully on an old leather sofa and waited for its owners, a Mr and Mrs Bevan, to make her the usual cup of tea.

The daps on her aching tiny feet were no longer white; patches of grass and waste ground had washed them into soggy blackness, and the rubber fender on each one was beginning to peel away.

She looked at Mr and Mrs Bevan and wondered what they would think if the Unicorn Insurance agent called for their twopenny premium with no shoes or stockings on, while Mr and Mrs Bevan looked at her and thought, 'Poor little soul. Why ever does she do her face up like that? She looks worn out.' They looked at the daps and tried not to sigh, but they exchanged glances. Mrs Bevan said, 'Is there no sign of John Davies coming back then? I heard he had pleurisy.'

Elsie nodded and took the cup of stewed tea Mr Bevan handed her in a thick white chipped mug. 'He's coming on fine though. Be back next month.'

'Nice,' nodded Mrs Bevan, who seemed to be an all brown woman, brown clothes, brown face, brown hair, brown eyes. 'As long as he's coming right again. Nice man. Reminds me of my brother. He only died last autumn, you know. It was pleurisy he had.'

Elsie wore her interested face. It was a habit she had learned easily. 'I'm sorry about that.'

'And he wasn't insured, was he Stan? God help too. His widow had to bury him on tick.'

There was a long sad silence, and Elsie drank the tea, not enjoying it, but glad of it. 'He was your brother?' she said then.

'Yes. Harry his name was. Harry Martin. Buried up the road here – '

Elsie nodded again in sympathy. Every Monday at this time Mr and Mrs Bevan gave her a cup of tea, then every

Monday she went up to the graveyard to sit on a tomb and eat the jam sandwiches she had squashed into her handbag. 'Everybody should be insured,' she said, and her grey eyes became bright and inquisitive. Did the Bevans have another brother, someone, anyone, who was not insured?

'Oh yes.' Mrs Bevan sat bent forward, her freckled hands smoothing her brown lisle-stockinged legs. 'We watch that now, don't we, Stan? We gave John Davies a load of new business as soon as Harry went. We learnt our lesson, didn't we, Stan?'

Elsie left them with good-natured waves and wishes all round. The tea had eased the dryness in her mouth that hours of talking always caused. It had warmed her too, and the sit-down had been nice.

She went to the graveyard and chose her tombstone. It was opposite a white angel on a pedestal so high it seemed heavenly against the undecided sky. Elsie ate and thought of money. She thought of a present for Bertie in exchange for the flowers, and a farm in Malvern for Ma, and about John Davies wanting his book back.

Soon the extra money she had been earning would stop. John had a big book, a big round. He could spec on thirty shillings every week, even in the quiet times, and in the good times he got almost as much as Bertie, and Bertie was a manager.

If I could be an agent, Elsie thought, and munched. If I could have a round like this I could send Ma to a farm . . . . And somehow she thought of Harry Martin and the fact that he hadn't been insured. Poor devil! She would have booked him up, if she had known. She would have booked him for twopence. Then she would have had ten times for commission. One and eightpence! She would have had an extra one and eightpence!

She crossed her knees, trying to ignore the coldness of the stone coming through the seat of her old tweed coat, lost in her dreams of affluence. What could she give Bertie for a present? A little something, just to show how much she loved the flowers.

133

Pensively she folded the brown paper bag her bread and jam had been in, and put it in her pocket. It would do again for tomorrow. She wondered why Bertie had made no advances to her since that night on the little bed. Hadn't he enjoyed her? Maybe he had told his wife about it. Maybe he had said, 'Come, my kitten, let me do with you as I will, or I shall once more bed my mistress.' Elsie flicked crumbs from her lap and got back onto her aching feet. She didn't think Bertie had done any such thing, but it was fun to dream, and she had time to wander around the graveyard, read the tombstones, see how many dead very old people there were among the continuous proof of very young ones. Some names were quite funny. There was an Olive Branch and an Ivor Cann.

She wondered if they had all been insured.

Later that afternoon she had to call in a little corner shop, and there were the Valentine cards. Elsie was delighted, inspired. That was what she would send Bertie, a Valentine card. She chose carefully, a little embarrassed, and walked out with a card bearing three small bows of ribbon, and three little verses.

'If to me you will be true,

Return to me this bow of blue.

If to me you will be wed,

Return to me this bow of red.

But if you think just friendship's right,

Return to me this bow of white.'

Elsie giggled to herself all the way home. Just wait until Bertie saw the card. What should she put on it? From an admirer? From Ready to be yours? Maybe she should just post it with nothing on it. But he wouldn't know she had sent it then. The problem and the delight kept her awake that night. She heard her father come in, his feet unsteady, his deep unhappy voice growling as he climbed the stairs. She heard her mother coughing, and she heard Tommy shut the kitchen door before he settled down on their old horse-hair sofa for the night One day she, Elsie, would buy a bed for Tommy, a proper bed with proper blankets.

134

She fell asleep, young, knowing, trusting and confident of the future.

She left the Valentine card amid the batch of letters waiting for Bertie's signature, then she sat at her desk taut with anticipation, waiting for Bertie to find it.

When he did so he frowned, puzzled. He picked it up, read it, let his eyebrows rise in amazement, turned it over, then stared at the three little verses again. It wasn't Kit's style at all. He looked at Elsie's back. She pored over her shorthand and something akin to pride enveloped him, together with the tenderness he usually felt towards her. She was a good kid, a good worker. If only she would stop plastering her face. He wiped a hand over his amused smile and his tongue felt around the inside of his cheek. He read aloud, 'If to me you will be true, return to me this bow of blue. If to me you will be wed – ah.' Carefully he picked off the bow of blue, a sliver of the card and glue coming with it, and still Elsie didn't look at him. She wanted him to love her, to come behind her and wrap his arms about her.

She needed the scent of him, the scent his soap left on his skin, the scent of his cigars, his cigarettes. Her inside hurt as she waited, needing him, wanting him, but he didn't leave his desk. He didn't understand. He had never been a dreamer, and he knew nothing of a young girl's yearnings. His energy went into his work, making a success of insurance, and his wife had trained him into a state of celibacy. He knew this wasn't the right moment to want Elsie, but he was flattered, amused, intrigued by her gesture, by her youthful, seemingly childish, happy guile.

'Now, let me see.' He played up to her, as he often did to his young daughters; a game of let's pretend. 'Who could have sent me this? Was it the fairies? Or, oh dear, maybe it was sent to my secretary and she inadvertently lost it amid these letters – '

Elsie whipped around to face him, unable to wait any longer. 'No Bertie! It's for you!' Her face was flaming. He had made fun of her gesture of love, and Bertie stared at her, startled, his well-meant humour gone, the little blue

135

bow held out. 'Hey – ease up – I'm sorry – I didn't mean –'

'I bought it for you. Special.'

'And I appreciate it. I love it. It's lovely. It's the first I've ever had.' He strove to make amends. 'But how could I know you sent it? It might have been the Queen . . . .' He relaxed, seeing the flush recede from her cheeks. And the teasing entered his dark eyes. 'There's no name on it . . . . Put your name on it . . . .'

She drew back, then laughed, left her chair and stepped forward, and her chin jerked up. 'All right. I will.'

He handed her a pen and the card and she scribbled quickly. 'From Elsie.'

'Now look,' he said. 'Here's the bow of blue. Is that what you wanted?' She took it, grey eyes entranced.

'And now,' he said deliberately, gently, 'I'll put the card in my wallet, and keep it here, in my inside pocket. Against my heart, for ever and ever.'

She watched as he did so. 'That do you?' He gazed at her and slowly understood what she needed. He stood up. 'Come here,' he said, and she went to him.

They embraced gently, like two people each needing the soothing of the other, and Bertie realised how emotionally barren the month of January had been. He had stood up and held his arms out to her like a father mollifying a daughter, but now she was becoming a desirable woman again, a small, pocket-sized, subtle creature with huge dark grey eyes and a lipstick rosebud mouth that trembled under his.

He moved her from him gently. His inner calm had gone. The girl had a fierce effect on his blood, it was coursing strongly, and this time he was stone cold sober on a cold, grey February day. He could not make the excitement of a party his excuse.

'Elsie,' he murmured, 'be a good girl and get back to your desk.'

She didn't argue. His wife was in the kitchen not so many yards away. There were horses, traffic, people, dogs, in the street beyond the little garden. Only in this room were the invisible bonds of love wrapping her and Bertie together. Her voice shook as she said, 'Did you see I got some new business this week?'

'Yes. You're a good girl. How did you manage it?'

She sat again at her desk, trying to stop her hands shaking, smiling shyly. 'People seem to like me, and I need the commission, so I can send Ma to a farm in Malvern.' Bertie's heart sickened. His blasted in-laws had stuck that idea into her head. What in hell chance did she have of affording a farm anywhere? 'A good idea,' he said, and wished he were a rich man, able to send people like Gwen Buckley to Malvern. He remarked, 'Some of the new names were odd.'

'Oh yes?' She looked up from her chair, her face as innocent as young Emma's.

'Well,' he smiled. 'If your name was Mrs Branch would you christen your daughter Olive? And there's an Ivor Cann. Poor man.'

'Yes,' Elsie sighed. 'I felt sorry for them too. Terribly sorry.'

And she looked down at her fingers. They were fondling the bow of blue.

*   *   *

On Monday, the 16th of February, 1932, there were two special letters amid the many that flopped through the Unicorn Insurance Company letterbox.

Elsie opened them both. One was on London's headed notepaper. It was typed, signed by someone in the office, and said that a Mr Z. Carruthers would be visiting the district and could be expected to arrive during the week-end of the 20th to the 23rd. Elsie put that on Bertie's desk. She had never heard of Mr Z. Carruthers, and so the letter contained nothing to fire her imagination.

The other letter was from John Davies, and Elsie sat to read it, John was returning to work. He would come into the office on Wednesday, the eighteenth inst., to see Mr

Hemsworthy and to collect his books and sheets. He enclosed a doctor's note proving he was now fully recovered from his bout of pleurisy and was fit enough to work.

Elsie sat with the letter fluttering in her hand. Within two days her salary would drop back to six shillings a week. And Ma had coughed up blood last night.

CHAPTER SEVEN

Carruthers arrived at the LMS railway station on Sunday night. It was cold, wet. Beyond the shunting-yard was the sea, spread on miles of sand. The sky was low and Bertie was hunched into his overcoat, his collar pulled up to protect his ears from the sharpness of the east wind coiling from Kilvey Hill. He had been on the platform early, watching rain fall on the rails and sleepers, feeling his fingers and toes go dead, smelling the stench of furnace steam as it shot from engines, hearing lone people call 'hello' or 'goodnight' to other lone people. The lighting was poor, the clock scarred by age and elements.

The Crewe train came on time, its round front breasting in with triumphant noises of pistons, its fireman peeping out beneath his blue cap. Bertie strolled to meet the carriages as doors opened and he saw the outsize Carruthers step onto the platform as one views a dancer, noticing the toe pointed to the step, the hem of coat-skirt flicking, one hand clutching the door's brass handle, the other with a large black suitcase. 'God,' Bertie thought, 'he's come for a year.' And the Chief Office Inspector turned his pebble gaze, searching.

Bertie and Carruthers bore down on each other, of equal height, but Carruthers was expansively rounded from throat to crotch.

'Albert, old chap. You look fit as a fiddle.' His extra two chins lay flat beneath his face and Bertie thought how naked Carruthers would seem without them.

'Have a good journey? She's on time.' Bertie took the suitcase.

'Yes, by Jove. Didn't expect it. Spot of fog up the line.

139

Manchester's a hell of a place.'

'I thought you'd have come from London.'

'Johnson's impending divorce. Unfortunate business. He's out. The Old Man told me to give him a week. I've given him a month. Poor devil. The Old Man is rigid on risks of scandal within the firm. It's too young, you know. He should have started fifty years ago. When he was twenty. Not when he was fighting off middle-age.' He thumped Bertie on the back and laughed chidingly. 'We, in the Unicorn, must be whiter than driven snow, Albert my boy. Whiter. Until the Old Man's second million is made – or his tenth.'

Bertie said nothing. Carruthers's personality could be overpowering. 'Manchester last week. York next.' Carruthers heaved his heavy shoulders, resigned. 'It'll be America one day the way we're expanding. The Old Man must be making money hand over fist.'

'Huh.' It was a sound of envy and derision.

'It's his sons we've got to watch. They've got ambition. I'm telling you on the q.t., Albert, it'll be God help us all the day they take over. They'll want gold blood out of every stone.'

'The Old Man – '

'Pss, he's a kitten compared to those two.'

They walked quickly, giving up their tickets and stepping to the street. A squall hit them and they squinted, cringing. Bertie lifted his arm and the taxi came, crawling, anonymous. Once inside it both men gasped. Carruthers was panting. Bertie said, 'Is that your chest I can hear? It's like a concertina.'

'Asthmatical for years.'

'I know, but it seems bad tonight.'

'I'm blasted dying.' Carruthers sat back. He put a hand to his heart and in the gloom his gaze sought sympathy. 'I could do with a divorce myself. Where I found the gall to sack poor blasted Johnson I'll never know. I'm breaking my neck to keep her in silk and satin and another bloke is rolling her over.'

In the semi-darkness Bertie mused on the irony of life.

Carruthers's wife liked bed too much and Kit didn't like it at all.

Carruthers hurrumphed and his stubby fingers probed inside his overcoat. 'Cigar?'

'No thank you – what did happen? Or is it taboo?'

'What do you think?' Carruthers found his cigar case and chose a cigar as a child chooses a sweet. He bit the end off it, his teeth gleaming in the spasmodic light as the taxi sped on, then he opened his top of the window to put the piece out with an expert flick of his lips and tongue. He replaced the case inside his coat and lit the cigar, his thumb and forefinger flicking the dead match out of the window.

He drew on the cigar then held it between his fingers as if examining the glowing end. 'Do you know, even if divorce was possible I wouldn't divorce her. I admire Johnson. The scandal, the cost. Where could he get another job? No reference. No chance. Not at his age. No, I'll ignore my wanton wife.'

Bertie spoke gently. 'Your wife isn't a whore, you know.'

'She is. I don't mind honest whores. I've known a few, but she – '

'I suppose she's found out about you.'

'Found out? Found out?' Carruthers's lips were loose and red, the whites of his eyes showing. 'There's nothing for her to find out. Told her. Honest as the day. Me? You know yourself. Always have been. Completely honest. Nothing hidden under a stone.'

'You're a bloody ram.'

Carruthers smiled, his jaw flattening into his chin. He placed the cigar to his mouth. 'No man ever had a finer reference.'

Bertie looked at the enormous shapelessness of the man, the blatant crudity, the honest acceptance of his animal lustiness. He said, 'I admire you.'

'Yes,' Carruthers said, 'I'm the you you'd like to be, but its not in your character.

Bertie looked away, at the black silhouette of the taxi-driver's head stuck on its narrow neck with its ears jutting like handles on an urn, all blurred beyond the glass partition. 'Quite true,' he said. 'I would like a wife who couldn't get enough of it.'

'You!' Carruthers's laughter rumbled deep in his belly. 'You've got used to your marriage – whatever it's like. You're used to Maggie but you're out of condition, man. Some knowledgeable person ought to write a book on technique. They'd make a fortune.'

Bertie stared at the glass partition, wondering if it was as sound-proof as he always supposed. 'D'you think that's the trouble?'

'Of course it is. You get a woman. Lay her on a bed, then wonder what in hell to do with her now you've got her. I still don't know. With the blasted light out, how can you see their faces? See if they're pleased or not? Anyway, who wants to see their faces, now I come to think of it. Not then.'

The taxi wheels sliced over the black and silver wetness of cobbles, the crashing of the gears jarring as the driver changed down to take the next turning.

'True,' Bertie said, and wondered why he had never thought of it the way Carruthers did. 'And women don't tell you. Shy, I suppose.'

He stared at Carruthers, wondering how he seemed to know so much. He didn't look like a casanova. Carruthers placed the cigar in the corner of his mouth, the tobacco, a special blend, well alight now, glowing scarlet like a million fiery particles in the darkness, the smoke strong.

Bertie said grudgingly, 'If rumours are anything to go by you've got in plenty of practice. You've even tried it on with Kit.'

'Of course, old boy.' Carruthers shrugged mightily. 'But have I ever touched her?'

'She said you tried.'

'Tried? Of course I tried. D'you want me to insult the

woman? It's a man's place to try. Of course I tried.'

'What if she said yes?'

Again they could hear only the throbbing of the engine.

'That would be a problem. All round,' Carruthers said drily 'One has to offer to do one's best after all. It's part of the game.'

'You're a bastard.' Bertie said lightly.

'Of course, but I'd rather me than you. What time are we out in the morning?'

'Nine-thirty.'

'Where?'

'Llanelli.'

'Llanelli, why not Port Talbot? Don't you want me to expand John's books?' Carruthers laughed low. 'Maggie might appreciate it.'

Bertie looked at the scudding dark street, a little exasperated. He could never appreciate Carruthers's capacity to include passion when discussing business. 'John has been ill. He's had pleurisy and my secretary has been collecting his books, so let him rest. You can go on his round next time.'

'Nice piece?' The words were casual, the cigar burning small now, Carruthers holding it daintily between fat thumb and forefinger. 'This secretary of yours?'

'She works hard.'

Carruthers waited for more information and got none. He said then, 'Ah . . . . So where did you say we were going tomorrow?'

'Llanelli.'

'I'm afraid not, Albert. That's why I'm here. To look over John Davies's book.'

'John's?' Bertie was startled. 'Whatever for?'

The fat man shrugged as if to imply the reason wasn't important. 'The Old Man gets these ideas. Sends me here and sends me there.'

'But John's as honest as the day!'

Carruthers stared, marble eyes bland. 'Did I mention the man's honesty?'

'No – but – '

'I do as I am told, dear boy. I get paid for obeying orders.'

'Well, there must be something – '

'Why must there be something?' Carruthers didn't wait for a reply. He went on, 'Tomorrow your secretary stays at her typewriter. You and I go over John's round.' The ash on the end of the cigar extended, scarlet, living particles, then died, grey ash, and he tapped it off into the ashtray on the door. 'Mum's the word. You understand?' He leaned back as if the worst of his visit was over. 'I have told you in confidence.'

'Thank you.'

'We'll see if we can get some new business in at the same time.' He patted Bertie's knee, laughing as if mocking, and when they got into the house he swooped on Kit like the branches of a falling oak. 'My temptress,' he called, 'are you aware I've already been threatened with my life if I so much as glance at you, dear lady?'

'Oh Carruthers!' Kit was pleased and impatient with him.

'So let me make the most of this moment. Enter into mine arms ye bundles of charms,' and he lifted her in a massive bear-hug. Her feet kicked back and her head stretched away as she tried to keep clear of him, but his great face plunged into her throat and he growled as he bit her. He stood her down and laughed into her eyes. 'By heaven you're a beautiful wench, Mrs Hemsworthy. I am your slave.'

Kit blushed and glanced at Bertie. 'The food's ready,' she said, 'if you'd like to settle in first.'

The two girls stood waiting, holding hands, and Carruthers transferred his full attention to them. He flung his arms up and exclaimed loudly, 'Well, blow me down if we haven't got two more ravishing beauties here,' and the girls laughed and reddened, adoration sparking from their eyes. Carruthers moved his head from side to side as if in disbelief. 'Most fortunate I brought gifts.'

144

'No,' Kit urged, 'you mustn't give them anything,' but Carruthers's soft palms were upheld, silencing her.

'I have here,' he said slowly, watching Emma and Linda, 'two beautiful gifts for two beautiful young ladies,' and he drew the tissue-wrapped objects from the depths of his overcoat pocket. He handed one to each child with deliberate attention, then watched the young fingers fumble and explore.

'A fan,' Linda breathed.

'Oh,' whispered Emma.

Kit said, 'Ah. Mother of pearl. How pretty.' And her pleasure was as genuine as her daughters'. 'They are, aren't they? Mother of pearl.'

'Yes.' Carruthers was pleased, his stomach even more expansive as he breathed.

'Oh they are lovely,' Kit purred. 'Linda, let me show you how to use it.' She took Linda's fan and flicked it open, its white satin binding ribbon overflowing down her wrist. 'Like this,' she said, and fluttered the fan before her face. Her eyes were dark with delight, uncharacteristically flirtatious as she gazed first at her daughters, then at Carruthers. Carruthers answered the signal with a raised inquiring eyebrow and a half-smile on his full red lips. Kit quickly looked away and lowered the fan. 'Now you do it, Linda. And you Emma.'

Bertie's smile was tight. Deep inside him was a hurt and he was angry, as if he had been slighted. He wondered just what was happening between Kit and Carruthers: why she could flirt with this grotesquely fat creature yet repulse him, her husband. He said sharply, 'Linda. Take your toy back,' and Linda's smile quivered, bewildered at the change in the atmosphere. Kit laughed, but the sound died as it reached the air, and the fan closed with a click as Linda took it.

Carruthers said, 'I shall get to the bathroom. These jealous husbands exasperate me.' He began shrugging out of his overcoat, exaggerating his struggle with it. 'Phew, I'm getting old – ' and both children reacted to his unspoken invitation, each reached excited, happy hands to help.

They went up the passage with him, seeming to crowd him with their chatter, and Bertie said, 'I'm sorry.'

'I don't understand you,' Kit hissed. 'You accuse me of being frigid, yet you suspect me of sleeping with someone else. A frigid woman sleeps with no one.' But she felt secret pangs of guilt, and there was also pleasure that she could still flirt with one man and make another jealous.

'I don't suspect you of sleeping with him – or anyone else.'

'Then why behave so childishly?'

'He kissed you.'

'He bit me,' and she rubbed her neck ruefully, grimacing.

'That's worse. The man's a bastard. He knows he's got me in a cleft stick. If I create too much he'll get me out and John Davies in.'

'Oh Bertie, that can't be true.'

'You know damn well it is. He's thick with Maggie. The slightest flaw on my part and I'm uprooted, sent to a harder area.' He took her hands, suddenly wanting her to understand. 'Look, Kit. He's come down to go over John's round.'

'Whatever for?' She was more attentive now.

'That's what I asked. He agrees John is completely honest so – '

'The Old Man wants a report on John's aptitude for a managership?'

'Could be. There's a vacancy in Manchester. That poor devil's been given the boot.'

'They'll send John up there?'

'Or me.'

'Not you! Surely?' Kit was alarmed. 'It's a terrible place. Worse than this.'

'Why not me? I don't speak Welsh. John does. I've got a feeling Maggie's written to him.'

'Oh she has. Sends him birthday cards and that.'

'Does she now? We're all crawlers, aren't we?'

'Why has the Manchester man been given notice?'

'Another woman.' Bertie stared deep into Kit's amber eyes as though his words carried another message, another plea for understanding. 'His wife is divorcing him.'

A long, slow gasp escaped Kit's lips and her gaze was horrified. 'The sack? For that?'

Bertie nodded. 'Carruthers reckons the Old Man won't brook the scandal.'

'There'll certainly be plenty of that. What on earth made her divorce him?'

He shrugged. 'Maybe she has another man waiting.'

'Maybe,' Kit whispered, truly shocked at the stigma of divorce coming so close.

'A big fat man,' Bertie grinned, releasing her hands, and she laughed softly. 'Can you imagine him in the raw?' She watched Bertie's face, and together they visualised Carruthers naked, Carruthers panting with lust-filled expectation, his huge stomach and wobbly chins shuddering above spindly legs, then they smiled smiles that extended to sniggers, each trying to stop the other thinking about Carruthers's real reason for being here. 'D'you honestly think he'd give John Davies your job?'

'John wants it. Maggie would give her eye-teeth for it. That and a baby.'

Kit sighed. 'So he comes to spy on us?'

'Of course he does. It's his job. He's called a canvasser, an inspector, but no one has said an inspector of what. Uh?'

'I'm sorry I twinkled at him. I didn't mean to.'

'He liked it. Maybe it did some good.' They smiled at each other, drawn together in this new fear of the future.

'How long is he staying?'

'I haven't asked. It might be a month, if he fancies you, or a day if I've offended him.'

'You haven't offended him. Your jealousy is a compliment to him. It means you think he's attractive to women.'

'He is, God knows why.'

Kit lifted one shoulder and turned down the corner of

her mouth. 'He makes a woman feel desirable, as if he's thirsting in agony for her lips and throat. I suppose that's what makes him a successful canvasser. It's nearly always a woman who opens the door to him. Have you noticed?'

Bertie nodded, and Kit's face was near to his own. She put her arms about his neck and he kissed her.

Kissing Kit was a unique experience: it was tender, loving, lingering, yet cool and without promise and, just then, Bertie asked for no more.

★ ★ ★

Next morning Bertie awoke early and lay wondering why. It was Monday, an inspector from Head Office was in the end bedroom, a man ready to pry into everything under the guise of finding new business, a man ready to seduce Kit, and maybe uproot the whole family, yet Bertie had awakened early, feeling happy.

He could hear a bird chirping in the tiny front garden, and he wondered if a crocus would appear today. He looked at Kit curled up beside him, her hair very black in the early morning February light, and he reflected that she had no grey hairs. She was gone forty.

Had he dreamed of Elsie? That would account for his feeling of happiness. He grinned at the drawn curtains; slicks of light were coming through, and he wanted to jump out of bed then run along a sunlit beach, as he remembered doing in his childhood, to splash into the sea, be loudly, ostentatiously happy.

He got out of bed quietly, breathing deeply and slowly, commonsense gradually taking over, his thoughts of Elsie and Kit and Carruthers mixed with the talk of divorce, its cost, its scandal, its trauma, the difficulty in getting such a thing, the church's ostracisation, and the outcome for the ex-manager in Manchester, poor fool. Could he ever divorce Kit for another woman? Throw away everything for love? Divorce? Divorce? What the hell was he thinking about? Fat yobs like Carruthers came down with the gossip

148

and already he was identifying himself with the morass. To have and to hold, his mind chanted, for richer, for poorer, let no man put asunder –

He reached for his dressing gown and slid into it. The bird in the garden was still chirping, but some of Bertie's happiness, his lightness of heart had gone.

Kit said softly, 'Stop scowling,' and he turned to her, startled.

'I thought you were asleep.'

'I was, but some elephant decided to get up.'

'I'll bring you a cup of tea.'

She snuggled her face into the pillow. 'Is it my birthday or something?'

'I just thought I'd spoil you.'

She nudged deeper into the pillow, her shoulder bare above the sheet. 'You've got a guilty conscience.'

'Tripe!'

'Been dreaming of Elsie Buckley?'

'Not at all.'

'Liar. I've been dreaming of Carruthers.' She began to giggle, peering at him from the soft depths of the white frilled pillowslip. 'Carruthers in longjohns with black socks and red suspenders, before he's shaved, and can't find a comb.' Her giggling grew stronger and she shook. 'Can you imagine it? My amorous knight in suspenders – all belly and blather?'

'Do you want a cup of tea or don't you?'

'You are developing a crush on Elsie Buckley, you know. And it could lead to big trouble.' The giggles stopped and she moved her head to watch him.

'At my age!' He was scathing.

'Particularly at your age. I've seen you smiling to your-self. You whistle a lot more too. Pretty lilting tunes.' Kit sat up. 'Throw my dressing-gown over. You're acting like a schoolboy and she revels in it. If you lived next door to her and were on the means test she wouldn't wish you a good day.'

'Stop preaching.'

149

Kit sighed, her black unplucked eyebrows up in resignation, and she took the gown from his outstretched hand. 'It's your funeral. I'll sink with you, but I'd be happier if you didn't sink the girls as well.'

'The girls! What have they got to do with it?'

'More than any of us.' She looked surprised. 'Gossip. The example you set. We struggled to send them to a private school so that they could make nice friends, then their daddy falls for a tart.'

'Oh, for God's sake!'

'It's up to you,' she said in mock airiness. 'It's a lesson you'll have to learn, when to back out of a threatening situation.'

'Nothing is threatening.'

'Give her the sack and get someone else. Someone less bold, brash, and awe-struck.'

'Give her the sack!' He stood glaring. 'What for? For fancying me? Let's give Carruthers the sack too, for fancying you.'

Kit moved her arms as if to sweep him and Elsie Buckley away. She couldn't understand herself. She didn't want to make love with Bertie, and was even a little relieved that Elsie Buckley might take that chore from her, yet there was a lump of resentment, jealousy, and, possibly, fear deep in her heart. She moved her head, resenting her mixed feelings. She put her fist where the lump was heaviest and said, 'I think I have indigestion again. If you'll get the kettle on and light the fire I'll wake the girls. The house is perishing,' and Bertie left the bedroom in silence.

At breakfast Carruthers appeared in fat but immaculate condition, and with a shock Bertie realised that the picture of Carruthers in longjohns and suspenders was imprinted on his mind. Carruthers wore the tie, cuff-links, and handkerchief set that Kit and Bertie had sent him for Christmas, the blue silk handkerchief perfectly folded as it cornered from his breast pocket.

'Beautiful morning,' Carruthers beamed, and tousled the head of each delighted little girl. 'Shall I sit here? Ah! Only a boiled egg for me please, Kit, my sunshine. I have decided to whittle down my magnificent form.'

'Since when?' Kit scoffed.

'Since this very moment. I have just realised everyone is squashed about this admirable table so as to leave ample room for me.' He laughed at the children, his loose lips not so scarlet in the morning light. 'And at what time do you have to present yourselves at the seat of learning?'

Linda blinked and considered. Emma spooned more marmalade onto her toast. Bertie said, 'They have to be in assembly at half-past nine.'

'Ah,' said Carruthers, and rubbed his fat hands together, looking at the clock on the mantelpiece then checking it with his pocket watch. 'They'll get a tram near here?'

'Yes,' said Bertie, and tried not to be irritated by the need for small talk. He, too, kept glancing at the clock, trying not to look concerned, but all the time he was waiting for Elsie. He told himself that when she came he would smile and say 'good morning' and it would be the start of another working day. No more than that. Yet each morning controlling his excitement was an excitement in itself.

There was now also an element of fear, placed there by Kit and his own commonsense, the fear his excitement would risk his marriage, and his job, but he stifled it, suffocated it with that part of his mind that remained sensible, that part of his mind that had kept him sane in the trenches; when the orders came to go over the top and he felt his guts would drop out from terror, yet they never had. He said now, 'We should do all right today. The sun will put everyone in good humour.'

Carruthers sliced his toast into fingers then wobbled his chins at the children. 'Soldiers,' he said. 'Now I am about to crown each one, then I will bite of his head.' He laughed, and the two girls watched him dip a finger of toast into the egg so the yolk rose about it then squashed and overflowed, streaming down the shell and egg-cup. Bertie watched, fascinated, as the soldier went into the soft, fleshy mouth, and the strong, off-colour teeth jammed into it, severing.

151

Bertie stood up quickly. 'Tea?' he said. 'Anyone ready for a cuppa?' And his straining ears heard the gate click. Again he glanced at the clock. Not yet half-past eight. She was early. He poured the tea, the sensible part of his mind holding him there, at the table, while his inside shook as if Elsie's aura was already touching him.

As the bell quivered and rang above the kitchen door, he heard his voice say, 'Linda, I think that's Elsie. Let her in, will you, please?' And as he gave Kit her tea his gaze met hers. Even the Elsie-dominated part of his mind saw the unhappiness between them, and he knew that sooner or later he would have to choose: Elsie and the excitement, or Kit and the security.

He heard Elsie and Linda greet each other, and felt amused that his secretary and his daughter should be developing a strong friendship. He could think of nothing they had in common. Then Linda was back at the table, happy and pink, her eyes not so loaded with painful styes lately and her features filling out a little.

Elsie was in the doorway. 'Good morning,' she called, and seemed to emit a new confidence. She stood erect on her tan high heels and her breasts were unfashionably shaped in her blue wool jumper. Bertie wondered if she had suddenly taken to wearing a brassiere thing and wondered why. The kiss-curls were there, each carefully stuck with sugared water before the small pink ears, and her eyes and lips shone at Bertie, the invisible something warming his being. She said, 'It's lovely out. Has the postman been?' And he found her very common-ness enticing.

'No,' said Kit. 'Why?'

'I just thought I'd do that first.' Elsie transferred her smile to Carruthers and he left the table slowly, one hand moving his chair back, the other using a serviette to wipe his mouth. 'By damn, Albert,' he breathed. 'You do find them,' and he took Elsie's hand, letting its smallness lie in his fatness. Bertie stared as Carruthers bowed and kissed the pink-tipped fingers.

'To youth,' said Carruthers. 'And the fascination it holds

for the mature taste.'

Kit's dark brows rose and her silent derision helped Bertie make his voice mocking as he said, 'You can keep your hands off my secretary, Carruthers. Her father also has six big sons and they won't stand for any hanky panky.'

'My dear fellow – ' Carruthers stood gazing into Elsie's shy but laughing eyes. 'Who mentioned hanky panky? I am serious, I assure you. Quite serious.' He was gasping slightly, as though bending had affected his lungs, and Bertie felt sympathy, even pity, for this man who played for every woman he met.

Bertie said lightly, 'There you are, Elsie. A chance for you when you need a reference. Carruthers isn't just employed by the Unicorn. He is a confidant of the Old Man.'

'Indeed I am,' breathed Carruthers, but Elsie's wide-eyed gaze had come back to Bertie, the laughter gone, shock in its place. 'Oh no!' she said.

Everyone laughed while Carruthers stood straight, his grossness seeming to fill the kitchen. Elsie blushed. Everyone knew by the way her gaze had shot to Bertie that she didn't see him as an employer; he was more, much more.

The letterbox on the front door rattled and the mail shot through. Elsie ran to collect it, her thoughts confused. Yes, she had known Z. Carruthers was coming, but who was he? She hadn't asked, and now his presence disturbed her. He had an air of such importance.

Carruthers turned slowly back to the table, his fat lips pursed in a soundless whistle, and Kit rushed to the iron kettle on the hob, tipping it nervously then placing it down again. 'More tea?' she urged. 'Anyone for more tea?'

'No.' Bertie was sharp. The little scene had upset him and he wanted to hurry after Elsie and explain, apologise for letting Carruthers make mock of her. 'We'll get off,' he said. 'Ready Carruthers?'

He strode to the office where Elsie was opening envelopes with shaking hands. 'That man,' she whispered, as her head turned to Bertie. 'Isn't he awful?'

'Not at all.'

'Are you taking him out this morning?'

'Yes. Port Talbot.'

She nodded quickly. 'In that case I'm glad John's back –' Then the expression in her eyes changed, and Bertie frowned.

'What's the matter?'

'Nothing.'

'Are you sure? You look – ' He stopped himself from saying 'frightened'.

'No. Honest. I'm fine.'

Bertie moved closer and put a hand on her shoulder. He didn't like the way her brightness had disappeared. She had come to the kitchen door happily, clear-eyed, ready to spring into the day, and now she was deflated, even depressed, with the make-up hard on her face.

He said, 'Hey, come on. You did your bit. You collected it for almost three months. If it wasn't for you John would have lost the lot.'

'Oh no. You'd have managed.'

He placed a kiss on her forehead, the Phul-Nana behind her ears reminding him of the party and bed, and his body filled with tenderness and longing. She was such a little thing, such a courageous, loving thing.

She said quickly, 'You'd better go then,' and her depression seemed less. He looked into the greyness of her eyes and liked what he saw. He kissed her mouth quickly, gently, and they heard Carruthers coming up the passage.

'Good girl,' he murmured, and saw her lips shape the words, 'Love you,' then he was striding to Carruthers, energetic, businesslike.

He and Carruthers grabbed their coats and briefcases, slapped hats on their heads and went with loud 'cheerios' to Kit and the girls, then they walked fast, like men who had been army trained. They got into the tram without speaking, and at High Street Station Carruthers panted to the platform then looked at his pocket watch. 'We've made

154

good time,' he said, and placed his briefcase on a bench.

They waited with small talk for the train to arrive, and when it came with a long whistle and a lot of steam they boarded quickly. Carruthers threw his briefcase to the net rack, then sat and undid his overcoat.

'Rum do,' he said finally. 'This effort with China declaring war on Japan.'

'Somebody'll make money out of it.'

Carruthers humphed, great chins squashed. 'Did you know they've collected a hundred and five million off us this year in income tax? Only sixty million last year. Think that'll put the country on its feet again?'

'Will it hell!'

'They've had our blood and guts in a war,' Carruthers pouted his lips. 'Now it's our money.' He sat back. 'Makes you wonder if it's blasted worth it, working, struggling . . . .'

They eventually left the train less happy than when they got into it. 'I suppose it could be worse,' Carruthers breathed. 'We could be like those poor devils getting blown up in a colliery.'

Bertie agreed. He didn't relish the day before him, even though the sun shone and one or two little gardens had grass showing skimpily green. His early morning happiness, like Elsie's, had gone.

He said, 'The streets here always seem longer than anywhere else.'

'Cock-eyed hole,' Carruthers said, and pushed open a gate. 'Shall we start here? Do a bit of canvassing?'

'Dead.' Bertie said. 'Nothing here but sand.'

'Plenty of that. Can't understand why they don't make something of the place. Turn it into a resort.'

'With the docks spewing muck?'

The house door opened and Carruthers swung into his patter, his smile wide and flattering. 'Good morning, miss. Your mother at home?'

'I'm Mrs and yes I'm at home. What're you selling?'

'Security, my dear. Security. Well . . . .' He smiled expansively. 'What do you think, Albert? Have you ever

155

seen a more fascinating piece of goods? Forgive me, madam, but my remark was unavoidable.'

The woman folded her arms over her floppy breasts and grubby overall. Her elbows were red and rough like her hands, and her shapeless jumper was thin and much worn. 'I don't want any,' she said. 'I can't afford any, but I'm naturally nosey. What is it?'

'I knew you'd be interested,' Carruthers beamed, his rotund front expanding as he straightened his back preparing for the fray. 'Intelligence always shows in a lady's face.'

'I've decided I don't want any,' she nodded. 'Good day,' and she stepped back, pushing the door forward in one movement, but Carruthers's foot was there. 'Hop it,' said the lady.

'I might have to,' said Carruthers. 'If I lose my foot, and all because you refuse your husband a decent funeral.'

'My husband's not dead.'

'I am deeply relieved. For two pence. Just two pence. You can be sure of ready money should your good man meet his demise next week.'

'Next week!' She grinned disparagingly.

'How old is he?'

'Forty-eight.'

'Ah.' Carruthers worked quickly with his puce pencil, making neat figures on a piece of paper. 'Next week,' he said, 'you would have paid my firm only two pence, and we would pay you ten pounds eight and six pence.'

'Ten pounds eight and sixpence.' She was interested.

'Ten pounds eight and sixpence.' Carruthers watched her face.

She scratched her ear. 'For two pence?'

'Sad as it is,' Carruthers moaned. 'Death is always with us.'

'Hmm,' said the woman. 'Sad it is.' The door opened a little further.

'Two pence,' Carruthers droned, his eyes becoming more bulbous as they concentrated on her.

She opened the door, wider. 'You'd better come in. He's been looking a bit off-colour lately.'

Carruthers and Bertie went in. They ignored each other now. Bertie said nothing. He would have the pen and proposal forms ready. Carruthers would gently break the news it was two pence a week – for life.

The day had begun.

Expertly Carruthers led the way, canvassing the houses he assessed as worth the time. He seemed to have an invisible antenna that waved and probed as he paused at a gateway or in the centre of a pavement, and he said, 'We'll try here.'

At lunchtime they met John Davies whose face was still almost as sallow as his crooked teeth, his once wide, hearty shoulders now thin and threatening to stoop.

Each man paid for his own pie and chips in a little corner cafe, then Carruthers lit a cigar, immune to the curious, even awed glances sent his way from other diners. Such opulence as displayed by Mr Z. Carruthers was rarely seen in such steamy little cafes.

John smiled, still afraid Elsie – or any other woman – would be given his job. 'Everything all right?' He wondered when Carruthers would be coming out with him, calling on his policy-holders instead of canvassing new calls.

Carruthers nodded, sitting sideways at the table because of his expansive stomach. 'I've done splendidly. Haven't I Albert?' And Bertie opened his briefcase and gave John the filled-in proposal forms. John smiled, delighted. He would get the commission on every ha'penny Carruthers had put on. He laughed at Carruthers. 'Thank you. Thank you.'

'Welcome,' Carruthers said, placid, watching like a bronchial buddha with a cigar in his mouth.

'Are you coming on the round at all?'

Carruthers removed the cigar. 'It's a possibility.' Carruthers was pleased with himself. For a chill February Monday morning he had done well. 'How is Margaret Ann?'

'Splendid,' John enthused. Surely they wouldn't send Carruthers down to increase his business if they intended giving the book to a woman. A woman couldn't handle it. Not if it got too big.

Carruthers said, 'You have had a number of claims sent through since Christmas, John.' And John looked at Bertie. He said quickly, 'Have I? I didn't know.'

'He's been ill,' Bertie put in. 'Very rough.'

'Ah,' Carruthers breathed, and he was like a toad, waiting at the edge of a pond for a fly to settle on its tongue. 'Yes, of course . . . .'

'Elsie Buckley has been doing it,' Bertie said, his eyelids lowered, suspicious.

'Yes,' said Carruthers. 'Yes, True. True. I had forgotten.'

* * *

On Wednesday Bertie sat at his desk and his agents came, one by one, to pay in, to tender their ledgers for checking, and their account sheets correctly balanced ready to be sent to Head Office.

Elsie sat at her desk, her fingers tapping as she used them to count columns of figures. This column balancing that, and both balancing with the ledger and the money handed to Bertie. Tomorrow she would transfer all these totals to another, kitchen-table size sheet and her fingers would tap faster, her brow would furrow, she would sigh and worry and Bertie would lean over her and help, his nearness a warmth that brought those lovely cuddly feelings up from the pit of her belly again, and his fingers would stroke the back of her neck so she lowered her head and forgot to keep counting, but today was the beginning. The end of one week for the agents, the beginning of a new account for the office, and Carruthers had taken to the streets alone.

He wandered up Wern View from the wrong end and eventually found number one. He stood for a while on the kerb staring, marble-eyed, at the scraped, poverty-stricken door, then he hunched his coat more comfortably on to his fat shoulders, licked his full lips and let his knuckles hit the centre panel. He waited. The street was silent, cold, dusty, grey, without gardens or trees, dispirited and dishevelled with darned curtains, and a striped cat blinking slowly from a window sill.

He knocked again, his senses telling him someone was in, but someone wouldn't open the door until they knew who stood there. It was a sign of the woman in debt. The woman expecting the bailiffs or the police.

Carruthers moved back to the kerb, deliberately looking at the road not the house; giving Mrs Travers the chance to see him, to get curious about him, and to finally open the door.

When she did so, she moved slowly, cautiously, her brows up, her nose pink with the cold, her sore red hands gripping the edge of the door as she stuck her face around it.

'Yes?' she said, and Carruthers straightened his back and beamed. He held out his right hand.

'Mrs Travers? Good morning. I'm from the Unicorn Insurance Company?'

'Oh yes.' She was tempted to shut the door again, but the memory of her fire claim calmed her. If their agent could wangle an extra couple of bob for her she could hold her door partly open for them.

'I was just on my way –' smiled Carruthers, 'and thought I would give you a call. Just to see if you are satisfied.'

'Satisfied?' She came from behind the door, skinny feet in tattered slippers.

'With Miss Buckley. She has been collecting your premiums.'

'Oh yes.' Mrs Travers glowed back at the fat man. 'Lovely girl she is. So understanding and all that.'

'She dealt with your fire claim all right?'

'Oh yes. Lovely.' Mrs Travers clasped her hands low before her. 'Who are you then?'

159

'From Head Office, Mrs Travers. I have been sent down just to see everyone is happy.'

'Oh yes.' Mrs Travers began to stare him out. She knew about the haves and have-nots and how the one begrudged every ha'penny the other one had. This man was, obviously, a have, and she was a have-not. From Head Office, was he? Spying on that nice little girl who had done the collecting? Mrs Travers decided she didn't like him. The door began to come forward and she began to slide behind it, while Carruthers wondered why. His antenna was busy again. He had come on a hunch and each second made him feel more certain he was on the right track. He dug into his inside pocket and brought out Elsie's official list of things burned. He handed it to Mrs Travers.

'These are the goods that were destroyed?'

She took the list and glanced at it. 'Yes. Why?'

Carruthers shrugged and laughed, but this woman was brittle; this woman wouldn't take flattery even if he gave it. He settled for the straightforward approach. 'Miss Buckley paid you out all right, I assume?'

'Well you assume correct, mister.'

'Ha . . . hum . . . .' Carruthers was stumped. He had expected her to deny that she had a fire claim. For a moment longer he and Mrs Travers stared at each other, he puzzled, wary, and she shrewd, defensive, then he shrugged, put the list back in his inside pocket and smiled again. 'I am delighted to have made your acquaintance, Mrs Travers. Good day.'

She watched him stride up the road, a huge man, sure-footed and confident, and she thought of Elsie Buckley increasing the value of the burned trousers from seven and elevenpence to eight and elevenpence, of Elsie increasing the list so Mr Jeffreys could be paid his one pound ten. Balls to Head Office! Mrs Travers thought, they wouldn't learn anything from her.

Carruthers went on, probing, learning nothing. The instinct of the poor kept them loyal to Elsie, to the secret that they too had been paid more then they were due.

160

He came to the little shop where Elsie had bought the Valentine card, and eight premium books were handed to him with one and fourpence. The shopkeeper was busy with his stock, not interested in yet another insurance agent.

Carruthers wobbled his chins and took his fountain pen from his jacket's breast pocket. 'Eight books?'

'Customers.' The man returned to a cardboard box and ripped it open, then began stacking its contents of tinned milk on to a shelf. 'They're all out working, so they leave it with me.'

'How very kind of you,' Carruthers smiled, and thought what odd customers they were. There was a Tom Smith and a Jack Smith. There was a Bill and Nellie Dean. Then there was Olive Branch and Ivor Cann.

Carruthers marked the books and pocketed the money. 'Thank you,' he said, and the man kept stacking the tins. Carruthers stood, supposedly viewing the stock, seeking something to buy, but the man didn't want to know. Carruthers gave a quick nod and said, 'Good day to you,' then went to the pavement. He had the oddest feeling, a stronger hunch than ever before. He stood watching the shop, thinking, frowning, puzzled. Then he sauntered away. The Old Man had sent him down to 'scout around', and Carruthers was good at his job. His invisible antenna worked miracles and rarely let him down. Today it was as vibrant as a harp string just plucked, and Carruthers was far from happy.

He didn't like the Buckley girl. Hadn't liked her from the moment he read Maggie's letter, her innocent description of forfeit-paying at the party, and he liked her less now. She was double-crossing Albert, but Carruthers couldn't find out how.

He walked faster, making for the station. He would have to come back. Alone. On the quiet. After he had thought about it, listened to his hunch.

He wondered about Kit and Albert. What was going on there? Kit's amber eyes were dull, even filmed over, but

161

Albert looked younger, lighter on his feet. The Buckley girl? Probably. Almost certainly.

Carruthers paused at a street corner and probed in one of his pockets for a cigar. He lit up, the briefcase at his feet, his eyes watching the traffic. It crossed his mind that although there were approximately three million unemployed in England and Wales he had also read somewhere that there were almost two and a half million motor cars licensed. He watched a pony between the shafts of a bobbing cart, and a man helmeted and goggled on a motorbike with sidecar.

Albert would have to dismiss Elsie Buckley. Blast it. The firm's office was right there, in the house where it was all going on. He mused on Maggie and John Davies, and their letter to him, a letter praising Elsie Buckley's handling of John's book but hinting at an affair between Albert and the girl. It was jocularly done, of course, alone the lines of ' . . . a wonderful party . . . . The new secretary stood on her head . . . . Bertie disappeared upstairs . . . . No sign of the secretary . . . . You know what parties are . . . . A marvellous time . . . .'

Carruthers did know what parties were. He also knew Maggie was ambitious. A big cuddly ball of lovely envy, and his red lips smiled around the cigar as he lifted his briefcase and marched on. It was often people like Maggie who retained his job for him. They helped him earn the approval of the Old Man.

He was lucky, Carruthers decided. No woman was likely to manoeuvre her husband into his job; he was away from home too much, it wasn't conducive to a happy married life.

Married life, he thought. Maybe he was lucky there too: a wife who found her satisfaction out of town: a most discreet woman, thank God, but a pity, a great pity that she had to seek amours at all.

He stopped walking abruptly, panting, only just realising how fast he had been moving: if a woman lay in front of him, her breasts and mouth uplifted, he could do nothing about it. 'Too fat,' he told himself yet again as he resumed walking, 'blasted belly in the way. Enough to deter a nabob with fifty wives.'

His teeth chomped on the cigar and he caught a train easily, almost lazily now. He sat and wondered about the size of the fire claims on John Davies's book since Christmas, whether Albert had noticed it and, if so, if he intended doing anything about it. He saw his reflection in the window as trees sped past, and Carruthers decided to instruct Albert to sack the girl, then watch Albert's face, let the antenna mooch around a bit, wait a while. See what happened.

When he got to Prince Edward Road Kit had a black eye. 'My dear lady!' he exclaimed, and his global eyes were as excited as they were concerned. Here was the proof that he must return to South Wales again, without informing anyone of his presence. Here was absolute evidence that all was not as it should be between the area manager and his wife. He nodded slowly, fleshily, as he gazed at the wound.

Cherchez la femme, he thought and added, the Buckley girl.

Kit laughed at him with half her face, her hand over the other half. 'It isn't anything!' she cried and, later over a cup of tea, 'Bertie did it . . . . It was an accident . . . . I bent down to get my shoe and Bertie's elbow came back. Wham!'

Carruthers's eyes protruded from their sockets, truly global. 'My dear lady! An accident? I am sure Albert was most upset!'

'Of course,' laughed Kit, and that night when she couldn't sleep for thinking of the pain in her face, and the loneliness and longings in her heart, she went downstairs to make cocoa, and a few minutes later Carruthers followed her. He was, he said, over-tired and unable to relax so, yes, he too would enjoy a cocoa with a fine lady.

For the rest of the week Carruthers was calmly polite and it put Bertie's teeth on edge. He couldn't think why the man had come here in the first place, not now, in February, with the east wind still blowing. It made Bertie uneasy, made him wonder if something was under way that he knew nothing about. He looked at Kit's black eye and cursed himself. It had been pure accident, and it had to happen now, with Carruthers here. He wondered whether he ought to explain, but he didn't, a small rebellious spark was igniting inside him; he wanted to tell Carruthers to go to hell, to stop snooping, and he watched Kit's black eye gradually turn green.

He had heard Kit come down in the night, and he had heard Carruthers follow her. He wondered what they had talked about. Him? Elsie?

On the Saturday, after a steak and kidney pie lunch, Bertie and Carruthers sat in the office, and Carruthers took a box of snuff from his waistcoat pocket. Daintily he tendered a pinch of the stuff to his nostrils.

Bertie tried not to feel irritable. The sun was shining, promising spring, and there was an oblong of clear blue sky between him and the roofs on the opposite side of the road. He said conversationally, 'You did well for John Davies. Maggie will be pleased.'

'Yes.' Carruthers put his snuff-box away and concentrated again on the file before him, the different coloured sheets flickering little sounds as he moved them. 'I worked it out once. Ten minutes with each householder over a period of six eight-hour days, not allowing for getting from one house to another – '

'What about that yearly?'

'I'll call there this afternoon, see if I can get it tied up before I leave. There's another fire I need to check on too. You do seem to be getting a lot of expensive fires lately . . . .'

'Expensive? I think they're all under ten bob.'

'Ten bob, Albert, is a lot of money.'

Bertie stared at Carruthers. 'It leads to new business. Especially around Christmas time. The firm can't afford to be penny-pinching.'

'D'you check them yourself, old boy?'

Bertie paused, still watching Carruthers's fat profile.

'Yes,' he said, but he sensed Carruthers didn't believe him.

Carruthers sighed. 'You will do as I ask, Albert, dismiss Miss Buckley.'

'I shall consider it.'

'We talked the matter over thoroughly this morning – '

'I said I shall consider it.'

'Choose someone mature.' Carruthers took a blue receipt from his wallet and slowly unfolded it. He held it out. 'Wouldn't you say this signature looks odd?'

'Another fire claim?' Bertie reached for the paper. 'Mrs Travers. I remember her. Got a lot of kids.'

'See anything strange about the signature?'

'Strange?'

'Strange, dear boy. Strange. Higgledy-piggledy.'

'If half your belongings had been destroyed by fire your signature would be higgledy-piggledy.'

Carruthers seemed to ruminate. 'Well over ten bob, too.' He took the blue sheet back and studied it. 'Might even be someone very old. Is it someone old? Doddery?'

'Mrs Travers isn't old, or doddery,' Bertie said, 'but could be illiterate.' He thought about it, frowned at Carruthers, then shrugged. 'Have you any idea where Elsie is?'

'Gone for cigars. While we discuss the matter.' Carruthers's chins wobbled and he smacked his lips. 'Which would you prefer, that you tell her? Or shall I, and make it Head Office official?'

Bertie studied the man, then he said with disgust, 'You know you're a hypocrite. To her face you put on one hell of a performance of near enslavement, and here you want to sack her.'

Slowly Carruthers lifted his head and looked into Bertie's eyes, admonishing. 'Hypocrisy, in the world today, Albert, is a clear requisite,' he added, gently, 'I am the Old Man's lapdog. You must have heard it said.' Bertie's lips parted, dry, accepting that some things seem inevitable.

Carruthers nodded. 'I shall tell her.'

Bertie heaved his shoulders, heaving away a mood, a

165

situation he didn't like. He said stiffly, 'What time train are you catching?'

'About four. It'll be late enough before I get home.' Carruthers took out his pocket watch and wound it, cumbersome in his movements, wheezing, his lungs emphasising his fatness. 'Where has the blasted girl got to? She's been gone half an hour.'

'Probably the shop is out of stock. Or they don't keep your brand.'

Carruthers closed the file and stood up, his face as set in distaste as Bertie's. He said pompously, 'I shall endeavour to obtain my supply in town. Then I shall have to come back here to see Miss Buckley.' He fumbled in his pockets, making sure he had all his needs.

'Does Kit know what time you'll be back?'

'I have already informed her. Yes. I shall be here in time to give your bit of floozy her marching orders, and to collect my bag.'

'She is not my bit of floozy.'

'Most relieved to hear it, dear boy. She gets the poke just the same.' Carruthers straightened his jacket over his enormous front. 'I suppose you haven't tipped her off?'

Bertie glared at him, and Carruthers turned like a sack of flour on the end of a rope pulley. 'Huh,' he breathed, 'merely mentioned the possibility. Could be that's why she's keeping away.'

Bertie picked up the file, putting it on a shelf, wondering if Kit had had the sadistic pleasure of telling Elsie Carruthers wanted her sacked? She would have done it nicely, helpfully, but in triumph.

He brought Carruthers's overcoat from the hallstand and helped the big man into it, then sighed as Carruthers left the house. Bertie went to the window, but Carruthers did not look back. The inspector strode like a man with a mission, the back of his fat neck squashed into rolls between his bowler hat and his overcoat collar.

Bertie stood for a while with his fists dug into his trouser pockets, watching a flimsy white cloud slowly change shape

166

in the blue oblong of sky. The sound of traffic seemed less harsh, as if making the promise of a good summer. He would have to get a car for Kit, take her and the girls off somewhere one week-end. He smiled, feeling better at the thought of a bathing costume and the thud thud of bare feet on hard yellow sand.

The phone rang and he jumped, startled, then unhooked the receiver.

'Hi there!' cried Elsie Buckley, 'I wondered how long Fatso would wait for his cigars.'

'Where are you? What the hell are you playing at?' Already he was laughing.

'I'm down the road. In the phone-box. And Carruthers marched right past me. Did you know he's got little legs?'

'You mean you've been waiting for him to go?'

'If I'm not there he can't sack me.'

'You need your backside tanning.'

She drew in breath, teasing. 'It'd be lovely. Bare bum, mind.'

'Get over here fast. You have work to do.'

'I'm not coming in.'

'What?'

'You 'eard.' She put on a mocking tone. 'Didn't yer mister? You 'eard.' Her laughter was happily naughty.

'You're in a funny mood.'

'I'm going down the beach.'

'Oh are you? And what if I tell Carruthers?'

'I shan't love you any more.'

His inside tumbled and the lump in his throat was exquisite. He stood undecided, then he called, 'I'll see you down there.'

'Where? On the beach? Now?'

'Now.'

'There's a bit of a cold wind for your poor old bones.' The teasing filled her voice.

'You're the one complaining. Not me.'

She gave a little squeal. 'We'll paddle. It'll be freezing.' Her voice was excited. 'Oh do come quickly before the sun goes in. It's lovely, lovely, Bertie. I'll race you there. To the other side of the iron bridge. Tara,' and she had gone. He smiled at the phone, at the desk, at the daffodils Elsie had placed on the filing cabinet. He strode to the door and yelled, 'Kit! I'm going out,' then his homburg was on the back of his head and his coat was over his arm as he ran.

Forty-seven? He felt twenty, even less than twenty. There was a cold wind, but the sun was warming towards spring and summer.

Tramlines and cobbles glistened, a car horn honked twice, and a flea-bitten horse neighed, shaking its head so its harness rattled, and it bared big yellow teeth. The pavement slabs slid past Bertie's pounding feet as he made the effort to get to the other side of the iron bridge before Elsie. He took the short cut through the lane, but a pony and cart was there laden with firewood. 'Afternoon,' he said to it, 'of all places to be. Blocking the gangway.' He stared into the pony's blinkered brown eyes. 'Poor old girl,' he murmured, and straightened her hat. 'Keep up the good work,' then he flattened himself between cart and wall. It became part of the joy, sliding along, trying to avoid snagging his clothes on the stones of the wall and the high wooden wheel with its steel tread, then he whistled and walked jauntily, knowing Elsie had won.

When he got to the beach the sand was glistening like a billion silver crystals on an orange carpet, its surface crusted by the winds, beautiful in the white treacherous sunshine of today.

Elsie was sprawled where the roots of the iron bridge dug into the sand, and he laughed at the thought of her having run up all those steps on one side of the road only to run down this lot on this side, in an effort to beat him to it. He flopped down beside her. She was still panting, laughing, in stockinged feet, her shoes where she had kicked them, her face bereft of makeup, and he suspected she had been in the bathroom using the Lux soap again.

She lifted her arms above her head so her breasts rose and

168

he put his hand on the flat of her tummy. 'I thought it was the fashion to be flat-chested, to be boyish.'

'You want me to be boyish?'

'I want to kiss you.'

'Go on then.'

'D'you mind if someone sees?'

She laughed gaspingly. 'There's no one here. Anyway why should I? I love you,' and with her eyes momentarily closed she accepted his gentle kiss.

'Well,' she said then, 'aren't you going to tell me?'

'That I love you?'

'Yes.'

'No.'

'Pig.' She rushed to her feet and ran from him.

'Hi!' he called after her, 'you've forgotten your shoes.'

'You fetch 'em,' she retorted. 'I'm going for a paddle.'

'With your stockings on?'

'I'll take 'em off.'

He lay on his back and her voice receded as she ran nearer the sea. The sky had large patches of deep blue that seemed to swirl up and into themselves the longer he stared at them. A seagull soared, and Bertie grinned at it, envying the bird's slow, graceful glide.

The promise of spring lulled him and he thought of fat Carruthers hurrying up some street, ever obeying the commands of the Old Man in Head Office, and of how sensitive Carruthers probably was under his official veneer, of the way he had referred to himself as the Old Man's lapdog.

Bertie closed his eyes, forgetting Kit's unhappy voice and pushing Carruthers's enormous bulk from his mind. He didn't hear Elsie return but he felt the ice-cold water trickle on his face, down his collar, and into his ears. His eyes jerked open and Elsie stood above him, her teeth like wet pearls between her lips as she smirked, squeezing the tide-soaked stockings above him. 'There!' she squealed. 'See if that'll revive the poor old thing.'

He sat up fast and she made to run, but his hand closed

on her ankle and with a loud yell she sprawled in the sand, her body racking with merriment. 'You pig!' she yelled. 'Oh you rotten pig!'

'Gutter language,' he retorted, and knelt above her.

'I'm the gutter type. Haven't you noticed?'

He wondered what to do with her now he had her down, then began scooping up sand, pouring it over her. She scrambled free, running on her knees, toppling and straightening again, glancing back as he stood and ran and grabbed her, then they were both standing locked in each other's arms, and he was saying, 'You're adorable, so alive, so vibrant. I'll die without you, Elsie, don't ever leave me . . . .' And then she was pushing him away as she coughed.

He sank slowly to the sand again, watching her, her handkerchief to her mouth, her eyes losing moisture as her face went red. He waited, frightened, telling himself not to be a fool, only women had thoughts like that, fears like that. Because her mother was consumptive it didn't mean she was; she wasn't underweight, she wasn't listless, tired.

She stopped coughing and blew her nose, then she was laughing again, the cold breeze making strands of her light-brown hair lift and glint with silken shades of gold, the kiss-curls long gone, lost in the tousled magic. She said, 'What's the matter with you? I'm the one who's coughing.'

'How long have you had it? The cough.'

'Don't be daft.' She fell to her knees beside him. 'It's not a consumptive cough. D'you think I wouldn't know if it was? I've heard my mother's often enough.'

He smiled, but the fear was there. She said, like a child, 'Tell you what though, if ever I do get consumption, I hope the doctor, or someone, will be kind enough to poison me or something. Without me knowing.'

He sought his cigarettes, unnerved, and she sat, letting the sand play through her fingers. 'I'd hate to be like my mother, knowing I'm going to die, that the hurt is going to get a lot worse.'

'Maybe she isn't going to die.'

'She is.' It was said flatly.

'I thought a farm was going to cure all that.' He was lying again, trying to appease her worry.

'Ah.' She leaned away, secretively. 'That's what I want to talk about.'

'Go on then. Talk about it.'

She shook her head, watching her fingers. 'Do I get the sack, or don't I?'

'Who told you Carruthers was going to sack you?'

'He did.'

'When?'

'Oh, he didn't say it, not actually say it. It's just the way he's been acting. I guessed. Ever since Kit started sporting that black eye. She told everyone you done it.'

'Did it.' He corrected gently. 'It was an accident.'

'It's a beauty. She told me first off that she hit the tap when she was bending over the sink to wash her hair.'

'I was raping her.' He smiled at his own joke.

'While she was washing her hair?' Elsie fell back and lay on the sand. 'You've got to rape your own wife? She must be batty.'

He chuckled. 'You'll believe anything, won't you.'

'I believe you love me.'

He turned from her, unwilling, unable yet, to commit himself.

Elsie said, suddenly, 'About the farm then. You haven't said I seem happy in spite of Carruthers.'

'All right. You seem happy in spite of Carruthers.' He turned back to her, squinting down at her. The beach was empty, the world seemed theirs, and he wanted to indulge her, ease her hurts and make up for his feelings of guilt and inadequacy. 'Why?'

'I've borrowed the money.'

'What money?'

'For the farm. The letter come this morning. Thirty pounds.'

'Thirty pounds!' He sounded hysterical. 'You only earn six shillings a week!'

'Look.' She sat up, intense now. 'It'll keep my mother on

171

a farm for months, and I'm goin' ter pay 'em back ten and a penny a week.'

He was shocked, stunned, kneeling before her. He said, 'You've mortgaged God knows how many years – ' He heard the sea moan and the gull shriek, but Elsie was triumphant.

'I got it. That's the important thing.'

He sat back on his heels. 'How the devil did they lend you that much? You have no collateral.'

'Good referees. And the Lender knew my mother when she was young. Fancied her a bit.'

'Good referees! Who the hell – ? Just what have you been up to, Elsie? You'll never pay that sum back. Good God!'

'If you give me a rise, I will. To ten shillings. Tommy'll help me.'

He stared at her, aware of the seagull strutting at the foot of the bridge, its beak orange and sharp. 'You are out of your tiny mind!'

'She chose the farm, Bertie..I couldn't say no. She thinks – ' She edged a little away from him. 'Bertie – Tommy and me – we let her think you and Kit were – are – paying for it.'

'And she believed you?'

'Rich people do, Bertie. Rich people always help poor people.'

'I'm not rich! I have a mortgage up to my ears and not two farthings to bless myself.'

'Your children go to a posh school.'

'And I pay the posh fees. Hell, I can't have it and spend it.' His voice seemed loud, filling the beach, and his hands lay helplessly on his thighs.

She said softly, 'You are rich to us. You have a lovely house with carpets – ' And he sighed. She went on, 'I'm not asking you for nothing – '

'Anything,' he corrected automatically. 'You are not asking for anything,' but she went on relentlessly.

'Ten shillings, Bertie. Ten shillings a week. And I'll work hard. I promise.'

He didn't know what to say.

172

Her fingers touched his. 'I didn't think you'd be cross.'

'I'm not cross.'

'Prove it then. Kiss me.'

He kissed her, but the sun was cold and his legs were stiff. She said, 'Will you come to see the farm? It's in Malvern. They'll look after her there until – well, until she dies, I suppose.'

'What about your father? What does he think of the idea?'

She moved her bare feet impatiently. 'Him? It oughter be him with consumption. And serve his right too.'

'So he doesn't like it.'

'You said it was a good idea.' She was accusing.

'Her going to the farm is, but not you borrowing money. Who is this lender? A bank?'

'No. A lender. A money lender.'

'Good God!' Bertie's jaw dropped, the horror of her foolishness incomprehensible.

'Why not?' She was ready to argue. 'Their money's as good as anybody else's.' She began to scowl, a child before his wrath. 'That's why I had to keep away from Carruthers. He mustn't sack me. Not till I found another job.'

'He'll sack you anyway, if not today then next week or the week after.'

She brightened, cocking her head cheekily on one side. 'In that case I'll worry next week or the week after.' She clasped her knees to her. 'Even if he did sack me I couldn't stop now. I promised Ma.' Her face was set. 'She might get better, Bertie. Miracles do happen.' She put her head on one side again, wheedling now. 'Can I be a part-time agent too? Heh? Please?'

'A what!'

'An agent. I can canvass. You know I can. I've proved it. I can build up a book of my own. I'll be quids in, I'll get times on all the new business. If I book up twelve penny policies I'll get ten shillings more in a week. That'll be twice the money – '

'My best agent only gets ten bob a week commission.'

173

'All right. I'll be better than your best agent. I've got to, Bertie, and I've got to do it quick.'

He had heard of women with peach-like complexions, had read of them in books, but he had never seen one until now. Elsie's cheeks were a particular shade of pink and a sort of fine down covered them. It caught the light and looked blonde, her lips were a natural pink and her lashes were thick and curling, dark golden brown.

He said calmly, 'Your eyes remind me of the sea on a stormy day, grey and misty.'

She relaxed quickly. 'And yours are like the sea on a summer morning, blue and brilliant, with flashes of silver.' She was laughing again.

'You worry me.'

'Make me a part-time agent.' She began smoothing his fingers. 'Please do. I'll be yours for ever and ever then. No matter what happens I'll just love you for ever, and never ask you nothing – anything– again.'

She was kneeling against him, but he moved away, sitting awkwardly with one foot beneath him. 'It isn't up to me,' he said.

'Yes it is.' She sat back on her bare heels and pouted. 'Kit can get round Carruthers. He has a yen for her. Poor dab.'

'You feel sorry for him?'

'No. For Kit. She loves you too.'

The beach was vast, the sand about them covered with dents and small hillocks, clean, dotted with cockleshells. The edge of the tide was thin and grey-looking now, without waves, sucking at the shoreline.

'It's on the turn,' he said. 'The day soon goes,' and he shivered again. 'We'd better be moving.' He looked at his pocket watch, then slowly stood up, trying to move the stiffness and cold from his legs.

'Will you, Bertie? Will you make me an agent? Please?'

'Get it into your thick nut,' he said without looking at her, 'first, Kit would never try to persuade Carruthers. It would make her feel obligated to the man. Second, if I actively try to stop you getting the sack I will nark

Carruthers, and for me to nark Carruthers is like asking for the push myself. Carruthers has pull in the right places. And although Carruthers and I seem to get on all right, I wouldn't trust the man any further than I can see him.'

'I thought you were friends! He stays in your house.'

'You have a lot to learn about life.' He began brushing sand from his trousers with both hands. 'I'll have Kit after me, sporting down here with you.'

'Kit won't say anything. She knows, and she's afraid of losing you.'

'Knows what?' He kept brushing his trousers, trying to sound casual.

'That we're in love.'

'Are we?'

She was silent and he had to look at her. The grey eyes were serious and enormous in the small piquant face, the lips apart, little furrows between the thinly plucked brows. 'Bertie – you are joking – ' Her voice became a whimper. 'Aren't you?'

He held a hand out to her and shivered again. 'Come on, It's getting colder. The wind is quite keen.'

She took his hand and kissed his fingers, naive and trusting. 'You haven't said you're pleased I came without any make-up.'

'I'm pleased.'

'Now say Elsie I love you.'

'Elsie I love you.'

'And I'll make you a part-time agent.'

'Come on. I'll walk you to the tram.'

'Say it! Say it! Please, oh please.'

'It.'

'Oh Bertie, you know what I mean.'

'Exactly. Now come along.' His voice was firm. He pulled her to her feet and she snatched up her shoes and wet sand-sodden stockings, then he walked quickly. He heard her following, the sand squeaking beneath them both. She stayed behind him, even when they reached the streets, and at the tramstop he turned to her. She was still barefoot, her toes stubby and pink. He said, 'If you don't stop sulking you'll get no help at all. It's bad enough having Kit pulling long faces without you starting the same tricks.'

'Kit doesn't want a part-time job.'

'No. She wants a car.'

'A car?' Elsie glowered, then a thought came to her and she half smiled, biting her lower lip. 'If you get a car we can go to Malvern in it. Take Ma to the farm! Oh.' Her enthusiasm grew and she chuckled, all sulks gone. 'We'll choose a lovely week-end, and you and me'll go. Easter! What about Easter? It's next month. Early. Just you and me, and Ma.'

'Here's your tram.'

'Hasn't it been a lovely day? I love you, I love you – '

'Your tram.'

He watched her board but doubted she knew what she was doing. She skipped up the stairs, her shoes and stockings swinging in her hand, her bare feet splashing sand everywhere, her knees still encrusted with the stuff. Bertie realised yet again she was a street kid, a kid who ran barefoot because shoes were kept for Sunday. She leaned from the top of the tram, laughing and waving. 'Cooey!' her teeth and cheeks shining, her eyes crinkled up with happiness. He saluted her gently, her pleasure pleasing him, the knowledge he could give her happiness or misery making his pride intense. He blew her a kiss.

He watched the tram go, saw it rocking as it always did, its antenna clinging to the overhead rail, and he hurried back to Kit. The sooner he got a car now the better.

Carruthers was waiting, sitting in Bertie's armchair beside the fire. Kit sat opposite him, her hands in her lap, patient, expectant, the black eye turning pale yellow.

Bertie was marching, whistling. He swung the door wide open and said, 'Aha, you two been talking about me behind my back again?'

Carruthers lumbered to his feet. He already had his overcoat on, and his bowler and briefcase waited on the table. He said heavily, 'Because of you I have missed my train.'

'Ah,' said Bertie, and in the firelit gloom of the kitchen his eyes shone darkly. 'Then you will have to catch the next one.'

Carruthers watched him disapprovingly, his red lips pouting thoughtfully, his lungs bronchial. 'Miss Buckley didn't come in this afternoon. In fact,' his lungs laboured hard, 'I am still awaiting my cigars.'

'Ah,' said Bertie again, and stuck his tongue in his cheek. He hadn't given a thought to the cigars.

Carruthers lifted the bowler and briefcase, holding them both in his left hand. He held out his right hand. 'Au revoir, Kit. Keep your chin up. There's a brave girl.'

Kit smiled, getting to her feet. Bertie knew he should be feeling guilty, even sinful, wicked, but he didn't. He felt light-hearted, almost happy. He said, 'Well, it's been nice having you, old boy.'

'I'm sure it has,' Carruthers said drily. 'You have sand on your lapels. Did you dictate many letters?'

Bertie kept smiling. 'It has certainly been a beautiful day.'

'I'm sure it has. Miss Buckley's notice is on her desk. See she gets it.'

Bertie's forefinger flicked sand from his lapel, and he could feel more sand down the back of his neck. He said calmly, 'It's none of your damn business.'

Carruthers moved towards the door. 'It's the firm's business. We cannot possibly endorse any risk of scandal within the firm.'

'Are you and yours so perfect?'

'Your insolence is out of character, Albert.'

'I took the girl on. I pay her out of my own grand salary of two pounds ten a week. I am employing extra help. That is my business.' Bertie's face was set. 'I gave her the job. I will say when it is to be taken away.'

Carruthers hesitated, looking from Bertie to Kit and back again, then he nodded. He tapped his bowler onto his

177

head and sauntered hugely up the passage. Bertie and Kit followed. They waved to him as he went down the street, and Kit said, 'He has almost an hour before his next train.'

'Maybe I ought to go with him. Soothe things over.'

'Don't put him in an awkward position, Bertie. He's a company man. His job depends on it, and his job is all he has these days.'

They watched Carruthers, his head high so the back of his fat neck was squashed into the familiar rolls. 'Poor devil,' Bertie said, and put his arm about Kit; he squeezed her to him. 'I bet he can't make hell or hide of us.'

'The kettle's boiling,' she said quietly, and Carruthers stopped at the end of the road. He looked smaller now, a dark square with a briefcase in one hand. He lifted his bowler in the air, shaking it like a tambourine in farewell, and Bertie waved with both arms. Then Carruthers had gone.

CHAPTER EIGHT

Kit had been worried about Carruthers coming down so much earlier in the year than was usual, convinced it was to do with Bertie and the girl.

She assessed the situation as Carruthers had presented it to her a few nights ago. Would Bertie give up his job, his wife, his daughters, his comfortable home, for Elsie Buckley? Because, on the face of it, that was her only fear.

Now she sat in her armchair opposite Bertie and watched him from beneath her lashes, her dark eyes barely open. For a few seconds the image of him copulating with Elsie made her inside twist into a knot that caught her nerve-ends and made her want to shriek. She swallowed hard and closed her eyes tightly, dispelling the unexpected anguish. It was the first time such emotion had seized her. She had experienced jealousy, dislike, even hatred, but that sudden griping of emotion was stronger than them all. She peeped at her hands, afraid their shaking was obvious, but the tremor eased as she exerted control. Then an odd thought crept into her mind. Was it possible she loved Bertie after all?

Her eyes flew open in alarm. Had she spent, at least, the last fourteen years loving him and not knowing? Believing she was tolerating him, as he was tolerating her; a hedge against loneliness, a need for roots, a belonging?

He was reading a magazine. His spectacles made him look different, and she thought the grey at his temples was more pronounced. He was sunk deeply into the battered old chair, its springs almost touching the floor, his body bolstered with cushions, that she had made. His face was without a line, without a furrow. She remembered the way he had first kissed her, gently, his strong, lean hands barely holding her, as if afraid of crushing her. Did he kiss Elsie like that? Her nerve-ends got strangled again and her tongue almost blurted, 'Bertie, I think I love you!' But pride was to the fore now. One didn't confess to loving as one did to needing a cup of tea.

She took a deep breath and said as calmly as her will-power could force it, 'Did your secretary have anything interesting to say today? Does she realise she's due for notice?'

Bertie looked up. He was enjoying reading; it transported him from insurance, from having to think, from loving Elsie yet needing Kit, from trying not to fear tomorrow and what it might bring: loss of Elsie and the excitement, the happiness of being with her; loss of Kit and the home, the comfort he had built up with her.

Kit's voice had been brittle, even quarrelsome, and he sighed, putting the magazine on the wide rexine arm of his chair. 'Elsie . . . ?' Across his vision came the sands, golden and empty but for a seagull, and he and Elsie; Elsie laughing, running, bare-legged, Elsie with a gleaming, teasing smile, Elsie against him, supple, small, warm.

He said calmly, even a little off-hand, 'She suggested we let her build up a book for herself. Apparently her mother's health is deteriorating fast and she wants her to go on a farm at Malvern.'

'Tch!' A mixture of pity for the Buckley family and amazement at Elsie's temerity made Kit sit up sharply. 'What a hope!'

'I think she'll do it,' Bertie said, and drew his hand over his face tiredly. 'She has a loan of thirty pounds to pay for the farm.'

'Good God! Did you tell her Carruthers wants her out?'

His face set stubbornly. 'She has guts. Carruthers can go to hell.'

Kit fet her body subside. So there was the answer to what she had thought was a hypothetical question. Would Bertie throw everything away for Elsie Buckley?

The answer seemed to be yes.

She said cautiously, 'Carruthers can be a nasty devil. He's left her notice on her desk.'

'I destroyed it.'

'Oh,' Kit said, and wished his obduracy wasn't over Elsie, because she, Kit, rather liked it. She touched her yellowing eye gently, murmuring, 'Ooh, my face does hurt,' and immediately Bertie came to the edge of his chair, immediately there was concern on his high-cheekboned face, a furrow between those clear blue eyes.

'Can I get you something?'

'Yes,' Kit said, smiling gently. 'You can kiss it better.'

Bertie's brows rose sharply in amused surprise, then obligingly he crouched before her and let his lips barely touch her closed eyelid. 'Better?' he queried.

'Better,' she said, and he went back to his chair, picking up his magazine. She asked, 'And what did you tell Elsie? About her wanting a book of her own, I mean?'

'I told her to go ahead,' he lied. 'She can build one up around her own area. St Thomas, Port Tennant, Bonymaen, that way. As long as it doesn't interfere with her office work.' Then he smiled at Kit. 'I thought our share of the commission on the new business could go towards a car.'

'Really?' She glowed at him, her pale thin face beginning to look alive for the first time in months; and when the car arrived, on the following Saturday, it was big and black with a hood that could be strapped back when summer came.

It stood at the kerb and Bertie and Kitty glowed at it, her black hair in immaculate plaits to the top of her head, his pale lips twitching in a secret smile. She said softly, 'Aren't you glad we live in such a long street?'

'No. Why?'

'So more people can see your masterpiece. All those who live up there as well as all those who live along here.'

'They have an even bigger one next door.'

'It's older and not such a nice colour.' She moved closer

181

to him, tall and elegant, linking an arm through his for warmth. He smiled into her eyes, forever amazed at the red flecks and the darkness of them.

'You know we're flat broke now,' he said. 'The deposit took all I could raise, and we're still paying for the carpet and three-piece in the middle room.'

'Then aren't you glad we didn't have another baby?'

He drew from her, still emotionally sore from her abortion, and she thought quickly, then asked, 'Shall we go for a run in your car?' She waited, smiling, as though enticing a child, and he shrugged almost imperceptibly.

'All right. Get your titfer on,' and she ran, her blue flowered apron flapping against her thighs. The children were watching from the bedroom window and as Kit went into the house she called them. They came down the stairs, eager, Emma concentrating on her feet, her hands sliding against the wall. They clutched their coats and scarves from the hallstand then ran, flush-faced to the street.

'Where are we going?'

The piled into the car, the celluloid windows sepia about them, and Bertie said, 'What about the Mumbles? Let's go to Bracelet Bay.'

Linda sat back smiling at Emma. Emma knelt on the back seat. 'I like Bracelet Bay.' And Kit nodded, the brim of her deep crowned hat making a pale blue halo around her face.

'It will be more fun than going by bus, go on then, Daddy. Drive us to Bracelet Bay.' And the Mumbles Road soon stretched long and wide before them, bending only with the bending of Swansea Bay.

Bertie drove contentedly. He felt emotionally comfortable, and the sea glinted in near sunlight on his left almost all the way.

Only once Kit spoke, and then it was with pleasure. She said, 'Oh my! Look at that view, those hills across the water. Isn't God good?' And everyone gave a gentle agreement.

In the cove known as Bracelet Bay the tide lashed white

against the cliffs, leaving trembling trails of silver. The ozone was strong, as if telling the world of the sea nurturing oysters and laverbread, of cockles hidden in the sand, and of mussels and periwinkles vying with limpets for clinging space around the rock pools.

Bertie breathed deeply, standing straddle-legged with his family amid the gorse bushes on the clifftop, squinting at the heaving waters.

'Turn left for Swansea,' Kit said lightly, 'and right for Gower.'

'Or swim straight on for Devon.' Bertie braced his shoulders. Life was good. He looked at Emma and Linda where they stood patting their chests, their pink faces into the breeze. He said, 'Let's go down. On to the sand.' And they all ran like children, down the steep narrow path.

'It's wet. The tide is only just going out,' Kit cried.

'We can pick periwinkles and eat them tonight. With a pin each,' Bertie quipped.

'Periwinkles?' Emma said.

'Like snails.' Kit laughed.

It was the day Dad gave the girls piggybacks in turn, and they all paddled in the tide that turned their toes into white dead-ends with cold. It was the day Bertie and Kit showed their knees, and olive-green and brown seaweed slipped across their feet and wrapped about their ankles.

That night Kit cuddled into Bertie and sighed. He smelled her hair and said, 'Has the Puritan soap all gone?'

'No. Why?'

'Your hair usually smells of it.'

'Does it?' She was pleased he had commented. 'I used the Lux. D'you like it?'

'Much better.' His arm drew her a little tighter.

She whispered, 'We have so much. I feel terribly sorry for people like the Buckleys. Life isn't fair. Oh thank God we are not like them.'

Sadness crept into Bertie's heart and his arm loosened from Kit. Now he felt disloyal to Elsie, and the agony of indecision went on in him. Was it possible to love two women? Two different ways?

He heard Kit slowly fall asleep, but he lay awake until dawn, hearing the milkman come on his cart, lifting his cans and taking the white jug from the doorstep to fill it, then replacing it, putting the saucer on top to keep out dirt, birds and other people's cats.

*   *   *

The sun shone. It was Easter. The office door was soundly locked. Bertie whistled and Kit sang. Emma sat on the stairs. She had awakened at five with excitement and now looked at her Mickey Mouse wristwatch with impatient concern. She counted carefully and noted the big hand and the little hand. 'Nearly nine o'clock,' she murmured, and started straight ahead, down the passage and through the open door to where the precious car demanded everyone else's attention.

'Emma!' Bertie strode past her. 'Stop sucking your thumb or it'll soon look like my big toe.'

Obediently she wiped her thumb on her petticoat then tidied the skirt of her new white dress across her knees. 'Are we going soon?'

A minute later Kit hurried past her. 'Emma, for goodness sake stop sucking your thumb, you'll soon have a mouth like a pig.'

'Can I get in the car?'

'Yes. Get a blanket off your bed. The seats are cold. You'll get chincough in your bottoms.'

Bertie was still whistling as they drove off. Kit wore a brown straw hat with a wide brim as if daring the weather to do its worst, and Emma kept trying to peer around it from the back seat.

Linda called, 'Why's there a blind here on the back window?'

'To pull down,' Bertie quipped, and Linda blushed while the others laughed. Kit said more kindly, 'To stop other car lights at night blinding your father.'

184

Bertie cruised the car very slowly over the New Cut iron bridge, its tyres rumbling and echoing, so Kit and the girls could view the docks and the great ships. So they could get a waft of the special smell: tar and grease and smoke and brine, all the acrid novelty of seafaring, while the water beneath them lapped thickly green.

When they drew up at the kerb near the great wall supporting the cracked houses of Salubrious Terrace, Kit stared blandly through the celluloid window at a boy sitting on the pavement, his bare feet in the gutter. 'He's damn near naked! Look at his pants. They're in ribbons.'

'And his legs are filthy too,' Emma said piously, her fingers twined in her lap. The boy stared back at them, vacuous, lonely, his dirty hands fondling two glass marbles, his nose running into his gaping mouth.

'I'm not getting out,' Kit said suddenly. 'I'll wait here with the girls. In any case I couldn't tolerate seeing that awful Tom Buckley again. Not after what happened at the party. He's vile!'

Bertie touched her knee. 'Oh come on. He might not be there. Gwen will be expecting you.'

Kit looked at the boy again and he half smiled, a mere twitching of his blue mouth. Kit said, 'God! What chance does he have?' Then she looked back at her two daughters, noticing Emma's inclination to plumpness, their confidence, even a little arrogance, and she felt proud they weren't sitting in the gutter.

She glanced at Bertie as he walked to the pavement, ignoring the boy, and she left the car and went to him, her hands clutching her cream woollen coat to her as if afraid it might wipe against the streaming, moss-pitted walls.

Tom Buckley came from his house as if he had been waiting for them, and for a while he stood, big, muscular, insolently rebellious as he watched; his striped flannel shirt open to his belted waist, the sleeves rolled up showing blue and red tattoos on strong, sinewy, forearms, then, as they reached the top of the steps he turned and walked away, pausing to turn and gaze once more, his eyes sunken into

185

defiant, disgruntled dark sockets.

Kit stopped. 'I'm not going in there,' she said, and Tom Buckley's face, the skin thickened by furnace heat, twisted into a derisive sneer as if he had read her lips. He went to a neighbour's window sill and sat, the stump of his hand resting on his knee.

Other doors opened softly, slyly, and people watched as though telepathy had called them out.

Bertie hesitated. He hadn't expected this. He was doing the family a good turn, taking Gwen Buckley to the fresh air of Worcestershire. He touched Kit's arm, gesturing her to wait, then he went to Tom Buckley, deliberately casual, one hand in his trouser pocket.

'Morning Tom.'

'Go to hell.'

'I probably will, but not yet. Is Gwen ready?'

'Look 'ere mister bloody moneybags – ' Tom Buckley didn't leave the window sill, his battered face a greyish-brown in the late March sunlight. 'You got no right to take my wife off of me, no right at all.'

'I'm not taking your wife – '

'You are. Stickin' your bloody nose in – ' Tom Buckley's eyes were questionably glossy, and Bertie saw the hopeless-ness in them, the tears that no strong man should shed.

Bertie put a hand on Tom's shoulder. 'D'you want to come with her?' Even as he spoke he wondered who would have to stay home to make the extra room in the car, what Kit would say if Tom Buckley moved from that window sill with a yes.

Tom Buckley didn't. He thrust Bertie's hand away. 'Go to hell,' he repeated, then he got up and brusquely strolled away, the big shoulders hunched, the stump of one hand nursed in the other.

Bertie stood for a while watching him, smelling the poverty about him, feeling the helplessness he so often experienced in his job, feeling even a little guilty at the fees he paid for his daughters' schooling, while these people starved, and knowing he wasn't going to do anything about it.

He went back to Kit and her amber eyes were anxious. 'Oh Bertie. He's horrid. Doesn't he appreciate we're trying to help?'

'No,' Bertie said. 'Come on. Let's get it over with.'

'He's like that kid, sitting on the pavement,' Kit whispered. 'They've both got the same attitude. As though it's our fault they live here.'

Bertie nodded to the neighbours and received more nods in return. He said quietly to Kit, 'If we lived here, on the means test, without hope, how would you feel?'

'Everywhere's so grey. The sun only makes it look worse.'

'They clean their windows and they scrub their fronts. Now come on – ' he drew her forward. 'Smile, Kit. For God's sake smile.'

Kit nodded, her face pallid with distaste, but she smiled while her amber eyes stayed sad.

Tom Buckley moved again. He went to the top of the wall, staring out over the road, his body unrelenting, as if made of concrete, and Bertie took Kit in, through the open doorway of Tom Buckley's home.

Bertie called, determined not to take his disquiet in to Gwen and Elsie, 'Hi ho, anybody home?' And a youth came, a youth wearing boots and grey flannel trousers held up by string. His ruddy face was flecked with freckles and he held out a hard hand. 'Mr Hemsworthy? I'm Tommy. Elsie's brother.' He jerked his head. 'Come on in,' and they gathered into the kitchen. It was thick with warmth, the smell of smoke, people, cabbage, consumption, and Phul-Nana.

Neighbours had come in to see Gwen go. She lay on the sofa, her head on a clean white pillow, her body covered with a home-made patchwork quilt, the stamp of death clearly on her face.

Her skin was tight, transparent, tinged with peach, her eyes were too big, too brilliant. She smiled with dry pale lips and her teeth were the teeth of a corpse.

Bertie had to swallow an exclamation. Her deterioration

187

was catastrophic. No farm, no fresh air, or good food, could save her. He heard the forced laughter of the well-wishers, was aware their knowledge of impending death was the same as his, and he bent to Gwen Buckley and gently kissed her between the eyes.

She laughed, breathless, weak, her hands clawing as if to grasp his strength from him, and her neighbours cheered and told her loudly Bertie had his eye on her. She ought to be careful. Keep her knees crossed. What a lucky woman she was having a young, handsome, rich man caring for her. And she was beautiful too. Looking better already.

Elsie came from the scullery and Bertie felt a wave of relief. She was made up, laughing, and she had put a beauty spot on her cheek. It looked silly and feminine, and far away from the death waiting on the sofa. She acknowledged him and Kit, then plonked a large pink straw hat on her head and turned to her mother. 'Well?' she said, 'I'm ready, willing and waiting.'

Bertie hesitated. He·didn't like this. Gwen should be allowed to die at home. He looked around at the faces of the people as they huddled back, giving him and Elsie room, and young Tommy was grinning at his mother, encouraging her. 'It's cured other people up there, Ma. They say there's foxgloves and a bird that goes pee-a-weet. They've got their own apple trees, dozens of 'em, and chickens . . . .'

Elsie cut in, 'Bertie, you carry Ma, won't you?'

He stared into her face and momentarily got lost in the hope he saw there, absolute, undoubted hope that this might be the beginning of a great miracle, the happening she hoped for so desperately that she had gone to a money-lender to get the money.

Bertie felt helpless. He looked behind him hoping Tom Buckley was there, he needed Tom Buckley to say go or stay, but he saw only Kit's white, startled face, then she too was saying the artificial things to Gwen Buckley. 'The air will soon clear those lungs of yours . . . . Just wait until you have a real ham-and-egg breakfast . . . '

Gwen put up an arm to Bertie and he leaned over her,

then lifted her. He felt the misery of all nations was cemented into him, and his face hurt as he made the effort to smile.

The burlesque that this was a good moment, a happy moment, the first moment to a healthy future for Gwen, continued, and on the terrace stood Tom Buckley. For a moment he and Bertie stared at each other, then Bertie said, 'Tom, aren't you going to kiss her goodbye – ' and wished he were in a hole somewhere, wishing he hadn't used the word, goodbye.

Across the paving Gwen smiled at her husband, her head against Bertie's shoulder. 'I won't be long,' she called in a thin voice. 'I'll soon be home again.'

Tom Buckley didn't move and Bertie carried Gwen down the narrow steps, and to the car. The feeling of sickness was thick inside him, and Elsie was the only one making a noise. She clucked around her mother, putting a pillow behind her in the back of the car, tucking the blanket in, then she got in beside her, and smiled at Linda who climbed in as well.

Emma went in the front on Kit's lap, and Bertie tied Gwen's cardboard suitcase to the grid on the back of the car. Then, keeping up the pretence that had been thrust upon them all, he squeezed the horn so its sound made a horse blow noisily, and more pot-bellied, undernourished children gathered to watch, to cheer and wave, as the women were doing on top of the wall, then he slowly drove away.

He could feel Tom Buckley's eyes boring into the back of his neck. He felt Kit's hand rest on his knee, and he wanted to cry.

Then there seemed to be absolute silence. Bertie was aware of the engine throbbing, of other traffic out there beyond the celluloid window, yet there was an uncanny silence.

He glanced around and each female gave a half smile. There was no excitement, no animation, as if they were five people trapped in a soundproof box that moved along the

189

bevelled, cobbled road of its own accord.

Then Kit moved her shoulders. 'Oh dear,' she said flatly. 'It feels as though the angels are passing over.'

Everyone agreed and normal, polite conversation began.

It was early evening when they turned into the drive leading to the farm. They had stopped for a snack on a grassy patch beside a five-barred gate. They had boiled the kettle on a primus and eaten Kit's ham sandwiches. The celuloid windows had made all views sepia, but now even Bertie exclaimed over the loneliness, the silent eeriness of the countryside where catkins hung, but nature didn't seem ready for spring.

The hills were grey-blue and already a mist was falling. The farm was hidden in a mass of trees, its thatched roof almost touching its bedrooms' latticed windows. As the car rattled, chugged and banged to a standstill, the farm's front door opened and a large woman dressed completely in white from mob-cap to shoes appeared.

Bertie had a feeling of anti-climax. He was cold and stiff, and he heard a long sigh escape from his passengers, then the woman he soon got to know as Maud was grinning at them through the celluloid, her flat nose taking up most of her face.

'Shwd ichi,' she said, bending her plump body in an effort to include them all in her welcome. 'You made it then. You found it all right. Good. Good. Good.'

'You speak Welsh?' Bertie exclaimed.

'Bless you. I am Welsh,' she returned, and suddenly stood and burst into song.

Bertie and his companions sat in astonishment as Maud gave vent to 'Men of Harlech' in Welsh, then he climbed out of the car.

'That is something I can't do. Speak Welsh.'

'Ah well, never mind cariad,' Maud soothed. 'I can speak English too.'

Then there was nothing but activity, getting Gwen out of the car, her skinny legs unable to fill the grey lisle stockings which hung, wrinkled about them; carrying her up to the ancient wide iron bed, making sure the two stone hot-water bottles were not too hot, seeing the flush on her face with the hard white lines that told of her fever, and seeing the utter exhaustion as she sank, like a doll, into the pillows; seeing her eyes, wide and staring, hopeful and frightened, glassy and unreal, beneath the spread of dying white hair.

Elsie cried, 'Ma, you look better already.'

'Elsie . . . ' Gwen murmured. 'Your dad . . . .'

'He'll be all right Ma. Next time we come up we'll bring 'im. Promise. Cross my 'eart and 'ope to die.'

Bertie and Kit let Maud show them their own room for the night, and neither mentioned the bulging walls, the slanting ceiling, the obviously home-made patchwork quilt, and the damp cold of Malvern at dusk in March.

That night they fell asleep cuddled close together, glad of shared warmth, of unspoken comfort, wishing they weren't there, yet glad they were, because only the flint-hearted could refuse to be.

In the next room Linda and Emma lay staring through the lattice window. An owl screeched, a fox called, and Emma's brows stayed up in a sort of delighted terror until, like Linda, she slipped into a healthy sleep.

About two o'clock in the morning Emma awoke. She gave a little cry and brushed her hands across her face. Then she screamed, 'Linda!' She screamed again and the sound carried on from the fears of strange pre-sleep sounds. 'Linda! A mouse! I think it's a mouse. In the bed, Linda! It's in the bed. It went over my face.' She curled up with horror. 'Oh Linda.'

Linda awoke with a startled heart banging in her throat, fear for her baby sister uppermost. She leaned to the chair beside the bed, her fingers seeking the matches. She knocked the candle over.

'Daddy! Daddy!' Their voices wailed through the thin plasterboard walls. 'Daddy! Daddy! Come quickly,' and Bertie sat up.

'Kit? It's the kids!' He had a torch on his bedside table and ran with it, bumping into the papered walls of the narrow passageway with sleepiness, his bare feet thudding on the uneven oilcloth-covered floor, his eyes half closed, his body unsteady. 'Linda? Emma? What's the matter?'

'Daddy, oh Daddy, there's a mouse in the bed . . . I'm holding the clothes down so it can't get out . . . .'

'It ran over my face . . . .'

He lit the oil lamp on the whatnot in the corner, calm now, smelling the earthy dampness of the old house, the mist seeping in from the marshes; and Kit was at the girls' bed.

'Bring the lamp over, Bertie. Let's see.'

The lamp smoked, flickered, then settled as he replaced the globe and adjusted the wick. His daughters sat huddled together against the pillows, their gaze on their mother, as if afraid to move their eyeballs in case it set the little intruder running again.

Kit whispered to them, 'Can you feel it now?'

'No,' they whispered back, and Bertie brought the lamp over. His inside was going odd. He had seen men die horribly in the trenches, and he had soon lost the habit of clenching his teeth and vomiting over the stench of blood and guts, but the thought of an intruder during sleep, even a minute one, caused him to erupt in goose-pimples.

He held the lamp high, the cold floor sticking to his bare feet; he hoped the mouse – or whatever it was – had run, lost itself in a hole, because he, Bertie Hemsworthy, couldn't, wouldn't, catch it.

Slowly Kit peeled back the bedclothes. Her black hair was loose about her shoulders, her profile sharp in the lamplight, her nightie a cloud about her, and Bertie was glad she was the hunter. Kit hunted the girls' heads for lice or nits regularly, making sure they were clean. Kit hunted the fleas off a visiting dog, and clicked them quite dead between her thumb nails after rendering them unconscious in a basin of water. She would watch the tiny body spurt, then wash her hands while talking of something else.

At this moment, as Kit hunted the mouse, Bertie sensed she was lethal, it was an instinct that seemed to come uppermost in her once the hunted was trapped. It passed through his mind that an army of men could be annihilated more torturously by an army of women than by any machine invented.

'Ah –' Kit sighed, and the two girls and Bertie watched, mesmerised. 'A spider,' Kit whispered. 'Not a little mouse at all. A whopping great spider.' The girls eased, their fear not quite gone, but their incipient squeals vanquished.

Kit put her hand down, onto the twill sheet, and the spider curled into itself hoping to be invisible, but Kit had it. 'Coo, isn't it a big one? Look at the stripes on it,' she whispered. Her long, thin, well-cared for fingers rolled it and presented it to each pair of eyes in turn, and Bertie moved to open the little window wider, making it easy for Kit to drop the spider out, onto the cherry tree climbing against the wall.

Kit didn't even notice his movements. Intently she balanced the fat little body between her finger and thumb. And squashed.

The two girls squealed, slammed their eyes shut and held their ears as if expecting the spider to scream.

Kit murmured, 'That'll teach him to keep out of your bed.' Then she flicked her hand out of the window before going to the wash-stand and washing her hands with the highly scented pink soap supplied by Maud.

Bertie said nothing. He hoped no one would ever know how squeamish he was, or how murderous Kit could be.

*   *   *

Bertie awoke early and took a while to get adjusted. The room was low with white distemper flaking from the ceiling. The wallpaper was smothered in pink roses and trellis. He sat up on the edge of the bed, the springs twinging from his movements, and he looked back at Kit; she was sprawled in a way he hadn't seen her at home and her eyes, half opened, were still dazed with sleep. 'Good morning,' she purred. 'This flock mattress has lumps in it.

193

Like potatoes.'

He smiled at her. She was regally beautiful, the high cheekbones forever emphasising the illusion of high breeding. There were no blue shadows around her eyes this morning, and her black lashes lay against a perfect matt skin. She turned to her side, cuddled her cheek to the pillow, and was fast asleep again.

Bertie thought of the spider, of Kit's satisfaction as she flicked her hand out of the window, and he went to the casement which was still partly open because the warped wood wouldn't let it close. He pushed the pink rose-patterned curtains to one side, then opened the window fully. The air came strong and fresh from the Malvern Hills and Bertie slapped his hands to his chest and breathed deeply.

Birds fluttered in and out of the ivy and cherry leaves peeping over the red sill, and Bertie caught sight of Elsie in the orchard. She was wearing the big pink straw hat, and her multi-coloured voile frock of blues and pinks flowed against her as she moved. The skirt wafted and she looked as if she was floating on the thick greenery of grass, the untrained trees like ungainly sentinels about her. She saw him and beckoned him to her, as usual giving the impression of excitement, of immediate delight at seeing him.

He washed quickly, tipped the icy well water from the heavy china jug into the large china bowl on the marble-topped wash-stand. He felt fit, strong, virile. He could smell April on the way, and the goodness of the earth in spring. He kissed Kit's nose and saw her lips move in a faint smile while she slept on, then he was hurrying down the narrow winding stairs, amused at the way they sagged and creaked.

'Hello Daddy.'
'Hello Daddy.'

The girls were already in the stone-flagged kitchen eating omelettes. 'Morning,' he said, and Maud Simms put her ample red hands on her ample round hips and beamed at him. 'Mornin' Mr Hemsworthy. Did you sleep well?'

'Very well thank you, Maud.'

'Ready for breakfast?'

'Not yet. If you don't mind I'll wait for my wife.'

Maud's white mob-cap framed her flat red face with a frill. She looked like a female Humpty Dumpty.

She moved to the black range that filled one long stone wall. 'And will you be here for luncheon?'

'No,' Bertie said. 'Once breakfast is over we'll be off. It's quite a journey.'

'And don't you worry about poor Mrs Buckley. I'll be looking after her.'

'Thank you Maud.'

'Oh don't thank me, Mr Hemsworthy. It's you paying for it,' and she smiled as he blinked. 'Ah,' she added. 'Mrs Buckley told me. Last evening. Thinks the world of you she does. But I'll care for her, never you mind.'

'I'm sure you will. Thank you.' He hesitated, like a child seeking an excuse to go out to play, then he hurried through the open door, into the denser scent of farm and country. He was paying Gwen's fees? He laughed, didn't women get cock-eyed ideas? He ran through the chickens, leaving them clucking and glaring, and he ignored the big white horse that watched him with slowly blinking eyes. He jumped the shallow stream where a gander stretched and a duck groomed her chest. Bertie made for the orchard.

Elsie was crouched in a bed of clover, her head bent, the skirt of the voile dress spread about her. He called, 'Looking for fairies?'

'No.' She laughed up at him, devoid of make-up or kiss curls; pink and shiny and enticing, her Phul-Nana perfume only a faint suggestion. 'A four leaf-clover. For luck.'

He crouched before her, aware of the lack of people, of the cleanliness of the air and the privacy caused by the branches about them. His fingers groped in the mass of cold green leaves. 'Here's one.'

'Can't be!'

'Why not?'

195

'You've only just got here. You couldn't find one so fast. I've been here for ages.'

'Ah well, I don't muck about.' He picked the clover leaf gently, holding it out to her. 'Put it in your bible.'

A twig cracked and he jerked up, listening.

'What's the matter?' Elsie asked.

'Nothing. Someone walking over my grave.'

'I have the oddest feeling too. It's this place.'

'It's the spring. Sap rising and all that.'

'I don't think it is.' Her face was dreamy now, sadly so. 'We all felt something before we set off. Remember? Kit said an angel was passing over.' She stood up quickly, then lifted her chin in challenge. 'Let's make love.'

'What, now?'

'Why not?'

'No reason at all.'

'I know the exact place. I found it earlier.' She caught his hand. 'I'm frightened, Bertie. As though life is suddenly going to change.' She kissed his fingers quickly, then they ran, he still a little bewildered by the speed of her ardour, but happy, and they struggled through the barbed-wire strands of a fence. He watched Elsie as though he was rediscovering her, and she led him on, intense, secretive, seeming to float in the blues and pinks of the voile dress.

At last she said, 'Here,' and the pine trees stood closely knit about them, the trunks so tall the sky was cloaked, hidden by the heavy branches of dark, dark green, the years-old carpet of needles making the ground soft and springy. There was no sound in Bertie's ears other than his blood pounding and his lungs labouring. Elsie was flushed, not smiling, and she stood before him and deliberately took off her hat, then she turned her back to him so he could release the hooks and eyes on her dress, then she slipped the dress down slowly, baring her shoulders, so there remained, soon, only the flesh-coloured French knickers, and the tiny unnecessary brassiere.

He said, 'Why take your dress off?' But she kept her hands slowly moving, taking off the satin French knickers

196

and the brassiere as though it had all been carefully planned. She stood naked with her arms held out to him and, in the silence of the trees, in the darkness of moist, ageless earth, in the pungent scent of pine and moss, her face was pleading and tender.

He didn't want to touch her. He wanted to gaze at her, imprint her on his memory as if today was the last day of their lives.

She took a step closer to him, her clothes strewn about her feet, and the pine needles sighed as she trod on them. 'I love you, Bertie Hemsworthy. I love you more than life itself, and I forgive you for not wanting to marry me, for never wanting to publicly accept me.'

'Elsie!' It was a whisper.

'I've thought about it. I've watched you with Kit.' Her low voice seemed to accentuate its Welsh accent. 'You do love Kit in a way, but I excite you, Bertie, don't I – ' And her body was warm and smooth as he took her to him. She undressed him, gently and caressingly, while the trees above them stood motionless, and a bird fluttered away as if to enhance their privacy.

Elsie murmured, 'No matter what happens I will always love you, and love you and love you – '

'And love you – ' Bertie echoed softly.

The pine wood was timeless, and when Elsie said, 'This place will be full of bluebells soon,' he and she were lying side by side on his jacket, staring up at the muted light in the spreading branches, feeling the gentleness of the pine needles-smothered earth beneath them. Bertie sighed. 'Isn't it nice being naked in the open air? As if I'm breathing all over.'

'I'd like it to rain again.'

'What? Now?'

'We could gloat in it. As if God was washing us, cleaning us.'

Bertie heard the cracking of twigs again and looked to his right.

Kit stood there, between two pole-like trunks,

silhouetted against a pale brown world of branches that were bare because they never felt the sun. Her black hair was thick and loose around her wide shoulders, so it made her face look smaller. Her cream woollen dress hung straight, her feet in plain brown court shoes. Her hands were clasped tightly before her, and her jaw was tense, as if it restrained her from hysterics.

For a moment Bertie stared into her eyes, into the depths of black anguish, and he thought he saw hatred, then she turned and walked away, tall, elegant and dignified.

Elsie sat up beside him, her dress clutched against her, her knees bent as if ready to lift her away, and Bertie heard her voice croak, 'Kit!' He got to his feet to go after his wife, then remembered his nakedness. He looked down at himself, and felt ridiculous standing there, covered in goose-pimples.

Elsie whimpered, 'She didn't say anything. Why didn't she say anything?'

Bertie gulped, grabbing his shirt, 'Maybe she doesn't really care.'

'Oh but she does.' Elsie tried to fix her brassiere, her hands shaking. 'By God she does. Did you see her eyes? She wanted to kill me, Bertie. Murder me – or you.'

And Bertie remembered the spider.

*   *   *

Elsie refused to walk with Bertie to the farm. She swerved from him when he tried to persuade her with an arm about her waist, and in her grey eyes was the expression of a fawn being chased by dogs.

Bertie put his hand through his hair. He felt harassed and furious, but not guilty any more. He walked slowly without Elsie, glad to be with neither woman.

So this, he thought, should be it. This should be the time and the place for a final choice.

He looked back at Elsie. She was dawdling, but following, her pink straw hat hanging from a limp hand.

He loved her. He wanted to console her, make her laugh again, yet he wanted to shake her, to tell her to grow up, to stop acting like a child.

She seemed like a schoolgirl on her way to the head-mistress's study, terrified of being caned, abused, punished.

He called gently, 'Come on, my love.' And she looked up at him instead of at her feet as they moved slowly over the grass. Then she ran a little, only to stop a few yards from him. Her mouth trembled. 'Bertie. Say you love me.'

'I love you.' He went to her, and she put her arms up around his neck.

Her kiss was anxious, demanding, clinging. His was detached, without emotion, and he cursed himself. Why couldn't he do what she needed now? Why couldn't he grip her dramatically and vow, 'My love, my love, to hell with Kit. You are all that matters.'

He felt empty, as if for months he had feared this moment, yet now it had come, there was only relief. No, he corrected his thoughts, not relief, not anything. Maybe shock. Maybe a sort of awe, but not relief.

He began walking again and she kept pace with him, her shoulders slumped, the hooks and eyes of the back of the lovely sweetpea-coloured voile dress not done up properly, because his fingers had been too impatient.

He couldn't think of anything adequate to say, and when he did speak it sounded inane and was out of tune with the day.

'You did well with new business this week.'

'Yes.' She watched her feet, listening to the slithering then she said petulantly, 'I told you I could be an agent.'

'True. You did.'

'I could be a good wife too.'

His inside cringed. He didn't want to be her husband. He didn't want to be anyone's husband. He breathed deeply. He wanted to escape, get away, stop his heart worry, stop it aching, stop it being split in two.

She said, 'I knew you wouldn't answer,' and he wondered if Kit would be standing in the little bedroom, the ceiling slanting and flaking above her, and her amber eyes shooting scarlet sparks as she quietly ground the words, 'It's her or me.'

In that instant Bertie knew that if she did, he would choose neither. He didn't wonder where he would go or when he would go. He just wanted to be completely alone.

He and Elsie went into the farmhouse together and Kit was sitting at the table preparing to eat ham and eggs and mushrooms.

Maud said, 'Ah, there you are then, Mr Hemsworthy. And you, Miss Buckley. If you'll sit yourselves down. The food is just ready.'

Kit ignored them, and, when a short while later he went to the bedroom, the suitcase was packed and waiting. He heard the girls saying goodbye to Gwen in the large bedroom along the passage, and he heard Maud wishing Kit a safe journey.

He realised it was time to go.

He went in to Gwen, and it was as if she knew, as if she sensed, there was a culmination. One thin white hand clawed the white fringed counterpane and her gaze was frantic.

He leaned over to kiss her brow and she put up her skeleton arms, her fingers clutching his face. 'Mr Hemsworthy. You've done so much for us. But our Elsie's never loved no other. Never.'

'Sshh,' he tried to calm her, moving her hands from him. Her lips were wet. 'You'll be all right.'

'Your wife don't know how much we've cost you.'

'No,' he said. 'She doesn't,' and knew that he and Gwen Buckley weren't talking about the same thing.

'Look after our Elsie, please – '

'Yes.'

'Look after our Elsie – '

He left the farm with a sick headache. Elsie sat in the back of the car with Linda and Emma. He could hear her softly sobbing.

Kit sat beside him, her hat pulled to one side so the brim

200

cut her from him. He drove for hours in a silence broken only by a shuddering sigh from Elsie and the whispered groan of, 'Oh Ma, oh Ma.'

His daughters sat as if they had been beaten, but he guessed it was because they knew instinctively that chatter wasn't wanted, that there had been, in their parlance, a row.

Within two hours of getting home the big double bed Kit and Bertie had shared for fourteen years had been dismantled, and in its place were two single beds, each partitioned and well-spaced from the other by the three-mirrored dressing-table.

Kit had still not spoken to Bertie, and now six-year-old-Emma sat up in one of the single beds and stared with bright inquisitive eyes at her father. 'I suppose,' she said, and her fringe stuck up where her fingers had threaded worriedly through it, 'that I'm in here because Linda and I talk too much. Even after we've said our prayers.'

'It's gone eleven o'clock, you ought to be asleep.' Bertie undressed in the discreet cover of the dividing furniture.

'Well, I don't like being in here.' Emma tightened her mouth so her cheeks dimpled, and Bertie got into the single bed allotted to him and groaned: it was hard, and he guessed he had a horsehair mattress. It was also cold with cotton sheets instead of the usual flannelette.

Emma complained, 'Linda didn't have to help Mummy move the beds. She could have said no.'

Bertie wetted his fingers and smothered the candle flame. The dark room filled with the smell of hot wax and he said wearily, 'Go to sleep Emma. Dad's tired.'

He heard her flop around angrily. 'We can't even have a proper light now. Mummy took the bulb out.' She banged her pillow. 'And she didn't tell Linda or me. We didn't know.'

'I didn't know either,' Bertie said, and in the next room Linda was peering from nose-high-pulled bedding, listening in the dark to her mother getting undressed, hearing the gentle slither of silk as Kit peeled off her stockings, the soft rustle of a chiffon nightie falling into place, then silence as Kit buttoned up the lace-trimmed neck.

'Night Mummy.'

'Get to sleep. It's late.'

'Why is Emma in with Daddy?'

'Go to sleep.'

Linda lay silent. She heard her mother sigh then whisper the twenty-third psalm: 'The Lord is my shepherd. I shall not want. He maketh me to lie down in green pastures . . . .' And the whispering suddenly stopped.

Linda listened hard, wondering why the prayer had stopped, and Kit began again. 'Our father who art in Heaven . . . .' Linda fell asleep and Kit lay awake, afraid to close her eyes in case it all appeared again . . . . He maketh me to lie down in green pastures . . . . Bertie and that girl lying – naked – in the centre of the little pine forest. Bertie and that girl chuckling together, contained in a private happiness: Adam and Eve. Each had had eyes lost in shadow, each had the pallor of having exhausted themselves, and each must have known, must have seen, how she, Kit, his wife, had felt.

Shocked. Electrified as if to death. Yet she had expected the scene, had gone searching for it. The shock was in experiencing her own passionate love for the first time. An overwhelming agony and realisation that bordered on hysteria.

So this was love. This hell. This mortification. This willingness to fight for a man, a determination to keep him when she should be discarding him. This unashamed admitting she needed him, even when he loved another. This jealousy of their nakedness, their capacity to copulate in the open air.

It had all engulfed her in a black trembling, while she hated Elsie Buckley from the depth of her soul: hated the young, lovely lively face, the rounded soft body, the ability to lie open to a man's gaze, shameless and adoring.

Kit writhed lower in the bed. Vicious thoughts spread

202

through her mind, schemes for revenge, for smashing the eighteen-year-old face, and sorrow at her own lost chances, the chances to keep Bertie for herself, the chances to enjoy passion, to banish the inhibitions that strangled her, to ease the terrible emotional frustration that, even there, among the heavy damp silence of the dark green trees, she had prevented from exploding.

She thought of the spider: its fat striped body between her forefinger and thumb, the pleasure of her slowly pressing, squeezing, and the moment of triumph when she flicked its uselessness away.

She would like to do that to Elsie Buckley. And to Bertie. The filthy beasts. Like animals in the wild. All the time, deep at the back of her mind, there seemed to be a wheel laden with thoughts that turned faster and faster, thoughts that told her it had all been her own fault, that she had created the forest scene by her frigidity, which wasn't frigidity at all, but a fear, a deep-rooted fear of everything carnal, of sinning, of dirt, of self-indulgence, of being possessed for lust alone.

She tossed. She envied Elsie Buckley, envied her laugh, her freedom to be happy in the middle of poverty and, dear God, she envied the way she lay, a hand resting lightly on her groin, in a pine wood in Malvern.

It was dawn before Kit dozed and by then all her fervour for revenge had eased away. She knew that she would do nothing. She would wait until their ardour had burned itself out. She would be steely, resolute, waiting like any spider in its own web, and then, when Elsie Buckley left, as Kit felt sure she would eventually do, she, Kit, would open her arms to Bertie, and start all over again.

*   *   *

It was Wednesday before Elsie was due in the office again, and Bertie and Kit waited for her with a mixture of emotions. Bertie wondered what he could say to her, and Kit wondered if she would have the audacity to come at all.

Elsie arrived at eight-thirty, as usual, and Bertie was already in the office. He was waiting for her, counting the seconds in an agony of suspense, yet when he heard the gate click as she opened it and his heart fluttered with relief and pleasure, he marched from the office to the kitchen.

Kit made no comment, and it was Linda who ran to let Elsie in, although there would be little for her to do. Because of Easter the agents would collect double next Friday and Monday, so there would be no men dallying, laughing, having their accounts checked today.

Elsie collected what mail there was from the coconut mat in the porch and took it into the office, before coming to the kitchen.

When, finally, they heard the ridiculously high thin heels coming along the passage Bertie's heart pounded deafeningly. Linda and Emma glanced at each other, then at their plates, while their hands kept busy with marmalade and knives and toast.

'Good morning,' Elsie said. There was no smile in her voice, no fear, no wavering.

Kit ignored her. 'Linda, do you want more tea?' And she became busy with the toasting-fork before the fire.

'No thank you Mummy.'

Bertie turned in his chair and looked at Elsie, and if ever he had doubted his love for her, he didn't now. It welled up in him like a full tide. She looked grotesque. The make-up was thick: not only the rouge and accentuated rosebud mouth, but black mascara in many layers, eye-shadow in deep blue, and an eyebrow pencil making black etchings where she had overplucked. Her fine soft goldy-brown hair was almost black with the amount of sugary water she had plastered on to it, and the stiff little kiss curls framed her face from earlobe to earlobe.

He exclaimed, 'For God's sake – !' Her gaze settled on him, huge and scared. 'You look like a bloody clown!'

Her scarlet lips hardly moved as she said, 'Thank you,' then she turned and hurried back to the office.

Bertie swore and Kit stood with her back to him,

watching him in the wall mirror. Bertie threw down his serviette and left the chair.

Emma said, 'When I grow up I'm going to dye my hair red. To match my rouge and lipstick,' and Bertie paused, smiled at his younger daughter, and a little gasp of self-derision escaped from him. He sat down again and Kit said calmly, 'More tea, Bertie?' It was the first time she had addressed him in three days, and Bertie wished she hadn't bothered.

'Yes please.' He pushed his cup and saucer towards her, avoiding looking at her. Her hands shook and the lid fell from the teapot, hitting his fingers. He moved them sharply and she rescued the lid and slammed it onto the teapot before replacing it on the hob. He was deep in misery. Here was his family. In the warmth of his home. All he had sweated to build up, and there was Elsie, her face beneath the atrocious make-up puffy with unhappiness.

'Blast! he gritted. 'Oh damn and blast everything,' then his gaze shot up, right into Kit's, and he saw satisfaction there. For what seemed a lifetime he absorbed what he saw: Kit, his wife, waiting for revenge, maybe a train of unconscious psychological revenges, like not putting the teapot lid on properly, then feeling satisfied when it fell in all its steaming heat on his fingers.

Bertie smiled without showing his teeth, and Linda was saying, 'Daddy! Look at Emma. She's spilled her tea in her saucer.'

Bertie left them and went to the office. In there the atmosphere was no easier.

He dictated letters, queried matters, made telephone calls, then said impersonally, 'You can finish at lunchtime. Take the afternoon off,' and Elsie turned, a pathetic child from the world of poverty and hopelessness, trying to hide behind a mask of Woolworth's cosmetics, the glass beads about her neck reflecting the grey light from the wide window. She said, 'I'm sorry,' and gulped.

'What for?' He leaned forward, his elbows on his desk, his face as grey as the light.

'You look awful too.'

'I feel awful too.'

'At least I tried to hide my face.'

'I'd prefer it to the one you have on.'

'It was my fault. I took you to the woods.'

'I am a grown man, Elsie. I chose to go with you.'

Her fingers fiddled in her lap and she watched them. She said, 'Coming home in the car was bad enough. Neither you, nor her, talking – '

Bertie breathed in deeply and sat back. He stretched his legs under the desk and crossed his ankles. He said quietly, 'When Kit and I married it wasn't for love, Elsie. War makes you do strange things. It heightens things like loneliness. You need to belong somewhere, to have a base, a home, you need someone, and I had no one. My parents are gone. They were in France, you know. Doing their bit.'

'Are they dead?' Her face was blank.

'I have no idea. I suppose so.'

Elsie looked at her fingers again; they were a typist's fingers, agile and quick. She said, 'Kit loves you.'

'No.' He reached for a pen because he needed something to hold. 'Kit doesn't love me. She loves what I can give her. What she married me for. A nice home, carpets, a car – that's all.'

'I love you.' She waited for his echoing avowal, but he said nothing.

'Bertie, I won't ever lure you on again. I promise. I'll be a good girl.' She licked her lips. 'Are you going to give me the sack? Carruthers said – '

The word divorce crossed Bertie's mind and was banished as fast as it came. He threw down the pen and rubbed the back of his neck slowly. There must be some way out of the morass. How the hell did he get into it?

He said, 'You had better get off home. I'll see you in the morning.'

She went to the door then stopped. She came back into the room. 'Bertie. I need loving,' and her voice trembled.

He left his chair and held out his arms. He needed loving

206

too, and she came to him. He kissed her, thrilling as she kissed him back, no longer a furtive cuddle in the office. Kit knew what was going on. Kit was accepting it. He grimaced at the cheap-scented taste of her lipstick, then waited while she rubbed it away with her handkerchief. He nuzzled her to him and tried to run his fingers through her sugar-stiff hair. He chuckled a little as the tension of the last few days began to ebb away.

'Tomorrow, Miss Buckley,' he said quietly, 'I want you in this office looking clean and natural. Do you understand?'

'Yes sir,' and her fingers on his neck were delicately sensuous.

'You have a lovely face, a beautiful face, Miss Buckley, and you must never hide it from me again.'

'It wasn't from you, Bertie. It was from the neighbours – and everybody. If they'd a' seen I bin cryin' all the time – '

He kissed her again and happiness was fleetingly reborn, warm and tender about them, then he held her away. 'You'd better be off. See you in the morning.'

As she went Bertie watched her from the window. She looked back and blew a kiss, and he felt a little wave of irritation; didn't she realise the neighbours might see? Then she was walking away fast with that odd little walk brought about by the too-high heels, and he wondered how they could possibly love each other. Was it a quirk of nature?

He rubbed a hand over his face. 'I'm forty-eight,' he mused. 'Thirty years her senior, and she talks of luring me on. Isn't it me leading her astray? Shouldn't I be shot for mucking about with a young girl?'

He sat at his desk, lit a cigarette, and tried to think clearly, but when he gave up he was merely more heartsick, and the telephone was demanding his immediate attention.

A week later Kit stood at the foot of the stairs and watched him fall down them. He landed on the hard cold lino against the hallstand then dragged himself up, onto the bottom stair, both hands grasping his ankle, his face twisted and scarlet. He glared up at Kit, ten days' enmity reaching snapping point between them, and he gasped, 'You bloody wished it on me.'

'It's God punishing you.'

The pain was shooting up his leg; 'Chr-ist, I've broken my ankle.'

'Good. Pity you didn't break your neck.'

'Bitch!'

'Beast!' She tried to move past him, to climb the stairs, but he refused to budge, crouched, the pain in his limb all-engulfing.

He glowered at her feet. 'Even the bloody breakfast was ruined.'

'It wouldn't have hurt you to keep an eye on the bacon.'

'It was black. Like a cinder.'

'And I broke your egg – ' Kit was nearer hysterics than Bertie would ever think possible, ' – of course. On purpose.'

He stood up, on one leg, leaning against the wall, not liking the disadvantage of sitting below his adversary, and Kit ran up the stairs. She began singing, and Bertie felt his control slipping. For ten days life had been hell. For ten days the house had been full of vindictive tension so thick he felt one could slice it.

And Elsie hadn't come out of the office to help him. Fury and misery fought for supremacy as he groaned with pain. He took the hook-topped walking stick from the hallstand beside him and used it to hobble to his desk, then he sat, depleted. He had had enough. Neither woman gave a damn about him and he, bloody fool, had almost let them ruin his life.

The telephone rang. Elsie answered it, watching him, afraid to speak in case she said the wrong thing. Each day his temper grew shorter. Each day she felt like a leper, and yesterday he hadn't kissed her at all. She put her hand over the mouthpiece. 'It's your mother-in-law. Mrs Nolan.'

'Tell her I'm not in.'

'She says she knows you are.'

'Tell my wife her mother wants to speak to her,' and he took the telephone while Elsie hurried away.

Lorraine Nolan's high-falutin voice came over the wires. 'Albert, I have just had the most frightful letter from Kitty. About an incident at Malvern.'

'Go to hell Lorraine. I have just broken my ankle.'

'Good. A pity it wasn't your neck.'

'Your husband's not so marvellous either.'

'He was abroad, Albert. He never insulted me by bringing his dung home . . .'. Bertie groaned. His brain was clogged with emotions, thoughts. He saw Kit come in, her face set with tight lips and flaring nostrils, followed by a timorous Elsie.

'Miss Buckley,' she snapped, 'kindly go into the other room and wait until you are called.' Elsie went, round-shouldered, and Kit took the phone.

Bertie rolled his trouser-leg up and his sock down. His ankle wasn't even swelling. He prodded it gently, hoping to prove it was broken, but it wasn't. He took off his shoe, gasping, and Kit finished the telephone call and marched out.

He rolled his trouser-leg down. A little tapping came on the door and he called, 'Come in.' Elsie did so, piqued he had forgotten she was in the other room, and she saw the impatience on his face because she had knocked.

She hurried to her desk and stared at her type-writer. 'Bertie,' she said plaintively. 'It's impossible, isn't it?'

'What is?'

'You and me – '

Then the gate clicked. There was a tramp of feet, the glass door opened with a rush. Heavy steps filled the passage, and Carruthers stormed in.

Bertie looked up in astonishment. 'What the hell are you doing here? You're barging in like you're raiding a den!'

'Orders,' retorted Carruthers, and sought a chair.

'Aren't you going to take off your coat? Or is this a flying visit?' Bertie tried to fit his painful leg into a different position.

Carruthers sat with his back to Elsie. He didn't acknowledge her and she bent low over her books, her thin brows
raised in mute fear. Carruthers opened his overcoat, then
his jacket. One could see his waistcoat creased deeply
where his chest should have been, and rounded out, taut
over his enormous stomach. He rested a fat white hand on
Bertie's desk. He was gasping and panting, purple-
cheeked.

'Did you walk or run from the station?' Bertie asked
drily.

'I took a taxi.'

'I think I've broken my ankle.'

'Good. Should have been your neck.'

Bertie groaned and Elsie glanced at him. He gave her a
silent message to carry on with her work.

Carruthers sat with his knees widespread, his globular
eyes shining damply. 'I'm returning to London as soon as
possible.'

'Must be something important that brought you down.'

'Could mean you going on the means test.'

Bertie's inside turned over with a terrifying jerk that left
him shaking. He kept his gaze on Carruthers's purple face,
his senses alert, instantly ready for any trouble that was
coming.

Carruthers said pompously, 'You appear to assume
that we in Head Office have been sitting on our back-
sides. Doing nothing these last weeks. There are changes
everywhere.' He took out a large white handkerchief
and mopped his eyes. 'Sometimes I am convinced the
Old Man is taking monkey glands. He is making a clean
sweep before he finally retires. Reshaping the whole
cahoots.

Bertie turned to the picture of his employer that hung
over the filing cabinet. It had been presented to him before
he'd even had a desk, and the Old Man's self-satisfaction
oozed from it: there he sat against a sepia background, one
hand resting on the top of a silver-knobbed cane, the other
on the plush arm of the chair, his face lifted, the trimmed

white moustache and goatee beard immaculate. Bertie had once seen him paralytic after a sumptuous dinner, so the airs in the picture didn't worry him too much – until today. Bertie said, his voice slightly uneven, 'So there are more signs of his sons coming into the firm?'

'One is in. The chinless wonder from Eton. That's part of the trouble. He's giving the Old Man ideas. Progress and modernisation. Wants everyone over forty out.'

Bertie leaned back and put his right hand in his trouser pocket. His fingers closed over the precious car keys, and there were the house keys, symbols of all he owned, all he had earned, all he was. He rubbed the keys, like Aladdin rubbing the lamp, hoping that nothing dreadful was going to happen, hoping for a miracle, then he said, 'Elsie. Make yourself scarce. Tell Kit that Carruthers is here, then fix up some sandwiches.' He watched her prepare to go, and couldn't think why he was sending her. Then he sat up, attentive, and took the gold watch from his waistcoat pocket. He said to Carruthers, 'You must have left London early.'

'Seven o'clock.'

'Will you lunch with us?'

'No. Thank you all the same.'

Elsie stood by the door, watching and listening, her soap-clean face anxious, her lips eager to speak.

Bertie said, 'Lunch could be ready in less then an hour.'

Carruthers shook his head so his chins quivered. 'I have more calls to make.'

Bertie nodded to Elsie, a gesture to go, and she almost smiled though her mouth was quivering with nervousness. 'If it's all because of me,' she sounded hoarse, 'because I didn't leave . . . .'

Carruthers still ignored her. Bertie said abruptly, 'Hop it! Make the sandwiches and let us know when they're done.'

She went, closing the door softly, the catch clicking into place, and Bertie said to Carruthers, 'How would a whisky and soda go down?'

Carruthers relaxed, his heavy jowls drooping. 'A tonic, dear boy, a tonic.'

Bertie hobbled to the filing cabinet and slid open the bottom drawer. He was trying not to think, not to jump to conclusions. He took the bottle of whisky and the soda syphon and, with two glasses in his jacket pocket, he went back to the desk. Carruthers said, 'What's the matter with your foot?'

'Fell downstairs. Just before you came. I told you. I've broken my ankle.'

Carruthers removed his coat and flung it over Elsie's chair. Both men drank; Carruthers quickly, then sucking his full tongue and staring at his near-empty glass. Bertie drank slowly, swilling the drink around his mouth thoughtfully before he swallowed. A group of youths passed the house, their voices and laughter sharp in the heavy April air. Bertie said, 'Right then. What's the trouble? Shoot!'

'She's chiselling the company.'

'Who?'

Carruthers stared at Bertie, and Bertie's look of curiosity turned to blank astonishment. 'Who?' he repeated, but he knew the answer.

'You know damn well who!'

'She wouldn't. She wouldn't know how!'

Carruthers sighed deeply then stretched and rubbed his fat palms on his waistcoat. 'I'm too old for this lark. Charging around. Trying to convince myself you're only a bloody fool and she's the thief.'

Bertie poured himself another whisky. It was early in the day, but a lot was happening. He took time before speaking. He had to get control over his voice, his movements, find out if Carruthers was bluffing, causing a stink in his efforts to get rid of Elsie, his efforts to save the firm's image from her lack of class.

'Well,' Bertie said at last. 'Come on. Out with it. What's it all about?'

'You've had her working as a part-time agent.'

'Very part-time. A few neighbours and friends.'

212

'You've let her investigate claims. Five fires and a death that we know of.'

'She's capable.'

'By God she is. Have you verified any of the new business she brought in? She brings in a hell of a lot for a girl who works in this office full-time and does her canvassing at odd moments.'

'Her brother helps her. He's quite good on the knocker. Has a pony and cart selling wood around the better houses. He talks insurance at the same time. The commission helps them.'

Carruthers's fat jaw dropped. 'Selling wood! Talks insurance!'

Bertie rested his arms on the desk, his face set in a hard smile that meant nothing, his eyes veiled of all expression. 'You'd better unburden yourself, old boy.'

Carruthers slapped his knee, exasperated. 'A lot of it is dud. A lot of her new members are already dead. She's been foxing you, Albert, pulling the wool right down over your blasted dozy eyes.'

'Bogey business?' Bertie felt a sledgehammer hit him.

'Bogey business. Bogey fires. This firm has been insuring names off gravestones. Go to that Danygraig cemetery. See for yourself. Your new customers are lined up neat and Bristol-fashion. With daffodils to show they're remembered.'

'No!' It was a cry. 'No, she wouldn't.'

'Yes! She would. She has. Wake up, man, wake up.'

'You're a bloody liar!'

'And I hope you had a good run for your money. The Old Man holds you responsible.' Carruthers held his glass for another filling and it took Bertie some time to realise what he was doing, then he said lamely, 'Help yourself, for God's sake.'

Carruthers did. He was cumbersome, wheezing, as he reached for the bottle. 'Not too much of the strong stuff, heh? More soda. My stomach won't take it. This investigation has sickened me, Albert. Literally.' He glanced at

Bertie. 'Shock to you?' And Bertie nodded. How could Elsie prove to be so two-faced? A thief?

'This one got you, old boy?' Carruthers poured himself another drink carefully. 'By the balls.' Then he savoured the whisky in his red mouth, giving Bertie time to recover.

At last Bertie said, 'It's hard to think straight – ' He shook his head, punch-drunk. 'How bad is my name in London?'

'Bad where the son is concerned. Not cricket, and all that. The Old Man's playing it softly. You've been a good worker. Built up this area from nothing. Have a good wife, and so on. I put a word in for you.' He watched Bertie with his protruding marble eyes. 'Get rid of the girl, Albert. See every ha'penny is refunded and your job might be safe.'

Bertie thought of Elsie in the pine wood, Elsie saying in a trembling voice, 'Bertie, I need to be loved,' and he had loved her. He might even have left everything for her, gone with her to the ends of the earth, trusting her, loving her, and all the time she was dropping him in it. All the time that she was smiling and laughing she was betraying his trust, ruining him, defrauding the company.

Carruthers was saying, 'I don't doubt everything will be remembered, to use in evidence against you evermore, but it is better than prison.'

'Prison?'

'Prison, old boy. Accessory after the fact or some such.'

Both men sipped slowly, Bertie trying to think, then Carruthers relaxed back as if relieved of a burden; it was over; he had said it.

Bertie stared up at the little oblong of sky beyond the window, and the red-bricked chimneys that helped frame it. He took a deep breath, then a corner of his mouth lifted in a derisive smile. 'You've got to hand it to her. It's been done so often one stops looking for it.' He gazed back at Carruthers. 'You just don't expect it to happen right under your nose.'

'She'll have the shirt off your back. They live by their wits, these types. You've seen them as kids over there, barefoot and brazen-mouthed. What made you blasted well think they could grow into young ladies?'

'I thought she was the exception – '

'We've paid out a fire claim to a policy-holder who was already dead and buried. You must have suspected. You must have sensed something.'

'No, I didn't.' Bertie frowned, trying to think. He hadn't known, yet, in the back of his mind, he had. He had seen her bring the new business in and attend to it. He had seen her come in too early in the morning so that she attended to the mail before anyone else, and she often replied to it as well. He had seen her nip out in the middle of the day 'to investigate a fire', then she had given him the quotation with a pen, and he had signed, every time, loving her, trusting her, only too glad to apportion tasks and responsibilities.

'She had characters out of books as well,' Carruthers said. 'Her characters insured with us, had fires, and we paid out on them. In three months she's caused havoc.'

'Three months?'

'Ever since she started collecting John Davies's book. She could book up a name, use her commission to pay the ten premiums, make a fast profit on a fire, then lapse the policy.' Carruthers leaned forward, his hands on his widespread knees. 'I also suspect that very few genuine claims got the total cash Head Office allotted to them.'

He stopped talking as a knock came on the door. Bertie sat back and called, 'Come in.' It was Kit, smiling, her old charming self. 'Shall I bring the tea and sandwiches? Or are the big white chiefs too engrossed in their pow-wow? Hello Carruthers. Back again?'

He stood up, awkward, ungainly and embarrassed. Bertie expected him to blush as well, but he didn't. 'Hello dear lady. I'm – er – sorry about this – '

'About what?'

'Albert will tell you.' He gazed heavy-lidded at her shining black hair, at the flame-coloured dress.

She said, 'Are you staying the night?'

215

'Unfortunately no.'

Bertie watched his wife and Carruthers smile at each other, then Kit backed slowly. 'I'll tell Elsie to bring –'

'No!' Bertie said sharply.

'Oh?'

'Shut the door.'

Kit did so then stood against it, her amber eyes glistening like a cat's beneath the strong black brows. 'It's about her?'

'Yes.' Bertie nodded. 'And bogey business.'

Kit's gaze travelled from Bertie to the fat man, then she said calmly, 'We understand why she did it, Carruthers. She's desperate for money.'

'She is not alone, dear lady. She is not alone,' Carruthers gruffed. 'Albert should have sacked her months ago.' He groped inside his jacket for his cigars and Kit opened the door. 'I'll get the food.' Carruthers paused, looking at the cigar, then lit up and Bertie asked, 'Have you any idea how much the bill is?'

'An idea. That's all. In excess of thirty pounds.'

'How much? That's a fortune!'

'Can't be far off it. From what I've seen. She'll have to pay it back.'

'She hasn't got thirty pence!'

'Head Office will drag her, and you, through the courts. The son is hell-bent on it as an example to all other evil-doers.' Carruthers speculated on the end of his cigar, and Kit came back with a rush, as if afraid she might miss the conversation. Bertie sugared his tea, thinking of Gwen in Malvern, and his agreement to take Tom Buckley to see her, to look after 'our Elsie'.

Carruthers said, as if guessing his thoughts, 'It's instant dismissal for her. Now. And the money returned within ten days.'

Bertie's blue eyes were appealing, still hoping there was a mistake. 'You can't demand money off her like that! You need proof!'

Carruthers laid the partly-smoked cigar on the black metal ashtray. It flickered minute red stars, then settled to

216

slowly burning itself out, wafting silent blue smoke. 'We have proof.' Carruthers took a sandwich and bit it. 'Salmon, Kit? Nice too,' then to Bertie, 'Remember me querying a signature on a receipt last time I was down?' His fat lips wobbled as he munched and his bulbous eyes were bland.

'Receipt?'

'A fire claim that had been paid. A Mrs Travers. Wern View. Our Miss Buckley forged it. Before Christmas.'

Bertie put an elbow on his desk, needing support.

'Forgery, Albert. Forgery as well as money by false pretences.' Carruthers kept looking at the rest of the sandwich. 'In that case the claimant really was a policy-holder, alive, but she was diddled. Diddled.' Bertie kept staring and listening. Carruthers went on, 'You let Miss Buckley investigate and you let Miss Buckley pay it.'

Kit asked quietly, 'What tipped you off? How did you start to investigate?'

'Margaret Ann Davies,' Carruthers said pompously, and tugged the knees of his trousers into greater comfort. 'Maggie. John's buxom wife. Maggie and I – er, get on quite well, you know.' He was smug. 'I received the usual card and note at Christmas, but this year I replied to it. She wrote me again.' Carruthers smoothed the underside of his many chins with a forefinger. 'I don't believe she realised what she was telling me. I just twigged. Put two and two together.'

'And made five.'

'Ah no.' Carruthers bent his head, his eyes looking up at Bertie. 'I only made three at that time. The two and two making five came later. I had previously commented on the number of claims on John's debit. Particularly the number of fires. I came down. Looked around. Met some policy-holders. Read some gravestones, that's an old gag.' He looked bulbously at Bertie. 'The girl is hogtied, Albert. And so are you for allowing it.'

Bertie pushed away the small plate Kit had given him.

He could smell Phul-Nana and feel the softness of a young naked girl in the cold spring dampness of pine woods. The pit of his belly was dragging and his legs were losing their strength. He looked at Kit and tried to balance his thoughts, to be sensible, not to rush to Elsie and shake hell out of her. He kept staring at Kit, telling himself how fortunate he was to have her, that she was his wife, dependable and trustworthy.

She stared back at him, and her eyes were accusing. Bertie put both elbows on the desk and his head in his hands. 'I'll sack her all right,' he said. 'She can get to hell out of it.' He thought of John Davies. And Maggie. Maggie with the big breasts and big laugh. He would have staked his life on Maggie's loyalty, yet she had done this. 'Maggie Davies,' he breathed. 'Who would have thought it?'

Carruthers flicked crumbs from his waistcoat. 'John dislikes you. He is also insecure. Expected the Buckley girl to usurp him. Every manager has an agent like that. Can't be helped.'

'He'll be out. On his rotten arse.'

'I think not.' Carruthers's fat face held a hint of sympathy. 'I think not. Finger up the right hole. I assume you know that.'

'You mean she sends Christmas cards to the Old Man as well?'

Carruthers nodded. 'The Old Man never replies, of course.'

Bertie rubbed his face, fury and frustration rising. He wanted to laugh aloud in self-derision; he had felt guilty about loving Elsie Buckley while John and Maggie Davies were licking the Old Man's backside, and Elsie was chiselling the firm. He muttered, 'By God, I'm a bloody fool!'

Carruthers said comfortably, 'Have you read the papers this morning? Over forty per cent of people in this county alone are out of work. Shocking state of affairs. Shocking.'

Bertie rolled his eyes. 'And me next. My neck on the chopping-block.'

'You took her on. You sack her!' Carruthers said, and made a massive sweeping gesture.

The anguish was flooding Bertie, drowning him, saturating him, and he went to the door, grimacing as his ankle hurt. His voice bellowed down the passage, 'Elsie! Here. At once!' And she came running, as though she had been listening and waiting for his call.

'Yes, Bertie yes?' Her unmade-up face was tense, haggard, the white lines deep from nostrils to mouth corners. She came into the room and stood with her hands clasped before her. 'Yes Bertie? Yes?'

'You know what it's all about! You bloody know!'

The kiss curls stuck stiffly before her ears, her pale blue dress not covering her knees. 'Yes . . . .' Her lips quivered and her grey eyes became immense.

Bertie's voice was like splinters of flint. 'You're sacked. Right now. Get the hell out of it before I kick your arse all down the street.'

She gazed quickly, imploringly, at Kit, then at Carruthers, then she turned, and they heard her at the hallstand, opening the small drawer and getting her thin cotton gloves. She came back into the room and went to her desk. She took her handbag from its deep drawer, and her face was soaked with silent tears. 'I'm sorry, Bertie. Oh Kit. I'm so sorry. I've always been a jinx on people. On anyone who ever tried to help me.' Her eyes and nose were wet, red. 'I'll pay it all back. I promise. As soon as my mother's better.' She fumbled with the buttons on her thin tweed coat. 'My father drank most of it. It kept him out of the house – '

'Get out!' Bertie gritted. He had loved her, trusted her . . . .

She rushed for the passage and Kit followed her. Bertie glowered at Carruthers and listened to the snuffling outside the door. He said, 'Your methods stink. Why the hell can't you investigate these things openly?'

The fat man shuddered. 'For me, next week will be worse. A widower with five small children. He's been getting away with it for years.'

'This bloody firm has never paid a decent wage. It could have paid Elsie over ten bob a week and not noticed it. Do you know it's only over the last year that I've had a salary? I started here with nothing. Nothing.' Bertie limped to the window, staring out. 'I got commission on what I collected. There were no members so I collected nothing.' He stormed on as Carruthers nodded, agreeing. 'Every damn member in these four hundred square miles is my work. My slog. While the Old Man gets stinking bloody drunk on the best, and sends his stupid sons to the finest schools. On my back!'

'It's a job, Albert.' Carruthers shrugged, his big face weary. 'One is free to leave and work elsewhere if one so desires.'

'Money! Power! All the time it's those with money and power trampling on those poor bloody fools without it.'

'You have money,' Carruthers said softly, 'and power. To a certain extent.'

Bertie stopped ranting to turn and stare, then he sighed. 'Yes, of course. In comparison to the Buckleys, I have money. And power.'

He looked back at that oblong of sky: a tiny piece of blue was threatening to split the grey. He heard Elsie's high thin heels hitting the tiles as she ran for the gate, then he watched her run along the pavement. She was hunched into her handkerchief. He watched her growing more grey, more distant, and he had an ache to run after her, to catch her to him, to nurse her, to tell her the whole bloody insurance world could go up in smoke as far as he was concerned.

Carruthers said, 'Well, I won't stay. There's an official letter in the post for you. I came to try and make it easier.' He stood up, clumsy, his lungs wheezing badly now. He struggled into his overcoat, and for a moment he patted his pockets as if unsure of his next move, then he crossed to Bertie and put a hand on his shoulder. 'Count your blessings, Albert. Count your blessings.'

Bertie didn't turn to him.

'So I'm going.' Carruthers stood, as if going was the last thing he wanted to do.

'All right,' Bertie said, and Elsie had gone from the street. Disappeared from his life, as though fate had finally made his choice for him.

'Anything I can do?' Carruthers asked.

'You've done enough.'

Bertie heard Kit let Carruthers out, and he came from the window. He felt bereaved. The lump of sorrow was a solid sickness beneath his ribs.

Kit said flatly, 'He's gone.'

'I heard him.'

'Would you like more tea? Fresh?'

'No. Yes. Anything you like.'

He heard her placing the used dishes on the tray, but he couldn't turn to look at her. He felt publicly shamed and betrayed, yet his love for Elsie was still there, pity and love, tangible and terrible. He didn't want to be in this office; he wanted to be with Elsie, cuddling and loving, saying, 'My love, my love, I need loving.' He was trembling. Kit paused at the door. 'I told Elsie you quite understood.'

'Thank you.' She could have been a stranger.

'I couldn't do anything else. The girl's demented.' Kit came back into the room, resting the tray on his desk. 'Bertie.'

He didn't answer, and she went on, her voice lacking its usual assured tone, 'I don't enjoy seeing you so heavily involved with another woman. I didn't enjoy seeing a younger woman naked – '

'For God's sake – '

'I'm trying to say that I'm making an effort to be compassionate, because – well, I'm no good to you in bed and – Bertie – did you know? She's got it too. The doctor told her last night. Consumption.'

Kit went out, leaving him. The phone rang and Bertie turned and watched it. It stood like a large black candle, ringing and ringing, but his arm wouldn't rise to answer it.

He went to the hallstand and put on his hat and coat,

221

ramming the hat down hard so it almost touched the top of his ears. Then he turned up the coat collar as if to hide in it, and called down the passage, 'Kit! I'm going to the beach.' He went out and was halfway down the street before he remembered his ankle. He swore and sat on the low wall skirting a house. He wanted to weep, overwhelmed by pain in his limb, in his chest, by mortification, fury, and by his complete and utter lack of comprehension of women.

CHAPTER NINE

Sometimes the longing for Elsie Buckley swept through Bertie in torrential waves that left him weak, and other times he deliberately thought of her, of the expression in her grey eyes and the quirk at the corners of her mouth, the way they had laughed together, the vary aura of her nearness.

Twice he drove over the iron bridge, unaware of the greasy green waters beneath him or the ships moaning in the blue mist, and he stopped the car opposite the great stone wall on which the terrace of little cracked houses was built, as if damming back the enormous black hill behind them.

He sat and watched the house, his hands gripping the steering wheel, ready to drive away if she appeared, drive away to avoid embarrassment, yet longing for her to appear, running, barefoot and laughing, shiny-faced, down the steps and across the puddle-filled, horse-dung-covered road to him. He would hug her, squeeze her into him, into his soul, make her part of his skin and bones so that she could never be separated from him again, the musky scent of her Phul-Nana swamping his nostrils and closing him safely into the world of happiness.

But she never appeared. One of the curtains in the bedroom moved once and Bertie stared, his head bent up awkwardly to see beneath the car hood, his heart suffocating him in case it was Elsie and she would wave, smile, blow a kiss; but no face ever appeared.

Twice he thought he saw her in the street, and he ran after her, touching her shoulder, panting, 'Elsie!' But each time a strange face turned to him, a strange and distrustful face. He wondered now, if ever he did see her again, would he touch her, or fear it wasn't her at all?

Sometimes he went to his club where Harriet of the aged wrinkled face and long yellow neck brought him a glass of whisky, neat, on a tray, followed by another glass, and yet another glass, then Bertie wandered a little unsteadily down Wind Street, skirting the docks, walking over the smaller bridge with its high arc sides, and the wind suddenly coming strong and fresh from the pier, gathering some of its smell from the fish market, the trawlers and the seaweed drying on the sand.

His inside was strangled with longing for her, and strangled with indignant fury at what she had done to him: made use of him to defraud the firm. He understood her, pitied her, yet he still couldn't forgive her.

She was a kid between the devil and the deep. Her world was of near starvation and consumption; diphtheria, scarlet fever, abortions, suicide; while in his world people gave him money, poured it onto his desk every Wednesday, and it was counted again every Thursday; shining silver, from tiddlers to half-crowns; notes crinkled, springy, brown ten-shilling notes, green pound notes, and sometimes the big white five-pound note; all handled, fingered into elastic bands, and him not expecting Elsie to be aware of what it could do for her and her mother. It was like showing a starving dog a slice of beef and expecting it not to touch.

Night was the worst time, when the house went silent, and he had to get out or go crazy. The beach was big. He could walk there alone. The sand slid beneath his feet. It was dark, black before him. The sea slithered in gentle waves, coming in curves that varied with the slope of the beach, and he heard the shells crunching beneath his shoes, felt his leg muscles tugging as he forced them to walk.

A terrible weariness had gripped him, deadening, dragging. He paused to draw breath; he who had run with Elsie feeling like a boy, now paused to draw breath, old, emotionally battered, so deep in grief that no common sense could drag him from it.

224

Tonight he looked up towards the wall where the black-ness in its shadow was infinite. There was no momentary movement, no sound of a voice. Up there the down-and-outs slept. Men who had protected their country. Had fought a stinking war in which millions died or were wounded. Men who had brought their scarred minds and bodies home to the mother country, only to have her mess rubbed in their faces. No jobs, no homes, and no money. Why should they need money, the means test said, they had no homes to keep up.

Bertie lit a cigarette, hiding his face and lighter in the top of his coat, his back to the strong breeze. He had a ridiculous feeling of satisfaction, of achievement. He had lit the cigarette first time, breeze or no breeze. As he straightened, a man appeared before him, grey, ragged, skeleton-faced, hunched and shivering.

'Evening guv'nor.' He touched his forelock.

'Evening,' Bertie said, and nodded, understanding. He threw the packet of cigarettes to the man. 'Share them,' he said.

The man caught the packet, his eyes sharp, accustomed to the darkness.

Bertie said, 'Want a newspaper?' He took the folded paper from his overcoat pocket and held it out. The man shuffled forward and took it slowly, suspiciously. One could so easily be run in for vagrancy.

'It's all right,' Bertie said, quietly. 'I don't need it.'

'Thanks guv'nor.' The man shuffled away, his toes jutting in shoes that had caps separated from the soles, and Bertie walked on. He hadn't read the paper. The man would need it as a blanket. When dawn came the beach would be beautiful, but icy; the homeless would be like fallen ninepins trying to sleep in the lee of the wall.

Bertie shuddered, not because he was cold, but because life was cruel, and sometimes life terrified him because men were bits of flotsam, and because he couldn't understand why, at forty-eight, he who had always been so level-headed was in this confused state over an eighteen-year-old girl who wasn't even of his class.

He avoided the spot where he and Elsie had lain; where she had run and he had gripped her ankle, where she had sprawled, squealing, the golden silvery grains in tumultuous movement about her.

He avoided the iron steps to the bridge that crossed the road. He took the slipway instead, crossing the railway track, then skirting the park, his footsteps echoing in the dark, breeze-ridden emptiness.

Prince Edward Road was long and he panted, his lips apart, and relief flooded him as he got inside his own front door, stood before his own hallstand in his own well-lit passage. He placed his homburg on its hook, then took off his overcoat and hung it beneath the hat. Kit opened the kitchen door. She was in her dressing-gown, ready for bed. 'Kettle's boiling,' she called, and his grief for Elsie had to be suppressed again, clamped down, hidden once more, curdled with the guilt of loving her at all when he was too old, married, and she was a guttersnipe no different from the pick-pockets in town.

He went to his chair and sank into it. One day he would turn it upside down, renew the springs, nail new canvas straps in place.

Kit handed him a cup of tea. 'Been down the beach?' she said.

'Yes, but it's nice to be home,' and he meant it.

Kit watched him. He looked nothing like the man she had married. His tiredness was like an illness and, at times, a dread that felt tangible gripped her, that he, too, was sliding into consumption.

Just as Maggie had worried about John, so Kit wondered what she would do if Bertie did go into the wasting disease. How could she save him? The sanatoriums were full and a long way out of town, hidden by banks of trees in hilly country where only volunteers ventured. Kit had read that consumption was caught through the mouth: a victim spitting in the street, the mucus drying, then being blown by the wind onto other people's lips and noses – or through kissing.

She turned her head away instinctively, not wanting to see Bertie's lips, nor to think of him kissing Elsie. The scene in the pine wood was indelible, like a tragedy from childhood that grows more terrible in the memory as time goes on.

She sighed, regretting his experience. He was stupid for not having heeded her warnings, but he was a man, and men did silly things, men were merely boys who had outgrown short trousers.

Kit swallowed. She was suffering too. The expressionless eyes of her husband made her feel she was standing before a butcher's window, watching the pig's head with an apple in its mouth and sprigs of parsley about its neck; the eyes were the same, unseeing, lost in this world.

Now, as she did a hundred times a day, Kit thought, 'Thank God she's gone. Don't let us ever set eyes on her again.' Her long thin white fingers curled into fists, squeezing so tightly her nails left purple ridges on her palms.

* * *

It was July when Bertie whistled.

Kit stood in the kitchen with the back door open and heard him. Gently she tiptoed out, smiling, her face eager to see this renewal, and he was snipping a half-opened bud from the cream tea-roses that climbed the old stone wall. He stopped whistling to put the flower in his jacket lapel, drawing it carefully through the buttonhole, and Kit relished the picture, not yet ready to disturb him.

The morning sun didn't touch the garden so Bertie stood in cool, dew-damp shadow, but the sky was a clear blue, and the mint was already thickly grown and glossy in its patch beside the night-scented stock.

Kit felt a wave of thanksgiving. This was her home, her garden, her man, her love.

She called to him, 'I think we ought to go for a drive

227

today,' and he turned and smiled at her. Again she felt the wave of thanksgiving: his gaze had seen her, had swept over the cream cotton dress, and had approved. She touched her hair, wondering if he had noticed she had worn it in a soft bun at the nape of her neck for some time now, and Bertie came to her, smiling, looking remarkably handsome in spite of his arrogant nose and the slight lift of his brows.

He laughed. 'Yes. I noticed yesterday. It looks nice too. Softer. More feminine.'

Kit blushed. The awareness of him was something new, not quite delicious, but exciting; and he could read her thoughts. He could confidently answer a question she hadn't yet put into words.

She didn't attempt to touch him. It was like watching a bird, maybe an eagle that was interested but might suddenly fly away if disturbed. 'Shall we?' she asked.

'Shall we what?'

'Go for a drive?'

'Why not?'

'As soon as the girls get in from school.'

He nodded and laughed. They went into the house together and up the passage to the office, ready to start the day's work, husband and wife, boss and secretary, man and woman.

At the office door he touched her. He put his hand across her back so she could feel its strength, its gentleness through the thinness of her clothes, and he asked, 'Did you buy yourself a bathing-costume?'

'Yes.' She nodded, feeling flirtatiously naughty. 'It's a navy blue with black bands around the neck and legs.'

'You devil,' he said. 'All we need now is an empty cove, heh?'

She laughed, still near to blushing, her heart hammering at the thought of undressing on a beach, hidden only by a rock and a towel, but it was a target she had set herself, on the road to being modern, an ambition she had nurtured ever since she had seen Elsie Buckley happily naked in a pine wood.

Bertie said, 'Will you get the mail?' And she hurried to oblige, opening the glass door, lifting the letters, then opening the front door, propping it back with the heavy coconut mat, letting the bright golden warmth of a summer morning glow in. There were letters from Head Office. There always were. She went to her desk and sat. Already Bertie was busy, drawing rolled sheets from pigeon-holes, making sure his pen nibs were free of fluff, and Kit opened the letters from policy-holders first. She separated them, some for answering immediately, some for filing, and some for Bertie's attention.

So it was gone ten o'clock when she opened the last one from Head Office and read it.

She looked at Bertie. He was standing, bent over the huge blue account sheet that covered his desk, his lips and fingers counting, the ruler at hand, ready for another red-inked line under a column of figures correctly balanced. She said, 'Bertie,' then cleared her throat as only a croak had come through. She tried again. 'Bertie.'

'Hmm?' He didn't look up, his thin face intent on the neat figures in their columns before him.

'There's a letter –'

'Hmm?'

'It's from the Old Man. Personally. Signed by him.'

Bertie looked up, surprised and curious, then he straightened his back. He put his pen down and held out his hand. Kit passed him the expensively stiff sheet of paper that had been meticulously folded in three, and he read it quickly. Then he frowned, slowly sat, and read it again, very carefully.

'Dear Albert,
It is with regret that I find it necessary to communicate with you in this vein, but I am under instruction from the Board of Directors concerning the matter of your ex-employee, Miss Elsie Buckley.

You will agree the firm has been most patient in this matter. Over three months have now elapsed and we feel it imperative that we take court proceedings . . . .'

'Court proceedings?' Bertie looked at Kit. 'What the hell!' Then he read on:

> 'To a certain extent the Company is bound to hold you responsible, and any court order would inevitably include you, maybe even suggest that you are wholly responsible in your position as District Manager for all claim investigations. We would, naturally, hope that the personal side of your association with this young woman could be overlooked, but as she is still under twenty-one . . . .'

'Good God!' Bertie gasped. Kit didn't move and he read on:

> ' . . . Enclosed you will find an account of moneys owed to this firm by the said Miss Elsie Buckley whom, I am instructed to point out, you employed personally. If the account is settled within seven days I will attempt to use my influence with the Board to get the matter dropped, but if not I doubt any regard I may have for you as a manager will be of any assistance to you. The Board will act as it deems necessary.
>
> Yours'

Bertie stared at the signature of the Old Man, then he read the letter yet again, fully absorbing the veiled threat. He said, 'I'm for the high jump, Kit. The means test.'

'No.' Kit fingered the paper-knife on her desk. 'It's all over now. Forgotten. It's almost four months ago. You don't owe the firm a penny.'

'Read it again. They hold me responsible. Pay up or else.'

'They can take her to court. Make her pay.'

'Not going by this letter. Not only would that be bad for the firm, but she is under age. I am responsible. Legally.' He stared at Kit, and she stared back, shocked dark eyes in a pale face, the hint of new-found happiness evaporating.

'Everything will go,' she gasped. 'The house, the car. We'll have to sell everything.'

'The house, the car – ' he echoed, staring at her. 'Me! I'll go. Be finished! Kaput! Christ! Can you imagine the talk, the scandal? Who the hell will ever want to employ me?'

'No Bertie! No!' Kit stood tall, at her most dignified in her determination. 'No, I won't let them. I love you and no one is going to harm you – !' She stopped, suddenly aware of the shock in his eyes, of the surprise, the disbelief, and he gently laid the letter on top of the blue account sheet before him, then he sat back.

They resembled two figures in a tableau as they concentrated on each other, blue eyes piercing into amber, a husband hearing his frigid wife profess to loving for the first time ever.

Then Kit looked down. Tall and slim. She felt ashamed of the way her self-control had slipped. She said self-consciously, 'I'll make a cup of tea,' but didn't move.

Bertie let the air out of his lungs through pursed lips, then he consoled, 'Well, maybe they can't hold me responsible. Maybe they're bluffing. Get the Old Man on the phone. I'll speak to him.'

Kit moved to obey, then she stopped. 'No,' she said, her chin lifted as if to rescue her pride. 'You landed us in this mess. You get us out. Use the telephone yourself.'

Bertie watched her go. The optimism of the last few weeks had brought back the gloss to her hair, enhanced the natural elegance of her walk, and begun to put flesh back to her bones. He called after her, 'Kit. We'll find a way out of it. Everything will work out right. You see.'

She returned to the door, her eyes accusing again. 'One thing is certain. I will not allow you to go and see her!'

He smiled. 'You're getting bossy in your old age.'

'Well, we haven't the money, so she certainly won't, either. Just how much is it?'

Bertie looked back at the letter, at the appended sheet.

231

'Thirty-nine pounds.'

'In seven days?' Kit scoffed, and put her hand on her hip.

Bertie examined the figures more closely, then said drily, 'They're even charging their expenses for the investigation. It's forty-seven pounds eighteen and sixpence in all.'

Kit jerked her head and there was panic in her eyes, then she went from the room, nowhere near as confident or calm as she wanted Bertie to believe.

He picked up the telephone, tapping the arm for the operator, his teeth gritted so his lips disappeared in thinness, and his nostrils flaring with desperation.

The Old Man was not available. The male secretary's voice was ready and impersonal as it came along the line from London.

Bertie said, trying to ease the tension from his lips, 'I'll be in London tomorrow. I'll call and see – '

'A waste of time, I'm afraid,' the voice replied. 'He is leaving for the north this morning.'

'Will he be back before the week-end?'

'I'm afraid not, Mr Hemsworthy. He has a rather full itinerary, conferences to attend. He is an extremely busy man.'

'Go to hell,' Bertie said.

'Yes, Mr Hemsworthy. Will that be all?'

Bertie hung up the mouthpiece then glared at it. He re-read the letter, then dropped it back to the desk. He slowly followed Kit to the kitchen, his hands sullenly in his pockets. He said, 'They've got me by the knackers.'

'Don't stoop to vulgarity,' Kit told him, and brewed a pot of tea. 'You're not to go,' she said finally. 'If you go to see that girl again it'll be the end of us. Everything we have built up together. I know it. She will ruin us completely and we mustn't let her. She's evil, Bertie. She is.'

'She can't do any worse than has been done.'

'We'll sell the car.'

Bertie stared at her, realising the sacrifice she was prepared to make. He said, 'We're still paying for it.'

'We'll sell it. Get rid of it. If we keep up the payments no one will twig.'

They stared at each other again, Bertie with his heart banging irregularly at thoughts of visiting Elsie with a valid reason, yet glad Kit was finding a way of preventing it. 'If we're caught . . . ' he said.

'It'll be no worse than it is now. But we won't be caught. We mustn't be. It's the only way.'

'I could try and borrow from a bank.' He wondered why Kit seemed to have grown in stature, why he felt she was suddenly the leader, the stronger? But he was too shocked to argue. Why the hell hadn't Elsie let him know she had made no effort to pay Head Office? Couldn't she have phoned, sent a letter? Surely she knew how he was having to carry the can?

The sickness was in the pit of his stomach. The shock of having her name appearing before him again, without warning, when he had been engrossed in something else, in rows and rows of figures, had made him sweat, yet he felt his inside shivering, trembling. Again his heart cried out for her, and the strangulation was deep in his throat.

*   *   *

He realised a cup of tea was being thrust into his hand, and Kit was saying, 'Pull yourself together, Bertie. It isn't the end of the world yet.'

Her jaw was set hard, a little nerve in her cheek moving almost imperceptibly. She felt herself fighting and was surprised. She had never fought before, and now she liked the experience, the way her blood coursed, and the way she felt determined to oust Elsie Buckley for ever, to keep Bertie to herself, as entangled in her web as any victim of a spider.

She said, 'We have never bothered with a bank. Even the collections go to London in a parcel. What bank would lend to us? And we'd have to pay them back as well as pay for the car, the house, the school. The rates are up again, and the electricity bill will soon be in. I haven't paid the instalments

233

on the suite for two months. They'll be taking us to court too if we don't do something.'

Bertie sat, feeling as old and battered as his chair, and the next evening the advertisement was in the local newspaper.

URGENT. MUST SELL WITHIN THREE DAYS 1928 MORRIS COWLEY. FIRST FIFTY POUNDS. CASH. SECURES.

On the fourth day after receiving the Old Man's letter Bertie let the car go for thirty-five pounds, to a little man in a near-orange tweed suit that had brown patches on the knees and elbows. It seemed no one had fifty pounds, cash, or even forty.

He sat at his desk and counted it all carefully, then he said to Kit, 'With this week's salary of two pounds twelve and sixpence, we now have thirty-seven pounds twelve and six,' and he put the money in Kit's purse as if that would help it to grow.

'Ten pounds,' Kit said thoughtfully, worriedly. 'Where can we get ten pounds?'

On the sixth day after receiving the Old Man's letter Bertie opened his desk's top drawer and saw the two five-pound notes, crisp and white.

He exclaimed, 'What's this?' and held them high, turning them in his fingers, a sort of exultation rising in him. 'Where did they come from?'

'John Davies brought them in. It's the first time he has ever seen two in the same month.' Kit wrinkled her nose. 'I bet there are people still stinking of the stuff. John wasn't sure how to handle them.'

'I suppose he had the sense to make a note of where he got them, and when?'

'Of course.'

'Mind you,' Kit went to her desk and drew a slip of paper towards her, then picked up a pen, 'I have a feeling John isn't short. Maggie does well selling eggs, and she flogs cabbages and swedes like mad. She never seems without a bob or two anyway.'

Bertie flicked the notes between his fingers, grinning at the pleasure holding them gave him, then an idea occurred to him. He frowned, sat back and crossed his ankles, rubbed his hand across his face, and eventually said quietly, 'Kit . . . .'

She was gently opening and shutting her lips so they made a soft rhythmic sound as she gazed at the figures she had written on the slip of paper.

Bertie said thoughtfully, his eyes hooded, 'Kit . . . I have an idea . . . .'

'So have I.' She looked up and yet again the telepathy was working. She said, 'If you are thinking what I am thinking, it's dishonest.'

He nodded slowly. 'Defrauding the firm.'

Traffic trundled past the window, echoing in the sunshine, a group of people talked fast and loud on the pavement, a car crashed its gears and horses' hooves sounded light on the cobbles.

Kit said, the end of the pen held to her lip, 'As I see it we have two choices. Not pay Head Office and risk a court case, losing the job. After all, the Old Man has been patient, when you remember his son is there chivying him on, so he's not likely to hold out any longer. And the second choice is – well – ' she lifted her shoulders in a shrug of resignation ' – we use those two beautiful fivers to make up the deficit.'

'Is it enough?' He glanced at the picture of the Old Man, assessing the Old Man's character and next action. 'He'll certainly do what he says. He hasn't built up an empire by being soft, and plenty of others could do my job.'

'We would need another six shillings.'

'Do we have six shillings?'

'I'll look in the kids' moneyboxes.' She went quickly, and came back with two white china pigs. Deftly she removed the corks from their bellies and emptied out the money onto his desk. Bertie watched her count it, one hand to his chin, his fingers moving slowly.

Finally she said triumphantly, 'Six and tuppence.'

There was a short silence, a moment of fear, a moment of resolution, then Bertie put both hands out and drew the money to him. He took a deep breath. A decision had been made. 'Right, Kit. Take a letter,' and he was dictating before she had grabbed the pad and pencil.

'Dear Governor.' He paused on the familiarity, then decided to let it stand. He continued:

'Enclosed you will find the full sum of forty-seven pounds eighteen and sixpence. A letter from you confirming that this unfortunate matter has now been closed once and for all will be appreciated.
                                                    Yours'

He paused then, watching Kit, watching her concentrate on the pad on her knee. 'No, wait a minute, add this bit. My wife and I recently visited Miss Buckley and found she is with consumption, the same as her mother. The publicity of dragging such people through the courts would have reflected badly on this firm. Now, Yours etc., etc.'

Kit typed fast, her classic-shaped face both worried and defiant at the same time, and now and again the tip of her tongue touched her drawn-in lower lip as if she still had doubts about the money.

She passed the typed letter to Bertie, still intact with its copy and carbon, and he read it, his hand firm and steady as he signed it.

Kit watched, frowning slightly, then she sighed. 'You realise we have now sunk to her level?'

'Her?' He looked up.

'Elsie,' she stammered. 'We are as bad as Elsie.'

Bertie looked down again quickly. 'I have understood all along how she felt, how easy it must have been for her to steal.'

'Yes,' Kit nodded shortly. 'So have I.'

'It's a case of there, but for the grace of God, go I.'

'Yes.' Kit watched him fold the letter and put it in a long

236

envelope, his fingers lean and strong. He addressed it, the pen nib making a scratching sound. Then he took the red pen and dipped it in the red ink. In large print he wrote on the top left-hand corner of the envelope, STRICTLY PERSONAL, then he flung it from him.

'Get it posted Kit. No. I'll take it. Get rid of the damn thing. Fast.' He stood up. He should have felt relieved, but he didn't. He felt as if he had descended into another quagmire of deceit, and a headache was coming on.

Kit stood, almost as tall as he, her gaze level. She said, 'There is another problem.'

'And that is?'

'We are now ten pounds short in next week's collections. John paid those fivers in as soon as he got them because he was afraid of losing them. His money, when he pays in on Wednesday, will be ten pounds short.'

Bertie stuck his hands in his trouser pockets and gazed back up at the Old Man. As if speaking to the picture, he said, 'As from today there is a new rule in this district. Every man pays in twice a week. On a Wednesday they bring in their Saturday, Monday and Tuesday collections, then first thing on Saturday morning they bring in their Thursday and Friday collections.'

Kit said nothing for a while. She twisted her body as if her inside was writhing, as if struggling for an escape from their dilemma, then she said, 'We post the accounts Friday. Money coming in on Saturday won't help us.'

'We'll hold the account over. Head Office doesn't get it until Monday morning anyway. As long as it catches the last post from the General in Wind Street on Sunday night, it will still arrive there on Monday morning.'

'It's terribly dishonest – '

'Each week a pound of my salary will go into the account. It should take ten weeks to get straight.'

'Oh God!'

He turned to her, almost casual in the weariness now overtaking him. 'Of course, you could ask Lorraine – '

'Oh no! I don't want them to know.'

'Or take another letter, telling the Old Man he can whistle for his money.'

Kit looked at the floor, then sighed again. 'We don't seem to have much choice.'

'I suggest a cup of tea. I think I will also have what will be my last cigarette for ten weeks. That will save something.'

Kit moved to the door and he went after her. 'You'll have to get out on the knocker, Bertie. Get new business in –' She didn't say, 'I'm desperate. We need money to live. We can't run around without shoes on our feet.' Neither did she say, 'It will all be worth it if I have kept you away from that girl,' but Bertie said, 'It's going to mean a lot more work for you. D'you think you can manage? Run the office on your own every day, and see to the house and the kids?'

'I'll manage,' she said, with determination. 'We'll do it.'

By the beginning of October they had returned the ten pounds to the firm. They took the two girls to the pictures to celebrate, and laughed at Laurel and Hardy. They went home carrying fish and chips. And Kit fainted as she reached the black and white marble front doorstep.

Bertie carried her into the house, and that night Emma went back to her own little bed beside Linda's, while Bertie pushed the two small beds in his room together, and he and Kit fell asleep wrapped in mutual concern and triumph. They were there. They had done it. The agents could revert to paying in once a week again. They were safe.

Kit's hair felt good against his cheek, and her feet cold and bony against his shins.

It was a week later that she fainted again. She was in the house alone and she couldn't get up off the floor. It was cold, and she shivered, her lips and finger-nails blue.

For a long time she lay there, silently imploring God to help her, listening for someone to call, for someone to walk in, and when she eventually got up the stairs on her hands and knees she told herself it was probably influenza.

Instinct brought Bertie home early and as he tipped his hat on to the hallstand hook, he carolled, 'I'm home,' and the house lay silent. 'Kit?' He went to the office and the morning's mail was on his desk, unopened. He went to the kitchen and out to the garden, then he loped up the stairs, two at a time, his hand gripping the banister as he went.

'Kit?'

She smiled at him and made an effort to get up, but he pushed her back. The light from the window struck her face and she looked sallow, her eyes sunken in black shadows. Bertie watched her, knew she was exhausted, knew this was reaction, the anti-climax to months of stress and overwork.

He patted the pink, deep satin quilt up around her and kissed her brow; it was cold and damp. He said, 'I'll get Sullivan here.' Kit smiled again, only too glad to let him take over.

Downstairs Bertie phoned the doctor, then made a pot of tea, and while it brewed he lit a cigar. It was his first in months and he savoured every movement: opening the brown cardboard casket, selecting the cigar that was no different from its mates, nipping off the end with his teeth, and placing the cigar between his lips. For a moment he let his mouth manipulate it there, rolling it, relishing it, smiling around it, his blue eyes like polished sapphires, then he lit it, slowly, and the smoke rose, rotating gradually, a tall grey-blue spiral.

Bertie put his hands in his trouser pockets for a minute more, just enjoying the cigar, enjoying the momentary freedom from stress, then he poured the tea, put Kit's favourite shortcake on a plate, and took it all upstairs.

Next day Dr Sullivan came, his bristly ginger brows drawn as he held Kit's wrists. 'Are you pregnant again, Kitty?' and she almost laughed.

Bertie turned away quickly. He didn't say, 'It would have to be immaculate conception,' but he thought it, and the doctor nodded, wise in the reaction of his patients, and diplomatic in his attitude to them. He said, 'Ha hum,' and unscrambled his stethoscope from the pocket of his frayed tweed jacket. 'Right then, Kitty. Open your nightie. There's a good girl. Now. In. Out. In. Out.'

She breathed obligingly and he listened, his head bent low over her, then he unplugged his ears, twisted the stethoscope up and tucked it laboriously back into his pocket.

His freckled hand reached out and a gnarled finger drew down her lower eyelid. 'Ha hum,' he said. 'I think she's a bit anaemic, Albert. Been overdoing it. Needs Parrish's Food. See she gets it. There's a good chap.'

Kit said, 'It rots the teeth.'

Dr Sullivan bounced his great head, ignoring her comment, then he looked shrewdly at Bertie. 'Your wife needs help in the house, Albert. That abortion last spring took the stuffing out of her. She rests up or suffers the consequences.' His attitude was of take it or leave it. He had more serious cases awaiting his attention. 'Kitty, how is your mother? Fine? Remember me to her – '

Then he was gone.

Bertie sat on the side of the bed and held Kit's hand. He remembered her blurting out that she loved him. She hadn't said it since, or given any hint that she had meant her words, and he made no effort to remind her. He still loved Elsie, longed for her with a hopelessness that lay dormant deep within him, but he respected Kit.

He said now, 'We should have expected it.'

'I didn't. I thought I was fine.'

'You had begun to put on weight, but you've lost it again.'

'Have I?' She was surprised.

Maggie Davies came to visit. She sailed in with her scarlet tent coat flying open and her scarlet cotton dress flamboyant about her, her breasts proudly oozing above the usual low neckline. Her face was full of the glee of leaving her Welsh black full skirt at home, and emerging like a glorious butterfly from a chrysalis into the home of her employer and his wife. She swooped on Kit and gripped her hand. 'Don't worry love. John and me owe you and

240

Bertie a lot. We'll look after you.'

John sat in the basket chair between the dressing table and the window, gangling, bony, smiling with his crooked yellow teeth. 'We never did have a chance to make it up to you.'

Bertie stood near the foot of the bed and said nothing.

'About Carruthers, I mean,' John went on. 'Mag writing to him. She never meant any harm.'

And so Bertie continued to go out five days a week canvassing. Maggie came almost every day and cleaned, and cooked, and shopped, and took the washing home to boil in the copper, put through the mangle, and dry in the mountain air. On Fridays she collected five shillings off Bertie in return.

Bertie employed a woman in the office who wouldn't know what to do with a man if she had one. As a secretary she was experienced and capable. She could even do the big account sheet, but she demanded the rate for the job, and Bertie paid her twelve and sixpence a week.

Money going out. Money he could not afford, and the bills kept piling up; mortgage, telephone, gas, rates, insurance, school fees, school clothing, instalments on the car.

Each Wednesday money poured from the pockets of the agents on to Bertie's desk, and each Wednesday Bertie realised afresh he had used company money to clear Elsie's debts; he could use company money to help clear his own.

One grey drizzle filled day he took four tattered pound notes from the white draw string bag, and he saved the telephone and gas being cut off. He paid part of the rates, he gave up smoking again, and he bought Kit a bunch of fat blue black grapes.

Maggie stopped calling each day, the secretary was given a week's notice, and the agents were instructed to pay in twice a week again. Bertie took to standing pensively below the sepia picture of the Old Man, confessing he was in the mire, and getting more tired of trying to struggle out.

Kit got to her feet, the double bed re-appeared in the

front bedroom, and each night Kit and Bertie sank into it, exhausted, drawn together by a united effort to exist; to keep up their standard of living, while the Old Man gazed down from his frame and watched the money being manipulated.

It was some time later, on the fourth of November, that Kit made love to Bertie.

He lay still for a long time, unwilling to believe what was happening, afraid of making her afraid, but when she finally lay naked and the tip of her tongue caressed his earlobe he couldn't stop the soft laughter that welled up inside him. 'Kit! You bitch!'

'Happy?'

'I'll never understand you,' and later he listened to the clock as Kit fell asleep with his arm about her. It hadn't been the most successful session in the world, but it had been willing and pleasing. The smile remained on his face all next day, and he was delighted to join the annual gathering on a piece of barren land not too far away, to agree with his neighbours that they were all working like mad to give the kids a good time.

The bonfire roared and crackled. The smell of paraffin poured onto cardboard, wood, and someone's derelict armchair turned to the aroma of Guy Fawkes night. At first the smoke was black and thick, but then it thinned, a grey ghost above flames that licked furiously towards the starlit sky. A jumping jack cracked and hopped on the hard black earth a few yards away, its sparks spitting, chasing the children who screamed in mock terror as they ran, hoping it would dive at them so they could talk of it ever after.

Kit was on the outskirts of the group, smiling to herself, her face flickering in the red and yellow glow. Bertie was at the fire, giving orders. 'Here nipper, take this paraffin can out of the way. Hey up, there, be careful, that piece of wood might fall on you.'

He chuckled, squinting in the hot light at his stocky little neighbour. 'Good show this year, Major.'

'Indeed it is,' the major preened. 'Another year gone by, what? Hey I say, your girls are growing into fine young women.' He nodded vigorously, glancing at the fire, then back at Bertie. 'The missus and I see them sometimes coming home from school. Damn decent place that. Wanted our grand-daughter to go there, but they sent her to one of those boarding places. Modern idea y'know,' and his ruddy face and small waxed moustache looked like a papier-mâché mask.

Bertie tut-tutted agreeably, watching the edge of the bonfire, making sure it didn't creep. He probably wouldn't speak to, or even see, his neighbour again until next Guy Fawkes night.

'Your lady around?' The major footed a smouldering branch back into the flames.

'Yes. Over there.'

'Always said. We are fortunate in our road. All damn nice people.' The major was self-satisfied. 'It's bad times. Afraid to leave the newspapers around.' He clamped his lips in a pout and looked up at Bertie. 'All scandal. Not the fit world we fought for, what!'

Bertie thought of Elsie, of the money he had borrowed from the firm, and he hurriedly changed the subject. 'The children have worked hard today, collecting wood.'

'Yes. Indeed. Called on us, begging anything to burn, anything old and worn out. Told them I was old. And worn out. They could take me, but they refused.' The major guffawed uproariously, his hands patting his belly.

'Daddy.' Emma tugged Bertie's hand. 'Linda's put a rocket in a bottle and it won't go up.' Bertie nodded, smiling at the major. 'We dads are on call tonight,' and he went to where Linda hovered, watching her failure. She was ash-splattered, as one with the smells of gunpowder and smoke. As Bertie tended the rocket Linda and Emma laughed a lot, over-excited, keeping their arms and feet moving, tapping.

Their young faces looked distorted beneath their untidy fringes as they grinned into the flames. A man shouted,

'Did you see Jarvis sent his old apple tree down?'

'God almighty,' called another. 'There'll be a mess to clean up in the morning.'

'The rain will do it. It's on the way. Look at that moon.'

Bertie put a match to the rocket. The blue paper flickered then flamed, and the rocket took off with a woosh. Emma clutched her hands together and sighed, while Linda loudly tried counting the stars that swam from the rocket's explosion.

Someone yelled, 'Here's the guy,' and Kit was in the group that stood aside to let Guy Fawkes through. He sat, tall and fat, yellow-masked, booted and gloved in a wheelbarrow.

Bertie felt Emma's hand reach for his and he smiled down at her. Her large eyes were wide, her other hand to her mouth in anticipated horror. Bertie called, laughing, encouraging the fun, 'On the fire with him!' and Emma gazed at the guy, her expression childishly sadistic. 'He's only a pretend man Daddy, isn't he?'

Together they watched two men grab the guy by his limbs, watched them swing him between them, grinning in the heat, the noise, the glare, chanting, 'Guy, guy, guy. Stick him in the eye. Hang him on a lamp post and there let him die.'

There was a moment's hush, broken only by the crackle of the fire, then Guy Fawkes sailed into the air, a big floppy bundle grinning in its mask, an old brown cap sewn to his head with string, crashing into the flames. Sparks soared, the burning debris began an avalanche. The men laughed and ran around followed by children, making sure all was safe.

Bertie and Emma watched Guy die, and Emma's hand gripping Bertie's kept slipping with sweat. 'It's only pretend, Daddy, isn't it?'

As the fire began to wane the excitement cooled, and when the hooter from Weaver's flour mills sounded hollowly over the town, it warned people that others were just changing shifts.

Kit came up with Linda. 'Did you hear that? Ten o'clock. Doesn't time fly? Come on you two girls, into the bath, then bed. It's just as well it's Sunday tomorrow.'

As the crowd dwindled the derelict patch of ground looked strange, splattered with dead fireworks, the fire smouldering low against the blackness. Bertie sighed. 'Come on then. Quick march. One two, one two.'

The girls passed him, obeying, arms swinging. The moon had gone, the air was damp. Kit said, 'The tide must be coming in. It'll bring the rain with it.'

At the corner the girls stopped marching and waited, then they held hands, all four of them, strung across the pavement, and broke into a trot, laughing. It had been a good night, but home could be better.

The telegram was on the mat behind the front door, its orange envelope causing panic before it had been touched.

Kit said, 'Oh dear, is someone dead?'

Bertie picked it up. 'There's no black band around it.'

The two girls went into the house, sensing the sudden tension and fear.

'Quick!' Kit urged them. 'Into the bath.'

'Can we go in together?'

'Yes. This once. And you can use the scenty soap.'

They half ran, half scrambled up the stairs, banging the bathroom door, arguing, agreeing, squealing now they were free of Kit and Bertie.

Bertie said, 'It's from Carruthers. The auditors are coming on Monday. He tried phoning this afternoon but got no answer.'

'Monday!' Kit took the telegram. 'Oh Bertie! They'll find out.'

'They must have already guessed or they wouldn't spring it on us like this.'

'But how can they know?' The excitement, the pleasure had gone from her face. 'Bertie? Would it be Maggie again? Telling him they pay in two days a week?'

He shrugged. 'We only owe the firm three pounds now. Can we raise three pounds?'

Kit gave a gasp of relief, then she smiled. 'You can have all the salary this week and we'll live on rice all next week.'

'Maybe Head Office doesn't suspect. Maybe they're just checking again because of Elsie. Maybe just a routine call.' But all the time he knew he was lying. A routine check wasn't sprung on you like this, a routine check was preceded by a letter asking you to make sure all relevant ledgers and sheets were readily available. Carruthers would have known about a routine check weeks ago, and it seemed he hadn't. His warning had come too urgently, too near the time of the auditors' arrival.

Kit handed the telegram back and they went into the office together. They stood in the darkness that was eased by the dim light from the street, and Kit's arm went about Bertie's waist. He never knew whether she was giving comfort or asking for it, but he moved from her. He told himself later it was a subconscious movement of not wanting her involved, but she hurried away, up to the bathroom and the gushing taps.

Bertie put the office light on and sat at the desk. Forty-seven pounds eighteen shillings and sixpence. It had all started with his needing to raise forty-seven pounds eighteen and sixpence, and it had gone on and on, a vicious circle. And he and Kit had paid that back. Almost killed themselves with work, but they had done it. They deserved praise, not the sack, not a prosecution case.

He went to the kitchen and brewed tea without wanting it. It was good of Carruthers to warn him. The man could probably lose his job for doing so. Where had they slipped up? Where might there be a clue for auditors to find? He heard Kit go with the girls to their room. She would be down in a minute, and he didn't want to talk to her, not yet. He hurried to the hallstand and put on his hat and coat, then Kit was calling, 'Bertie? Where are you going?'

'To think.'

'But it's starting to rain. Can't you hear it on the window?'

'I won't be long.' She came beside him and he let his lips

brush her cheek. 'I'm sorry Kit. I've got to get out.'

'Well,' she tried to smile, 'at least we've kept paying for the car.'

Bertie stared at her; if someone found out about the car, his selling what still belonged to the finance company . . . .

He lowered his head and made for the door. Kit followed him. 'Bertie – ' But he was marching quickly, and he could hear the rain spitting on the brim of his hat, the cobbles and tramlines already glistening with wet, the street empty, eerie, silent.

He made towards the club then stopped abruptly; it was after hours; stop-tap. He held his face towards the sky and spots of rain fell lightly, gently, but threateningly onto his skin. He remembered he had been messing with the bonfire; his face was dirty; he had caught a glimpse of it in the hallstand mirror.

He saw a rocket go up beyond the roofs, soaring into the blackness, silent from here, then dividing into stars, blue and red, all sinking, floating back to nothingness.

He turned, walking quickly, his hands in his overcoat pockets now, wishing he had remembered his kid gloves. He went past the house. It looked strange, cold, uninviting, high and wide, Victorian. The only light was the dull glow from the fanlight above the front door. It made his guilt reappear. It was all his damn fault, his blasted mistake, and the terrible ache for Elsie was still there. Was she alive? Was she dead? Had the consumption killed her? He groaned. At times like this he didn't want Kit, he wanted Elsie: Elsie's laugh, Elsie's teasing, Elsie's boost to his ego, Elsie's sharing of eager loving.

Then the guilt got worse. He had married Kit for better for worse, till death us do part. She loved him. His thoughts of Elsie horrified him and he moved faster. On the beach the air was steaming from his mouth and, in the blackness, he could dimly see the tide coming in. He went towards it, the sand showing pale orange as his vision improved. He walked awkwardly, even stumbling a little, and the waves were high, menacing, crashing, starkly white at the fringes, like the lace on Elsie Buckley's French knickers.

He turned, following the tide-line as if it were a marker, hearing the undercurrent dragging at the shingle, and a ship's deep-throated call beyond the docks.

He looked sideways, to where the sea wall was invisible in the darkness, and he wondered how many poor devils lay up there tonight wrapped in sacking and newspapers. There, but for the grace of God, go I: no jobs, no homes, all because of a war and strikes, and Ramsay MacDonald's National Government being as much use as a nut to a starving elephant.

He winced at the thought of the major and his missus next door; the wondering that would ensue if the auditors tumbled to what was going on, if the story got around. He frowned, trying to think of another reason for the auditors coming without warning, and he saw, yet didn't see, the black shapes halfway up the beach. They were like sodden logs washed ashore, pieces of flotsam that hardly imprinted on his gaze.

He tramped past them, lost in his own world of concentration, and the rain became insistent. He thought of the Old Man calling him to London, telling him how he regretted their parting, and somewhere outside himself he heard a call, but it didn't register. His feet kept plodding, crunching in the sand that was caking with wet.

'Mr Hemsworthy! Mr Hemsworthy! Just a minute!'

Still he tramped, mentally alone, locked in his private world of worry, but it came again.

'Mr Hemsworthy! Please listen!' The voice was young and strong. A youth's voice, desperate, pleading, in the damp darkness. The ship moaned again in the channel, muffled in the mists out there, and a wave placed a glistening ribbon of seaweed against his shoes. He moved quickly, irritated that he'd allowed himself so near the water.

'Mr Hemsworthy?'

He looked up the beach, into the blackness, then back the way he had come, and one of the dark shapes was

248

getting up, sitting, as if not too sure, then standing, excited, an arm waving, then running towards him, heavy-footed.

Bertie went back towards it slowly, suspiciously, and Tommy Buckley's face was shining with wet and anxiety, his hair stuck to his head. 'Mr Hemsworthy! I'm glad you've come, sir. I've been hoping every night. It's our Elsie. She's bad.'

Astonishment hit Bertie first, then excitement caught him the strongest, low in the crutch. His breathing stopped. A fear of Elsie coming back into his life swamped him, yet he welcomed the joy and the delight of hearing news of her.

'Tommy! What the devil – '

'Pa threw Elsie out, Mr Hemsworthy, after Ma died. I came with her, but she's bad. It's the consumption like Ma had.'

'What're you doing down here, for God's sake!' Bertie walked back with the boy.

'There's others down here.' Tommy was white-faced, puffy-eyed. 'They're all up in the dunes though. It's warmer up there, but Elsie wouldn't go. She says there's creepy things in the grass, and she's afraid of the men.'

Tommy kept talking, then he stopped and knelt, sniffing the rain away from the tip of his nose. Elsie lay on the sand on her side, her knees up, covered with an army blanket. She didn't turn. Bertie crouched low, staring, as if he couldn't believe the glistening wet dead-looking face was real.

'Elsie!' Her body was a dark bundle, inert, and the mixture of his emotions grew worse. Her cheeks were sunken and her eyes opened, feverish like her mother's had been.

'Elsie! For God's sake! Why didn't you tell me? Let me know?'

'Go away.' She pulled her head down, further into the blanket, hiding.

He knelt beside her, wanting to lift her, to love her, but

249

her voice came, muffled, 'Get 'ter hell out of it Mr Hems-worthy,' and slowly Bertie rose and walked away, then he stopped, aching physically, mentally, emotionally, and he looked back. The boy was still kneeling, staring after him, a black statue on an even blacker wet beach. A foghorn wailed, the banshee of black waters, and the smell of the crashing sea and sand was strong. The rain made thudding sounds on his hat and shoulders. He opened his overcoat and groped in his trouser pockets. How much did he have? Half a crown? Five shillings? He called sharply, 'Tommy. Come here,' and the boy came scrambling. 'Yes, Mr Hems-worthy?' He pulled his sleeve across his cheek as if with relief.

'Can you get Elsie into a bed-and-breakfast place?' He held out the money, and his voice and hand shook.

'Oh no, Mr Hemsworthy. Nobody'll take us. We got no bags and she's coughing all the time. She's bad, Mr Hemsworthy.'

Bertie stared at Tommy. 'How old are you?'

'Sixteen now.'

'Still selling wood?'

'No. Pa sold the cart – and Montague, my pony.'

Bertie felt the shock of the boy's sorrow. 'I'm sorry,' he said.

'It doesn't matter, Mr Hemsworthy.' The boy swayed from one foot to the other. 'I can go in the army. I can be all right. I can be fine. It's our Elsie. He threw her out, Mr Hemsworthy. Not me. I come with her.'

'Why? For God's sake. Why? Why throw her out?'

Tommy looked towards the dunes and licked his lips. He moved his wide shoulders uncomfortably. 'Well yer see – '

Bertie watched him closely. The lesson had been painful: Elsie was a liar and a cheat. Was her brother the same? What yarn would he come out with now?

'She said you must never know, Mr Hemsworthy . . . . She said . . . . It was me made us come down here, Mr Hemsworthy. In case you come along like . . . . Not Elsie . . . . I heard you tell Ma once you come down here . . . .'

'You'd better explain, Tommy. What happened?'

'She – our Elsie – she's got a bun in the oven, Mr Hemsworthy. It's due in January.' His words speeded up. 'She's over seven months gone, Mr Hemsworthy. She could have it now. Down here . . . .'

Bertie didn't speak. It was as if his eardrums had gone hollow, buzzing.

'It's yours, Mr Hemsworthy. Elsie says it's yours,' and horror curdled in Bertie's throat. The boy seemed to be floating from him, yet the urgent voice went on, 'So Pa flung her out. She didn't tell him, Mr Hemsworthy. She didn't tell him it was you. She's been working as a skivvy, but she's getting big now, and they wouldn't keep her on.'

Bertie never remembered running, or even moving at all, but he would never forget the feel of Elsie's ice-cold face against his as he lifted her. She was murmuring, crying. 'Oh Bertie, I thought you'd gone. Oh darling, I thought you'd gone,' and he was sobbing against her, 'You fool, you bloody little fool. Why didn't you tell me?'

She didn't cough at all and his hat went skew-whiff. His fear of her returning to his life had gone, forgotten, and all he felt now was relief and happiness; surging, glorious, wonderful happiness. He heard Tommy traipsing behind him, and he wanted to sing, to whistle. His feet squashed the sand noisily and she clung to him, her eyes enormous as she gazed into his face. She was too light for a grown girl, but he would feed her up, get her to a good doctor, a specialist, cure her of this consumption, give her the will to live, make her fight. God, what if he hadn't come down the beach tonight? She would have lain there, wet and cold. It was November.

'I love you Bertie.' It was a whisper, a sighing. 'With all my heart and all my soul I love you. I didn't want to land you in trouble. I'd have worked for you, Bertie . . . . Done anything for you . . . . I knew it, right from that first day, when you opened the door to me . . . . D'you remember?'

He let her ramble on; he had carried more than one man like this during the war, his legs stomping on as if they had a will of their own. He avoided the steps, taking the slipway over the railway track.

'I do love you, Bertie. I'll never love anyone else. I never have loved anyone else. I've missed you so terribly . . . . I can walk, my love. Please put me down. I'm all right. I'm not dying or anything. I was only tired.'

But he didn't put her down. It was like a penance for deserting her, carrying her now through empty streets, the rain falling like a silver-beaded curtain about them, just him and Elsie. It was as if Tommy wasn't there, he kept so far behind, the blanket that had covered Elsie bundled under his arm. Bertie held her closer. She said, 'Are you pleased to see me?'

'Very.'

'Liar.' Her head snuggled closer to his shoulder.

'Why ask if you don't believe the answer?' He smiled down at her, unaware he was panting.

'Where're you taking me?'

'Home. Where you belong. In the spare bedroom.'

'You can't! Kit will be upset. She'll throw me out.'

'Kit never throws things. She is civilised.'

'I'm not civilised. I throw things.'

'I bet you do.' He had never noticed the slope before; he always thought the road was flat, but he kept going.

'I can walk. Let me walk.'

'I'll carry you.'

She giggled, rubbing her wet cheek against his wet coat. 'Have you ever tasted rain?' Her small red tongue licked. It was pointed and wicked. 'It's lovely. Cool and clean.'

At the gate of the house he put her down, then kissed her gently, their lips raindrop wet. He said 'I will love you through all this life and the next. I make a promise,' and Tommy was beside them saying, 'I'd better go then. I'd better go.' He looked at Elsie, awkward, too big for his years, and her eyes went wild, staring as consumptive eyes do. 'Don't go, Tommy, don't leave me. Don't go back, not there.'

'Open the gate,' Bertie said calmly to the boy. 'You need

252

supper. And be quiet as we go in. Kit might be sleeping.'

But Kit wasn't. She appeared at the top of the stairs as they walked in, the three of them bedraggled and soaked, and her gasp of 'Oh God!' was loud and clear. She hesitated then came down quickly, her hand to her mouth, her pink chiffon negligee floating about her. 'I'm not having that girl here! Take her out. I'm not! I'm not!' Her voice cracked, screeched.

'She's ill.' Bertie took his hat and coat off, not looking at her, his mouth a straight line.

'So will I be, and your children! Take her out!' Kit glared at Elsie's obvious pregnancy, and Elsie turned towards the still open front door. Bertie put out an arm and stopped her. He looked at Kit, and she stood on the bottom stair, a monument to anguish.

'Kit. I want her here. If she goes, I go.'

Elsie pulled against his arm. 'No Bertie. No – '

'Shut up!' he snapped, and dragged her back. 'Tommy, shut both doors. Bolt the front one. We'll talk sensibly in the morning.'

'The morning?' Kit derided. 'We'll all talk now.'

Tommy closed the doors and the bolts rammed home.

Bertie said, pleading now, 'Put the kettle on, Kit, for God's sake. Tom Buckley threw them out. I found her and the boy sleeping rough.'

'On the beach?' It was an accusation. 'She knew where to go. She knows you walk down there. Accidentally finding her on purpose.' Kit's hands were wringing, she was appealing, her dark eyes even darker in spite of the furious red sparks in their amber. 'It's not just her and you, it's the consumption. We'll all have it. And she's pregnant. Look! You can see it. Let the father look after it. Find him . . . .' And slowly her voice ebbed away. Her gaze fastened into Elsie's.

'A cup of tea, Kit,' Bertie repeated. 'I'm buggered too.'

'There's the workhouse,' Kit said, softly now, not wanting to believe her instinct. 'Get her to the workhouse.'

Elsie said quietly, 'I'll go to the workhouse, Kit.

253

Tomorrow. I'll go.' And for another moment they stared deep into each other's eyes. It was Kit who put both hands to her face and turned away. 'Oh my God!' she muttered, then, 'I'll make a cup of tea,' and she hurried to the kitchen. Bertie followed her. He said, 'You should see the poor sods on that beach. Homeless.'

'The poor sods on the beach!' Kit turned on him. 'What about the poor sods here? Us?' Then she looked at Tommy, then at Elsie, their hair flattened black, their clothes drenched, their faces drawn with stress. She seemed to make a decision and drew a deep breath, lifting her head. 'Bertie, if they have to be here, get the rum out. The kettle is boiling. You two. Get your wet clothes off.' She banged a lot, clattering the cups and saucers, deep furrows between her dark brows. She scowled at Tommy. 'Are you consumptive too?' And when he shook his head, she snapped, 'Get those wet boots off. You'll have sand everywhere.'

He did as he was told then sat on a hard chair, his body bent with weariness. He sniffed and Bertie wondered in horror if the boy was going to cry. Tommy's hair was cropped short, as if his father had cut it, his ears were scarlet with cold and his face had a purple hue, his grey trousers were too big, held at the waist with string. Kit looked at him and a little of her displeasure died. 'Dear heaven,' she sighed, 'what a mess the world is in.' She poured tea quickly, nervously, then hurried away as Bertie splashed rum into each cup. She reappeared with a warm nightgown and a pair of pyjamas that would drown the boy. 'Here you are, you two, never say I don't give you anything.' They took the clothes but made no other movement. Tommy seemed stunned and helpless. Elsie was sunk in Bertie's chair, her pregnancy looking much bigger there. She was shuddering, her face misshapen with cold.

Kit was in charge. 'I'll get a hot-water bottle in the spare bed for you, Elsie. Tommy will have to kip on the settee.' She hurried around, her negligee wafting, her soft red slippers appearing and disappearing beneath it rapidly as she walked. She produced blankets and took the boy to the sitting-room. She put a match to the prepared fire and piled coal on with the brass tongs, then she shepherded Elsie up the stairs.

Bertie sagged into his chair. It was midnight. In about thirty-four hours the auditors would be here, and he had two women and three youngsters to feed. Kit found him still there an hour later. She scowled at him, her voice frosty. 'Come to bed, Bertie. Leave the worrying till daylight. They're here now.' She took his hand and led him to the bedroom, then she got into bed and watched him undress. She said quietly, aware of the children sleeping in the next room, 'You do go out of your way to find trouble, don't you?'

'I couldn't leave them down there. I did try.'

'D'you still love her?'

'Yes. That's the main trouble.'

'D'you love me? Maybe just a little bit?'

He didn't answer and she lay watching him, one corner of her mouth up-tilted in question. 'Do you?'

'In a way I suppose I must. I stay with you. I'd be lost without you.'

'Just remember that. In the days to come. Remember that Bertie, and we'll have nothing to fear.'

He smiled at her without pleasure. She seemed indefatigable. She said, 'She won't last long. It's on her face. Death. Six months.'

'Don't be a callous bitch.'

'What about the baby? I suppose it's yours. Has she said?'

He didn't answer. He rubbed his chin and it scraped. He needed a shave. He also needed a wash.

'Bertie?' Kit sounded cross, yet kept her voice low. 'Has she said who the father is?' The curtains made a little sound on their rings, as if a draught was trying to come through.

'Yes,' he said. 'Me. I think I wanted it to happen. It might be a son.'

Kit hit the quilt about her, scowling again. 'So it's all my

255

fault. Because I nearly died not having the last baby.'

Bertie busied himself at the dressing-table, unwilling to get into bed with her, thinking, It *is* all your damn fault. You knew I wanted a son. Every man needs a son, but he said nothing.

'When?' Kit demanded. 'When?' Then she calculated. 'Easter. March the twenty-eighth. That loving scene in the pine wood.' She counted on her fingers. 'May, June, July, August, September, October, November – hm – ' Her voice rose a little, but still considerate of the girls sleeping next door. 'I'll not let you take the responsibility for it. I won't. She'll ruin you. And us. She's blaming you for someone else. She's had someone else. Maybe any number of someone elses. She's on the make. You're the one she thinks is made of money – '

'Shut up.'

'Bertie!' Kit sat bolt upright, all attempt at patience gone, and he turned on her.

'Kit! Shut up. For God's sake, shut up!'

They glared at each other, both weary and bewildered, then she pushed his side of the bedclothes back. 'Come on in. I'm not going to quarrel.'

He got into bed, the sheets cold, and Kit moved her legs away from him. He said, 'We're in one hell of a mess.'

'She won't live, you know.'

'For Christ's sake stop it.'

'You stop it. Stop thinking about her. Stop it. Stop it.'

'You want her in the workhouse. Have you ever seen inside that place? With my baby – '

'Every day people advertise their babies for sale.'

'And almost half the babies born die before they're five. Is that what you want?' He was still glaring, his hands on his blanketed knees, ready to shout and rage. 'Well, mine won't die. And mine won't be up for sale.'

'In the workhouse they'll put it up for adoption. Rich people will have it.'

'Shut up Kit. I've warned you.' His voice had lowered, more menacing than if he had shouted, and Kit slid down into the bed, stiff with anger but silent.

Bertie lay for a long time, aware he had left the light on, yet feeling incapable of finding the strength to leave the bed and put it out. Eventually the shilling in the meter ran through and the light faded, going dim, then dying completely. Bertie thought Kit was asleep and he didn't move, but she said quietly. 'You are MY husband. Father of MY daughters. Do you understand?' And Bertie struggled to sit up again, to see her in the darkness. He said, with steel in his voice, 'Elsie is ill. Sick. Dying. Dying. And we will be kind to her. The same as we would to a stray cat or dog. All of us. If you aren't kind to her, Kit, I will leave you. I will go. I will take the two girls and Elsie and go. To hell with the job and the house and the whole bloody lot. I realised it tonight, when I saw her lying there, huddled in that filthy bloody blanket.'

Kit began to sob quietly, and he put a hand on her shoulder, wanting her to understand. 'My duty was here, so I stayed. Please accept that, Kit, then shut up about it all. Do you hear? Shut up!'

The room became icily silent. Kit was still, and when Bertie settled down to sleep, she was still lying, unmoving, without sound.

CHAPTER TEN

Kit might have fallen asleep sometime before the dawn, but the kitchen door creaked. She listened. She hadn't heard anyone go downstairs. Quickly she left the bed and put on Bertie's dressing-gown; it was heavier and warmer than the negligee she had worn since late summer. She padded down to the kitchen.

A candle burned on the mantelpiece, but Kit's hand went, automatically, to the electric switch and pressed. No light came on and she sighed, 'The bob's gone.'

Tommy looked up from where he was sitting on the edge of her armchair. He had been forcing a sockless foot into one of his boots. The other boot was still on the fender before the open oven door where Kit had put them to dry. He stood up quickly in respect.

Kit's voice was sharp but not loud. 'Where are you going?'

'To the beach. Mrs Hemsworthy, to collect wood.'

'Wood?' He was only an inch or two shorter than she was, and she was tall. 'The tide threw a lot up last night.' Kit didn't speak. She didn't understand him. He smiled. 'It might help you, like, pay a bit for Elsie and me.'

'Wood!'

'Firewood, Mrs Hemsworthy.' He stamped the foot with the boot and Kit nodded at it.

'You had better get that on properly.'

'It's stiff. Like cardboard it is.' He sat again and drew the other boot to him, forcing his foot into it, flattening the misshapen tongues against his arches, then lacing deftly.

'Don't you want breakfast?' Kit was amazed at her own question, and he stood again, grinning, his face not drawn this morning, covered in freckles.

'Oh, yes please. Can I?' He clamped the few paces to the pantry beside her, and stepped inside. He took the loaf from the tin and sawed a thick slice, then he smothered it in black current jam. He turned to Kit, grinning, then he sank his strong, big teeth into it, his eyes bright. ''Slovely, Mrs Hemsworthy. We never have this at home, not Hartley's blackcurrant. They won't give you that on a means test chitty.'

'You must not talk with your mouth full, Tommy, it's bad manners.'

'Yes, Mrs Hemsworthy.'

Kit stared at him as he relished his breakfast. He was a new breed to her, subservient yet cocky, polite yet rough, common yet acceptable. She turned from him quickly. 'There's a coalshed out the back. Second door on your right. You might find a sack there. You can borrow it. To put the wood in.'

She watched him go, still holding the bread and jam before him, his string-supported grey flannel trousers very creased and baggy. 'You need a candle.'

'Got matches.' He grinned back at her, then went, a gust of cold air filling the room as he opened and closed the back door.

Kit sank to her chair and he returned, chewing the last of the food. He said, 'Shall I light the fire afore I go, get the coal in?'

'No thank you.' She spoke sharply, not willing to accept him, yet she asked, 'Are you likely to be long?'

'No, once this is full.' He hung the sack about his shoulders, cape-like, and caught it in front with a huge safety pin. 'Then tomorra I gotta go down Wind Street. I'm joining up.'

'The army?'

'Yes, Mrs Hemsworthy.'

'You're too young.'

'They won't know.' He grinned again, and Kit looked away from his level gaze. 'I won't tell them.'

He strode to the passage, then tried to creep in silence, his boots heavy, and she followed him, watching him slowly unbolt the front door, then he was clumping down the empty lamplit street, out of place in this reserved neighbourhood.

The rain had stopped, but the pavements and cobbles still shone black wet and the sky was a mass of brilliant stars.

Kit turned back into the house and a sound made her glance up. A white shadow, almost a nothing, flitted across the landing. Kit frowned; the place was dark except for the candle glowing in the kitchen at the end of the passage. Was it a trick of her imagination? She listened, standing motionless. Someone was there. Her skin tingled. She felt herself being watched, then she hurried to the kitchen, moving quietly.

She took the candle from the mantelpiece and went back up the passage, one hand shielding the flame from draught. She went up the stairs, her eyes seemingly sunk into her head as the light played on her jaw and throat. She watched the landing and listened.

Elsie's bedroom door was open, inviting. Kit paused on the landing, her shadow a grotesque thing stretching along wall and ceiling. She tiptoed to the bedroom and peered in.

The candlelight danced as she held her hand away from it, and the room was silent, the three mirrors of the dressing-table reflecting black and silver, the wardrobe mirror reflecting her, tall and straight, her face white, long with suspicion and tiredness, and the form of Elsie was in the bed, huddled, deep in clothes.

Kit stood for a moment more, than she turned away, weary for bed herself, yet loath to go back to Bertie. She was stunned at his stupidity, his selfishness, his audacity at bringing that girl home. She feared the future and regretted her past.

She hurried back down the stairs and into the kitchen. She lit another candle, placing one at each end of the mantelpiece. She made herself tea, then she sat hunched in her chair, wondering about herself – and about Elsie Buckley, wondering if her imagination was going to make her hell worse – and upstairs Elsie nipped into Bertie's big double bed, drew up her knees and wiggled her ice-cold toes against his bottom.

He moved from her and she moved her feet with him. He sighed, then at the very edge of the bed he opened his eyes furiously, the feet plonked square on his cheeks.

'Kit! For Christ's sake stop bloody tormenting me. It won't solve anything.'

And Elsie giggled.

Bertie frowned, thinking, then slowly turned in the darkness, not believing that even Elsie was so bold. His hand touched her face, feeling like a blind man, her hair, her ears, her neck. 'Elsie . . . .' He could only gasp, then she was in his arms, snuggled warm and close, laughing in a little suffocated way as her nose got buried in the sparse hairs on his chest.

'Bertie, isn't this lovely?' She quivered with naughtiness and delight.

'Elsie.' He laughed too, softly, deeply, secretly. 'You'll get me hanged, drawn, and quartered,' but her body against his was like a miracle, the mound of her belly fitted into him as he curved to her.

There was no passion. There was just the feeling of belonging, of being in the midst of infinite warmth: of a deep calm that was almost spiritual.

When they talked they whispered, telling of the last months apart. She of washing dishes, and he of Carruthers. She snuggled tighter to him then, frightened.

'Oh Bertie. And you paid them?'

'Me. And Kit.'

'Yes. Of course. You, and Kit.' He felt her sag, crumble; she said, 'I'll never be able to pay you back.'

'If the baby is a boy, you will have paid me back over and over.'

'You'd like to have him?'

'Of course. He would be my son.'

'No. You can't. Kit would hate him . . . .'

There was so much to say. So much to tell each other.

'You told me you were sterile, that you couldn't catch.'

'Mm . . . .' She snuggled close again, moving herself against him, her hands caressing beneath his pyjama jacket. 'I'd planned, Bertie. I'd planned. I wanted a little Bertie.'

'You're a nut case. What if I hadn't come along tonight?'

'I'd still have had a little Bertie.'

He sighed, loving, resting his head against hers, and when the whispering stopped he knew he could sleep.

She crept from his bed and flitted back across the landing. She pulled the bolster out of the bed and re-arranged it, smiling at her own deviousness. The bolster had looked like her, all lumpy and tucked up.

She got into bed and drew her feet up into the nightie Kit had lent her. She shivered. It would soon be dawn and she would have to climb Mount Pleasant hill to the workhouse.

She put her head down, determined not to think. Bertie loved her, had missed her, wanted the baby. She re-said her prayers, but she didn't ask for anything, and at breakfast she kept her gaze down and her voice modified. She had been a naughty girl, and one day the devil might have her, but she had enjoyed the naughtiness, and would do it all again, given the chance. She stole a glance at Bertie, and he winked.

Kit concentrated on feeding them all. 'Tommy. D'you want more bread and jam?' Already Kit realised Tommy lived on bread and jam. The bacon, eggs and tomatoes she had supplied had been a luxury he enjoyed, but he still looked for his bread and jam.

By dinner-time Kit felt she was presiding over a large family. Two more in the kitchen, two more at Sunday table, made the place seem crowded.

Bertie carved the joint, wondering whether to leave some for a cold meal tomorrow or to use the lot. For a moment he almost asked Kit, but stubbornness took over, and he carved the whole joint, then forked the slices onto every-one's blue and white plates. 'Another slice Tommy?'

'Yes please, Mr Hemsworthy.'

'Elsie?'

'No thank you.'

'Pass your plate.'

'I said no thank you.' She wanted to quarrel, the situation had become more humiliating as she ate what she saw as Kit's food, yet she wanted to laugh; he was trying to feed her up, and no one had, as yet, pushed her off to the workhouse.

Bertie ordered, 'Pass your plate,' and Tommy did it for her, grinning, confident he was on the winning side.

Kit took her place with her back to the scullery door, and as she picked at her food she watched everyone else. Bertie looked ill-tempered, his jaw set hard, his head averted slightly from her, his eyes now and again softening at the sight of Elsie Buckley. Emma and Linda seemed excited, verging on giggling, as they kept throwing glances at Tommy Buckley, then back at each other.

Tommy's table manners upset Kit. He held his face over his plate, and scooped great forkfuls of food into his mouth as if afraid the lot would be taken from him. He was also noisy, chewing, lip-smacking, swigging from his water glass while his mouth was full, then swallowing like a dog bolting food.

Kit was fascinated yet horrified, then she watched Elsie. Elsie was being polite, eating because the filled plate was there. Kit thought of the climb up Mount Pleasant hill to the workhouse. Elsie was round-shouldered, weary, her short hair that had once proudly presented sugared kiss curls was lank, yet in that swelling belly was Bertie's baby. A baby that might have Tommy's strong, young, cocky attitude to life, blended with Bertie's air of breeding, his air of gentle elegance. Kit thought of the comments made by Carruthers; would Bertie leave her, his home, his job, everything for Elsie? And Kit nodded to herself. He might not have done so before, but now that Elsie was pregnant, he most certainly would.

She looked back at Bertie, and for an amazing moment

she realised he wasn't master of this house any more. She was. She could force him away or lure him to stay. She could break this family asunder, or bind it together. She, Kitty Nolan, was the power: the judge and the jury.

She sat, not eating, a small, perfect green sprout pierced at the end of her fork, and she looked around the table as if seeing everybody, everything, in slow motion. She had power over all four of these people. Each was so interlinked with emotions that she could make or break every one of them. Elsie was going to die. Bound to. Everyone with consumption did, so what long-term danger could she be?

Kit served the rice pudding briskly. She felt more sure of herself. The shock of seeing Bertie come into the passage with Elsie last night was wearing off. She was beginning to think clearly again.

She served coffee and watched Bertie offer Tommy a cigar, watched the boy hesitate, grin as if he didn't believe it, then watched him take it. Tommy imitated Bertie in the ritual of nipping and lighting and savouring; laughing, abashed, while Emma and Linda watched with delight, and Elsie smiled, wondering when they would tell her to get her old tweed coat and go.

Then Tommy coughed, a short burst at first, spluttering, like a rousing sneeze, the cigar held above his right ear like a bomb about to go off. 'Ooo – gawd – ' he managed, then doubled up with a paroxysm again, his mouth agape, his tongue full and scarlet and shaking.

Everyone looked at him, amused, curious.

Bertie quizzed, 'Too strong for you?'

Tommy shook his head and put the cigar to his lips once more, then he drew on it as if it were a weak cigarette. 'Oooo gawd – !' His eyes opened like those on a ventriloquist's doll and his skin went mahogany.

Everyone began laughing. Linda ran and thumped Tommy on the back.

He tried to laugh and cough at the same time, tears streaming down his freckled cheeks.

Linda cried, 'Tommy! You'll be sick!'

'No, he won't,' Bertie replied. 'And how do you know, anyway? Have you been trying them?'

Elsie called, 'Tommy! Throw that cigar away. Give it back to Bertie,' and Tommy struggled from his chair.

'Go to hell,' he spluttered. 'I'll smoke the bloody thing if it kills me.'

Bertie roared with laughter as he stood with his back to the fire. It was as if an explosion of tension had taken place, and Tommy played up to him.

The boy staggered about, his cough exaggerated now, his body bent in the old grey shirt and trousers, one fist thumping his chest. He leaned against the pantry door, sagging at his baggy knees, his turn-ups caught on the tops of his battered salt-stained boots. He rolled his eyes and gasped, then looked at Bertie, wet-faced. 'Poo – and you smoke these things? Old socks they are, mun. Oooo – my gawd . . . .'

Emma and Linda cupped their hands to their mouths in laughter and sympathy, their eyes brilliant, like blue fires above their white fingers, while Kit's dark brows lifted in concern and begrudged laughter. Her lips wriggled against the desire to join in the fun but finally she, too, looked almost jovial. Her voice came deeper than usual as she chided. 'Bertie, you should not have given it to him. He'll be ill.'

'Tripe!' Bertie gurgled. 'If he's going to be a sergeant he'll smoke worse than my cigars,' and Kit went to the scullery. Still smiling ruefully, she washed the dishes, and Elsie stood beside her and wiped them. One woman tall and thin, the other short and pregnant. Neither woman acknowledged the other, but Bertie and Tommy talked easily in the kitchen, about the army: what Bertie had done while in it; what Tommy hoped to do when he got into it.

Darkness came early. Tommy put more coal on the fire and Elsie prepared tea. Kit sat with the Sunday papers and, at nine o'clock, Elsie stood between the back of Bertie's chair and the door to the passage: the door to her coat and the workhouse, but also the door to the stairs and the spare bed in the back room. She twisted her hands together and drew courage. She said quietly, nervously, 'I'd better get up to bed, then,' and no one answered. She took a stifled breath and found more courage. She said, 'Shall I be in the office in the morning?' And Kit lowered her newspaper and looked at her, then she looked at Bertie and he was watching her, waiting.

On the mantelpiece the clock ticked, in the fireplace the red and orange coals made a little hissing sound, and Elsie felt her chest so tight her lungs couldn't move to breathe.

Kit drew her lips in, then loosened them. She knew the question Elsie was really asking, and she knew Bertie was waiting to know his future. She hated him, loathed him, yet she loved him, needed him, and knew that if she had to have him at all, it had to be on his terms.

She glanced at Tommy. He sat on the settee, a cowboy magazine of Bertie's held before him, but Kit could feel him waiting too.

All of them waiting for her, Kitty Nolan, judge and jury, to pass sentence. She smiled, as ladies do when they drop pennies into beggars' tins, and she said, 'That would be a good idea, Elsie, but be out of there by half-past nine. The auditors are coming at ten o'clock.'

Elsie felt the blood drain from her head, and the baby kicked. She was suddenly afraid she would faint. She put her hands to her belly and turned quickly. She left the kitchen door open and ran up the passage and stairs to the bed. There the coughing took over. Her tears of relief ran with the saliva of her cough, and she struggled with a small white handkerchief. Then she climbed into bed, too spent to undress. She would wait until she was rested, then she would put on the nightie and sleep. She longed for Bertie to come to kiss her goodnight, but he didn't, and as she thought of Kit, of the auditors coming tomorrow, of the weight inside her and the tension about her, she half wondered if, maybe, the workhouse might have been better.

267

The auditors came at ten o'clock as promised, two fresh-faced young men who thought coming to the backwoods of Wales a hilarious adventure.

Bertie opened the door to them and they were all laughter and clear complexions, the grey pin-striped suits with accentuated padded shoulders as identical as their grey trilbies.

Laugh they might, Bertie thought, but they were no fools. The books and papers were already laid out for them, and Kit brought tea and biscuits. Bertie said he had calls to make, put on his overcoat and homburg and went out.

Tommy had instructions to come back from Wind Street quietly, and Elsie was to stay in the kitchen. The auditors settled down to auditing.

Would they like Kit to prepare lunch for them? No, they said, looking at chrome watches worn on clean hairy wrists, they had other plans and would be back about three.

Kit smiled, the perfect hostess, in her best mustard-coloured woollen dress, and they went.

The silence that had struck the kitchen all morning broke into chatter. The recruiting sergeant had looked like a totem pole, honest injun, straight all the way up with a peaked cap on top, and yes, of course, they'd accepted Tommy. He would hear in about six weeks' time.

No one mentioned the workhouse. The wood Tommy had brought was stacked in the coalhouse, all chopped into pieces that would fit deep in the grate, and Elsie thought she might do some more office work.

Kit had five minutes on the bed which lengthened to an hour, and it was manna to hear someone else hitting the typewriter keys. She told herself she didn't really hate Elsie Buckley, she pitied her; she wished to God the girl had never entered the house in the first place, but the unpaid labour was welcome – just until Elsie went home to her father again. Bertie would have to see to the matter, visit Tom Buckley and get the stupid man to see sense. That would, at least, be more merciful than the workhouse.

Then the auditors came back at half-past two instead of the promised three o'clock. They walked in fast, like young men who dance through life, and they found Elsie with her big belly and her white consumptive face at the small desk.

She jumped up, looking as guilty as a child caught in the mud, and they eyed her curiously. Kit came rushing, panic-stricken – if they told Carruthers that the girl was here . . . !

They turned to Kit smiling, each with a desultory hand in a trouser pocket, young men who had been to university and so were, socially, far above the peasants, and Kit, as well as Elsie, felt very much in awe at that moment.

Elsie edged to the door, also smiling, her hands making a silly effort to hide her pregnancy, and Kit came into the room while Elsie escaped behind her.

One auditor remarked laughingly, his eyes calculating, 'Your daughter is shy.'

'Yes,' Kit said, for want of something better. 'She is,' and a long awkward silence made one auditor idly tap the leg of Bertie's desk with the toe of his immaculate black shoe. Kit jerked herself back into life. 'Did you have lunch? A nice meal?'

'Thank you,' they said. 'Yes thank you.'

At four o'clock they went. Kit stood on the doorstep and waved them away. They had been in the office for only a few hours, not long enough for a full investigation, so they had come because of only one or two things, and they had found their answer easily. Kit wondered what it had been. Their voices carried as they left the gate. They were talking about Piccadilly Circus and the way it was lit up now, with coloured electric lights. Kit closed the front door and went to the office. Books and papers were strewn everywhere, the pigeon-holes emptied. She sat at Bertie's desk, depleted. She thought of her kitchen, no longer empty for her to escape to for a quiet cup of tea, and she put her head in her hands. At that moment she had no emotions left; they were completely stifled, love, hatred, jealousy, fear, all deadened, yet five minutes later, she was swamped with her daughters charging home from school, navy blue melton coats undone, navy blue velour hats kept on by elastic under the chin.

'Mummy. We're going to do Grecian dancing, and Miss Evans says we must have pink dresses with –'

Kit smiled. 'Into the kitchen,' she said. 'Elsie's made a coconut cake.' It seemed a perfectly natural thing to say.

A few days later on Armistice Day, Friday 11th November, 1932, Kit gave Tommy money to take Elsie to the talkies.

There was great excitement and much chatter. Laurel and Hardy used to be marvellous, and no one could better Charlie Chaplin, but talkies . . . .

Elsie sat before the three mirrors of the dressing-table and dipped her fingers into a basin of sugared water. Carefully, systematically, she brought the kiss curls back into being. She used a pencil from the office to fleck in arched eyebrows, and she used one of Kit's pink lipsticks to colour her cheeks and re-draw her lips. She had to study the latter, contemplating her face in the mirrors. She looked different, older. There were no lines or wrinkles, in fact the skin seemed tighter on her bones, but unhappiness had left emotional scars that reflected in her eyes, as they do in those of an injured dog, and even when she laughed there was a sadness.

She sighed and decided. The heart-shaped mouth was out, no longer fashionable; Clara Bow, the star who began it all, belonged to the age of silent films. This was 1932, almost 1933, the age of the talkies, and she, Elsie Buckley, would draw herself a different mouth.

She went downstairs feeling self-conscious about the change in herself. She didn't feel ill. Her baby kicked, and Bertie gave her a shilling for chocolates.

Tommy waited for her, his grey flannel trousers held up by a pair of Bertie's braces which were hidden beneath one of Bertie's blue and green Fair Isle jerseys.

Kit stood smiling, watching them, amused at the pathetic pleasure surrounding brother and sister as they

270

admired each other, then she said, 'Have you decided where you're going?'

'Oh yes,' Elsie replied. 'The Castle. To see Anna May Wong and Clive Brook in *Shanghai Express*.'

'No,' Tommy said, 'the Rialto's best. It's Johnny Weissmuller and Maureen O'Sullivan in *Tarzan the Apeman*.'

For a few moments Tommy looked down at Elsie, then he shrugged, his face showing his caring for her. 'A'right. We'll see Marlene Dirty Bitch,' he agreed.

'Don't say that.' Elsie scowled. 'She's lovely.'

'It's only a joke.'

Elsie pouted, and the warmth, the closeness between her and Tommy kept Kit and Bertie watching.

'A'right,' Elsie moved quickly and took Tommy's arm, 'we'll go to the most amazing adventure film ever seen.'

Bertie stood before the fire, interested in the difficulty of their decision. 'Is that what it's supposed to be?'

'Yes.' Elsie grinned at him. 'Jungle thrills and jungle romance.'

'Oh, that's it, then,' Bertie laughed. 'That's the one to see.'

He and Kit stood, listening to them go in much the same way as they often heard Emma and Linda go, then the doors had closed, the gate had clanged, and the house was silent.

'Linda gone to Girl Guides?' Bertie asked.

'Yes. And Emma to Band of Hope.'

They settled to a quiet evening and it was Kit who said eventually, 'Bertie,' as her long white fingers crocheted a scarlet beret for Emma.

'Mm?'

'I've been thinking.'

He looked up from his magazine, then stretched. It seemed years since he had known such peace.

'Don't you think you ought to go and see Tom Buckley?'

'Tom Buckley?' Bertie's brows lifted in question.

'Yes. About Elsie and Tommy. He must wonder where they are.'

271

'I doubt it.' Bertie looked at his magazine longingly, but Kit persisted.

'I still think it would do no harm to go.'

'All right.' Bertie began reading. He didn't mind going to see Tom Buckley if it pleased Kit. He read on, turning a page, then he looked up again, thinking, wondering which way Kit's mind was working, and one side of her mouth tilted in a half smile.

'He might miss the two of them,' she said. 'Want them home again.'

Bertie heaved his hips up from the depths of his battered chair and struggled to get his handkerchief from his trouser pocket without standing up. He didn't need the handkerchief. He was playing for time. He blew his nose, thinking, looking at the fire, feeling its heat on his shins. He went through the same manoeuvre to put his handkerchief away, and then he said, 'All right,' and Kit's fingers didn't falter with the crochet hook, the scarlet wool being caught and twisted with concentrated dexterity.

'I think it will be best,' she said, and Bertie felt he had suddenly become involved in an invisible game of draughts. Kit's black had just jumped his white. He would have to be more wary in future. He smiled, his eyes deceptively bright as he looked at her, and she glanced up at him. She was a beautiful woman tonight, her thick black hair drawn softly back to the nape of her long smooth neck, her high-cheekboned face tranquil, her eyes challenging as if she knew he knew she was out to win the game.

'Yes, of course,' Bertie said amiably. 'I'll go tomorrow. See what I can do,' and next morning he ran for the tram still hoping an idea would come to him, that he would think up a valid, honest reason for Elsie staying near him. He needed her.

There were still moments when he felt the urge to run away with her, be forever alone with her. He wanted her in his bed, but it was Kit who snuggled between the sheets, Kit who fell asleep with her arm across his waist like a lasso that held him; and being on the tram, rattling across the

New Cut bridge, seeing the dark green waters lapping at the slimy dock walls, wasn't solving his problem.

The wind came from Kilvey Hill and turned his nose red, and he ran up the worn stone steps, not only in an effort to get the task done, but also to warm himself. He thought now of Tom Buckley, the big, burly, bald man who had nothing, not even his pride. He had lost his hand, his job, his wife, his son – and now his daughter was pregnant, unmarried. Maybe, Bertie thought, that had been the last straw: Elsie's pregnancy.

The terrace of houses seemed to be bending even more with age and decay, and Bertie wondered what he was going to say when Tom Buckley opened his front door, or if he would have time to say anything before Tom Buckley hit him. He also wondered how he, himself, would react if ever a married man got Linda in the family way, and he didn't like his thoughts.

The aspidistra was still there, in the window, dusty, not too healthy in its green glossy china pot on the tall wooden stand. Bertie saw his reflection in the window, with a white-grey sky, and he threw the last of his cigarette away. He raised the knocker and let it drop, then he turned his back on it, looking out over the road that ran below the supporting wall. He waited for Tom Buckley and nothing happened. Cautiously he turned and knocked again, more definitely this time. He peered through the small black vertical letterbox and, inside, the house was still, the kitchen door slightly open. Bertie knocked again, harder, waiting, but he knew the house was empty.

Through the parlour window of the house next door a flustered face peered out and a hand flicked, then went. Bertie waited. The neighbour came out, small, thin, cold, her skimpy orange hair drawn back in a small straggly bun, a Welsh flannel shawl across her shoulders, tied in a knot on her flat chest.

'Hullo.' She twinkled up at him. She was toothless. 'You're Mr Hemsworthy, aren't yer. Of the Unicorn Insurance.'

'Possibly.'

'D'yer want the key then?'

'Do you have it?'

'A'course.' It was as if she expected him to know. 'Tom said as how you'd be coming sooner or later. For Elsie's things. I packed 'em, not that she 'ad much, poor thing. He told me to throw out Gwen's things, but I didn't.' She pushed a Yale key into the lock. 'I gave 'em ter the jumble at the church.' Bertie followed her into the house and she moved in small quick jerks, looking at him, at the walls, the ceiling, the narrow dark stairs. 'The new people will be in on Saturday, it's a good job you've come now.'

'New people?' He was in the kitchen. The grate was full of dead cinders, there was no furniture. 'What happened?'

'Sold it. Sold it all. Had to have a couple o'bob to go with, now didn't he? I said as how he ought to sell Gwen's things too, but he wouldn't. It wouldn't have done 'er no 'arm, would it?'

'Where's he gone?'

She grinned at him, brown-necked and half-starved. 'You don't know then? Gone ter Dagenham ter get a job.' She nodded and folded her arms in satisfaction. 'In that new car works. Car works. Walking. A whole crowd of 'em gone. All walking there. All the way to England. They need the work, see.'

'Do you hear from him?'

'From Tom Buckley?' The question astonished her. 'Never. He's gone now. New life for 'im. Bloody good luck to 'im I say. Nice man though. Always generous, if you know what I mean. Anybody down the Brown Cow'll tell you.'

'Yes,' Bertie said. Then sadly, 'There's no need for you to stay. I can see to things myself, thank you.'

'Elsie's bags are up the stairs. In the front bedroom.' Her bright gaze probed.

'Thank you, you have been most kind. I'll take them.'

'I'm glad she's got a good 'ome. With you now then, is she?'

274

Bertie stared at her woodenly and she backed, feeling for the door behind her.

'Good day,' he said pointedly.

Still she dithered. 'Yes, well, tell Elsie I was asking about her. And the boy. The boy all right?' She twitched her almost hairless head to one side, the toothless smile still in place.

'The boy is fine, thank you. Good day.'

'I allus said they were lucky 'aving you – a rich man – '

She went then, pattering up the passage, slamming the front door after her.

Bertie listened to the echoing silence and smelled the damp and decay. The stone floor was glistening with globules of condensation, the wallpaper was bleached where the sofa had been. On the high mantelpiece lay awful crepe paper chrysanthemums, red and yellow with long green stems. He took them down and shook them, grimacing, holding them away as the dust rose in a cloud, then he took the small sheet of cheap notepaper that had lain beneath them. It was a letter in Elsie's handwriting. With no qualm of conscience Bertie read:

'Dear Pa,
Do not worry about Tommy and me. Mr and Mrs Hemsworthy have taken us in. Do not worry at all. I will put the baby up for sale. You can get as much as ten pounds for one if you advertise in the right paper. I am sorry I am not yours because I would have liked to have been. Ma told me before she went to Malvern. She said for me to forgive her for having bad blood and to look after you. I did try to look after you, but you are a stubborn fool sometimes. I am sorry I am not yours. Tommy says he is going to the army.
Love,
Elsie.'

Bertie stood near the grimy window that faced a big grimy black wall and read the letter again. So Gwen had

had a lover. Poor Gwen. She had probably carried her sin hard. Maybe it explained her acceptance of Tom's aggression, his drinking. Maybe she felt that as a woman with 'bad blood' she deserved nothing better.

And what of Elsie? The guttersnipe who had needed loving desperately, yet had been unwanted by her natural father, unwanted by Tom probably, unwanted by Gwen, and was now unwanted by Kit.

Bertie's heart literally ached; it felt heavy and tight and he put a hand to it, rubbing gently. A feeling of hopelessness permeated the house, and he lit a cigarette in a vain effort to comfort himself, to calm his mind, to make the place seem less empty, less an emblem of the times, with its gloom, depression and poverty.

He put the letter into his pocket then went up the stairs, still gripping the flowers. He found a suitcase, and a shopping bag with a green skirt sticking out of it, and he hurrried out of the house. Elsie would have to stay with him now. There was nothing that could separate him from her.

She was in the office, alone, at her desk, and he presented the chrysanthemums to her, leaning over her shoulder and kissing her ear. She took them slowly, as though they were roses he'd brought her, and he told her that Tom had gone. She smoothed the awful crepe paper petals between finger and thumb and smiled, while her eyes stayed dull. 'They're nice, aren't they?' she said. 'I made them. Did I tell you?'

Bertie shook his head, and immediately decided the paper flowers were beautiful. He washed a vase for them, then gave them to Tommy to put on the mantelpiece in Elsie's bedroom. He thought she was looking better. Her face wasn't so drawn and the kiss curls were as defiant as ever. She sat well back from her desk, put her hands on her swollen belly, and smiled. 'I'm sure he'll be on time.'

'Maybe he'll come for Christmas.'

She laughed and stood and went into Bertie's arms.

He felt the bliss of her body against his, and the tension seeping from him as his face gently rubbed her hair. He said, 'No Phul-Nana these days.'

'No. I haven't any.'

'I'll get you some. For Christmas.'

He could smell the consumption on her, a warm, cloying, body smell, but it had become a natural part of her, and they kissed lingeringly, tenderly, no longer passionately but like two people who know their love is forever.

★   ★   ★

Maggie Davies plonked the scarlet straw hat on the top of her head, stuck a long silver-knobbed pin through it, and yelled from the rickety back door to the lamp moving down the dark garden. 'John! Cut yellow ones. They look more cheerful and they bring good health.'

At the bottom of the half-acre John kept clipping the chrysanthemum stems with the big rusting scissors, then he took the bunch into the warm kitchen. 'How's that, heh?'

'Lovely.' The flowers were wet, smelling strongly. 'And the bottle of plonk. What have we got?'

'Parsnip? Elderberry? Potato?' His crooked teeth matched his crooked nose, his illness of a year ago gone and forgotten.

'The first two.'

'Two?'

Maggie put her plump hands on her scarlet taffeta-covered hips. 'It's a party we going to. Don't be mean.'

'No – I was only thinking – '

'That's it then.'

She turned, nodded to the fire, the cauldron hanging as usual from the chimney hook. 'There's fine they'll be when we get back.'

'How many have you got in there?'

'Two. They're the best Christmas puddings I've made yet, I can tell you. Brandy in them. Did you taste it yesterday?'

'Marvellous,' he enthused, wrapping the flowers in tissue

277

paper. 'Let's take one of them and all.'

Maggie and John stood like Jack Sprat and his wife. He gangly, lean, bony, and she oozing soft rolls of flesh everywhere, in the low-cut dress she had worn to last year's party, an artificial daisy jutting from her cleavage. She chuckled indulgently. 'Your conscience troubling you then?'

'Well, they're in a mess, aren't they, mun?'

'Poor dabs. Who'd have thought Elsie Buckley could end up like this?'

'I suppose it is Bertie's?'

Maggie humphed and got a pudding in its large white china basin from her larder. 'Get a bag to put this lot in. One thing's certain, boyo, it's not the Holy Ghost's.'

John got the bag and shook it open, holding it for Maggie to slip the pudding into. 'Bertie's in a hole,' he said.

'Now you keep your mouth shut. I didn't even send any cards to London this year, so we can't be blamed if anything goes wrong.'

John packed the bottles and pudding and flowers together. 'It's going to be embarrassing, mind. It's bad enough when we go to the office. There's Kit, queen of all she surveys, there's Elsie with her big belly; and Bertie with bags under his eyes you can put these bottles into.'

'We'll laugh,' Maggie ordered, 'and play hunt the slipper, and pretend we believe that damn silly yarn about Elsie's lover gone to China and got himself shot. Right?'

'I suppose so.'

'Have you locked the back door?'

'Yes.'

'Have you got fags to hand around?'

'Yes.'

'Now, let's see . . . .' She rummaged in her enormous handbag. 'Get me my coat, there's a love. My best one. God, I haven't worn it since their last party. Remember that one? Elsie standing on her head showing all her fanny . . . . Have you got the presents for the kids? I hope they like bracelets. I couldn't think of anything else to get. It's

278

no wonder Bertie strayed, you know. Kit's hard. Hard as nails. You can see it in her. Wonder if he ever loved her.'

John held the coat for her to get into. It was a big expansive task involving the waving of dimpled arms and jerking of breasts, rustling of taffeta and quivering of cleavage daisy.

'Some managers are like that.' Maggie did the coat up, standing straight, trying to hold in everything from bust to knees, then she gave up, laughing. 'I've never liked Kit Hemsworthy. There's something there – I don't know – '

'She's the manager's wife – '

Maggie glanced around the kitchen, making sure all was secure, the lamp wick lowered, the fire dampened down, then she and John went out, into the blackness of the mountain night, picking their way on the unmade road, waiting for their eyes to become accustomed to the dark before putting out the torch.

Comfortably she took his arm. 'Maybe we've only got oil lamps,' she said. 'Not electricity and chandeliers, and we don't have a baby either, but at least we are true to each other.'

His arm squeezed hers to him. 'I'd like to have been a manager, Mag. It's like just waiting to grow old and die if you don't have some ambition, but I wouldn't be in Bertie's shoes now. Not for all the tea in China.'

They caught the train, smug in their contentment, not admitting a sense of satisfaction about the way fate had overtaken the previously successful and respectable Hemsworthys.

'Still,' Maggie frowned, and her brows were as black as her dyed hair, 'they're lucky they've got us. We are good friends to them, John, aren't we?'

John agreed. The train picked up speed and the winter night rushed past the windows that reflected like mirrors. 'We'll cheer them up,' he nodded. 'I got a couple of good jokes to tell.'

★   ★   ★

The only person in number 300 Prince Edward Road who wanted another party was Linda, and she had pleaded to go into town alone to buy herself a new dress.

She bought it to please Tommy.

'What's your favourite colour?' she had asked him coyly.

He had thought for a long time, knowing why girls asked such questions, then he had laughed at her, mocking her young earnestness, her guileless desire to please him.

'Yellow,' he had said then, 'like the buttercups in Singleton Park. My Pa grew a sunflower once. In a pot out our back. It was bigger than me.'

Linda gazed up into his freckled, happy face in awe and adoration. Her voice squeaked, 'Higher than six foot!' And her lips were faintly tinted with lipstick.

Again there came his laughter. It was superior, indulgent, but, in a way he was unaware of, affectionate. 'I wasn't six foot then, duffer, I was only a tiddler. About seven, I think.'

'Seven . . . .' The thought of Tommy being only seven, about the same age as Emma, made Linda sigh, and her mothering instinct came to the fore. 'Did your Pa love you a lot?'

'Not a lot,' Tommy said, and didn't add, 'but he loved me more than he loved Elsie,' and when, on new year's eve, Linda came down the stairs in her new lemon-coloured net and taffeta dress, with an artificial yellow rose in her dark brown hair, Tommy felt like a lord. He went to the stairs to meet her and took her hand, as he had seen courtiers doing in films, and he let his lips rest lightly on it, while she curtseyed a little, each of them playing an innocent game of enticement and pleasure.

Elsie watched wistfully from the half-light of the landing. They were free to love. Linda didn't have to hide away because of a shameful big belly, and soon Tommy would be marching to a life of independence and adventure.

Elsie went back to her room and sat on the bed. She felt enormous. The smock she wore had been Kit's, and so it

280

was beige, a nondescript colour that made Elsie feel the same way. She saw her reflection in the wardrobe's big mirror. She was slumped, round-shouldered. She heard Kit going into the bathroom, the taps running fast, she smelt the scent of pine bath-salts filling the house, and Elsie thought of Malvern pine woods, and regretted nothing. She hugged herself and remembered the feel of cold air on her skin and the warmth of Bertie inside her.

When the door opened slowly, and Bertie peeped around it, she laughed quietly at him. He was so furtive, and he chuckled as he scuttled in, exaggerating the naughtiness of it, because it was wonderful to see her face lighting up, her grey eyes twinkling with subdued laughter.

She switched off the table lamp beside her and held out both arms to him. She whispered, 'Have you come to seduce me while your wife is in the bath?'

'I've forgotten how to,' he whispered back. He sat on the bed beside her, then she lay on her back and he lay beside her, his white shirt gleaming and stiff with newness. They heard the tank emptying in the bathroom, heard the splashing as Kit began cleansing herself, and the gentle kisses they exchanged were manna.

'Bertie?'

'Sweetheart.'

'D'you think the agents believe my lover was killed in the army?'

'Does it matter?'

'It must be awful for Kit.'

'Yes,' he said, and wished his women wouldn't be so concerned with each other. He let the tip of his tongue tickle the lobe of Elsie's ear, his hand resting lightly on her belly.

She lent her head on him, lovingly. 'D'you think they've all guessed you're its daddy?'

'Shall I tell them?' His tongue stopped teasing. He watched her, and she turned her head to him, shocked at his suggestion.

'You wouldn't! Kit would have a fit!'

281

'I'm beginning to think Kit could live in a harem. She never says a damn word. No quarrels. Nothing.'

'You think she doesn't mind?'

He leaned up to look into her eyes. 'Mind you being here, you mean? Mind me loving you?'

'She does mind, Bertie. She's just waiting. Sometimes she frightens me.'

'Waiting?' He sat up. 'Waiting for what?'

'I dunno. To get her own back I suppose.'

He laughed again, but not happily now. It was a sound of gentle derision that hid a deeply rooted fear. He had the same impression about Kit. He too had seen the dark brooding in her eyes, and had wondered what was going on behind them. He said, smiling, 'That's the trouble with pregnant women. They imagine things.'

She turned her head from him and asked seriously, 'D'you believe there's a hereafter?' And he stopped to think, to weigh his words.

He said, 'Does it matter? Sometimes I'm so tired I dread the thought of still existing, of going on, even after death, but other times, when I'm happy – '

'Are you happy now?'

'When I'm with you – '

But it was as if she didn't really want his opinion. She said, as she stared at the ceiling, 'I believe there is a hereafter, and that we all come back together. In a new life.'

'Reincarnation, you mean?'

'Right from the beginning of time we're all in one group, and no matter how many times we live and die, we still stay in that group.'

Bertie lay back. There wasn't a lot of room for them both on this single bed, but he said nothing, glad to be alone with her, puzzled at the turn of her thoughts, even a bit surprised that Elsie of the bare feet and ragamuffin up-bringing could become a philosopher.

She went on quietly, 'Maybe in the last life I was your wife and we were very rich, while Kit was a begger and our butler sent her packing, so in this life she'll pay us back.'

He laughed a little then. 'So what's going to happen in the next life?'

'Will you wait for me?' Her head turned sharply, unexpectedly, and her stare was serious, demanding. 'Will you, Bertie? Next time don't marry anybody else. Only me.'

He nodded, willing to agree his soul away. 'I won't marry anybody else.'

'Even if I'm a horrible old lady and you are a young and handsome man?'

He frowned, perplexed by her earnestness. 'I'm a very old man now, and you are a young and beautiful lady, in this life, yet we love.'

'But you didn't wait for me. You married Kit.'

'All right.' He pecked her cheek, his lips wanting to cling to hers even as he drew them away. 'I'll wait for you. No matter how old I get. As long as you promise to wait for me, no matter how old you get.'

She smiled, utterly believing, but then she frowned. 'What if what I believe is a little bit wrong, and we don't meet in the next life?'

'Then I'll remain a bachelor and you'll become an old maid.'

She gurgled with delight and cuddled up to him, her head propped on the pillow, her belly like a mountain, and he said, 'D'you feel better now that's all sorted out?' And the corners of her lips quirked so that for a moment her face was that of the young girl who loved to run barefoot through the market, making rude signs to the men who bawled their lust and admiration after her.

'I feel as I have always done.' Her expression emphasised an innuendo. 'When your hands are near me. Shall we try it?'

'You are an obscene little witch.'

'Love me?'

'Lots.'

'I wish it was over. I've had awful backache all day.'

'Another three or four weeks – '

'Oh Bertie – ' and in an instant her mood had changed

again. 'I am frightened. Of everything.' She turned, clumsy, and their arms gripped each other, the scent of the Phul-Nana he had bought her for Christmas mingling with the scent of his shaving soap and toothpaste. He worried that he could feel her spine through her clothes, but she rarely coughed in the day now.

He whispered, 'Have you taken your slippery elm food?'

She nodded into his throat. 'And my raspberry leaves. And my bile beans.'

'Good.' They cuddled close and he felt the baby kick. 'Coo! He's going to be a footballer.'

*   *   *

In the bath, Kit sat for a while and listened. The tank had stopped refilling. The house was suspiciously still, like the ominous quiet before a storm. She guessed Bertie was with Elsie and wondered what they were doing. She squeezed the soap between both wet hands so it began to ooze its soft pink surface between her fingers, and a little sound of agony escaped from her lips.

She moved her long pale legs, watching the green pine-scented water sway, then she replaced the soap in its holder, swilled herself and stepped out of the bath. She dried herself and put on her dressing-gown and slippers. She hesitated, standing, panting with tension, then she opened the door a few inches. The silence was uncanny. She moved back to the bath and pulled out the plug. The water began to rush noisily away and Kit peered around the door, waiting. She saw Bertie stealing from Elsie's room, his eyes squinting against the unaccustomed electric light. He was tidying his hair and buttoning his shirt.

Kit began to sing, tunelessly, not too loud, and opened the bathroom door with a flourish, then she came out, tall, thin, wide-shouldered, shining, vibrantly clean, her smile beamed at him, artificially cheerful. 'You ready, Bertie?'

'Almost. Won't be long.'

'Good. I won't be a tick either,' and they went to their

bedroom together, neither of them mentioning Elsie Buckley.

Elsie lay on her bed and listened, then she turned her face to the big bay window as if trying to turn her back on the rest of the world.

The sky was dark purple and, in a house opposite, a naked bulb showed through the net curtain of an upstairs room, spreading a golden glow over the intervening gardens. A cat screamed and Elsie thought of Salubrious Terrace and the evenings she and Ma and Pa and Tommy had spent in the comfort of the firelight. Now it was all gone, Ma, Pa and son, Tommy and herself.

Elsie might have fallen asleep then but she heard the front door bell clang in the kitchen beneath her, heard Maggie Davies all ready to whoop it up with a big red mouth, and Elsie smiled reminiscently. Maggie in her own mountain home, the place that was once a farmhouse, and the Maggie who came here, to Bertie's parties, were two different people. It sounded as if everyone was arriving together. Elsie felt the cold air from the open front door rush up the stairs and into her, then she sat up.

She supposed she ought to go to the bathroom. She had backache and was tired, and hoped the luxury of hot water would help. She didn't bother with make-up, glad of the bath, more Phul-Nana behind her ears, and Kit's strong bristle brush to sweep through her hair.

She went back to her room, switching on the main light, then she crouched suddenly as a darting of wind caught her. As it passed she straightened up and stared in the mirror at herself. She was all belly, and the beige smock was as dull as a wet day. She looked around the room for inspiration, something to cheer herself up, and then burrowed through the drawers of the dressing-table.

She giggled as she explored, her feet wonderfully bare on the warm red carpet, and music floated up from below. It was the lovely lilting tango Jack Buchanan made famous, 'Good night Vienna . . .' and it sounded as if everyone had arrived. The women had stopped scurrying past her door, bringing their outdoor things to the girls' room, and the scent of cigar and cigarette smoke was filling the house.

Elsie sat on the dressing-table stool and sewed fast, biting the cotton between her big strong teeth, then she dressed and put on stockings, but no shoes, and went downstairs. She walked slowly in case the effort made her cough, and she went into the party.

Bertie saw her first, maybe because he had been waiting for her, and as she appeared in the doorway he whistled, low and teasing. Everyone followed his gaze. The wireless loudspeakers hung on the wall, a man's happy voice was singing, 'All the horses in the zoo, cock up their tails so why shouldn't you?' but no one laughed. Elsie was framed in the doorway as if in a portrait, her eyes big, too bright, but laughing; her head was wrapped in a white scarf, turban style, with a large blue brooch in front, while the hem of the beige smock waved with the weight of the red and yellow crepe paper chrysanthemums.

Kit gasped. Here was the epitome of Salubrious Terrace, the cheapness, garish common-ness and lack of taste. She laughed at Bertie, illogically expecting him to laugh with her, but he didn't.

Bertie did for Elsie what Tommy had done for Linda. He went to her and held out his hand, took hers and kissed it. Kit moved forward, indignant and hurt. On a previous occasion Elsie's face had publicly shown her love for Bertie, when Carruthers watched, but this scene was far more emphatic: this was Bertie enslaved by Elsie, and Elsie adoring Bertie.

Instinctively Maggie clapped, trying to ease the sudden tension rather than endorse what she saw.

Linda cried, 'Oh Elsie. You are pretty.' Elsie curtseyed and lifted her shoulders in a gesture of apology.

'I can't bow. My son won't let me.'

The wireless made loud noises on instruments. 'So horsey, keep your tail up, keep your tail up . . .' And Tommy was before Elsie with a filled glass held out to her. The men made a passageway for her to come further into the room, and

286

women left their seats so she could choose where to sit. Glances were exchanged everywhere, some silently remarking on her boldness, and others on her courage.

'A plate!' Maggie called as if Elsie's arrival had reminded her. 'Where's the tin plate? Come on everybody. Sit in a circle. On the floor. Let's play spin the plate.'

Emma came running with a plate. Already, at almost six years of age, her baby plumpness was disappearing. Like Linda and Kit, she was going to be tall and leggy.

Kit wore a navy blue woollen dress with a high mandarin collar, and a wide green sash at her waist. She watched Elsie take her place on a stool for the game, and felt deflated. Elsie seemed keyed up, energetic, a little flushed and unusually confident. Someone turned the wireless down and Bertie took off his jacket and gave everyone numbers.

The game began slowly, as though the guests were selfconscious, caught up in the embarrassment of a boss with his wife and mistress, but as Linda supplied the drinks, they began to forget, to laugh more easily, and when the plate suddenly received a faulty twist and fled under the settee, John Davies stretched out his legs and gasped, 'Phew – !' while Bertie lit a cigar.

Emma wriggled on her stomach, making a great exhibition of trying to retrieve the plate, her legs flailing in the air, while Linda gazed at Tommy, and Tommy smiled at her.

John Davies said conversationally, 'I would hate to go to a nudists' wedding,' and everyone except Emma turned to stare at him.

There were a few minutes' silence and John sat there, on the floor, his arms folded as he leaned easily against the armchair. His mouth moved in its crooked smile over his crooked teeth, and Kit's voice called, 'Oh? Why?'

There was another silence and John bided his time, then he said casually, 'There'd be too much hanging about.' Another momentary silence followed as everyone tried to equate his remarks, then there was laughter, roaring, dirty, and Maggie threw a cushion at him. The party had truly begun.

'Out!' Maggie called, just before midnight. 'Oh darro! Nineteen thirty three will be here before you go. John. Go on cariad. We'll tell you when to come back in!'

Bertie turned to Elsie, wanting to cuddle her, to tell her the New Year was coming fast, and her gaze lifted to his, longing, yearning, yet she said nothing, small without her shoes, big with her pregnancy. He turned fleetingly to Kit and smiled, 'Tara then,' said Kit called after him, 'Put your coat on. You'll catch cold.'

The men went out, through the kitchen and scullery in a noisy, happy stream stumbling, not too sober, along the garden path, then out through the side door, in the wall, and around to the front. Already the male neighbours were there.

'Hello there!'

'Hello. By Jove, this year has gone quickly,' and in the house the women clustered in the passage and the office, looking through the window, giggling, chatting, laughing, making remarks about their menfolk on the road.

Only Kit and Maggie remained in the middle room with Elsie, and both the older women looked hard at her. Maggie said, 'You all right, love?'

'Yes,' Elsie said. 'I'm fine,' but then the gripe came again, and she added, 'except for the wind. Ooh,' and she bent.

'Wind?' Kit and Maggie said together. 'Where?' and the wireless chimed midnight. The town's hooters and sirens wailed the old year out.

The men pulled the bell as if to snap its wire, banged every inch of the door, yelled, 'Open up for 1933! Open up there!' and gaffawed loudly amid the neighbours' echoing shouts of, 'Happy New Year! Happy New Year!'

Kit and Maggie knew Elsie was in labour.

They stared at each other, wondering what to do. Kit whispered hurriedly, 'How often, Elsie? How often does the pain come?'

'I don't know.' Elsie caught their panic, then she said, 'D'you think it'll come now? How does it come out?' and Kit's face went ashen.

'Elsie! You don't know? You don't know how babies are born?'

Elsie's eyes were enormous, glassy, catching Kit's contagious fear. 'Will they cut me open?'

'Oh *Jawch*!' Maggie cried. 'Someone should have told you.'

'Me, I suppose!' Kit was frantic. 'Me!'

Maggie was furious. She took Elsie's arm. 'Come on, cariad, up to beddy byes. I hate doing this, but someone's got to. Oh *Jawch*! I'll tell you.'

Elsie went with her, too bewildered to argue, and Kit followed up the stairs. In the bedroom Kit said, her voice becoming calm now, even steely, 'You saw me have an abortion. The baby came out the same way as it went in – ' Her amber eyes glittered as she switched on the light, and Maggie reached for Elsie's nightie, her buxom body radiating disapproval.

Maggie said, 'Kit, your bitchiness is showing.' Then to Elsie, 'Never mind her, love, you get undressed. Who's your doctor? Bertie can go and get him. And the midwife.'

Kit leaned against the dressing-table. Now the baby was coming, now that Bertie's child was forcing its way from this girl's womb, she had no doubts about her own feelings. Elsie Buckley disgusted her. The baby would be a bastard, and her inside was convulsed with jealousy, jealousy of Elsie and jealousy of the unborn child, and an unreasonable fear that it would be the son Bertie wanted.

They heard the men pouring into the house. The wireless seemd too loud. Harry Lauder was singing. 'Keep right on to the end of the road . . . ' and Kit felt her life was shattered. She said softly, almost gently, 'Elsie. I will never forgive you. Never. Never.' Elsie gave a little cry and clung to the bed. 'Oh Jesus,' she groaned, forgetting to be better than she was. 'Does a baby – a whole baby – have to come out like an abortion does?' and Bertie came into the room.

'Elsie!' His gaze darted from face to face, and his own blanched as he guessed the situation. 'Elsie! You said January!'

'It's now. Oh Bertie. it's now.' He strode past Kit to take Elsie to him, to soothe, to calm, to whisper, and it was John and Maggie who put on their coats and went for the midwife, while Bertie made sure the kettles were filled and the fire was built up.

Tommy made a fire in Elsie's room, drawing it up fast by holding a large sheet of newspaper across the grate to act as a blower, and downstairs the agents and their companions quietly took their leave, whispering their good wishes as if attending a funeral.

Kit went to the front bedroom and sat in the pink basket chair. She was shaking, great tremors that prevented her clasping her hands together, great tremors that hurt her chest and shook the sickness that was stuck there. She wanted to cry, but no tears would come. She wanted Bertie, but he was with Elsie, holding the girl's hand, pleading with her to be brave; and when Maggie came with a tot of rum, Kit took it as if she had ague and swilled it down her throat. Maggie wrapped a blanket around her and had Tommy light another fire, in here.

The midwife came and the bewildered horror showed on Elsie's sweating face. 'Oh God! Oh God! Oh Ma, Ma, why aren't you with me? Oh Bertie. I didn't know it would be like this!'

About six o'clock that morning Dr Sullivan came, his pyjamas peeping from his jacket sleeves and trouser bottoms. His gingery brows bristled as he opened his bag at the foot of the bed. 'Well, Elsie, my girl, this lad won't give a damn who he disturbs, heh? Getting me up before dawn on New Year's Day.'

Elsie heard the midwife whisper. 'It's breach, doctor,' then she screamed, and the attack of coughing came. She struggled for breath, to make diseased lungs work, and Bertie cried, 'Can't we have an ambulance? Get her to hospital?'

Elsie gasped. 'What's a breach? What is it? Tell me. Please?'

'Sshh,' Dr Sullivan said, and lowered his great head like

290

a red bull about to charge. 'The baby'll be all right. You're acting like a brand new father, Albert. Pull yourself together, man.' He took off his jacket and pulled up the striped sleeves of his pyjamas. He put his hairy hands into the waiting bowl of hot, soapy, Dettol-smelling water, then he said, 'You'd better get out of the room, Albert. There's no doubt your wife needs you. Go on, man. Get out.'

Bertie backed to the door, Elsie's glazed eyes watching him, her head almost lost in the pillows, her face scarlet and glistening, still bewildered at the wracking of her body. She panted. 'Tell Kit. She was right to have an abortion. Tell her – '

Dr Sullivan waited, the midwife watched, then she gave Elsie a spare pillow to squeeze. 'Bite it, dear,' she advised. 'Jam your teeth into it. It'll soon be over now,' and Bertie went to where Maggie sat on the stairs. She looked up at him, her dyed hair like a floor mop now, her scarlet lipstick smirched. She sneered, 'Bertie Hemsworthy, you're a swine. A stinking, rotten, filthy swine.'

Bertie stared down at her: she was fat, her breasts oozing in the low red taffeta neckline, her throat loose with flesh as she looked up at him. 'Do you know,' she accused, 'that poor little sod didn't even know how babies are born? Expected an operation, she did. An anaesthetic.'

Bertie turned from her. He had no control over his feet. He wanted his cigarettes but didn't know where they were. He could smell his own body odour, feel his own heat burning from him.

Elsie shrieked and Bertie gripped the banister rail. What if she died? What if he lost her? All for a few minutes of happiness last Easter. He wanted to beat his chest, tear his hair; he went to his bedroom and Kit was like an old woman, slumped in the chair, the blanket fallen from her, the fire too low to give out warmth.

Bertie touched her cheek and it was frozen, hard, like marble. He took her hand: it was limp, icy cold, unresisting. He knelt before her and his blue eyes, dark with worry and self-condemnation, looked into hers, wishing the red sparks would return. 'Kit. I'm sorry. Dear God, I am sorry.'

Her other hand touched his cheek. She said, so softly he almost didn't hear, 'Sometimes I love you, but mostly I hate you, and all the time I hope that one day I'll forgive you.'

Bertie put his head in her lap and cried. His body went numb, yet he didn't move, and Kit's hand caressed his greying dark hair.

When the cry of a new baby shrilled through the house he was too cold, too stiff, to move, and it was Kit who murmured, 'Come on, my dear one, we must make cups of tea.'

Maggie was in Elsie's room first. Maggie was the first to hold the baby. Maggie was the first to hold out her arms to the midwife and plead, 'Give it to me.'

'It's a boy,' Elsie murmured. 'A son for Bertie.'

Tears coursed down Maggie's fat cheeks. 'Oh Elsie, love,' she cried. 'I could be so happy. Give him to me. Please give him to me. He'll want for nothing. Before God, I swear. He'll want for nothing.'

Elsie smiled at her, depleted, and downstairs Emma snored in the depths of her father's old chair, while on the sofa in the middle room, Tommy suffered pins and needles in his arm rather than move it and disturb the sleeping Linda, who was still cuddled into him.

CHAPTER ELEVEN

Bertie stood at the office window and stared out at the tiny purple crocus that stood proudly in the little front garden.

It had been a mild winter. Christmas Day had been clear and sunny and now, in the middle of February, it looked as if maybe there would be another summer like last year, hot and long.

Bertie expanded his chest in a subconscious movement of satisfaction. Soon he would be out on the knocker again, forever increasing his kingdom and improving his pay packet. His son was six weeks old. His womenfolk seemed to be settled into a peaceful routine. Linda was nursing a crush on Tommy, who should be off to the army soon, and Emma was enchanted with a baby brother.

The only thing Bertie felt in need of now was more money. Money to feed them all and keep a roof over their heads. He also wanted Elsie to pick up in health. He looked at the sky, his mouth shaped to whistle a little dancing tune. He wondered if a herbalist could cure her consumption. Maybe there was a plant somewhere, a seed, a flower, or perhaps a leaf that would give her strength.

Even as he thought of her she opened the office door behind him and peered around it. 'I'm off then, Bertie.'

'Off.' He swung around. 'Where to?'

'The clinic.'

'Ah!' He never did know what to say when she went to the clinic in Grove Place for her check-ups. 'Have you told them it's time they cured you?'

She smiled, her teeth seeming bigger, less white now her face had lost its plumpness and its colour. 'There are worse than me in there. All hoping. And the Poor Law not

293

caring about any of us.'

Bertie gave a low laugh. 'It's not the Poor Law now, you know, my love, it's called Public Assistance.'

She stood firmly looking at him, doing up the belt of her old tweed coat, and he approached her. 'Did you hear about that man?' she said. 'They burned all his bedding because his little girl died of scarlet fever in it, then they wouldn't give him anything in place of it. The sods.'

'Shssh! I thought I had turned you into a young lady.'

'They came to us once.'

'Only once?' He was teasing, wanting her to laugh, to stop worrying.

'Pa kicked him out. And a good thing too. D'you know what the man said?' She pulled one of Kit's soft, grey, and too big, cloche hats onto her head, so it reached her plucked eyebrows.

'No,' Bertie shook his head, playing up to her, indulging. 'What did the bad man say?'

'He said we had three saucepans and that was too many for three people, so we had to sell one and the money from that could keep us.'

Bertie stood with his hands in his trouser pockets, looking at her. She was a fighter. She had to be. 'Soon,' he said, and kissed her cheek, 'you'll be galloping to the beach again, racing me over the bridge.'

She laughed then and lifted her face so he could let his lips touch hers. He raised his hands, wanting to squeeze her to him, but was afraid to, a hug could set her coughing again, as if her lungs could be disturbed by her movement against him.

'Berty Hemsworthy. I love you.'

'Elsie Buckley. I love you.'

They laughed together, breathlessly, each concentrating on the other, longing to hold, but not daring to touch.

He said, as if to ease his emotion, 'How d'you feel?'

'Like I always feel – ' she answered pertly ' – when I'm near you. Want to try it?'

He chuckled deeply. 'You really are a wicked one.'

'And nice with it?'

'And very nice with it.'

They kissed again, more intently now, his hands on her shoulders, her hands against his chest. She smiled. 'I'm glad I got these high heels on. It stops you having ter go on your knees to kiss me.'

'I didn't hear you cough last night.'

'I didn't. I slept the sleep of the dead.'

His face, too, was thinner, paler, his once straight mouth was now perpetually turned up at the corners as if determined never to be glum, but incongruous with the arrogance of his nose and dark brows. The glass door of the porch opened and the postman carolled. 'Post.' Elsie laughed, and reached for the letters he held out. 'Thank you.'

'Thank you.' He touched the peaked cap that was square on his head, and tramped, whistling, back to the street.

Elsie laughed, 'Second post,' as Bertie took the letters from her. 'I'll be off then,' she added. 'Tara,' and went.

She seemed diminutive, the old tweed coat hanging loose at her rounded shoulders. Her walk was stilted because of the ridiculously high-heeled shoes that had been saved from wear and tear by her use of daps and going barefoot. Today she was dressed up, in the best she could concoct, to see, and to be seen by, a specialist.

In the street she turned and waved, the consumption having crept into her so insidiously that he found it difficult to realise how ill she was. She didn't cough as much as her mother had, and she never coughed up blood.

He watched her walk down the road and a tram passed her. He frowned. Why the hell was she walking? Then he remembered – money. She probably had no money. He contemplated running after her, giving her a shilling, but he didn't. He would get Kit to pay her later on.

He turned back to his desk and the letters. He found his spectacles and put them on, then took the little ivory paper-knife from the flat drawer before him and calmly opened the envelopes. The contents were run-of-the-mill. 'Dear

Sirs, My line broke and all my things got burned on the Dover stove . . . .' 'Dear Sir, My children's dresses were on the oven door . . . .'

He smiled at them – spring was coming, people wanted money for new clothes – then he frowned over a death claim. He didn't like people dying, not even people he didn't know.

The long brown envelope was last. Bertie sat, then stared at it, a sixth sense telling him it held bad news. When he opened it, he read it, put it down and lit a cigarette. His first instinct was to call Kit, to show her, but he didn't. He finished the cigarette while staring out of the window, at an attic window that was open across the street. He tried not to think too much. Not to panic. He should have expected it. He should have remembered. He looked back at his desk and the words jumped at him from the typewritten page.

'H. F. FINANCE COMPANY . . . .
RE LOAN FACILITIES TO MISS E.
BUCKLEY,
LATE   OF   SALUBRIOUS   TERRACE,
SWANSEA. ·
It is with regret we find it necessary to bring this matter to your notice . . . .'

Bertie's foot tapped gently under the desk with irritation. Why were people such hypocrites? The writer regretted nothing.

' . . . We understand Miss Buckley is now in your care . . . . We are fully aware you realise your responsibility to the contract I now have before me . . . .'

Bertie's foot stopped tapping and he blew through pouting lips. What contract?

He re-read the letter more slowly. There had to be a mistake. He hadn't signed any contract with a finance company.

He went to the kitchen and Kit was bathing the baby in the white enamel bowl on the kitchen table. He made himself a pot of tea and watched her. She was laughing gently. He wanted to tell her about the letter, tell her Elsie still owed the money-lender twenty-nine pounds, and that the money-lender was after him, Bertie, for his pound of flesh. He also wanted to tell her she looked lovely, like a Madonna, with that expression in her eyes, but he knew from recent experience that if he did, that expression would whip away and she would turn on him with a hiss, demanding to know if she was expected to drown the child, simply because it was 'Hers'.

Instead he took the tea to the office, and he didn't feel Kit watching him go, her face puzzled as she sensed his mood. A short while later he called down the passage.

'Kit! I'm going out.'

'Will you be long?'

'I don't know.'

'Will you be in for lunch?'

'Probably.' He put on his hat, using both hands to fit it accurately, his blue eyes assessing seriously in the hallstand mirror while his mind worked on dates and figures. Elsie borrowed that money a year ago. Thirty pounds. He felt sure she had said thirty pounds. Yet she had managed to pay off only one pound? So, where had the money gone that she had fiddled from the firm? On her mother? To her father? Certainly not on herself. She was destitute.

He got into his overcoat, deep in thought, then he moved fast. He had to find out.

The money-lender was in the arcade, above the piano shop. Bertie paused long enough to gaze at a piano. It was twenty pounds and had a head of Mozart on its lid. A card said hire purchase could be arranged. Kit had wanted a piano, years ago. She used to play quite well before they were married. He had refused it. Said he couldn't afford it. Twenty pounds too much. Yet what had Elsie cost?

The steps to the money-lender were of ornate iron with a banister of carved leaves and roses, all dirty now but once painted silver and pink. They led up to a narrow verandah skirting the tops of the shops, and the money-lender's door was half frosted glass. Bertie turned the black bakelite handle and went in.

There was a long counter that was well worn where others had leaned against it, their hands spread on its surface with worry or relief. Bertie didn't touch it. He stood very straight, his hands to his sides. The air was cool, musty with a smell of paraffin. A small blonde girl with thick round shoulders and a heavy bust sat at a table that served as a desk, and she lifted her face, inquiring.

'My name is Hemsworthy. I received a letter from you this morning.'

Her expression clouded for a moment, then she nodded. 'Oh yes.' She didn't sound too bright. 'You want to see Mr Fligginbottom then?'

'Do I?' Bertie said flatly.

The girl opened a flap in the counter and gestured him through. She had no interest in him, and even as she directed him to another half frosted door, she was looking at her table and the papers spread on it. 'He's in there,' she said, then turned her back and closed the counter flap with care.

Bertie suddenly wondered what he was going to say, yet knew no words would come until he was confronted by the person he was dealing with, saw the type who leeched on the poor. He went into the second room. He was prepared for a fat, flat-nosed Jew who said vat for what.

'Good morning,' said the voice in the gloom. It was pleasant, even cultured.

'Good morning.' Bertie closed the door behind him.

The light from one small, dingy window fell on the large desk; Mr Fligginbottom was somewhere behind it. 'You wish to see me?'

Bertie stared and the old man leaned forward, into the light: he was a Jew all right, with a flat triangular nose in a sallow face, but he was shrivelled, with a sunken chest and egg on his waistcoat.

'I am Mr Fligginbottom.'

298

Bertie wanted to smile and say, 'Never mind,' but he sat as indicated and plucked the legs of his trousers away from the tightness above his knees. He put his hat on Mr Fligginbottom's desk and said, 'I left the house in a bit of a hurry so didn't bring the letter with me, but I received it from you this morning.'

'Yes,' Mr Fligginbottom nodded, 'Mr Hemsworthy,' and his head kept nodding.

Bertie wondered if the man had a method of hearing all that was said in the outer office.

Mr Fligginbottom said, 'Miss – er – Buckley isn't it? A bad risk. For a small amount maybe, but for thirty pounds – ' Mr Fligginbottom pushed out his mouth like an ape wanting a kiss. 'Too much. Much too much.' He gripped the narrow wooden arms of his chair. 'I knew the family, years ago. Sad. Sad. Did she – ah – Gwen Buckley – ?'

'Yes, she did. She died, of consumption.'

'Then they might not have used the full thirty pounds, heh?' He watched Bertie, awaiting reaction.

'I don't know. Your letter was unexpected.'

The money lender watched, nodding almost imperceptibly now.

Bertie said, 'Do you have the guarantor papers here? I don't recollect signing any or giving permission for my name to be used.'

'And Miss Buckley? She doesn't remember either?'

'Miss Buckley wasn't available this morning.' Bertie looked at his hat on the desk, his hands were between his knees now, thumbs running against each other. 'She's consumptive, you know, like her mother.'

The money lender sat back, his lips thick and supple; he moved them in and out, then licked them. 'Sad. Sad. Consumption? Her father now – er – evicted er – ?'

He paused again and watched Bertie carefully, his eyes wary under sagging heavy lids. 'That was when we traced the – er – young lady to you.'

The door behind Bertie opened and the blonde came in. She handed the Jew a folder. She went out again without

299

anyone speaking or looking at her.

Mr Fligginbottom opened the folder, spreading it on the desk. 'You need to see your signature, Mr Hemsworthy?' He slid a large double sheet across and pointed with a grey-nailed finger. 'There. Your signature.'

Bertie stared. It was not his signature. His name, but not his signature. He looked up, right into the Jew's expectant, waiting, bagged and hooded eyes. The Jew seemed to understand. As if to fill the awkward moment, he said, 'She was a most attractive girl – Miss Buckley's mother.'

'You knew each other?'

'Well. Yes, very well.' His loose lips almost smiled. 'We danced good together, but – ' he shrugged. 'She was not of the same faith as myself. You understand?'

Bertie nodded, imagining the delicate Gwen in this man's arms.

The money lender withdrew the paper slowly; it scratched and rustled as it slid across the wood. 'A forgery?' he said, and kept nodding, but gently now. 'Ah yes, well,' then he smiled.

Bertie said without expression, 'She paid you regularly?'

'She was very good for a while, but you know, in our line of business, so little goes off the capital. We can't force our clients to pay more than they can afford. A penny or two. It's the interest.' The money lender seemed comfortable now, in charge of the situation.

Bertie said, 'What was she paying you?'

'Ha hum,' said the money lender. 'Let me see, mm, yes, ten and a penny a week.' He smiled. 'And she did manage a little extra now and again.'

'How much had she paid you in all?'

'Six pounds three and tuppence.'

'And she still owes you how much?'

'Twenty-nine pounds,' said the money lender calmly.

'Out of thirty pounds?' Bertie said disgustedly. 'The ten shillings of the ten and a penny a week you asked, is interest?'

'Of course.' The money lender spread his hands, the

300

palms up, pale grey and hollow, the pads of his fingers, corrugated. 'I try to help the poor. I am not a hard man, Mr Hemsworthy.' His unhealthy eyes rolled. 'You would find the rent I pay unbelievable. You also sent me a letter. Were you aware of that? A letter of recommendation.'

Bertie couldn't speak. He hoped his anger wasn't showing, anger with men like this, and anger with Elsie for keeping the matter to herself, for not telling him on the beach that day that he had been the good referee.

The money lender asked, 'You would care to see it?'

Bertie shook his head and picked up his hat.

The money lender said quietly, 'She – ah – Miss Buckley was your secretary, I believe.'

'She IS my secretary, and friend of the family.'

'Ah.' The money lender seemed relieved that something was true. 'So you will consider the matter?'

'What if I don't pay? What if I deny the whole damn business?'

The money lender laughed, rubbing his hands. 'You have one way of finding out.' He left his chair and moved to the door. 'I trust you will consider carefully, Mr Hemsworthy.'

'What do you want, exactly?'

'A continuance of the payments. That is all.' The money lender spread his hands again, palms up. 'It's quite a simple matter. We are a kindly firm. You will understand, naturally, that the interest has accrued during the defaulting months – I had to bring the matter to your notice – '

'Of course.' Bertie heard assurance returning to his voice.

'And you, being a gentleman of discretion – ' The money lender opened the door, smiling, inclining his body in half in a deep bow.

'Yes,' Bertie said. 'I'll attend to the matter.' He moved quickly, his arrogance at its most supreme, his wide shoulders straight and proud and furious. 'I will attend to it, Mr Fligginbottom. Good day.'

He didn't look at the girl in the outer office yet was aware of her face lifted towards him. He sensed sympathy which made him move faster, lengthening his stride. On the iron verandah his shoes clanged and he hurried down the steps. He marched with his head high, the length of the arcade, then he hit the fresh light of the high street.

There was noise, horses, traps, men shouting and whips flicking, wheels trundling against the tramlines, cars tooting, people smiling and scowling, shoving and dodging. He couldn't go home. Not yet, not to face Elsie, not to face Kit.

He turned and the pub was beside him, open, with men sitting on the window sill with mufflers about their necks and chests. The street here was filled with the scent of beer and horse manure. Bertie put a half smile on his face and went into the pub, through the narrow brown passage, to the brown bar where sawdust lay clean on the floor and a small fire glowed orange in the little black grate. He ordered a brandy and took it to a table. The walls about him were plastered with photographs of boxers. Bertie sipped the brandy and let his emotions thaw while his brain struggled with the problem. He should have realised she couldn't keep up the payments. He should have thought. He should have gone to see her, guessed the mess she was in; God, she was only nineteen now, how could she be expected to cope?

He tried not to think of her, big with the weight of his son, working as a skivvy; she and Tommy struggling to pay the money-lender. He stared at the spittoon on the mantelpiece. It had a handle and a lid, the same shape but bigger, heavier, than the one she used.

If only he was single. If only she hadn't gone into consumption. If, if, oh Christ! If only he had never set eyes on her. The ache for her was terrible, combined with the belief that loving her, being obsessed by her, didn't make him like her.

She was a defrauding street urchin, the type who could easily have slipped into pickpocketing as she fled, bare-legged and laughing, through the market crowds on Friday and Saturday nights.

Bertie didn't feel disillusioned. He felt sad for her, and

cross with himself for loving her. Maybe, he thought, he was a little jealous. It might be exciting to scorn respectability and scuttle through crowds, pitting your wits against other people's purses, but, right now, he wanted to shake her, ram commonsense into her silly little brain, and he tried not to remember the day she had told him she had got the money. The sheer youthfulness and rebellion of squeezing icy water over his face on the beach still made him smile.

She was a hell of a girl. Which didn't solve anything. There was only one thing to be done. He had to find the money. He resolved there and then that he would not tell Kit. He couldn't face the rows that would ensue – and neither could Elsie.

He went again to the street and listened to a youth who leaned against the pub wall playing a concertina. A tall man with a peg leg was holding out a cap. Bertie dropped a silver sixpence into it and turned from the smell of dirt and sweat and booze. It was then he saw the hat. It was coming up the street towards him, amid the caps and trilbies, a red and purple straw that could not be missed. It sported a large white feather that flounced in the February sunshine, and he knew that only one face could be beneath it.

Maggie Davies!

He shook his head slowly in wonder. Maggie should have gone onto the stage. She led a double life so successfully. He had no doubt that, only a few hours before, she had been swamped in her funereal black skirt and Welsh flannel shawl, feeding her chickens and collecting the eggs. Now she was dressed to kill, strolling with all the full-breasted splendour of a variety songstress.

She saw him and moved faster, a big scarlet open-mouthed smile squashing her face into a mass of folds.

'Bertie! Have you recovered from the birth of your son? John told me you look terrible – ' She paused, watching him, ' – and you do, too.' She glanced behind him, to the beggars and the pub, the sawdust that had been trampled to the pavement, and she smelled the brandy on his breath. 'You haven't been in there, have you?'

303

'Very nice too.'

'Oh Bertie Hemsworthy. You're going to the dogs, that you are.'

'And you?' One dark brow lifted inquiringly as he remembered Maggie sitting on the stairs the last time they met. 'Where are you going?'

'For a coffee,' she smiled. 'To the Kardomah with a handsome man. Come on. I'll treat.'

'You forget. I'm that stinking, rotten swine.'

'Oh Bertie.' The smile went and she flushed. 'It was a bad time, wasn't it?' She thrust her arm through his and tugged. 'Come on. I'm sorry. We're all sorry.'

He went with her. He liked being persuaded. A man doffed his hat to Maggie, and the white feather in her red and purple straw bounced as she nodded a happy acknowledgement. The man glanced at Bertie, and Maggie's arm tightened in his. She walked grandly, proud of her size and her companion, and the warmth and the aroma of the Kardomah coffee house enveloped them like a sheltering blanket.

He led Maggie to a corner and held a chair for her. She lowered her ample body splendidly, and the young waitress in the brown dress and coffee-coloured cap and apron took his order. He sat gazing at the wonder of Maggie Davies, his left hand, with his wedding ring glinting, on the table, and Maggie put plump warm fingers over it. She said quietly, 'Now Bertie, tell Maggie. Why a pub before lunch? Why d'you look as though you've seen a ghost? And can I help?'

The question startled him. 'Help?' and he drew his hand from her.

'I never have,' she said. 'You kept John's job open all the time he was ill. You didn't draw me over the coals for writing to Carruthers. We owe you a lot, John and me.'

'Tripe!'

'The baby *is* yours, isn't it?' He half smiled. Maggie never had beaten about the bush.

'And you're going bald with worry.'

'Am I?' He touched the top of his head, fearing her words were literal.

She opened her red coat and her cleavage was framed in a white frilled blouse. She drew a handkerchief from between her breasts and laughed. 'I didn't mean it that way.'

The place was full, and people were chattering like magpies. The waitress brought their coffees and hurried away. Bertie lit a cigar, and watched Maggie watch him light it. As the first waft of blue smoke rose Maggie breathed deeply. 'Smells delicious,' she said, and Bertie smiled, beginning to recover from his visit to the Jew.

'You are looking splendid,' he said, and she nodded, in full agreement.

They talked, mostly about nothing, until Maggie finished her coffee. Then she said, 'Now,' and pushed her cup and saucer away. 'Is it money?'

'Money?' Bertie was blank-faced, uncomfortable with her interest in his affairs.

'Money.' She rubbed a finger and thumb together suggestively. 'The stuff that makes the world go round.'

'I thought that was love.'

'Then you thought wrong.' She watched him, letting her mouth grimace into various shapes as she speculated, and he drained his coffee cup and shook his head. She said, 'How much d'you need?'

'Maggie.' He didn't look at her. 'You keep your egg money. The tax man might come after it one day.'

She straightened in her seat. 'All right.' She replaced the handkerchief. 'But if you want it for Elsie and her baby, it's yours.'

'Thank you,' he said, not avoiding her gaze now. 'It's kind of you to offer, but it is quite unnecessary.'

She nodded, but he felt he hadn't convinced her.

She opened her huge red handbag and applied new lipstick to her mouth, then she said, 'Will you be wanting John to pay in twice a week in future?'

'What the hell . . . .' He glowered, and she put the

lipstick away and snapped the bag shut.

'Bertie!' she retorted. 'Don't be a bloody fool, love. I saw you earlier on. You were climbing the steps in the arcade. I watched you. You went in to the money-lenders.'

He ground out the remains of his cigar in the metal ashtray. He felt hounded and cornered. His mouth was jammed tight and the tips of his fingers hurt where he had pressed the hot rolled leaves into brown shapelessness.

Maggie stood up, her heavy eyelids lowered. 'It's all right. I shan't tell. Does Kit know?'

'No.'

'Elsie?'

'No.'

Maggie buttoned her coat. 'Well, remember my offer when Fligginbottom puts the thumb-screws on. He's notorious.' Then she smiled, relentless. 'You really are a bloody fool, Bertie. They don't come any duller than you. You have let that girl ruin you and change you completely.'

'Thank you for your opinion.'

'I'm going.' She picked up the bill and swept away. 'I'll tell John. Twice a week in future. Like last time.' She went, but Bertie stayed, shocked. He appreciated she had made the offer, but he was mortified and humiliated; she was the wife of his employee, and she had offered him a loan.

He lit another cigar, then went to the street. Of one thing he felt certain, he loved Elsie, but he was disliking her more, disliking whatever it was that held him to her, disliking the chains of obsession. He swung himself onto a tramcar and went home.

As he opened the glass door and went in, Kit came to the top of the stairs. It seemed dramatic. The landing was gloomy, the daylight flooded from Elsie's room, and Kit stood, stiffly tall and thin, in the midst of it.

'Bertie?'

'Yes?' He put his hat on the hallstand and looked up.

'Dr Sullivan is here.'

Something curdled in Bertie's throat, and he went up the

306

stairs fast, his long slim body arched forward in his need to reach that room.

Elsie was in bed. She seemed unconscious. Bertie ignored the doctor who stood near the big window, and went to her. He took her hand and patted it, calling her, and she moaned.

For a startled, frightened moment Bertie glanced at the doctor, and then at Kit. 'What happened? What's wrong with her?'

'She collapsed in town,' Kit said, moving her shoulders helplessly. 'Some man brought her home in his car.'

The doctor bent his shaggy gingery head as he turned from the window. 'I can't understand it, Albert. She shouldn't be this bad.'

'You mean it isn't the consumption?' Bertie sat on the edge of the bed, all his attention on Elsie. He called her again. 'Elsie! It's me, Bertie. Have you a pain? Where d'you hurt? Elsie? Where's the pain?'

Through the darkness of unconsciousness Elsie heard him and tried to nod, to speak, to move her head towards the right groin. 'Here.'

She felt someone pull back the bedclothes. The air was cold. Kit's voice floated from far away. 'Appendicitis, doctor?'

'No-o.' He drew breath deeply. 'Is it just there, Elsie girl?' And his forefinger touched her.

Her hand gently rested on the side of her belly, and the word, 'There,' was more an escaping of sound. For her the darkness became infinite, and she relapsed deeply, away from Bertie and the room.

Dr Sullivan covered her again, then prowled, thinking, and Bertie sat in anguish. Kit said, 'Haven't you any idea at all, doctor?'

'None,' he said honestly. 'None.'

'Isn't that where the appendix is?'

'No. That's lower down. And she'd not get the pain where it is now.' He rubbed his chin hard. 'And she seemed to be holding her own too. What was she doing in town? Where had she been?'

307

'To the clinic in Grove Place.'

'Ah.' Dr Sullivan nodded, pleased at being reminded he had another authority to refer to. 'I think I'd better get in touch with them, then. Find out if they know anything.'

Kit laughed uncomfortably. 'Consumption doesn't give you a pain in the tummy!' And the doctor let his eyes roll up in his bent head as he looked at her.

'Depends on where the consumption gets to, Kitty girl, doesn't it?'

Kit followed him out, down the stairs, thanking him for coming so quickly, then he was gone, and Kit came up again. She put a hand on Bertie's shoulder. 'I'm going to make a cuppa. Would you like one?'

*   *   *

By the end of February Elsie lay in a twilight world, her belly slowly swelling as water filled it.

'But can't you get her into hospital?' Kit entreated Dr Sullivan, and he nodded.

'I could. Into Craig-y-nos, but they couldn't do anything. It's too late. No one knew she had it in the intestines. No one expected peritonitis. She hadn't told anyone. You see Kitty, girl, we can only go on what the patient tells us. We don't have X-ray eyes.'

'Craig-y-Nos!' Bertie gasped. 'It's miles away. Lost in the mountains . . . .'

Dr Sullivan shrugged slowly; so often he went through the selfsame scene with others. 'It's so easy, y'see,' he tried to explain. 'If the patient swallows the sputum instead of spitting it out, it can spread the disease to other parts of the body. The intestines, obviously.'

'Yes,' Bertie said. 'Yes.'

'She must have known,' Dr Sullivan went on. 'She'd have had the yellow diarrhoea for a while now. And the pain.'

'Yes.' Bertie said again. 'Yes,' and watched the doctor go.

*   *   *

308

Bertie took a white mug with a spout and held it to Elsie's dry lips. 'Drink, my love, please drink a little. It's warm milk and honey. It will do you good.' Sometimes Elsie took a little, but usually she didn't.

Each Saturday the agents paid in for the second time, and each Monday Bertie sent a pound to the Jew. Kit helped him to do the accounts on Saturday afternoons, and she took them to Wind Street each Sunday evening, thrusting the package into the wide mouth of the letter-box in the General Post Office, making sure it caught the nine o'clock collection, so it would be in London next morning.

She didn't ask Bertie why. She was afraid to. It was something to do with Elsie. It had to be, but Kit didn't want to get cross with Elsie now, not while the girl lay helpless, probably dying, and the baby was learning to laugh.

Kit worried a lot, especially about the baby not having been christened, and she told Maggie Davies when Maggie came with John on the second Saturday in March.

Tommy stood before the kitchen fire, straddle-legged, his full freckled face grinning at Linda. 'A sergeant I'll be, mun. Three stripes by 'ere.' He gestured to the top of his left arm.

Linda sat in Bertie's chair and gazed up at him, her hair longer now she regarded herself as grown up, held back with a wide brown ribbon bow.

They heard Kit welcome Maggie and John in, and they stopped talking, listening, as John went into the office to give Bertie the collections he shouldn't part with until next Wednesday, and Kit brought Maggie down the passage.

Maggie held her arms out in greeting, her red coat open, loose, like a fur-collared, heavy cape.

'Children, you both look well. Indeed you do.'

Linda jumped up, eager to tell, one finger to her chin, a part extrovert, part shy young girl. 'Tommy's had his papers.'

'He has?' Maggie cried, as though no one had ever

309

expected Tommy to hear from the army again, and her sparkling encouraging gaze settled on him. 'That means you're really going then.' And when he nodded quickly, still grinning, she exclaimed, 'Well, well. Fancy that,' and everyone laughed.

Kit said quietly, 'On Monday. First thing. He'll be away.'

'Well, well,' Maggie sparkled again. 'Well, well,' and for a few moments all four stood as if in a silent communal ecstasy, then Kit said, 'Mm . . .' and moved her hands. She asked. 'Tea or coffee, Maggie?'

'Tea or coffee?' Maggie scoffed. 'And our very own sergeant going off to defend his king and country? Sherry, surely.' Then quickly she added, 'If you have some.'

Kit bristled. 'Of course we have sherry. Tommy, go and fetch a bottle from the cabinet in the middle room, and Linda, get the glasses.'

Maggie moved to the high black and chrome pram in the corner and looked down at the sleeping baby. She clasped her arms under her bosom and breathed, 'Elsie any better?'

'No. She is still in a coma.' Kit came beside her, speaking softly. The baby slept on, his eyelashes and brows so light in colour they were almost golden, the little bit of hair on his almost bald head still in the cockscomb Kit had patiently brushed there.

Each woman held her body at an angle to watch and admire. Then Maggie whispered, 'I could take him today, couldn't I?'

Kit went on gazing at the baby, smelling the talcum powder she had put on his bottom, the baby soap she had lathered over his body, and Maggie said, 'Couldn't I? She wouldn't know.'

'Mm?' Kit looked at Maggie. 'Sorry, dear, I was thinking of something else,' but she had heard, faintly. It was just that she didn't believe it. She said, 'What was it, Maggie?'

'The baby. I could have him christened in three weeks.'

'I would like to see him christened too. It worries me that we can't ask Elsie's opinion.'

'Oh but I have her opinion,' Maggie said, and both women stood, almost nose to nose, each in shock that Maggie knew something Kit didn't.

Tommy brought three bottles of sherry and Linda brought stemmed glasses. Tommy called cheerfully, 'Sweet, dry or medium?'

'Take them away,' Kit said. 'We don't want them. Kindly go to the middle room. Maggie and I have business to talk about. Privately.'

Tommy and Linda went, backwards, exchanging wide-eyed, astonished glances, the bottles and glasses held at arm's length, then Kit quietly shut the door on them. She didn't put her hands on her hips, but her attitude was demanding, her throat long and creamy smooth as she raised her chin in superiority. 'Now, Mrs Davies, please explain. What have you done behind your employer's back again?'

'I have done nothing behind anybody's back!' Maggie's breasts rose and expanded with indignation. 'Elsie must have told you. So don't you go trying to wriggle out of anything. She has willed the baby to me. That's why he's not christened yet. I'm going to call him Buck.'

'You are going to call him Buck!'

'Now don't you start trying to make a fuss, Kitty Hemsworthy. He's mine. To take. And you know it.'

'That child is not leaving this house. He belongs to my husband.'

'Your husband's name is not on the birth certificate. I've seen it. There's a blank space where the father's name should be.' Maggie clasped her hands, then unclasped them, and Kit sank to the arm of Bertie's chair.

Maggie breasted to the door. She opened it and called, 'Tommy! Linda! Those bottles and glasses, please. We're going to wet the baby's head,' and Kit suddenly marched past her.

Kit stormed up the passage and into the office, red sparks like darts shooting from her amber eyes. 'Albert!' She demanded, and he looked up in near fright. Never before had Kit called him Albert, never before had she been so forceful.

He sprang to his feet like a schoolboy caught cheating. 'Kit! What's the matter?'

'You had better come into the kitchen. She has been up to her devious ways again.'

'Who?' John stood more slowly, moving his chair back with one hand.

'Your fat deceitful wife.'

'Kit!' Bertie cried, she was so out of character, then he was hurrying to the kitchen, his face set hard and white. 'Maggie? What's going on? What is it?'

Maggie had the baby in her arms, its tiny pink mouth puckered at being disturbed. She said, 'He's mine, Bertie. Elsie should have told you. It isn't my fault that she didn't.'

'Maggie! You're out of your mind! How dare you!' He was gasping. 'Put that child down and get out! Out! John, please get your wife out of my house. Now!' and he was remembering Maggie writing to Carruthers. Maggie sitting on the stairs calling him a stinking, rotten, swine. Maggie watching him go to the money-lender's.

John leaned against the closed door and the kitchen seemed oppressively hot. Kit was aware of six faces; Tommy, Linda, Bertie, John, Maggie and the baby. She also knew that she had begun to shake. The trembling that cursed her while Elsie was in labour was with her again. Her lips and chin quivered. 'They can't just take him, Bertie. He is your son.'

Maggie jerked her head towards a paper on the table. 'All signed and sealed,' she said, and her eyes glittered with triumph. 'By a solicitor. The baby is mine. Paid thirty pounds for him, I did.'

'Thirty pounds!' Bertie cried. 'You what!' He snatched the paper up. 'Good Christ! You bitch! You fat, deceitful bitch.'

'Hey now!' John stopped leaning against the door. 'There was nothing deceitful about it. Maggie met Elsie in town. Planned it themselves, and they went to the solicitor

312

together. It was for Elsie to tell you. Not us. We thought she had done.' He nodded to Tommy and Linda, his crooked smile almost showing without the slightest amusement. 'Get two more glasses, kids. And whisky. If there is any.'

Tommy went and the silence in the kitchen was terrible. The clock ticked fast, the kettle hissed, and the fire made a little singing sound, yet the silence seemed like a suffocation.

Bertie sat in Kit's chair, slowly, as if bending hurt him, and Kit sat on the arm, her hand on his shoulder.

They watched Tommy pour the drinks. 'Whisky for the men?' he said, and included himself. 'Sherry for the – ah – ladies?' and he included Linda.

John was the most at ease. Maggie swayed the baby against her, crooning, waiting, knowing the child was hers. She said, more calmly now, 'The solicitor has the thirty pounds. Elsie told him it was to be sent to Mr Fligginbottom on the day I took the baby. Just thirty pounds.'

Bertie gasped, 'My God!' as the meaning of her words really sank into his shocked brain.

'She knew,' Maggie said. I met her before I saw you, Bertie. I asked you about Fligginbottom. Remember?'

Bertie wanted to swallow, but couldn't. His mouth and throat were dry.

Maggie went on. 'Elsie confided in me about the money. Everything. She was terrified he would write to you – '

'He had done.'

'She said Kit would throw her and Tommy and the baby out.'

Kit listened, the glass of sherry in her white, thin hand; her head lowering.

'So I guessed what you were doing at Fligginbottom's,' Maggie said. 'That was why I was willing to pay some off for you.'

Bertie's whisky went down in a gulp. He held the empty glass out and Linda took it, then she sat on the other arm of the chair and her hand met Kit's on her father's back.

Maggie said, 'I'm sorry, Kit. I'm sorry, Bertie, but I had to have the baby.' She glanced at John, the soft folds of he face slumped in despair, but she became resolute again and the baby went back into the pram, re-covered, snug and warm. Maggie said, 'I don't need his things. I've bough everything new,' then she was manoeuvring the pram through the doorway.

Tommy grabbed her arm. 'Hey! You can't do that!' But John pulled him away.

'You mind your own business. It's all signed and sealed Legal like.' Then he was following Maggie, easing the pram over the black and white marble front doorstep, and heading for the station.

The kitchen door closed yet again and Kit put a handker chief to her face and sobbed. In her heart swelled the old hatred of Elsie Buckley. Elsie had stolen her husband given him a son, then sold it away, to Maggie Davies, for thirty pounds, and not said a word. 'I hope she dies soon,' Kit sobbed. 'God forgive me, but I hope she does die soon.'

Bertie stood up and cuddled her to him. His desolation was immense. When, eventually, he turned from a quiet ened Kit, he lifted the sheet of watermarked paper with its red seal and read it. He saw the date and recognised it.

It was the day he had received the letter from Fliggin bottom, the day Elsie had collapsed in town. The day she was supposed to have been to the clinic for consumptives She had not told him before she went, and she couldn't tell him when she got back.

He said softly, 'Maybe this is why she collapsed. Oh, she was ill, but maybe this is why she suddenly gave in and prepared to die.' He sighed heavily and put his hand to his head. 'It isn't easy giving up your baby – not even to pay off a debt you incurred trying to save your mother.' His voice broke and he could say no more.

Kit asked, 'Is that it?' And slowly, gently, hoarsely, he told her all about it, about his visit to the money-lender, and the payments he had been making since.

Upstairs, Elsie lay in her coma, the pains in her swollen.

water-filled body dulled by a brain that could take no more.

And on the Monday Tommy walked out. He was a man. He tried not to show emotion. He kissed Elsie and ordered her to be up and fit by the time he came home on leave, but she didn't hear.

Linda went with him to the station and received her first grown–up kiss. She waved him and the other recruits away, while the train belched steam and smoke, while it blew its whistle and shunted off like a triumphant dragon, then she went home, and as she enterd what seemed a silent, empty house, Carruthers arrived.

Carruthers marched in wearing a loud grey and green check suit, his fat face in rolls of ill temper. He ignored Linda and she ran to the kitchen, seeking her mother.

Bertie stood up, the residue of Saturday's money on the desk before him, ready to be counted and bagged.

Carruthers held out a pale fat hand, palm up. 'You can hand the lot over to me, Albert. It belongs to the company.'

Bertie flushed with fury. 'And the company will have it!'

The fat fingers flicked, urging movement, and Bertie sat again, his weight making a flopping sound as it hit the chair. He reached into the bottom drawer and brought out two cloth bags, one black and one white. He handed them to Carruthers. 'It's all here,' he said. 'On the desk.'

'Not all, surely,' Carruthers growled. He was breathing heavily, his bull-like shoulders hunched so his open jacket seemed shapeless. 'You posted your account again last night. Why? You've been posting it on a Sunday for weeks. Why? How daft d'you think we are? Did you think we couldn't read postmarks? You know blasted well it should be posted on a Friday. A Friday, Albert.'

'For God's sake, Carruthers. Get off my back.'

'It's my job, Albert. The Old Man says jump and I jump. He says you're on the fiddle and so you're on the fiddle. He's given me the blasted job of proving it.'

'The auditors came – '

'The auditors came and saw and reported. That was months ago. And even then your floozy was living here.

You were given time to get straight. The Old Man could have kicked you out then, Albert, but he didn't.'

'Kick me out then? What the hell for?'

'What the hell for?' Carruthers's damp red lips quivered. 'Think we're all as thick as you are?'

Bertie stood up again, strength returning to his body and fury to his eyes. 'Carruthers, I am fed up to the teeth with everything. They're a lot of bloody shit-arses. And you could have warned me.'

'And you could keep your maulers out of the till.'

For a while Bertie and Carruthers eyed each other, then Carruthers unexpectedly dropped the black and white bag on the desk. 'I'm tired,' he said, 'I hate this blasted job.' He used both hands to heave his belly, then he looked at the window. 'How much did she land you in the crap for this time?'

'Forged my signature on a loan with a money-lender.'

'You blasted fool.'

'It will all be paid back today. A solicitor is seeing to it . . . .' Bertie lifted a pen, then threw it back to the desk. 'I need a cup of tea, Carruthers. She's dying.' He strode to the door and opened it. Kit stood in the passage, her arms limp at her sides. She said, 'I've been listening.'

Carruthers turned to her, like a bell on a rope. 'I'm sorry, Kit. The Old Man is definitely retiring this summer. There's a hell of a shake-up. Right through the firm.'

They went to the kitchen, three unhappy people, and Linda was in Bertie's sagging chair, her eyes red from crying. Bertie beckoned her away. 'Go upstairs,' he said, 'and stay there until I call you down – or go to school. Tell them why you missed this morning.'

She looked sideways at Carruthers and slid away. Carruthers tousled her hair and laughed, 'See you later beautiful,' but she went self-absorbedly, deep in her loneliness.

Kit stood as if she had forgotten what to do. She said, 'I suppose the son wants us out.'

Carruthers filled her armchair opposite Bertie. 'Not just

you. All the old ones. Any excuse will do.'

'Old?' Bertie echoed.

'Old,' Carruthers echoed.

Kit made tea and poured it, her hands shaking. 'Will they take us to court? Send Bertie to prison?'

Carruthers raised his eyebrows as though perplexed, his fat lips pursed, his chins squashed against his chest. 'A chap in Yorkshire is doing three years for ten pounds. Your bill has been a lot higher.'

Kit sat hurriedly near the table, a teaspoon glinting between her fingers as she trembled. 'Do they know that?'

'The lot,' Carruthers said. 'So I think.' Then he shrugged and sat back with a humourless smile. 'At least I hope they know the lot. If there's any more you had better make a clean breast of it, P.D.Q.'

Bertie sipped his tea then sat staring at it. It tasted of soap. He wondered if Kit and Carruthers would taste soap in theirs too. The clock on the mantelpiece sounded tinny. Ticking his life away. He wondered, for no reason at all, if Elsie had died. He saw Kit and the shaking teaspoon and Carruthers staring at the toe-caps of his brown brogues. He took another sip of tea and the soap taste had gone, but the tea was cold, thick, clinging to the cup. He gulped it down, afraid now of hurting Kit more, of accusing her of making soapy, cold tea. He took the cup and saucer to the scullery and his legs felt a mile long and slow, not properly joined on to his heavy feet.

He turned on the tap and watched the water rush into the cup then spout out again, splashing. Silently he moaned, 'Oh Christ!' and turned the tap off. He wanted to smash the cup.

He went to the garden that Kit had nursed all through last year's drought and heat, and he stared at a rosebud: just one cream rosebud, now, in March; only partly open, sheltered by the stone wall, bowing gently on its stem. He took the small pearl-handled pen-knife from his waistcoat pocket and cut the flower. He sniffed it, knowing it was too young, too soon, to have perfume. He blew a black speck from a petal. He thought the flower symbolised sanity and all things fine and lovely.

His mile-long legs took him back into the house. He suggested Kit and Carruthers smell the rose. He could feel his face smiling while his inside was sick. No job, no income, no baby, three million on the dole. On the ash-tip.

Irrationally he wanted Elsie. He wanted Elsie's warmth, Elsie's voice, Elsie fit and well. He couldn't look at Kit. She moved to take the rosebud from him, her face drawn though tender, but his hand pulled it away.

He went upstairs, hearing Kit call after him, 'Don't disturb her. She's just had one of those little pills.'

On the landing guilt hit him like an earthquake, the sickness rising in his throat. He leaned against the wall, feeling the hard white paint cold against his face. It was all his fault, the whole bloody mess.

His fist thumped the wall and he was near to sobbing. His mind was fuddled, maudlin. I'm forty-nine, he thought, forty-nine; embezzlement, prison for ten years, fifty-nine, fifty-nine years of age, no job, no references. Oh Elsie, my love, my love, console me, oh Kit, forgive me.

He went in to Elsie and she lay quite still. He crept to her side and stared down at her. She was not yet twenty and her body was already dead, dark grey, turning black. She sensed him, and her eyes opened just enough for him to see their glassy blindness. He put the rosebud beside her head on the pillow, cream against the white, and he leaned down, his cheek against hers. 'Hello my sweetheart.' He blinked quickly, dreading his voice would break. 'You go back to sleep.' He put his hand on her where it rested on the quilt. 'I only came to tell you I love you.'

She made no sound and he gazed at her, at the contour of her face, the young curves of her cheek and chin, the tight smoothness of her skin, the grey marble coldness of her dying flesh.

'In all my life,' he whispered, 'I have loved only once. And that was you. I will never love again. Never.'

He heard the slight creak behind him but didn't turn. Kit glided past the bed, her face set, her lips and mouth straight and small. She caught Elsie's hand from him and pushed it under the sheets. Her voice was smooth as she said, 'Off to sleep, Elsie, there's a good girl,' then she was pressing his shoulder. 'Come along,' she said. 'Elsie needs rest,' and she lifted the rosebud from the pillow and held it before her, torturing the stem so the flower revolved and flopped.

He obeyed her, moving from the bed, and on the landing Kit faced him; there were hollows of purple shadows beneath her flashing eyes. She hissed, 'If it wasn't for her we wouldn't be in this mess. She's the cause of it. Can't you see that?'

'Kit. Please.'

'Pull yourself together. Start being a man again.' Then her words trailed away and her hands twisted before her, the rose caught in them, being mangled. 'Bertie, can't you see? I need you. Am I to lose everything? Even you?'

He took her to him, smoothing the thick black hair that had come loose and hung untidily to her angular shoulders, wishing he could undo the last two years and put everything right, wishing Kit could give him the warmth and comfort he needed.

'Go down,' she said then. 'Carruthers want to talk to you. I'll follow in a minute.'

Bertie nodded and left her. He didn't want to see Carruthers. He wished the fat man would go, and not come back.

But the fat man was there, waiting in Kit's armchair, resplendent in vulgar checked suit, his legs stretched out, crossed at the ankles, his fingers linked on his chest.

Carruthers said, 'Would you care to stay long enough to hear the good news?'

'What good news?'

'You're being transferred.'

'Transferred?' Bertie felt for a chair and found one near the table. His stomach was beginning to churn.

319

Carruthers looked at his toe-caps again. 'The Old Man insisted on a sort of last request. Do not sack our Albert.'

Bertie still didn't speak.

'It'll be somewhere rough, old boy. No salary. Start from scratch again. But it's not prison. Or scandal. It'll be cold canvassing, and no more hokey pokey.'

'Good God!'

'You're a lucky bounder. Got your finger in the right hole.'

'Good God!'

'There are other words in the English language, Albert.'

'Yes. Yes, of course. Have you told Kit?'

'I'll leave that to you. It'll probably be Merseyside. Or Glasgow. Bad places just now,' but Bertie was up the stairs faster than ever before. Two strides took him across the landing and he burst open Elsie's door, his mouth open to tell all, and Kit was bent over Elsie's head.

Kit's terrified, startled dark eyes looked up, and slowly Kit's long thin, white hands took the pillow off Elsie's face.

Bertie's mouth opened wider, as if a knife stabbed at his throat. Kit said, 'It was better this way. It was best.'

'Christ almighty!' And he thought of the spider at Malvern, of Kit squeezing slowly, deliberately.

'She's dead, dear. Gone.'

'You killed her!' It was a croak. 'Cold-bloodedly. You've murdered her!' He moved to the bed as if punch-drunk, staring at Elsie's half open eyes. 'Elsie? My love! My love.' He grabbed her wrist, seeking a pulse, then tapped her face. 'Elsie? Elsie?'

Kit moved his hand away, then drew the sheet over Elsie's head. 'You murdered young boys during the war, Bertie, young healthy boys like Tommy, who had everything to live for. So stop being a hypocrite. I did her a favour.' Her amber gaze fixed on him. She said, 'I couldn't stand it any more. Watching her die. Now it's over. Like everything else. Finished.'

She led Bertie down the stairs, but at the hallstand he gestured her from him. 'Carruthers has something to tell

320

you. And you had better phone the doctor. I have to get out.' He escaped from her, from the house, from Carruthers, trying also to escape from his past.

He felt the fresh air of the early spring street, heard the traffic, and he walked fast, like a man who had somewhere to go. A bicycle brushed his coat, but still he didn't stop. He went to the beach and looked at the tide; it swept in white curves to where the black seaweed was strewn and shells glittered wet like a beaded stream. People strolled with their dogs, a boy flew a kite, and Bertie sat and watched the waves. He vaguely heard the deep-throated call of a steamer and a dog barking, someone was shouting, a girl was laughing. She was alive, flirting, And Elsie was dead. Gone.

Bertie let his head drop between his up-bent knees, and he cried, not bothering to wipe the tears away.

The beach emptied and the air was chill. Dusk crept up like a multi-coloured veil. He hadn't seen the tide go out, and Kit came and sat beside him, her hand ice-cold on his.

She said gently, 'Would you believe me if I said I loved her too? Even though I hated her as well?' Bertie put his arm up and Kit rested into him. She said, 'Elsie told me once she didn't want a long slow death, yet that was what we were giving her.'

Bertie felt the sand moving beneath his feet, and a gull screamed above his head. He remembered the afternoon he and Elsie had spent up near the foot of the bridge. He could see her face now, hear her voice, unusually serious, saying 'I hope the doctor, or someone, will be kind enough to poison me or something. Without me knowing . . . .'

He said now to Kit, 'Did she see you – ? Do you think she knew – ?' and Kit shook her head.

'She was unconscious. Absolutely.'

The seagull glided languidly about them, then came lower. It landed before them, its grey legs straight and strong, its sharp eyes seeking the remains of a picnic.

Kit murmured, 'We still have each other, Bertie. And the children. We can start again. All of us. Tommy as well.

321

He needs a family too.'

He didn't reply. He felt numb with cold.

Kit said, 'Come on, Bertie, let's make a cuppa,' and she stood up, then helped him to his feet. 'She changed you, Bertie. You aren't the same person.'

'Nor you, Kit. Nor you.' He sounded like an old man.

The sky was pink and lilac behind them, sending delicate colours onto the sea as they walked up the beach and he let her lead him home, to where the fire was glowing, the kettle boiling, and Carruthers had gone.

CHAPTER TWELVE

For two further Wednesdays the agents came with defer-
ence, paid their collections across the desk, waited for their
accounts to be checked, then left, doffing their hats or
touching their brows; all whispering, making sure nothing
disturbed the homage paid to those bereaved.

Now, on the Saturday, Kit stood in the passage and
listened to the hush. Even from the foot of the stairs she
could hear the clock on the kitchen mantelpiece; it ticked
neurotically.

She hurried up to the big front double bedroom and, in
the semi-darkness of drawn curtains, stripped the bed.
Last night she had turned and cuddled into Bertie. He had
put his hand on her hip, and his lips touched her hair. The
contact had brought a feeling of promise, as if something
was coming back to life.

She remade the bed, punching the great feather underlay
into shape, making sure there were no bumps where Bertie
didn't like them, then she caught sight of the dark outline
of herself in the tilt of the dressing-table mirror. She had
worn black up to and during the funeral, but not today.
Today she wore French navy, and rather liked it, with the
white Peter Pan collar, but she was pallid.

Mourning had gone on too long.

She hesitated before touching the curtains then, with a
heave, as if with great resolution, she swished them back.
Brilliant sunshine flooded in, and Kit smiled. The palms of
her hands rested on her hips, then slid down over her thighs
as she drank in the glory of the golden glow. It was all over.
God knew what lay ahead but, at this moment, she experienced a challenge, a complete new beginning.

She wanted to sing, but not too loud. It was too soon. A blasphemy. But more than two weeks of silence, of darkly cloistered rooms, of slippered feet, or rubber-soled shoes, had proved hard because, she told herself, she was in the house all day. The children went out. Bertie went out. She, Kit, had taken the full brunt of mourning.

Now was the right time to stop.

The sun showed up the dust on the dressing-table, across the washing-stand, and on the whatnot with its collection of small ornaments in the corner. Kit told herself not to notice. Not today. Today was her day of release.

She strode across the landing and her hand reached for the knob of the door of that back room: Elsie's room, and for a few seconds her heart pounded with an irrational fear. She had to draw breath before she could turn the knob, but once done, she was inside.

The place smelled, not of consumption now, but of staleness, lack of air, of darkness and despair.

She crossed to the window, touching the cold brass of the foot of the bed as she passed. Then there were those long dark curtains.

She stood looking up at the white wooden rings on their white wooden pole. It was as if she was about to desecrate a grave. Then rebellion, the need for self-preservation, took over, and the curtains were flung back.

There appeared grey-blue roof tops, the backs of other houses, and there was the sky. Blue. Blue. Preparing for summer.

Kit put her hands together and entwined her fingers. How beautiful the world was. How wonderful to be alive, to feel her heart beating, to know that Elsie had gone, but Bertie was still here.

She heard the door of the office open, heard the soft sounds of him going to the kitchen. Looking for her? She went to the landing and called gently, 'Darling? I'm upstairs,' then she waited to see how he would take her actions. Would he be furious she had ended mourning so abruptly, or would he understand?

324

He stood on the slip-mat at the foot of the stairs and gazed up at her, a tall, too thin woman with lines of suffering etched into her face, and behind her was bright daylight, the door of Elsie's room open, brilliant, almost blinding in its sudden shock.

Bertie's left hand gripped the nub of the banister rail and, like Kit, he knew the length of mourning had to end. This was as good a time as any.

He came up the stairs slowly, as if resignation was predominant, and Kit turned so he followed her into Elsie's room.

Kit went back to the window, unlocking the clip, then lifting the sash so fresh air scudded in, eager to cleanse, and she saw Bertie straighten his shoulders and gaze around.

He said calmly, 'You stripped the bed, then?'

'Yes. Straight after the funeral.'

'And the bedding?'

'For the chapel. For their charity store. Some poor family might be glad of it.' She laughed as if afraid he might think she had done wrong. 'I had it fumigated and laundered properly first.'

'Yes,' Bertie said, and drew in air until his chest expanded, accepting the inevitable. 'Is her stuff still in the drawers?'

'I haven't touched anything like that.'

The gaudy paper chrysanthemums that Elsie had made were still in the china vase on the black mantelpiece, their colours fading, dust clothing their petals, and the chimney smelled strongly of soot, as if the weather was about to change.

Bertie strolled to the ottoman and lifted the lid. 'They should all go,' he said, then averted his eyes from the few clothes folded in there.

He opened the wardrobe and a black patent handbag fell out, so did a pair of silly shoes, shoes that had high thin Spanish heels, and were so small his school-aged daughter could wear them.

Kit came quickly, replacing the shoes, then stood,

holding the handbag. For a moment her fingers hovered about the clasp, then she looked into Bertie's blue eyes. 'You open it. She'd want you to do that,' and Kit left him. A woman's handbag was the most private thing she possessed; only a husband, or lover, would encroach on such privacy. She called back, 'I'll make a cup of tea.'

'All right,' he said, but she knew by the tone of his voice that, already, he had found something of interest.

She hurried to the kitchen, to the big iron kettle that rarely stopped boiling, then she took her time brewing tea, preparing the cups and saucers, and almost praying that no one would telephone, no one would knock at the door, no one would interrupt these few minutes her husband was sharing with this dead love.

A spasm like a silent sigh rushed through her. She had never loved like that.

She gazed at the coals that were kept glowing because a fire meant home, and not because the weather was cold. 'Could I ever love like that?' She put her hands to her face, thinking of nights needing love, yet not able to accept because it was dirty, not nice, and thinking of days weighted with guilt because she didn't feel a proper wife. She was a mother, a housekeeper. Not a lover. She had never been a lover.

'Elsie,' she whispered. 'In worldly goods, I have always had so much more than you, yet you were able to give Bertie so much more than I ever could.'

The coals slipped, dropped, and scarlet, glittering speckles fell to the ash-box.

Kit sighed. The past was gone. The future was a vision.

When Bertie came down he didn't come silently. He strode along the passage, the black patent handbag swinging between his forefinger and thumb. He said, 'We can burn this. It's no good to anyone. She probably kept her handkerchiefs in it.' He put the handbag on the fire. He stood and watched it catch alight, slowly at first, then burning more avidly, the flames reflecting in his eyes. Then he turned to Kit. 'She left me a letter.'

326

'Oh yes?' Kit's hand shook as she gently poured milk into the waiting cups. 'Anything interesting?'

'You can read it.'

'I'd rather not.'

'She wanted you to.'

Kit and Bertie sat, opposite each other in their own comfortable, battered chairs, and Kit opened the sheets of folded lined copy-book pages, then she didn't know whether to smile with amusement and tenderness, or blush with a sort of embarrassment. 'Are you sure you want me to see this?'

Bertie nodded.

Kit sighed, took a sip of tea, then sat forward, intent on the rounded young writing of the girl she had both hated and loved, but mostly been so jealous of.

She silently read, 'My darling, darling, darling, darling. Be happy. I will sit on a cloud in heaven and watch you. When Saint Peter gives me harp lessons I will try to pay attention, but I know I will be spying on you to make sure you are happy. I hope my Mum will be with me and she won't be coughing. She will be all right. We will both be laughing at you still working down there.

Tell Kit I did not want to steal you off her. I only wanted to share you. I know you love her and I wanted her to see this letter so she knows I know. She is strong and will live longer than me, or you, so look in her eyes and see she does love you in her tinpot way, and you love her too. If you did not you would have left her for me. I am sorry I sold our baby to the Jew but he wanted his money. Give the girls a smacking kiss from me.

Lots of best love from

Elsie Buckley. (Sitting on a cloud watching you.)'

Kit lowered the letter to her lap and began to laugh, a quiet yet almost hysterical laugh, so the tears came streaming down her face. 'Oh Bertie! What a knowing child she was!'

Bertie beckoned her and stood up, putting his cup and

327

saucer on the table. 'Let's find the kids. Go out. It's a lovely day.'

'They're over the road. New people have moved in. With sons. They're on the phone. I'll ring them now.'

They caught the tram, running for it with hands linked, and at the big wide gates of Singleton Park they split up, and Linda and Emma ran on.

Emma turned when she was at the old Gorsedd stones, and her piping voice echoed among the new-leafed branches of many trees. 'Daddy? When we move, can we have a puppy?'

Bertie grinned. His younger daughter hadn't sounded a bit sad at the idea of a move. To her it evidently meant not his demotion, but an adventure.

He called back, 'What sort d'you want?'

He felt Kit's hand reach for his and he took it, squeezing her fingers.

'An Alsatian,' came the reply.

'Never!' Kit cried. 'We couldn't afford to feed the brute!' and she didn't sound as if it was the end of the world either.

Linda came closer. 'Daddy?'

'Yes?' How fast she was becoming a woman.

'When Tommy comes home, he won't see me!'

'You're writing to him, aren't you?'

She nodded, brown hair glinting in the sunlight.

'There you are then. Invite him to stay with us. He could find a better life in England than he found in Wales.'

Bertie watched the pink steal into his eldest daughter's cheeks, saw the sparkle re-enter her eyes. 'Oh Daddy, I think you're wonderful!'

'So do I,' he said, without humour, and Kit was swinging his hand.

'How much d'you think we'll get for our house? And what sort of place d'you think we ought to look for?'

He turned to her in amazement. 'Aren't you upset about it? Depressed?'

'No.' She returned his gaze soberly, her height making it

unnecessary to look up at him. 'I'm just relieved it's over. I'm glad we'll be getting away from the gossip.'

'Gossip?' His astonishment grew.

'Bertie!' She was remonstrating. 'The agents knew. They talk. Do you suppose they never told outsiders? D'you suppose the neighbours never wondered?'

'Kit. There'll be no salary!'

'There wasn't here at first.' Her tawny eyes flashed those red lights of fire, of inspiration. 'It'll be like when we first married. Renting a house. Building dreams. Canvassing. The excitement of swopping notes, seeing how we've done . . . .'

And he knew she meant it. He couldn't stifle the rueful laughter that welled inside him, the curdling of excitement her words evoked in him. 'You're darned right!' he exclaimed. 'God! What have I got to be so blighted about?'

He took her in his arms, there, in the centre of the path through Swansea's main park. He heard a duck on the pond go quack-quack and, although Elsie could not be banished, he was here, with Kit, with his in-love-with-Tommy daughter, and his can-we-have-a-puppy daughter.

'Kit,' he murmured, and a young couple strolled past, too involved in their own romance to notice that of an old married couple. 'Perhaps our lives are only just beginning.'

'Of course,' she said. 'A new phase. We've been in a rut too long,' and Bertie thought how beautiful she looked. Worthy of a man who had the initiative, the courage, the acumen, to open yet another new area for the company. 'I'll never be unfaithful to you again,' he murmured. 'There'll always just be you and me and the kids.'

'All three of them,' Kit challenged gently, and Bertie shrugged as he let her move from him.

'We'll have to see,' he promised. 'We'll have to see.'

They strolled on, a family that had survived, and planned to continue doing so.

THE END

DIANE PEARSON
THE SUMMER OF THE BARSHINSKEYS

'Although the story of the Barshinskeys, which became our story too, stretched over many summers and winters, that golden time of 1902 was when our strange involved relationship began, when our youthful longing for the exotic took a solid and restless hold upon us . . .'

It is at this enchanted moment that *The Summer of the Barshinskeys* begins. A beautifully told, compelling story that moves from a small Kentish village to London, and from war-torn St Petersburg to a Quaker relief unit in the Volga provinces. It is the unforgettable story of two families, one English, the other Russian, who form a lifetime pattern of friendship, passion, hatred, and love.

'An engrossing saga . . . she evokes rural England at the turn of the century with her sure and skilful touch'
Barbara Taylor Bradford

'The Russian section is reminiscent of Pasternak's *Doctor Zhivago*, horrifying yet hauntingly beautiful'
New York Tribune

0 552 12641 1   £2.95

CORGI BOOKS

CSARDAS
by Diane Pearson

'A story you won't easily forget, done on the scale of
GONE WITH THE WIND'
Mark Kahn, *Sunday Mirror*

'Only half a century separates today's totalitarian state of
Hungary from the glittering world of coming-out balls and
feudal estates, elegance and culture, of which the Ferenc
sisters — the *enchanting* Ferenc sisters — are the pampered
darlings in the opening chapters of Diane Pearson's
dramatic epic CSARDAS. Their world has now gone with
the wind as surely as that of Scarlett O'Hara (which it much
resembled): hand some, over-bred young men danced
attendance on lovely, frivolous belles, and life was one long
dream of parties and picnics, until the shot that killed
Franz Ferdinand in 1914 burst the beautiful bubble. The
dashing gallants galloped off to war and, as they returned,
maimed and broken in spirit, the Hungary began to emerge
like an ugly grub from its chrysalis. Poverty, hardship, and
growing anti-semitism threatened and scattered the half-
Jewish Ferenc family as Nazi influence gripped the country
from one side and Communism spread underground from
the other like the tentacles of ground elder.
Only the shattered remnants of a once-powerful family
lived through the 1939-45 holocaust, but with phoenix-like
vitality the new generation began to adapt and bend, don
camouflage and survive . . .'
Phyllida Hart-Davis, *Sunday Telegraph*

0 552 10375 6 £2.95

THE MARIGOLD FIELD by Diane Pearson

THE MARIGOLD FIELD is a story of poor, proud, high-spirited people . . . people whose roots were in the farming country of southern England . . . in the bawdy and exuberant streets of the East End.

Jonathan Whitman, his cousin Myra, Anne-Louise Pritchard and the enormous Pritchard clan to which she belongs, saw the changing era and incredible events of a passing age — an age of great poverty and great wealth, of straw boaters, feather boas, and the Music Hall . . .

And above all THE MARIGOLD FIELD is a story of one woman's consuming love . . . of jealous obsession that threatened to destroy the very man she adored . . .

'An exceptionally good read. One of those *comfortable* books you can live in for a while with pleasure.' — *McCalls Magazine*.

'When Maxi takes Anne-Louise home on Sunday, when his relations assemble loudly at the meal-table . . . there is an instant of the finest, broadest comedy . . .' — *Sunday Times*

If you have enjoyed this book, you can follow the continuing saga of the Whitman family in SARA WHITMAN, the superb sequel by Diane Pearson.

0 552 10271 7   £2.50

SARAH WHITMAN by Diane Pearson

The continuing story of the Whitman family . . .

A 'God is an Englishman' kind of novel — about a very human kind of Englishwoman, a woman who fought her way up from domestic service to schoolmistress and whose life was touched by three men, one who taught her what it was to love and be loved, another who waited for her in vain, and a third — the strange tormented man who was to be her destiny.

Rich in adventure, history and human passions, this is a novel of astonishing breadth . . . an enthralling panorama of life and love between the wars . . .

'The very stuff of reality . . . SARAH is superb.'
Norah Lofts

0 552 09140 5   £2.50

BRIDE OF TANCRED by Diane Pearson

Miriam Wakeford was full of hope when she arrived to take up her new appointment as needlewoman and companion in the bleak, windswept house of Tancred, high on the South Downs. Her strict Quaker upbringing was no preparation for the experiences which awaited her there . . .

John Tancred, a widower, was a mysterious, moody figure, frequently harsh and sometimes surprisingly kind. His young daughter, Esmee, seemed unbalanced . . . John Tancred's mother was an imperious old lady who ruled the decaying mansion from her wheelchair. Above all, the atmosphere was filled with the evil, violent presence of John's dead farther, Richard, who by his excesses had brought ruin, infamy and tragedy to the name of Tancred . . .

0 552 10249 0   £1.75

THE DAFFODILS OF NEWENT
by Susan Sallis

They were called the Daffodil Girls, spirited and bright, enduring, loving and dancing their way through the gay and desperate twenties.

APRIL   who married the tortured and sexually suspect David Daker, convinced she could blot out his memories of the trenches.

MAY   pregnant by her handsome music hall star husband who did'nt want to settle down.

MARCH   loved and betrayed by the man who had farthered her child, and who still wanted her.

The Daffodils of Newent — three wonderful girls whose story began in A SCATTERING OF DAISIES.

0 552 12579 2   £1.75

A SCATTERING OF DAISIES
by Susan Sallis

Will Rising had dragged himself from humble beginnings to his own small tailoring business in Gloucester — and on the way he'd fallen violently in love with Florence, refined, delicate, and wanting something better for her children.

March was the eldest girl, the least loved, the plain, unattractive one who, as the family grew, became more and more the household drudge. But March, a strange, intelligent, unhappy child, had inherited some of her mother's dreams. March Rising was determined to break out of the round of poverty and hard work, to find wealth, and love, and happiness.

0 552 12375 7   £2.50

A SELECTED LIST OF FINE NOVELS
AVAILABLE FROM CORGI BOOKS

THE PRICES SHOWN BELOW WERE CORRECT AT THE TIME OF GOING T
PRESS. HOWEVER TRANSWORLD PUBLISHERS RESERVE THE RIGHT T
SHOW NEW RETAIL PRICES ON COVERS WHICH MAY DIFFER FROM THOS
PREVIOUSLY ADVERTISED IN THE TEXT OR ELSEWHERE.

☐	12281 5	JADE	Pat Barr	£2.
☐	12142 8	A WOMAN OF TWO CONTINENTS	Pixie Burger	£2.
☐	12637 3	PROUD MARY	Iris Gower	£2.
☐	12387 0	COPPER KINGDOM	Iris Gower	£1.
☐	12503 2	THREE GIRLS	Francis Paige	£1.
☐	12641 1	THE SUMMER OF THE BARSHINSKEYS	Diane Pearson	£2.
☐	10375 6	CSARDAS	Diane Pearson	£2.
☐	09140 5	SARAH WHITMAN	Diane Pearson	£2.
☐	10271 7	THE MARIGOLD FIELD	Diane Pearson	£2.
☐	10249 0	BRIDE OF TANCRED	Diane Pearson	£1.
☐	12689 6	IN THE SHADOW OF THE CASTLE	Erin Pizzey	£2.
☐	12462 1	THE WATERSHED	Erin Pizzey	£2.
☐	11596 7	FEET IN CHAINS	Kate Roberts	£1.
☐	11685 8	THE LIVING SLEEP	Kate Roberts	£2.
☐	12607 1	DOCTOR ROSE	Elvi Rhodes	£1.
☐	12579 2	THE DAFFODILS OF NEWENT	Susan Sallis	£1.
☐	12375 7	A SCATTERING OF DAISIES	Susan Sallis	£2.
☐	12636 5	THE MOVIE SET	June Plaum Singer	£2.
☐	12609 8	STAR DREAMS	June Plaum Singer	£2.
☐	12118 5	THE DEBUTANTES	June Plaum Singer	£2.
☐	12700 0	LIGHT AND DARK	Margaret Thomson Davis	£2.
☐	11575 4	A NECESSARY WOMAN	Helen Van Sylke	£2.
☐	12240 8	PUBLIC SMILES, PRIVATE TEARS	Helen Van Sylke	£2.
☐	11321 2	SISTERS AND STRANGERS	Helen Van Sylke	£2.
☐	11779 X	NO LOVE LOST	Helen Van Sylke	£2.
☐	12676 4	GRACE PENSILVA	Michael Weston	£2.9

*All these books are available at your book shop or newsagent, or can be ordered dire
from the publisher. Just tick the titles you want and fill in the form below.*

TRANSWORLD READER'S SERVICE, *Cash Sales Department,*
61-63 Uxbridge Road, Ealing, London W5 5SA

*Please send a cheque or postal order, not cash. All cheques and postal order
must be in £ sterling and made payable to Transworld Publishers Ltd.*

Please allow cost of book(s) plus the following for postage and packing:

UK/Republic of Ireland Customers: *Orders in excess of £5; no charge.
Orders under £5; add 50p*

Overseas Customers: *All orders; add £1.50*

NAME (Block Letters) ....

ADDRESS ....

....